# HOMME FATALE

# HOMME FATALE

# FATALE

PAUL MAYERSBERG

ST. MARTIN'S PRESS NEW YORK

*Design by Dawn Niles*

Library of Congress Cataloging-in-Publication Data

Mayersberg, Paul.
   Homme fatale / Paul Mayersberg.
     p.  cm.
   ISBN 0-312-06996-0
   I. Title.
  PS3563.A9552H6   1992
  813'.54—dc20                                   91-33307
                                                        CIP

First Edition: July 1992

10 9 8 7 6 5 4 3 2 1

This Book Is for
Bobby Littman

# HOMME
# FATALE

# PART ONE

# 1

# IN THE MIRROR

She was pulling the body along by the arms, moving backward step by step. The body was heavy for her, a dead weight on the floor of the hallway. She paused for a moment to glance around. The narrow passage was deserted. She changed her grip from the upper arms to the wrists. She started again to pull. There were small clicking noises as the bones moved in their sockets, hers or the victim's joints it was impossible to tell. She wore no shoes. Her black net stockings wrinkled around her ankles as she moved on the dark red nylon carpet. She was much thinner than the body she was pulling. She might have been an insect hauling its dead to a burial place.

The woman's face was a tense mask, very pale under the white fluorescents in the passage. She seemed almost bloodless, a pale, Oriental look. Her short hair and bangs formed a black helmet. The hair was so solidly black and so immaculately cut that it looked like a wig. There was something doll-like, artificial about her. The thinness of her uncovered arms and angled legs gave the impression of a marionette con-

3

trolled by invisible strings. When she looked round, her eyes were sooty marbles, showing neither fear nor desire.

Only her lips suggested a conscious concern for what she was doing, and how dangerous it would be if she were seen. The lips moved independently from the rest of her face. They tightened with her exertions. When the body she pulled moved more easily along the passage, her lips relaxed. Her impassivity could have been interpreted as satisfaction.

Her thin dress matched her hair and suited her limbs. As she bent to rearrange her grip on the body, her small breasts were visible. Delicate glands, they seemed extraneous to her narrow torso. Having moved only a few feet, she paused again for breath and a look around. In her black dress, stockings, and neat hair, she looked as if she was going to, or had come from, a party. She was pale and cool. There was no sign of sweat on her forehead.

The temperature outside the small hotel was above one hundred degrees. It was desert heat, New Mexico in July. At the end of the hallway the blinds were down over the window. Under the window was a humming air-conditioning unit. Outside was an old railroad track unused this Sunday. Beyond the track the small town of Artesia shimmered in the hair-dryer heat. Having gotten behind schedule, they were working Sunday shooting a scene in a local church. I had visited one of my clients on set earlier that day. Mike Adorno had a small part in a TV movie called *Ghost Town,* a supernatural modern western. But whatever they were shooting, it couldn't match this as an essay in the bizarre. A great opening scene for a movie. I would suggest it to Paul Jaspers when I got back to town. Paul was a young writer client for whom I had high hopes.

Watching the woman's progress, I found myself unable to breathe. I had come out of my room and almost immediately seen her and her victim reflected in a mirror set at an angle at the junction of the hallway. I watched her face, unable to look away. What would happen if she looked up into the mirror that linked us so clearly and saw me? My skin tingled. I continued to examine the mask face; I could feel the thin arms between my fingers. I could smell the lemony perfume trail she had left. She must have passed my door just before I came out. She must have pulled the body right past my door.

4

To begin with I had hardly glanced at the victim. She was wearing a white miniskirt, a blue denim shirt, and white sneakers. No stockings. Blond hair. Biggish breasts, I guessed, although the angle in the mirror made it difficult to see her properly. In any case, I was watching the woman in black. The girl must have been either unconscious or dead. Later, I thought she looked a little like Barbara.

Then the woman looked up as she took a deep breath. I jumped back to the door of my room. I fumbled with the key which was still in my hand. Had she seen me?

I went back into my room. I closed the door very slowly and quietly and waited. Waited? What for? Wait a minute. Why was I hiding? Why didn't I go down the passage to see what was happening? Now. Quick. If the woman was disposing of that girl's body, shouldn't I report it to the hotel, if not to the police? But then I didn't want to get involved. It was none of my business, even if it was a crime.

But I was intrigued, and being intrigued cast me in the role of detective. So why, if I was the detective, did I feel guilty? As if I were the criminal.


# 2

# BARBARA'S FAIR HAIR

I came back into the room and closed the door. At the end of the bed the television was still on. No sound, just the visual antics of two aggressive cartoon characters, a big dog and a small cat trying to destroy each other because it was supposedly in their natures.

Barbara was in the bathroom.

"Did you get it?" she asked.

"They didn't have any."

"No beer? That's ridiculous."

When I left the hotel room it was to go out to get two beers. I didn't get them because I was stopped by what I had seen in the hallway.

5

"Are you all right?" Barbara was suddenly concerned. I must have looked strange. I bent and kissed her breast softly at first, then with sucking energy. I pulled half of her breast into my mouth. The suddenness excited her. I put my hand under her buttocks and started to squeeze her flesh. Again I saw the woman being dragged along the hallway outside. I imagined the victim without her clothes, her bottom sliding on the rough carpet.

Sex with Barbara started better than it finished. She loved to treat me like a baby, enfolding me, cuddling me, nursing me. It gave her enormous pleasure. But by the time we were back on the bed and she had finished undressing me, I no longer really wanted her. I wanted to rerun the scene I had witnessed outside in the hallway, stop it and examine it closely when I felt like it, and rub myself as and when I wanted and then move on inside the scene. What I had seen had unlocked a special kind of desire I hadn't known since adolescence when searching books and photographs for sexual excitement.

Why had I settled with Barbara? *Settled* is the wrong word. And untrue. I hadn't settled for anything. Until Barbara, I hadn't lived with any girl for more than a few weeks. I enjoyed my freedom with women. I got easily bored. When I moved in with Barbara and stayed it was a shock. To me.

At thirty-three years of age was it domesticity? It was certainly pleasurable and convenient living with her. I had the occasional fling, but I didn't enjoy lying to her. She was naturally faithful. I was enough for her. We had the occasional fight. She thought I ought to merge with a bigger agency. But I needed my independence. The thought of having someone over me was not acceptable. I had to admit she was a shade too conventional. With Barbara, what you saw was what you got. But then, if what you got was what you wanted, what was wrong with that?

She continued to mother me with her mouth. I lay back with my fingers inside her and did next to nothing until she brought herself to the brink by rubbing my penis between her breasts and licking her fingers to help.

The memory of those two women was indelible now. Had I seen the aftermath of a murder? Was it the end of a lesbian fight? Or was there some simple, innocent explana-

6

tion? I couldn't think of one. I was intrigued by the arousal. It was unexpected, wild. The stimulus was intense. I didn't want it to go away.

One of Barbara's rings scraped my groin. She wore six or seven rings at any given time. She had scores of rings, because she made them and sold them in a small boutique in Santa Monica. On several occasions when a woman admired one of her rings, usually in a restaurant, she would offer to sell it. Barbara was a model for her own work. Some women were surprised that she would wear jewelry that had no significance for her. I was sometimes surprised how unsentimental Barbara could be.

She sighed deeply, closed her eyes, and stretched. She put her hand between my legs in a gesture of thanks. When she felt that I was hard she opened her eyes.

"Come inside me," she said lovingly.

I was still watching, feeling almost, the thin strong hands of the woman in the hallway, gripping not the wrists of her victim, but holding mine as I lay back.

"Is that what you want?" Barbara asked, putting her jeweled hand at the back of my neck and exerting a little pressure. "Come on."

I grunted. I moved close to her sticky skin. The room was airless. I touched her shoulder-length blond hair. I wanted it to be black and short and slightly oily. I moved my other hand to her fair pubic hair, which hardly concealed the opening of her vagina. When I first saw the soft hair between her legs I thought I would never tire of looking at it, touching it, penetrating it. But at this moment the light color seemed obvious, see-through like a close-up in a girlie magazine, without mystery. I half-loved Barbara. I wanted her because she had wanted me. Barbara closed her eyes again.

I thought I heard a sound outside the hotel-room door. I caught my breath. Had the woman seen me before I ducked back into my room? Had she now come to explain, to beg for my silence, to offer me anything not to report her? I waited. There was no further noise.

"What is it?"

"Nothing. I thought someone was outside the door."

"It's wonderful to spend a weekend away like this, even in a crummy little hotel."

7

"Yes," I said.

"Ouch, careful." She twisted as I pushed into her. I held her shoulders down on the bed. I had no intention of hurting Barbara. I just needed the release. The sound outside the door had made it urgent. I closed my eyes and saw black and red. I came quickly. This got her started again. I had injected her with passion. She wanted me to come again. Her desire was blatant. I went slack. She stroked my balls. It worked but it made me slightly uncomfortable. I did not want her to want me now. I felt what it was probably like to be a woman resisting unwelcome attentions. Barbara started to cry but without tears, out of pure desire.

There was a news bulletin on the television. I pressed the remote to hear what was going on in the world. Almost immediately, the phone rang beside the bed.

In that second before I said "Hello," I knew it was her, the woman in the passage. I felt cold.

"Mr. Elliott?"

I exhaled audibly. It was the deskman's voice.

"There's a message for you, Sir."

"A message?"

"An envelope, Sir. I'd send it up, but the boy's on an errand and the maids have left for the day."

"I'll pick it up." I hung up.

"What is it?" Barbara got off the bed.

"Someone's left me a note." I shrugged as if it had no importance. "I don't want that beer anymore. Why don't we get dressed and try and find a proper drink. We can visit the set if you like. They'll have booze." Anything to get out of that hotel room.

Barbara agreed and went into the bathroom, pulling the door shut. Had she noticed a change in my behavior?

The hallway was deserted. The aging elevator was in use or else out of action. I went down the stairs two at a time. I almost slipped on the loose carpeting. I came up to the bald deskman in the lobby.

"You've got a message for me. Mr. Elliott."

"Yes, Sir."

The guy took an envelope from under the desk. He handed it to me. I started to open it, hesitated.

8

"Did you see who delivered this?"

"I didn't see them. I was taking a call. I found it right here." He patted the stained desktop.

I opened the envelope carefully. My name, "Mr. Elliott," was neatly written on it in ballpoint pen. Inside was a piece of plain white paper. The unsigned message was unambiguous: "I know you saw me."

# 3

# LAND OF ENCHANTMENT

The film crew was just about to wrap when Barbara and I arrived at the church. Mike Adorno, my client, was a guy with a brutal face and a sweet disposition. He insisted we have an early dinner with him before we left for Albuquerque and Los Angeles. I looked at every woman on the set, from the leading actress to the script supervisor. I couldn't help myself. None of them looked like her. Barbara took Mike's arm and led him on ahead as we crossed the Santa Fe railroad on our way to dinner.

I thought of making some excuse and going back to the hotel to look for her. She had to have been staying there. I considered going from room to room, smashing down doors to find her. I was walking on a sand dune. I could feel my own blood running around in my veins and bubbling in my arteries. Find her if you dare. That was the injunction. "I know you saw me." Was it possible she might be somewhere out there looking for me?

The three of us went to the El Rancho Cafe for dinner. It was a Chinese restaurant with Mexican help. I couldn't handle the food. The specialty of the house was deep-fried chicken gizzard with sweet-and-sour sauce. None of us ordered it. For me the conversation during the meal was like skimming the pages of a script.

"I'm sure amber jewelry is staging a comeback," said Barbara.

"So you'll talk to him about my per diems," said Mike.

"I should have bought some turquoise while I was here. After all, New Mexico is turquoise country," said Barbara.

"This fish was a mistake," said Mike. "How can you have fish in the middle of a goddamn desert?"

"You know, there are more sightings in this state than in the rest of the country put together." Barbara had gotten this information from an airline magazine she picked up on the plane coming out.

I agreed with her. But you don't have to look up in the sky for a sighting. In this state you can see things in the narrow passage of a rundown hotel in a small town.

"It's the Land of Enchantment," said Mike. "That's the state motto. You can see it on all the old car license plates. Land of Enchantment."

After leaving Mike happier, flattered that among all the actors on the production only his agent had bothered to visit the location, Barbara drove our rented car back to Albuquerque. The long straight desert drive in the evening sunlight was pure Georgia O'Keeffe. Every detail was clear as crystal. The tall fingers of cactus, sentinels in silhouette, the mauve clouds fiddling with the sinking orange sun, the rim of the far mountains challenging you to guess their distance and height, the spread of lost farms where nothing seemed to grow, the tethered horse alone for the night miles from his owner's house, the three-legged dog so adapted to his disability that he had forgotten the truck that hit him and still strayed onto the highway. Every sight was etched and distinct but at the same time composed a dreamlike image. Just like the picture in my head.

During the night flight from Albuquerque to Los Angeles, I left my seat on three occasions and wandered up the narrow aisle of the plane. I was restless. It was crazy. I was half-consciously looking for the woman.

I went back to my seat and pulled out a script I had promised to read. I got through all of ten pages in an hour. Barbara was into her second martini. She was absorbed in her fashion magazines and, unusually for her, silent. I stared at the legs of the cabin attendant as she went back and forth maybe thirty times.

I finally gave up on the script altogether and picked up

one of Barbara's foreign glossies. The pictures of the girls together in their underwear that wasn't really theirs produced a violent erotic charge. I started to make up the story. I stopped feeling like a criminal and turned detective. Examining the way those girls held each other so formally, one in black panties, one in white, goaded my imagination. Working backward I began to see what must have happened.

They were both staying in the hotel, the woman and the girl, by chance. The woman had noticed her on Saturday morning at the desk when she was enquiring about messages. She fell in love with the girl's neck and shoulders, the way one folded into the other like a swimmer's torso.

They were both from out of town. The woman was a dress designer traveling to Texas, the girl a graphic artist taking cliché Georgia O'Keeffe pictures of the desert. Neither had come to New Mexico with a man.

"You're gay," the girl said, later that night.

"I don't hate men."

"I'm not that crazy about men myself. Not right now."

"I see that," said the woman.

Their relationship, the way they spent the day and the night, became clear to me in fragments. It wasn't like a dream. There was nothing surreal or impressionistic about it. I could see real scenes from their life, extracts of what had happened.

After six o'clock on Saturday, yesterday, the woman followed the girl to a bar. She knocked over her drink in a contrived accident and bought her another with apologies. As in any successful pickup, dinner followed. Another bar until one-thirty in the morning and then back to the hotel. They went to the woman's room where she had a bottle of wine. The girl smoked a joint. The woman came out of the bathroom in her white robe. The touching began. The swimmer's neck and shoulders. Then the first request.

"Take off your shirt. Let me see you. You have a wonderful torso."

The girl felt awkward, as Barbara might have. But unlike men, women are not instinctively afraid of each other.

The girl's large pale nipples made the woman shiver. They reminded her of her mother's breasts. She showed the girl her own delicate breasts with their small dark nipples. The girl was moved. So was I. Then came the first kiss.

11

"I've never done this before," the girl said.

By the time she was naked facedown on the bed, her breathing became quite irregular. The woman was aware that for all her physical size and strength the girl had poor circulation and a weakness in her back. After the long massage the girl was on the brink of unconsciousness. She had never been so aroused in her life.

I thought of the girl in the hotel hallway as a heavy lump. If she sat on you it would hurt. The thought of the woman sitting on me, as I saw her climb onto the girl's thighs, produced a sensation of weightlessness. She had no weight of her own and imparted that lightness to the person she was with, to the girl on the bed and the man now in the air over the mountains of New Mexico. A few minutes after the woman rolled the girl over onto her back, the girl blacked out. She had come in her head.

The woman was frustrated at this inertness. She tried to revive the girl by manipulating her tongue with her fingers and at the same time opening and closing her hand inside the girl's vagina. I was beyond jealousy now. I despised the unconscious girl. I came close to hating the woman. How could she have made such a dumb mistake? What did she want with this creature in the first place?

I could see her dressing the girl when she woke in the morning. Those pale thin fingers pulling the girl's panties over her muscular buttocks, taking the silly breasts and fitting them back into the bra, tugging the strap at the back to clip it.

When the girl regained consciousness in the night, the woman sucked her dry. This was the beginning of the end. The girl began to make heavy, fair-haired love to the woman. She understood nothing. She did it out of gratitude. It was a clumsy mess of a seduction and the woman was appalled. The woman did not want to be touched. That ought to have been obvious. She wanted only to touch. In the touching she was stimulated herself and was satisfied.

She stopped the girl's confusion by removing her hands from even the outer folds of her vagina. The girl started to cry. As she sobbed, the woman untypically felt sorry for her. She kissed her tears and stroked her carefully to soothe the blotched pink flesh.

12

Midmorning they were in the tub together. It was too small for comfort. The woman washed the girl's neck and shoulders. Then she climbed out of the bathtub. The girl now had room to lay back comfortably in the warm soapy water. The woman bent over her and sucked her nipples with increasing diligence. The girl closed her eyes. The lids flickered as she received this natural electric-shock treatment. The girl's head sank down below the surface of the water. She did not close her mouth. As she sucked in air she sucked in water. She gasped and spluttered and her body went rigid in orgasm. Her body shook and she slumped against the side of the tub for support.

Time stopped. Then the woman saw that the girl had not surfaced. For the first time she was scared. She hauled the girl's head out of the water.

"Don't be dead," the woman ordered. "Don't be dead!"

The girl wasn't breathing. The woman gave her a desperate deep sucking kiss on the lips, the kiss of life. Seeing the woman's mouth gulping to save a life was more sensual than purely sexual kisses. The woman's lips contorted and her throat strained. Her cheeks were alternately sucking and blowing in a disciplined frenzy. I twisted in my seat. The girl did not recover consciousness.

The woman did not panic. Now she became coldly efficient. It took her fifteen minutes to pull the girl from the bathtub. She slipped and slid impossibly. She began to dry the girl's body very carefully, every crevice gently, every hair vigorously. Then she wrapped her in her own robe and put the girl on a towel, which she then pulled to the doorway across the tiled bathroom floor. It was hard work getting her to the center of the bedroom. Exhausted, she sat and looked at her victim, taking deep controlling breaths.

Looking at the girl, she couldn't resist it. She opened the white gown and, imagining she was kissing her dead self, brushed the girl's body, from hair to toenails, with her lips and hands. The body was warm. The woman had never touched a dead person before. It made her quiver. She parted the lips of the girl's vagina and felt inside. It was warm and damp but not wet.

The woman decided to take the girl back to her own room. She decided quite specifically what to do. Drag the girl

13

along the passage just after three, when most guests would either have checked out of the hotel or would be still out to lunch, or napping or fucking. After three was definitely the safest time of Sunday. Then I saw her.

"I know you saw me." Yes, and now you know that I know that you saw me. So where does that leave us? Wherever you are, you must realize that I know what happened but I'm not going to report you. You're safe with me.

We picked up my car at LAX airport and drove to the Pacific Palisades. We lived in a small house that belonged to Barbara. I wasn't looking forward to going to bed. I didn't want to dream some irrational crap. I wanted to remember and remember, to stay awake with her and relive what I saw and what I knew. I wanted to be alone with my mental photo album, to experience again the thrill of being criminal one minute, detective the next.

Barbara put her hand on my crotch. It was unexpected.

"When we get home I want to make love to you."

"Oh."

"I want to start from the beginning, as if I'd just brought you home for the first time. I'll make you a cup of coffee, light the candles. We'll watch a movie on 'Showtime.'"

"What's the movie?"

"Then I'm going to undress you. I'm going to unzip your pants and take all your clothes off one by one. Then I'm going to stroke you and kiss you. And I'm not going to let you do anything. You can imagine that you're all chained up."

Was this the result of a short visit to the Land of Enchantment?

I laughed. "Barbara, what's happened to you?"

"It's what's going to happen to you. I'm going to seduce you. I'm going to do everything you ever dreamed of. You're not going to do anything. Nothing. I'll do it all. Mason, I'm going to make you explode."

The lights turned red. I braked. I looked at her again, wondering what had prompted this release of sensuality. She had somehow picked up on my own charged sensuality and was responding to it by osmosis.

Barbara looked straight ahead. She was determined.

14

"I'm going to show you a thing or two," she said. Then she sniffed. "Can you smell perfume?"

"I don't think so, just your usual . . ." I stiffened. Now I could smell it. I sniffed again. My intestines twisted involuntarily. From its effect the perfume might have been ammonia.

"It's kind of lemony. Verbena, isn't it?"

Christ Almighty! The woman had been in my car.

# 4

# WHO'RE WE GONNA GET?

F irst thing when we were inside the house, we checked our machines. I went into the spare bedroom where I kept the machine that I alone answered. Barbara had her own in the living room. It was inside a hand-painted jewel box.

The little red eye of my machine was winking in the darkness. There was just one message: "Mason, it's Paul. Look, I had a weird call from some woman called Felicity. Do you know her? She told me to leave you, that you were a useless agent and ought to be a writer. I tell you, she sounded kind of demented. . . . Who is she? Whoever she is, boy does she have it in for you. Anyway, I'm telling you this 'cause I don't intend to leave. . . . I got the impression she'd called quite a few people, before she got round to me. I'll talk to you when you get back. Hey, read my screenplay yet?"

That was the message from Paul Jaspers. Felicity was up to her old tricks again. God knows how much she'd had to drink and how many people she'd called. I was sure I'd find out over the next few days. I still had to figure out what to do about Felicity.

Barbara was as good as her word. She didn't let me sleep. She tried everything. It didn't happen. So I faked it. As she slapped my face with her breasts I arched my back, pushing her thighs a foot off the bed. Then I fell back. Almost immediately Barbara fell asleep like a happy dog.

I thought of the woman, herself dissatisfied, taking pity on the girl. Barbara and that girl were so alike it was uncanny. I had never faked an orgasm in my life before. I wondered about it. Women supposedly did it all the time, although never with me. Never?

I fell asleep thinking of the woman in black, holding her arm. Sadly, I don't think I dreamed about her. I dreamed about the house burning down.

At dawn I showered and dried my sweat away. I thought of calling Felicity, but I'd work to do first. I drank three cups of espresso and got back to Paul's script. Somehow I managed to concentrate. It was called *Who're We Gonna Get?* None of Paul's screenplays had yet been filmed, but I knew one day soon he'd make it. This one was a black comedy about the making of a movie. Each time the picture got to the firing line, someone in the cast or production either died or got sick or just didn't turn up for work. At each stage the producers sat down and said, 'Who're we gonna get?' Needless to say, in the screenplay the picture never gets made.

It was pretty funny for most of the way, but there was something jaundiced about it all. Paul had put too many of his own frustrations into it. But maybe an independent would pick it up. It had the makings of a cult hit.

In the warm mist of this West Side morning I contrived to put the woman in black out of my mind. Weaving my way down from the Palisades she didn't seem so real. By eight-thirty I was sitting comfortably in a traffic jam on Sunset, and the lemony perfume had gone, if it ever really existed. Nothing can last very long in L.A. Except the traffic, which is eternal.

I took advantage of the jam to call Os Yates. I wanted him to leave his agent and join Mason Elliott and Associates. I'd known Os Yates for eight years, since I was a junior at ICM and he was a struggling actor of the punk era. Now Os was pulling down a million five a picture. By the time I got my own agency, he had already signed with Larry Campbell. Os had always said he'd join me, but just before his contract was up and he was ready to come over, something stupid happened and the deal fell apart.

16

He was dating this alcoholic starlet named Rosie Elman
I represented. I got her a part in a soft-core picture called *A
Hard Life,* in which she took her clothes off a few times.
When Os saw the picture he went ape-shit seeing his beloved
with her legs akimbo. He blamed me unreservedly and swore
never to talk to me again.

Then he joined Larry Campbell and like a dummy signed
a five-year contract. Five years. Two would have been fine.
So Larry represented Os just as he started to climb the lad-
der. Eventually we made it up after he discovered that little
Rosie had been screwing his half-brother. He then found out
that Larry knew about it and had been concealing this fact
from him for months. Os hated Larry for that and tried to
leave him and come over to me. But Larry wouldn't let him
out of his contract, which still had two years to run. However, every Monday morning I called Os because I was determined to represent him one day. I like him. And then there's
the additional factor that 10 percent of Oswald Yates would
improve my status.

"Os, did I wake you? . . . You were dreaming about
me? Good things, I hope."

He told me his dream. This was spooky. In his dream
Os had come into a hotel room somewhere, his hotel room
it seemed, and found me in bed with a woman. The woman
was very thin, pale-skinned with a Louise Brooks hairdo, like
a black helmet. *Black helmet,* those were his words. It was
scary. He must've picked up my fear in my questioning voice.

"What . . . what happened? . . . What did you do?" I
had to know.

Os had only a poor recollection of what he did in his
dream. All he could remember was that the woman got out
of the bed, put on a black silk dress, and was gone.

"And then?" I was asking. "You've got to remember."

But Os couldn't remember.

The traffic was moving again. The woman in black was
in my brain again. There'd been an accident. I felt that I had
been in it. Os's dream spooked me.

Next, someone had been sick all over my parking space.
Beverly Hills on the weekend was another town. I walked
along the first-floor passage to my office, still thinking about
Os's dream. It had to be just a crazy coincidence.

As I arrived at my office I ran into Kate Maddox. She was a psychotherapist who had the office down the hall from me.

"Mason, you're looking beautiful."

"Kate, men don't come any prettier."

About a year ago we had found each other arriving together at the bathroom door at the end of the hall. We had been on nodding terms before. This was the first time we had laughed together. Kate was an academic type of woman in her late thirties. She had always appeared somewhat remote before.

That evening when I left my office I saw her door was open. Kate was packing papers for the weekend. I couldn't resist her or her couch. It was instant, healthy, and unneurotic fun. We fucked our brains out for a few hours that evening and had dinner at the Mandarin across the street. Afterward, we came back to my office for more. And that was it. I had the feeling Kate wanted rough treatment. I wasn't up for that. To me it was more worrying than pleasurable. I guess we both saw that. Nowadays, we just joked together.

"You're wasting your time as an agent," she said. "You should be an actor."

"And you should become an artist's model, strictly nude work, and quit being a shrink."

We laughed and went our own ways.

I pushed the office door. It was locked. So Alexis wasn't in yet. That was strange. Alexis, my secretary, and I had a pact: She would always be in by eight-thirty on Mondays, in return for which she could leave at four on Fridays. I looked for my key. Alexis had been with me since I started the agency. She was efficient, kind of dull, but utterly reliable. When she had very painful period cramps she would rest up odd days here and there, but that was it. We had a very good relationship.

I saw the envelope propped up against the word processor. It was addressed "Mr. Elliott." Instant panic, as I recalled the letter in the hotel, even though this was typed. I tore it open. I read the letter inside. It was from Alexis, typed on my word processor and on Mason Elliott and Associates paper.

Dear Mr. Elliott,

I spent almost the whole weekend here in the office writing this letter while you were in New Mexico. Don't be too angry. I just can't work for you anymore.

For months I have been tortured by these visions (I can only call them that), yes, visions of the two of us together. I sit at the desk answering the phone and I feel your arms come around me, your hands in my hair, everything.

Of course, part of me knows that you've never really touched me but I feel that you have. I can't help it. The night we had dinner at the Imperial Gardens, I don't know whether you noticed but I was in tears. Really. I felt so lousy. I know I drank too much. I couldn't help it.

Afterwards, when you drove me home, I asked you up and, well you know the rest. . . . It was wonderful, wonderful. But the thing is now I can't face you anymore. I've got to get away. Don't misunderstand all this, will you? I know it's a vision of mine, but I just can't help it. Forgive me please. Please. I'm so unhappy. Reading this, you must think I'm really dumb. I didn't want it to happen, but it did.

So now I've told you. I've written this because I couldn't bring myself to tell it to your face. I must be a coward but I love you. I want you. I feel warm all over with you.

I'm going to my mother for a few days back east. I suppose I'll want a reference from you if that's all right. I hope you'll give me one even if you're angry now. On a professional level I've loved working with you and I think I did a good job. Thank you for everything.

Good-bye,<br>Alexis

P.S. Felicity called on Sunday at 3:15 P.M. She was very angry that you hadn't called her. She swore a lot. I'm used to that, as you know, but it upset me very much because she accused me of having an affair with you.   A.

Fuck Felicity. I had to go sort her out. I started to read the letter again. It was so depressing. Alexis gone. Gone, dammit. Now who was I gonna get?

# 5

# FELICITY

I had never laid hands on Alexis, never even thought about it. Or had I? Somewhere, at some time, perhaps, I had maybe considered seducing her, when I was tired or bored. When I look closely at a woman, at some point I think about sleeping with her. Everybody has their fantasies, and they're harmless enough. Except not so harmless for Alexis. She must have been sitting there at the desk torturing herself for months. She invented the love of her life. Me. It was pathetic. Although perhaps I should be flattered that I was the focus of all this passion. I had never received a letter like that in my life. A few notes of affection from Barbara and some others, but nothing like this. It must have taken some courage to write this kind of thing down, to commit it to paper.

The phone rang. It was Joe Ransom, a producer of down-market but not-uninteresting independent movies.

"Hey Joe, what's happening?"

"I've a not-uninteresting project. I'm looking for a writer. Somebody young."

"And cheap," I said, knowing Joe.

"More like experimental."

"Haven't you heard there's a strike on?"

The writers' strike was now in its third month. It had affected everyone in town, and in some areas not for the worse. Paul Jaspers would not have written *Who're We Gonna Get?* on spec if he had had commissioned work.

"Find the right guy and I'll pay him in Europe, in Hong Kong, cash in a brown paper bag, I'll pay his grocer's bills or his mortgage."

Joe's voice was as high as his state of mind.

"You sound serious, Joe. Why don't you send the material over and I'll read it."

"There's nothing to read, kid. Let's just meet. I want to move quickly on this. Lunch tomorrow at The Grill."

"Twelve-thirty."

"Make it twelve-forty-five. I don't finish with my analyst till midday and you know what the traffic's like from the Valley."

This could be something for Paul. I hung up and made a note on my blotter diary. I ought to call him about Felicity's message. Later.

I opened Saturday's mail. I made a few notes on the blotter for replies. Then I read Alexis's letter again. I wondered what would happen if I wrote a crazy letter like that to the woman in black?

To work. I looked up the number of the agency Alexis came from. Fast Finders. I spoke to a voice there.

"What exactly are you looking for, Mr. Elliott?"

"Reliability above all. I want a girl who can be trusted to do everything she's supposed to. The one I really don't want is the one that lies and says she's done it when she hasn't."

"Age?"

"Totally unimportant. Not over thirty-five."

I put the machine on and locked up the office. I drove into Hollywood.

I grew up in Hollywood. As a matter of fact, the apartment where I lived with my mother after my father's death is still there, and empty. A few years ago she said I could have it when she herself moved to a larger, more baroque place. But she never got around to making it official and turning the deeds over to me.

"You live there," she said. "I don't want to go there ever again."

She knew well that my memories of the place were unhappy. She knew I would never actually live there. So it has remained dustily embalmed since then. I thought of renting it out, but never quite got around to it. For myself, I rented another place for a couple of years before moving in with Barbara.

A wave of loneliness came over me. I remembered the places I had lived in, addresses more than places, and the people I had lived with. Living now in Barbara's house, I realized that if I had had a home of my own, it was the office. The office was the place I was most attached to.

Out of loneliness I wanted to visit the old apartment right now. It was on the second floor of a street of largely Spanish-style houses that were once middle class, then fell into disrepute, while she and I lived there, and in recent years have come up again with the yuppie influx.

I unlocked the outer door of the building and climbed the stairs. There was a strong smell of rotting plants. I pressed the timed light button. The bulb was inadequate. They hadn't changed the fixture since I lived there twenty years ago. "They?" There was no they. The place was ours for all eternity, mine and my mother's. The carpet on the stairs was very springy. For some reason, my mother had it renewed after she left. I turned the key in the door. At that moment I knew why I had decided to visit the apartment.

To look at the mirror in the bedroom. When my mother was out, which was not very often, I used to creep into her room and look at the mirror. This mirror was full-length, built to the height of my mother, in an Art Deco pink and apple green plaster frame. The left-hand side of the frame was wider than the right. The top of the frame was thicker than the bottom. When I came into the room like a burglar to go through the drawers of the commode, I would glance into the mirror so I could see if my mother was coming into the apartment. It was angled so that with the bedroom door open, it reflected the length of the passage right across the small hall to the front door. While my mother was out, I would run a bathtub of water and take my clothes off, ready to wash or be washed. Naked, I would ritually examine the room. When I saw or heard my mother coming, I would head for the bath and leap into the water. So that when my mother found me, I seemed to be doing a sensible, late-afternoon thing. Once upon a time I spent a lot of time in the tub. Now as I looked again in the mirror I saw not my mother but the woman in black and her Barbara-like victim in the hotel passage. The vision wasn't a shock. It was dreamy.

The mirror remained, but precious little else did. The yellowing lace curtains were still there. The worn patterned Arab rugs, whose designs reminded me of gardens and

22

mazes, were as slippery as ever on the oak flooring. A coffee table thick with dust. A tall lamp with a thin bead chain to pull it on or off was now a spider's home. There was a pile of newspapers, brown with twenty years of local history, which had never been thrown out. The kitchen, which my mother used as a bar rather than a larder, retained its peculiar smell of cat and cat food, despite the fact that we never owned a cat. I looked around for a souvenir to take to my mother. I found nothing. I picked up the old vulcanizate phone. The line was long dead. But not my mother.

Her new apartment was older than the old one. It was in a classic Hollywood building where Mae West lived until she died. It had a heavy, senseless character. My mother lived alone in five rooms, fingers of a splayed hand. She used only two fingers, a bedroom that with the exception of the mirror was identical to the old one, and a living room that was devoted to music and books. Several hundred volumes and several hundred records and cassettes constituted the furniture, together with ten thousand dollars' worth of hi-fi equipment, all of it British in make. She had an obsession with British manufacturing. She never explained it beyond asserting that it was the best. I put this down to the influence of my father, who was originally from England. She refused on principle to buy a CD player.

The woman who opened the door was a familiar but still startling sight. Fifty-six or fifty-seven years old, claiming always not to know her real age, my mother was a young-old woman. Long black hair without a hint of gray made her look girlish. Her face, lined, grooved almost, presented an aging mask to the world. Her body was thin and angular, incredibly preserved, like a dancer's, and belonged to a woman of thirty. She always wore a black lace blouse through which her good breasts and broad amber nipples were quite clear. Her bony hands had the light brown spots of age. The tight black skirt, midlength and showing off her ageless legs in black stockings, was somehow out of time, beyond fashion. Her dark red, immaculately painted lips smiled at me. Her black eyes looked me up and down as usual.

"Hello, Felicity."

"Come in, Mason." She sounded drunk, but wasn't. Her

drinking voice had remained over the years so she always sounded as if she were halfway through her second bottle of the day, even if she hadn't had a drink.

I followed her into my damaged past and closed the door with its seven locks.

"Where have you been? I wanted to talk to you."

"I went away for the weekend to New Mexicio."

"Did you go to Taos?"

"No. Albuquerque."

"Albuquerque? What the fuck for?"

"To visit a client. I went with Barbara."

"Why don't you dump that bimbo?"

Here we go, I thought. My mother had only seen Barbara twice and was violently rude to her on both occasions.

"She's just the kind of dumb broad your father went for, don't ask me why. All feeble and yellowy. You know, Mason, I sometimes think that if you found yourself a proper woman, you'd perform a lot better. She can't be any use to your work and when it comes to fucking I'll bet she doesn't know which end is up."

Now it was my turn.

"What the fuck do you mean by calling up my clients and telling them to quit?"

"Somebody's got to tell them." She fell into a chair and put her stockinged feet on the coffee table among the six or seven books she was reading simultaneously.

"Just remember, I'm the first fucking woman you met on this planet."

I looked at her. With her feet on the table I could see up her black dress. I couldn't see if she was wearing panties or not. Probably not. She knew what I was thinking. Mother or not, she brought me up thinking, like herself, of everything in sexual terms. Not just men and women but objects too. "That chair's no good," she would say, "you couldn't fuck in that." "That's boring music. The rhythm's all wrong for screwing to." Light fixtures, door handles, kitchenware, carpets; everything was viewed by Felicity in terms of sexual significance.

"Do you want some coffee?" she asked. "I've got some new coffee beans from an Italian place in the Valley. They're real black and slightly oily. Like little animal turds."

24

I declined this appetizing offer.

"You look nervous, Mason. What's happened?"

"My secretary's just quit." When I said it, I knew it was a mistake.

"Why? Didn't she want to fuck you anymore? I kind of liked her voice. It was sexy."

A thought came into my head: Why hadn't I tried to call Alexis, to have the thing out with her? Maybe I was relieved in some way that a relationship was over. Was I unconsciously looking for a new face in the office?

"You said you wanted to talk to me." I tried to sound firm and businesslike. It sometimes worked. Given a subject that interested her, Felicity was capable of talking sense, even of insight. In another life she might have become a female guru, a marabout in Arabia.

"I was looking through some old shit the other day and I found this." She rummaged around on the coffee table and found a sheaf of typed pages. She handed them to me. "Recognize it?" she asked.

I looked at the pages. I did recognize it. She had kept some of my work when I was still struggling to write.

"Take it away and reread it. It's pretty shitty but there's something in it."

"I remember."

"I want you to stop what you're doing, Mason. Go back to writing. But for fuck's sake quit this nonsense now. An agent is a shitty thing to be."

"Felicity, listen to me. I like my work. I enjoy what I do. I get a charge out of helping my clients. Get it through your head, I'm not a writer and I never will be."

I threw the pages back onto the table. I was used to her craziness, her loony sexuality, but her constant carping was too much. Becoming an agent was probably the sharpest thing I ever did. The job gave me a sense of myself. It allowed me to enjoy my limitations.

Felicity got up. "You know your trouble, Mason. Your trouble is you never found anyone you really wanted to fuck. You never wanted a woman, except me. You never wanted any fucking thing, not really wanted it. Maybe I'm all wrong. Maybe being an agent is perfect for you. It lets you want what other people want. You've no fucking desire of your own, so you live through other people's. I'm showing you a way out."

I'd had enough. I seriously considered taking Felicity and throwing her out of the window. Instead, I kept my temper and went to the door.

"Darling mother, I know the way out."

I opened the door with seven locks.

"Don't call me that, Mason!" She was furious. "I've never been a mother to you."

I turned at the open door. I looked back at her. Felicity, my mother, a portrait in black.

"That's true. So stop trying to run my life. If you call any of my clients again, I'll come and beat the shit out of you. I swear it."

"I'm going to put you out of the agency business if it's the last thing I do."

I slammed the door. Leaving the apartment, I breathed deeply to control my anger. I considered going to the pool at the Bel Age hotel for a dip. I kept my swimming shorts and robe in the trunk of my car. I unloaded tension when I swam. Well, I was tense enough right now. But the relief I needed most was to find a replacement for Alexis.

I got back to the office around three o'clock. Os had called and left a message on the machine. I called him back, but he was out. A good thing. I no longer wanted to talk to him about his dream. Our dream. I opened the mail and waited for the first potential replacement for Alexis. By coincidence the first applicant had worked for Os's agent, Larry. In truth, I was more interested in him than in her.

"Mr. Campbell was a very difficult person."

"In what way?"

"He would fly into crazy rages over nothing."

"There's a lot of tension in this job, you know." I smiled to myself. Not just from the job.

"Mr. Campbell's tensions didn't come from the job, not in my opinion." She read my mind.

"From where then?" Everything about Os's agent interested me.

"From his head."

I didn't take to this girl. I didn't trust her. There was something vaguely criminal about her. Whatever she told me about Larry she'd eventually tell someone else about me. She had dyed hair, auburn, and a thin-lipped mouth, painted shocking pink. Also, I could see the triangular line of her panties' elastic cutting into her buttocks. Then she started to quibble about the money. That was it. At the door I shook her soft hand. She winked at me slowly. At least I thought she did.

"How was your day?" Barbara asked later.

I made it simple. "Alexis quit."

"Quit? Why?"

"She had problems at home, back east."

"Men problems, more likely," Barbara said, uncharitably I thought. "What exactly did she say?"

"She didn't. She just left a note."

"That's a real pain in the butt," Barbara said. "Poor you."

# 6

# MY LUNCH WITH JOE

The Grill was crowded at lunchtime. I stopped at three tables before I made it to Joe's booth. It was a relief to get away from the office calls Alexis used to field so well. In two days I had found out just how reliant I had been on her.

Joe Ransom was a surprising man for a producer. He had an Ivy League background and looked like it. He had a thin face, elegant manner, high-pitched laugh. He was well read, spoke good French, and did pills with everything. As I sat down he swallowed something, washing it down with a gin and sugar-free bitter lemon. He told me the pill was to counter the effect of alcohol. All his pills were antidotes. When Joe ate a steak he took something to break up the fat.

27

With his bread roll he ate a starch blocker. With his glass of water he swallowed an Aqua-Ban. Joe told everyone that he had always wanted to be a singer.

"This is a real unusual project, Mason." He handed me a book of photographs by a New York photographer called Sigismund Helman. It was called *La Belle Dame Sans Merci.*

"Do you know Helman's work?"

"Yes, I think so. Mostly advertising, isn't it?"

"Half and half. This book has sold thirty-two thousand copies in hardback at thirty-five bucks a throw. That's not nothing. Take a minute and have a look."

The pictures were mostly black and white with a half dozen color photographs spaced at intervals. They were all in Helman's familiar style. Pictures of narrow-hipped, impossibly elegant women dressed invariably in black, leather or velvet, with stiletto-heeled shoes, black stockings. There was little nudity, as such, but the positions of the women, who usually came in twos, were suggestive. Through Helman's camera eye, legs crossed were more erotic than legs apart.

In one photograph there was a woman lying full-length on a polished wood floor in a black cocktail dress with her legs crossed. Beside her was an open book. Slumped in an armchair across the room was a second woman with her legs wide apart. One leg hung over the arm, a black shoe still on her foot, and the other leg, without a shoe, bent to the floor. This woman wore a funeral veil. In the open doorway stood a man in a tuxedo, holding the other shoe. The room looked like an elegant hotel suite in Rome.

In another photograph a woman was standing with her stiletto heel pressing into a man's shoe. Her face was calm. His face showed no pain. There was something erotic in the absence of expressed emotion. It was as if they were performing some private ritual in which pain was banished and any outward sign of pleasure forbidden.

The picture that struck me as the strangest was also the simplest. It was one of Helman's ambiguous sets, perhaps a hotel room, perhaps an office, perhaps a borrowed house, painterly and theatrical at the same time. The room was empty. The light from the tall window suggested twilight or dawn. Near a tall Italian black metal lamp a woman was bending over, her back toward the camera and the viewer.

Her head was out of sight, masked by her body. Only one arm was visible since she was apparently picking up things from the carpet. The woman was naked, but her skin was so pale that her torso and buttocks looked like smooth white stone. It made you want to put your hands on the stone-skin surface. I had the impression it would be cold to the touch, but if you put your hand between the faintly shadowed buttocks you would feel the warmth, and if you pushed your finger further inside it would be hot and liquid. This woman's body was cool on the outside, fiery in the center.

"You understand," said Joe, "all these pictures have the same theme, a woman who treats the man with plenty of disdain. She can have anyone. That's the story I want, a relationship where the man, not the woman, is the replaceable one."

Then I saw something I hadn't spotted to begin with. There was a man in the photograph. At the far end of the room by the door was a mirror. A man, wearing only his pants, was visible in the mirror. He was looking at the woman's back. Perhaps the man was Helman behind the camera, or an image of the man looking at the photograph from within. Or me.

"Mason, are you listening to me?"

Joe's voice was distant. I was absorbed in this picture as if it had been music heard through Stax headphones. The outside world didn't register. I leaned forward, bent my head down, to look at the man in the mirror. I saw myself there. Perhaps it was the mirror in the hotel hallway, the mirror in my mother's bedroom. The man in the picture and I watched the woman together. We were doubles.

In the last few days my life had become a series of remembered photographs. In my head I turned the pages of an album of frozen images. The woman in the hotel hallway. Alexis's letter. Felicity's face at the door of her apartment.

"Hey Mason, are you all right?"

I came out of my dream.

"It's an interesting book, but I can't see how there's a movie in it. Who's the central character? What's the story?"

"That's the point. There's no plot yet, but there's plenty of scenes. And that woman in black could be quite a femme fatale."

"But you'd have to invent so much."

"Everything."

"There's not enough there."

"If there's nothing there, Mason, why were you staring at the picture? You must've been looking at it for three or four minutes."

How could I explain it to Joe? So I said: "The girl reminded me of someone. Is she a model?"

"I don't think so. The women he uses are just ordinary women. Well, maybe not ordinary but they're not professional models. Sigismund told me they're mostly friends of friends or people he meets. I guess he meets some great-looking women and spins one or another of his little fantasies around them."

"Now that would make a story."

"Okay," Joe said.

"There's a young writer I know who'd go for this. His name's Paul Jaspers. He's very imaginative."

"You mean he hasn't had a script made."

"Correct. But he will."

"So he's not expensive."

"Fifty for a draft and a set."

"Ten for a treatment. Twenty for a draft. Five for a set."

"Get out of here," I said.

"Remember, Mason, the theme has to be that the girl's the center of the story. Get her character, her story right and the rest'll take care of itself."

We both turned at the ringing sound of a slap. It was like a gunshot in the restaurant. The babble of conversation stopped. Three tables away a fair-haired girl I didn't recognize was attacking Larry Campbell, who hadn't been there when I came in. Her white shift dress was torn. One of her breasts was visible. She was swearing in French at Larry, who bellowed back at her.

"You sleazy little tramp. You think sex is going to do it for you, well it won't!"

The headwaiter tried to quiet Larry down. The production executive from Columbia who was lunching with Larry and the girl held the girl's arm.

"It's a good thing Larry can't understand what Sophie's saying."

30

"You know her?" I asked.

"She had a small part in *Coincidence*."

"Is Larry her agent?"

"Until now."

Larry grabbed hold of Sophie. He was fit to be tied. A woman at the table next to them threw a glass of iced water into his face. Larry stopped. He let Sophie go. Sophie said some more words in French and stormed out of the restaurant, pushing past waiters and the people around the bar who were watching the entertainment. A waiter by their table bent down to pick up her white shoes. She must have kicked them off.

"Larry's a violent pig," Joe said. "You should give Sophie a call. She's a good little actress. I've got her number in the office."

"I've got enough clients right now. Enough small ones, anyway."

"Small ones can become big ones," Joe said.

Larry dried his red angry face with a towel brought by the headwaiter. He stood up and left the restaurant. The studio executive whose name was Mark something-or-other also prepared to leave. He finished a call on his phone.

"I would have thought you'd known her."

"Sophie?"

"Yes. She's Os Yates's current squeeze."

Why didn't I know that? Os never told me. Joe popped a pill to help digest some of the other pills. I returned to the subject of *La Belle Dame Sans Merci*.

"With this kind of subject matter what kind of rating would you get?" I asked. "You don't want an X."

"I don't need a rating at all. With this picture I wouldn't even submit it to the MPAA. Nonunion, we'll make it for under three million. The video market for this is huge worldwide."

"This must be the first picture ever made based on photographs."

"Film is a visual medium, Mason. What's so strange about basing one on photographs? People respond to photographs nowadays more than they respond to written stories. Nobody reads anymore. You know that. Remember, Mason, I want the thing bold. We can play up the lesbian angle. Boldness!"

"What about the women's groups?"

"What about them? Sigismund doesn't care about the feminists. His pictures are about women turning each other on. Men are fascinated and women are intrigued. Every woman has at least thought about making love to another woman. What I'm looking for is a picture that's actually about sex, about people's sex lives, their fantasies and so forth. Just like these photographs. I want to make a real sex film, not a movie with sex in it or a cheap porn pic. This isn't a love story. It's a sex story. But it has to have class. This one must appeal to women as much as to men. Girls like to fuck too, don't they?"

I looked again at the photographs. I thought about Larry and Os and that French actress. Joe was right. Sex was everywhere. Take Alexis, I thought. Sex had changed her life. And maybe mine.

"What about fantasy?" I asked. "Do you see scenes of sexual fantasy in this movie?"

"Sex is fantasy," said Joe.

I looked again at the photograph of the bending woman and then at the man in the mirror. I could have sworn he moved.

# 7

# URSULA

There was a knock on the outer office door. I was on the phone to Mike's producer about his per diems. It was long distance and the line was poor. I was straining to hear and had my finger pressed into my left ear to block out the sound of construction work across the lot outside the window. I assumed that the knock was a bike messenger, so I didn't call out. They know just to come in.

Then I smelled the perfume, the lemony, verbena scent that had haunted me from the hotel in Albuquerque. My scalp tingled. I heard another knock, this time on my door, which was ajar. In my head it was the warning beat of drums.

"I'll call you back on a clearer line."

The door opened and she came in.

"I'm from Fast Finders," she said. It was her, of course, but she was quite changed. She wore a scarlet dress. Her lips and fingernails were neatly painted red. The stockings were skin-colored, the high-heeled shoes were black and matched her handbag. She wore a black cardigan so I couldn't see her arms, but the thin fingers and the black helmet of hair were unmistakable. Her smile was worried but cheery. She wasn't quite so pale. She made no sign of recognition but merely waited for me to speak. It was difficult. I plunged in.

"I've seen you before, I think."

"Oh." She looked genuinely surprised. "Well, it's possible. This is from the agency." Her voice was low. I had expected that. She handed me an unsealed envelope. I couldn't take my eyes off her. I opened the letter. It was a recommendation and a résumé of her past work. Her name was Ursula. Ursula Baxter.

"Please sit down, Miss Baxter."

She sat comfortably, without embarrassment. She crossed her legs. The stockings rubbed against each other silkily.

"Have you ever been to New Mexico?" I couldn't help myself.

"Well, yes, I was in Taos once. Why?" She was surprised.

I started to doubt myself. Perhaps I was totally mistaken. Or this woman was a brilliant liar.

"It's just that I feel I've seen you before."

"Have you? I haven't actually worked in the movie business before. I hope that doesn't disqualify me."

"No, no it doesn't." Nothing could disqualify her right now. "My former assistant was new to the business when she came to me. She turned out just fine."

It was true. Alexis had come from a real estate company.

"But she left."

"For personal reasons." I didn't bat an eye. "Let me tell you a little about the job, Miss Baxter. This is essentially a one-man operation. Me."

"Oh." She seemed surprised. "Outside it says Mason Elliott and Associates."

"Well, about two years ago I had a partner. But it didn't

33

work out. I like to do everything myself with the help of an assistant. Which is really what I'm looking for. More than just a secretary, an assistant.''

"Someone you can train." She smiled.

That disconcerted me. She made it sound sexual. Or was that just my imagination?

"Yes, in a way. I used to work for a large agency. But I found I was in business for the agency rather than for my clients. And that wasn't why I became an agent.''

She was watching me intently. It was as if I was applying for a job with her. Don't let her faze you.

"So I decided to go it alone with my few clients. That way I can guarantee them my full attention. I treat my clients as friends.''

"That must be quite rare in this business," she said.

"I guess it is." Was she trying to flatter me?

"It must be exciting to watch your clients develop. It's refreshing to find someone in this town who's not just profit minded. Someone who's not just interested in the quick kill.''

I couldn't have wanted someone with a better attitude. Still, I was worried. If she was the woman in the passage, had she come here to scare me? How had she found me? It all seemed impossible.

"It sounds like exactly the kind of job I'm looking for. I don't mind working late if it's necessary. I want something that involves meeting people. In my last job in a lawyer's office I didn't get much chance to do that. The thing that worries me is that I don't know all the names and companies in the movie business. I'd have to familiarize myself with them. I'd have to be, well, broken in, wouldn't I?''

"I wouldn't put it quite like that," I said. "It doesn't take very long. A few weeks in this office and you'd know my whole life.''

I had to smile. I hadn't meant to say that.

"I'm a fast learner," she said. "After all, I'm from Fast Finders." It was a joke. My woman in black wouldn't make jokes. Also, Miss Baxter had a sweet smile.

She had nothing of the smoky presence of the woman I thought I knew. I began seriously to think I had been mistaken. But I couldn't take my eyes off her face. It was impossibly similar. Then there was the perfume. That was proof. No, no, this was the woman all right. Why was she here?

"I know you saw me," the letter had said. I shivered. This was no coincidence. This was part of the plot. She was here to explain what she was doing with the girl.

"Is there anything you want to know about me?" she asked. A serious question, no hint of a second meaning or irony. What an actress. Now come on, Mason, think of a question. Nail her.

"May I ask why you left your last job?"

"At the law office? Frankly, I was bored. I was spending too many hours at the word processor. And actually, my eyesight was getting weaker."

"Do you wear contacts?" It was an excuse to stare into her dark green eyes.

"I'd like to, but I can't get along with them. I use these." She opened her handbag and took out a case from which she pulled a pair of thin, black-framed half glasses. She put them on.

"Don't laugh. I know I look funny."

"Not to me," I said. "They suit you."

Ursula Baxter was the perfect secretary, composed, serious, meticulous. She was a cliché.

She took off her glasses and stood up.

"Well, Miss Baxter, I'm still seeing people for the job and I'll make a decision in a couple of days. . . . I'll let Fast Finders know. Thank you for coming to see me."

I held out my hand. Was it shaking? This was it. She put her hand to mine. I gripped the fingers and palm carefully. It was a shock. Her hand was not cold as I had expected, but quite warm, almost sticky. Her grip was pleasantly firm and to me intensely erotic.

I saw her to the door, watching her legs, reminding myself of those thin limbs straining in the hotel passage.

"I hope I see you again," she said at the door. She meant it.

"I hope so too."

She was mine. Mine.

I watched her walk away down the passage, cool, measured, sensible. The walk. The legs. The stockings. The heels. And the imagined parts. Ordinary madness. She must

35

have known I was watching her. Of course, she didn't turn around. She was innocent. I wasn't. At the sound of the phone I had to go back into my office. While I was talking I thought, Well, Ursula Baxter, you've got the job.

I opened the unsealed envelope she had brought, this time looking for clues to her life. I prayed that it would contain something handwritten by her, so I could check it against the note from the hotel. There was just a typed page. Disappointed, I read it.

Ursula Baxter. Born Portland, Maine. There was no date. Wide secretarial experience including . . . There followed a short list of companies Ursula Baxter had worked for. I decided to check the last company for a reference. I called the law firm and reached her ex-boss.

"Ursula is very efficient. Very. From the professional standpoint I can't recommend her highly enough."

"And from the nonprofessinal standpoint?" I sensed a hint of reservation in his response. There was a pause.

"The only thing I would say is that she had a somewhat disruptive influence in the office."

"What did she do?" I was excited.

"She? Nothing, nothing at all. The men in the office got on great with her. But some of the women found her . . . difficult. Difficult to relate to."

"In what way difficult?" So I wasn't so far off in my guess at what could have happened between her and the girl.

"She seemed to get them all jealous. But as far as I know she didn't do anything specific to any of them. It was just that she was incredibly attractive to the men."

"An interoffice affair?"

"Nothing like that. I can't really put my finger on it. The girls just didn't go for her. If you have other women in your office . . ."

"No, I don't," I said.

"Well, then there's no problem. She's a dream."

"Then why did she leave?"

Another pause. "Between ourselves, there's a partner here, a woman, who just didn't like her at all. Maybe something happened between them. I really don't know. But my partner wanted her out. So she was with us just a short time."

"You fired her?"

36

"No, I didn't. I didn't have to. She understood the problem and suggested that she go of her own accord."

"Is she gay?"

"Mr. Elliott, I have no idea what her sexual preferences are and frankly it doesn't interest me."

It fascinates me, I thought. And that was the end of the conversation. I had the impression that her ex-boss had begun to wonder if I was really a potential employer at all. I guess I sounded more like a private dick. In a way, that's what I was.

Ursula Baxter, my mystery woman, my murderess, would soon be sitting over there at Alexis's desk. For eight hours a day, five days a week, she would be mine.

# 8

# DAY ONE

Her first day in my office was one of the happiest days of my life. Ursula's presence calmed and reassured me. My fears and the tensions of my memory and imaginings were massaged away. I was quite curious about her past, but the violent desire to investigate, to get to the bottom of the mystery, to realize the suspicion, faded through her being there. Close to, she was a different person from the woman in the mirror.

Ursula answered calls, took messages, made a list of things for me to do, typed intelligent draft replies to my mail, made the coffee, ordered the caffeine-free Coke for the fridge, and ploughed on with the filing. Ursula made Alexis look like a slut; she was that organized. She had an instinct for what I wanted. She eased the pressure.

Os breezed in after lunch. He was impressed with Ursula. Who wouldn't be? But she didn't appear to recognize him.

"Where's Alexis? Who's that?" They were Os's first questions when I closed the door of my office.

"Alexis left. She had some problems at home. This is my new girl." I felt proud of Ursula.

"Boy, you'll have trouble keeping your hands off her," he said.

"That's the way to lose them," I said.

"With her, I'd say the world would be well lost."

"What would Sophie say?" I couldn't resist it.

Os reacted predictably. His lustful smile vanished.

"How did you hear about Sophie?"

"I was in The Grill when she had that fight with Larry."

"That scumbag! There are times when I seriously wish he was dead."

Os was a big man and he wore clothes that made him look even bigger. He had a joking manner that could turn without warning to rage. I thought of reminding him about his dream but I didn't want to get into it now that the dream was here.

"So when are you going to leave Larry and come over here?"

"Larry's such a prick. He might just've lost me a film at Universal. He's asking two mill and ten points. Of the gross! They're just not going to pay it. I know they won't. It's absurd. He's pricing me out of the market."

"Why don't you tell him that?"

Os stood up and did an impersonation of Larry Campbell in action: "You motherfucking slime, before I took you on you were making shit. You were fucking nowhere, playing scumbag roles in crocks of shit. Your agent was a cunt lapper and you were total shit. A hundred grand a picture. Shit. Now what're you getting? A million fucking five. Don't tell me they won't pay it. Those pricks'll pay what I tell them to pay. When I call up they start shitting bricks and they don't fucking stop till I've finished with them. My job is tearing their balls off every fucking day. And I do it for you. So, no shit from you, please."

"Maybe that's the coke talking," I said. Os's rendition of Larry Campbell reminded me of Felicity in action. There was madness in it. No question, Os was a superb actor. I had to sign him. Ursula knocked and came in.

Os said, "Sorry about the screaming."

"Can I get you anything?" she asked, as if she had heard nothing. "Coffee, tea, Badoit?"

"Have you got a beer? Screaming is thirsty work."

I shook my head. "We don't. But we can get some. Ursula, I wonder . . ."

"We have it," said Ursula. "Becks, Budweiser, or Dos Equis?"

I was impressed.

"Dos Equis," said Os.

When I looked at the fridge later I saw that Ursula had stocked it with all kinds of stuff, from Lite beer to Stoli. She had also bought some snacks and smoked salmon from Greenblatt's.

"I took it out of petty cash. I didn't think you'd mind."

"You're brilliant," I said.

Ursula brought the Mexican beer in a chilled tankard.

"What service!" Os said. When Ursula had gone back to the outer office he went on, "You've definitely got something there, Mason."

I agreed.

"What happens if you just quit, break your contract?"

"Then he'll sue me. No question. He's in a vile mood. His wife was in the office the other day when I was there. She was in floods of tears. He'd beat her up the night before."

"What about Sophie? Does she have a contract with Larry?"

"No, she hasn't signed yet. She's lucky."

"Is she looking for representation?"

"She's not for you, Mason."

"Why not?" I was hurt.

"Representing women is not your strong suit. You're better with men than women. As an agent, that is. I can't answer for your sex life."

"No one can answer for their sex life."

"Don't worry, Mason. When I leave Larry, I'll come to you." Os was jealous of Sophie.

When he had left the office, brightened by the beer and by Ursula, I explained the situation to her. If she was going to work for me she had to understand the business. I wanted to take her into my confidence.

She said, "There must be a way to get him to come to you."

"If you can figure it out, let me know."

"Barbara called. She said she's at home if you want to call her about tonight."

"I'll call her later."

At around five that afternoon, Paul Jaspers came into the office. He had expected to see Alexis. He introduced himself to Ursula.

"I liked your screenplay very much," Ursula said.

I had given her *Who're We Gonna Get?* for an opinion. I explained to her how to read a screenplay, that it wasn't like a book, and she said she'd be interested in reading it. I hadn't expected her to have read it, not in office hours.

"How did you find time to read it?" I asked.

"In the lunch hour," she said. "I'm a quick reader."

"And you really liked it?" Paul was flattered.

"I laughed. Is the movie business really like that?"

"Pretty much," I said.

"You're new to it, are you?" Paul Jaspers was curious about her; I could see it in his face. He was twenty-five, long dark hair, designer stubble, dressed in L.A. clothes. He looked like an actor.

"Would you like something to drink?" She knew what Paul was thinking.

He looked at his watch, then at me. "I thought maybe we could go to the Magic Mushroom; I could use a drink."

But we didn't go out. Ursula brought him a vodka on the rocks and some smoked salmon canapés.

"It sure is a changed atmosphere in here," Paul said. Then, just as Ursula was going back to her desk, he said, "Was there anything about my script you didn't like?"

Ursula hesitated in the doorway.

"Go on," I said.

"I don't think it's my place to—"

"Go on. Tell us."

"Well, I thought the woman was a bit weak, the producer's girlfriend. She just seemed to be along for the ride. Perhaps if she had a relationship with the young actor . . . it would make things a little more . . . I don't know. Tense. Excuse me."

40

The phone was ringing. Ursula went to the outer office to answer it, closing the door behind her.

Paul turned to me. "Not a bad idea."

I told Paul what I thought of *Who're We Gonna Get?* and then started in on Joe's project, *La Belle Dame Sans Merci.* I showed him the book of photographs. He knew Helman's work and liked it. He had an idea how to treat the subject.

"It's the story of Macbeth and Lady Macbeth. She has a hold over him, a kind of sexual grip on his mind through his body. She humiliates him in small ways. For instance, in a room full of people she could dig her stiletto heel into his shoe. No one notices and he has to hide the pain. Basically, she can always get him to do what she wants."

"Okay. But why doesn't he leave her? I mean, sex can't hold people together forever."

"He's dependent on her. When she's not there, he's lost, doesn't know which way to turn."

"What is it she wants? Hopefully not money."

Paul sipped his vodka. "Not money. It's the power, the power over him."

"I'll set up a meeting for you with Joe, when you feel you're ready. He'll commission a treatment. If he likes it, he'll go to screenplay."

"How much for the treatment?" Paul asked, a true writer.

"I don't know. Ten thousand, maybe fifteen. And possibly forty for a first draft with a set of revisions."

Paul was looking at the glass of vodka. "There's lipstick on this glass."

I looked at it. He was right.

"That must be Alexis," I said. The lipstick was red. But Alexis never wore red lipstick, always pink. Ursula wore red lipstick.

"It's all right. I don't mind."

"I'll get another glass."

"No, no, leave it. It's kind of sexy. She's kind of sexy."

On his way out Paul talked to Ursula. I didn't know what they said. By then I was on a call to New York. A woman casting director I knew was recommending an actress who had recently come to live in L.A. and was looking for representation.

"She's very good," the casting director said. "I think you'll like her. Her name is Silvia Glass. I've given her your number. She'll call you in a day or so. Silvia's done some stage and commercials. I think I sent you some pictures and her rés. She's a bit eccentric, but don't be put off."

"How eccentric?"

"She talks a lot about boxing. She's very athletic, tough but vulnerable at the same time."

"One day I'll meet an actress who's tough but not vulnerable," I said.

It was six o'clock. I went into the outer office to tell Ursula she could go home.

Ursula was kneeling on the floor, her back to me. Every facet of her bottom was visible through the material of her dress. I couldn't see exactly what she was doing. She was hardly moving. Her body was a solid sculptural shape, identical to that in one of Helman's photographs. In the picture you couldn't tell whether the woman was spontaneously caught by the camera or whether she had been carefully placed by the photographer. The inescapable sensation was that she was offering herself. You want me like this, don't you? was what the photograph said. Ursula's pose was identical.

I felt dizzy. I had to speak because if she turned suddenly to see me standing, watching her, she'd be embarrassed. I'd be embarrassed.

"What happened?" I asked.

She didn't jump at the sound of my voice, as I had half-expected her to do. She didn't move. It was as if she hadn't heard me. She froze like the image of the photograph. I walked forward. She slowly turned her head, then moved her body round on her knees. I now saw what she was doing. She was picking up cigarettes. There must have been twenty or thirty on the floor. She was putting them into a gold paper box. They were English cigarettes.

"I dropped my cigarettes." She wasn't embarrassed. Her tone was oddly flat, a statement of fact.

"Let me help you."

"Oh no, that's all right, Mr. Elliott. It was clumsy of me."

"I didn't know you smoked."

"I don't, not in the office. I'm sorry about this."

"I don't mind if you smoke, Ursula."

"No, I wouldn't dream of it."

I watched as she put the cigarettes back into the box. It was a ritual, one at a time. She was asking to be photographed.

"I just wanted to say it's six o'clock and you can go home."

"Are you sure there's nothing more I can do?"

"Nothing, thank you. You've done wonderfully today. I'm very pleased."

She smiled as she stood. That thin body. She straightened her blood-red dress. It was immaculate, her second skin.

"These are the letters for you to sign." She handed me the folder. "I'll wait and then take them to mail."

"No, you go. I'll mail them myself when I leave."

She carefully covered the word processor with its plastic protector and picked up her handbag.

"Good night, Mr. Elliott. I have enjoyed today."

I wished her good night and watched her go. My anxiety returned. Physically attracted to this woman, I couldn't help recalling my vision of the other in the hotel mirror. Were they one and the same? They had to be. Did it matter? No. Yes. I felt the beginning of an erection, the thrill of desire.

I signed the letters without really reading them. They looked perfect. She had stamped all the envelopes. I touched one of the stamps that wasn't quite straight. Under my two fingers the stamp moved minutely. The gummed side was still damp, sticky with her saliva.

At dinner Barbara talked compulsively about men and women and love with a capital *L*. It was unusual for her not to discuss the jewelry business at all. She even started to sound jealous, as if she suspected I was having an affair. But maybe that was in my imagination. So many things were.

"You know what you mean to me," she said. "Do I mean that much to you?"

"Yes," I said, "of course you do."

All through the meal I thought about Ursula. It was impossible that Barbara suspected anything, yet she seemed unaccountably scared of losing me.

"I never really liked that girl, Alexis," she said.

"She was very efficient."

"She seemed kind of shifty to me. I don't know. I'm glad she's gone. What's the new girl like?"

"So far so good."

# 9

# THE JACKET

You're a clotheshorse," Barbara said at breakfast.

I had put on a new Cerruti suit, a faintly striped, dark green-blue mixture. With soft narrow lapels, it gave off a matt sheen. I had bought it several weeks ago, but I couldn't decide when or why to wear it. Today I had an eleven o'clock appointment with my bank manager. I was going to hit him for a loan of seventy-five grand. Barbara stroked the shoulders of the jacket.

"You're a dish," she said. That was her old-fashioned term of affection and, I guess, admiration.

We were sitting in the kitchen, up at the counter. Like every room, like each piece of furniture in Barbara's house, it wasn't quite large enough for people. It was a Melrose-antique Disneyland, built to three-fourths scale.

"I went to see Felicity."

"She's truly nuts, isn't she? What did she say about me?"

"Nothing."

"She hates me, I know. But I don't take it personally. She'd hate any woman you were with. When I think of her I feel sorry for you."

"Don't," I said vehemently.

"All right. I won't. But I don't see how you could have a mother like that and not be affected by it. You didn't exactly have a normal childhood, did you?"

"Look, I don't want to get into a discussion."

Suddenly, Barbara's approval of my suit seemed like a preamble to her criticism of my mother. It was intended to soften me before needling me. She sometimes adopted this technique in the early mornings. I had no idea why. Maybe it came from things she had dreamed.

"Okay. You still look good enough to eat."

"You did that last night."

"Don't be vulgar. It doesn't go with your suit."

The night before, I had tried to make love to her. It was a little desperate. She must have sensed it. She took over. I kept seeing Ursula bending in her red dress.

After Barbara had fallen asleep I had gone to the bathroom and masturbated, imagining photographs of Ursula bent, naked, on the floor. It was an electric feeling. I was an adolescent again, making a sexual discovery about myself.

On my way out of the house Barbara said, "I'll take your jacket and pants to the cleaners."

"I can get the new girl to do it."

"Give her a break. She's not Alexis."

"What do you mean?"

"I mean, Alexis was like your servant. She loved taking your stuff to the laundry. Not all girls want to be servants."

"True."


It was nine when I arrived at the office and found myself walking toward her. Ursula was waiting at the door. She was dressed in black and smiling.

"You don't have to get here until nine-thirty, you know."

"I know." She sounded apologetic. I thought about waking up beside Ursula instead of Barbara.

"How long have you been here?"

"About ten minutes. Someone gave me a ride."

"I must give you a set of keys," I said. Who gave her a ride? A man? Someone she'd spent the night with? A woman?

We went in together. Now she was completely the woman in black. For a moment I believed she was mine and always had been. She bent and picked up the junk mail from the floor. I wanted to put my arms around her and hold her tightly and still for a few moments. I wanted to thank her. I wanted to tell her I didn't care whether she was the woman in black or not, whether she had done what I imagined or not. It didn't matter.

"What are you looking at?" she asked. I was staring at her without realizing it. I thought it had been just a glance.

"Is it my dress? Does black depress you?"

"Not in the least. Black's my favorite noncolor. It suits you."

"Thank you, Mr. Elliott."

I wanted to say "Please call me Mason," but it could have sounded wrong, insinuating. Instead, I became stiff with formality.

"And Ursula, I meant what I said last night. Please smoke if you want to."

"If I absolutely have to, I will."

There was a smell of cigars in the bank manager's office. The last client obviously had a taste for Havanas. Probably someone I knew. Half of Beverly Hills banked here. There were no secrets from the manager.

"Seventy-five thousand," the manager said. "Over what kind of period?"

"Eighteen months. Maybe two years. It depends on how long the writers' strike lasts."

"What's the prognosis?"

"Three months. Six. No one knows. It could end next week."

There was a pause. I knew he wasn't going to turn me down. I was a good, reliable customer. I'd had a loan before and paid it back on time. So why the pause?

"For that kind of money in today's market, the bank would be looking for some kind of security."

"All right. I have my apartment."

"What's the market value?"

"I don't know. Maybe two fifty."

"Is it encumbered?"

"No."

"Good enough. Can you let me see the title deeds?"

"Sure."

He made a couple of notes on his pad. The deal was done. I had expected him to ask me what the loan was for. But he didn't. He smiled.

46

"I kind of admire you, Mason."

"Why?" That was a surprise.

"You must have had offers to join a larger agency. To merge."

"Yes, I have. But I like my independence."

"I know. But independence comes expensive in this town, especially in your business."

He was right. I'd been told many times that my solo days were numbered. Perhaps the one really valuable and romantic legacy from my unromantic mother was the desire to go it alone.

I walked back to the office. I remembered that while the apartment was mine, my mother hadn't actually given me the title deeds. I'd have to ask her for them. That would be a scene I'd have liked to avoid.

As I approached the office I heard Ursula's voice on the phone. I often left the hall door open during office hours. I heard her say, "Yes . . . I'll see you tonight. No, I don't, but I'm sure I can find it. . . . No, I'll go home first to change."

I smiled at her and went on past her into my office. I heard her finish the call. She obviously had a date for tonight. Well, why not?

Ursula had set out all the mail on my desk for me to read. She brought me some coffee and a Danish.

"First get me Joe Ransom."

"Mike Adorno called. Said he'd received his per diems. Everything's fine."

"Oh good." I was surprised because I hadn't called the producer back.

"I took the liberty of calling Mr. Sohl myself to remind him while you were out."

This woman was incredible. "I didn't know you even knew about it."

"I saw a note you wrote to yourself on the blotter so . . . you don't mind, do you? I was very polite."

"I'm sure you were, Ursula. Thank you."

After lunch I found a Fed Ex package from the casting director in New York. I looked at the photographs of the actress she had recommended. Silvia Glass. She looked vaguely like Barbara. And she reminded me of the girl in the hotel

47

passage, the same blond hair and neck, the look of a swimmer. Right now I didn't need a new client without real experience.

Some construction work had just started up in the alley when I heard Barbara's voice in the outer office. The door flew open, banging against the rubber stop. I jumped. Barbara charged up to me.

"You asshole!" She threw two folded sheets of paper across the room.

"What's the matter? What's happened?" I had never seen her in a temper like this. Normally, when Barbara was angry she was sullen, playing with her rings, taking them off and dropping them. This shouting was new.

"You asshole. How long have you been fucking her? Months! How could you do it?"

Barbara ignored Ursula, who was standing in the doorway. I picked up the two sheets of paper. It was the letter from Alexis. Fuck. How had she gotten hold of it?

As if to answer me, Barbara said, "It was in your jacket. Well, I burned the jacket. I shoved it in the incinerator. I wish you'd gone in with it. What was it like fucking her and then coming home to me? Well, don't try to come home. If you want some action tonight, try her!" Barbara pointed at Ursula, who closed the door, leaving us to our row. It didn't last long.

"Barbara, if you've read the letter properly you'll know it was just a fantasy of Alexis's. Nothing happened."

"'It was wonderful.' Does that sound like nothing happened?"

"Fuck it, Barbara. Alexis imagined it, all of it. Read the letter, you'll see."

There was no way of reassuring her.

"I don't want to see you again!" She was crying now. "I feel sick. Sick to my gut. How could you do it, fuck your own secretary. It's like some crummy cliché. You can pick up your things anytime and leave the keys. But just make sure I'm not there when you do. No wonder you didn't want to fuck me. It was her."

"Barbara, just read the letter. You've got it all wrong."

"You make my skin crawl."

48

She charged out through Ursula's office and slammed the front door. The phone started ringing. I stared at the letter. I don't remember putting it in my jacket. Shit.

"Mr. Elliott's in a meeting," Ursula was saying calmly, "he'll get back to you."

I couldn't look at her. I went back into my office and closed the door. I sat at my desk. I looked at the smiling face of Silvia Glass.

# 10

# LULU

A fter the first shock of Barbara's outburst, which lasted numbingly through the afternoon, I felt an unexpected sensation of relief. It came as I watched Ursula at work, answering calls, typing letters, crossing and uncrossing her legs. There was something extraordinarily calming in her apparent indifference to the scene. My first instinct had been to explain what had happened, how it was all a misunderstanding. That would have been close to an apology.

Ursula's lack of inquisitiveness massaged my insecurity. Her very presence soothed me. She was above it, superior to Barbara. And she made me feel superior as well. My embarrassment at the incident, going back to Alexis's letter, just vanished. I experienced a sense of freedom. If Barbara wanted to believe Alexis's fantasy, let her. It was her mistake, not mine. A pity perhaps, but there it was. I was grateful to Ursula. Saying nothing, she had fulfilled the role of a good friend.

As she prepared to leave the office at the end of the day, I remembered her talking to a man on the phone when I had come in earlier. I was jealous. I would like to have invited her out myself, had dinner, gotten to know her. My suspicions about the woman in black seemed irrelevant. Now I wanted Ursula Baxter. Tonight. My renewed desire was less abstract than before. She was a real woman. Of course.

49

When I recalled my erotic and even criminal imaginings about her, I had to laugh. That woman was a creature of my mind, someone I invented, just an image.

While she was freshening up in the bathroom at the end of the hallway, I resolved to ask her to have a drink with me this evening. As I waited, I realized I hadn't yet given her the office keys. She ought to have a set. Had Alexis taken her keys with her? I looked in the desk drawers. Shit, where were they? I opened drawer after drawer, rummaging about among the paper clips and staples. Suddenly, I was aware of Ursula standing in the doorway watching me. I could see how it must have looked to her, my going through her desk, her things, looking for what? I looked at her. My smile collapsed. Ursula had changed back into the woman in black. Once again, she was the pale-skinned, thin-armed doll from the hotel. Her black dress shone like metal. With her helmet of black hair she looked like a warrior. And she had put on the lemony scent that filled my nose with chloroform, sweet and druggy.

"I was looking for the office keys," I said. "You ought to have them."

"They're here," she said and went to the locked filing cabinet. "I put them in here for safe keeping."

I closed the drawers of her desk. She retrieved the keys and held them out to me.

"They're yours," I said.

"Thank you." She opened her black handbag and dropped them in. The bag snapped shut. She smiled pleasantly, but looked me straight in the eyes. "Is there anything else I can do before I go?"

"No, nothing. Have a good evening. I'll see you in the morning."

"Good night, Mr. Elliott."

And she was gone, leaving me with only the fading sound of her heels clicking along the hallway.

Silence. I felt completely alone. I had not asked her out for a drink. Having unsettled me, having reassured me, this woman had now unnerved me again. Was it my weakness or her power?

I turned to my friends the fish. I saw that the gold and white one was now floating among the green lilies on the surface of the tank. Why hadn't I noticed it before? I took him

50

out and held him in my hand for a moment, resisting any inclination to make something symbolic out of his death. Things happened in life. They just happened. Only a writer like Paul Jaspers would look for significance in everything. When I threw the dead fish down the toilet at the end of the hall, I could smell Ursula's scent.

I drove to the apartment, my mother's apartment. I was disoriented. I had an invitation to a party later. I debated with myself whether to go. I decided not to. All I wanted was to know where Ursula was having dinner and with whom.

I called Barbara. I couldn't just leave things. She wasn't home, or she wasn't picking up. I left a message.

"Barbara, listen. You have completely misunderstood the letter. Alexis was talking about her fantasies, not, repeat not, what actually happened. I've got it here with me. Let's sit down and we'll read the damn thing together. You'll see. Please call me." Maybe she'd call, but my guess was she wouldn't. But then, how could she call me? The phone in the old apartment wasn't working. So I'd have to go over to the Palisades and talk to her. But I didn't feel like doing that right now. I would spend the evening putting my mind in order.

The apartment was depressing. I spent an hour sitting and pacing, trying to avoid memories of my past in the place, the terrible times with my mother when she went through a phase of taunting me by bringing home men.

I would get up in the morning to go to school and the place would stink of whiskey and sex. My mother would be in bed with someone or other. One morning there were two of them.

How was I going to live here? No way. I went out for a meal.

I ordered too much sushi and didn't finish my beer. I decided I wanted a distraction. I went to the party. It was a predictably dismal affair in West Hollywood. Too many actors and the inevitable questions.

"Barbara not with you? . . . I heard Alexis walked out. . . . What happened? I thought she was a permanent fixture. . . . Apparently your new secretary's terrific. Paul told me she was quite amazing."

I nodded and lied and dodged until I caught up with Paul.

"Given any more thought to that idea of Joe's?"

"I think I figured it out. Set up a meeting and I'll pitch it. It's really exciting."

"Tell me," I said.

"It's really a classic tale of humiliation that ends in destruction. It starts innocently enough. He meets her. He falls for her. She starts to take over his life, bit by bit. She reorganizes his life. She makes him change everything. He leaves his old apartment. She decorates the new one. She gets him to cut his hair differently, wear different clothes, eat new kinds of food that he didn't like before. Everybody tells him what's happening but he can't see it."

"Why can't he see it?"

"He sees it, but he likes it. He thinks it's all for the better. And see, here's the point. In many ways it is for the better. He becomes more confident, more successful. His friends even begin to envy him. Then one day she suggests that he kill someone."

"Just like that?"

"Yes. But it has a purpose. She wants him to kill someone who's in the way, some business rival. He's scared, of course. He won't do it. But she threatens to leave him, abandon him. He tells her he can't kill anyone. So she leaves him. Now his business starts going downhill. He goes to pieces, drinks too much, gets into fights. Eventually, he has to go back to her. He agrees to the murder. They plan it together. They do it. She rewards him with all kinds of sex. With the dead guy out of the way, his business takes off. But now she's in charge. He becomes her lackey. Their roles are reversed. Now she runs things. He becomes her assistant."

"What about the murder? Do they get caught?"

"Now here's the switcheroo. Someone else gets arrested and tried for the murder. There's a trial and he gets life. The woman is now completely dominant and our man becomes just a fixture. She's got what she wanted and he's happy."

"Why is he happy?"

"Because he's the kind of guy who all his life secretly wanted to be dominated. She uncovered that part of him and satisfied it. That's why he's happy at the end."

"Joe'll never go for that. It's so black."

"No it's not. It's a weird love story with a happy ending."

52

"Do you really think this is commercial?" I asked Paul.

"Of course. It will be. Remember what you told me the first time we met. You said, 'Everything is commercial if it's well done.' That's what you said, Mason."

It was true. I did say that. I didn't want to argue specifics with Paul.

"Okay. If that's the story you want to tell. I'll call Joe in the morning and set up a meeting."

"Don't be depressed. You'll be quite surprised. I'm going to call it *Lulu.*"

I left the party early. I went back to the apartment. There was something about Paul's storyline that seemed to me truly shocking. Could anyone be happy when they were under the thumb of someone else?

I switched on my mother's mauve-glass bedside lamp. I wanted to reread Alexis's letter. I wanted to be able to quote chapter and verse to Barbara. She won her point so easily in the office, and in front of Ursula. I looked at my watch: Ten forty-five. Ursula would have finished eating dinner by now, wherever she was. Was she drinking? She didn't look like a drinker.

On the second page of the letter I stopped and went back to reread it from the start: ". . . Afterwards, when you drove me home, you asked to come up and well, you know the rest . . . it was wonderful." Wait a minute. That wasn't right. Alexis had written something like "I asked you up." She hadn't said I asked to come up. Then I went back. I read this: ". . . Part of me wishes you'd never touched me but I know that you have . . ."

"Wishes you'd never touched me." Alexis hadn't said that. I remembered her phrase clearly: "Part of me knows that you've never really touched me . . ."

This whole letter was different, altered around.

The stinger came at the end. I read: "P.S. Your mother called on Sunday at 3:15 P.M. She was very angry that you hadn't called her. She swore a lot. She knows we're having an affair. A."

Was I deranged? I could not have misread the letter so completely. Yet there it was. Now I could see why Barbara reacted like that. This letter wasn't the letter Alexis wrote. It had been changed.

# 11

# THE RED AND THE BLACK

When I let myself into the office I could smell her lemony scent. I switched on the lights. There was a sudden small splashing sound as the fish woke up. Had she killed that fish as well? I started on a thorough search for the letter, Alexis's letter. I went through everything, my desk drawers, the files, piles of trade magazines, even the stationery drawers in Alexis's desk. Now I was looking for the letter not in places I might have put it but in places she might have hidden it. I was back in my detective's role. In the morning I would confront her with my suspicions.

"Why did you do it? I know you did it, but I don't know why. What do you want from me?" I would be cool, not accusing but concerned.

After a while I gave up the search for the letter. If she had taken it and then retyped it, she wouldn't leave the incriminating original in the office.

I was closing the desk drawer with the paper clips and Scotch tape when I saw a small cellophane package. I took it out. It was a pair of women's red satin panties. Hers.

I turned the package over and pressed my fingers into the cellophane. I opened the package and took out the panties. I felt the soft shiny material in my hands. I pulled the elastic wide, imagining her putting them on. She was sitting on the side of a bed somewhere. She was wearing a red blouse. I couldn't tell if she had on a bra or not. She bent to slip the panties on. One leg bent toward her blouse, she pushed her foot through the hole. I watched. Her pubic hair glistened in a flickering orange light, a fire or candles. She had just had a bath or taken a shower. I could smell it. Her skin was faintly shiny from the oil. She lifted the other leg, balancing on the side of the bed for a moment. She was exposed. Between her legs was the mouth of a peculiar animal. She stood up, slowly pulling the scarlet material across her skin. Her pubic hair was probably still damp. I could hear the slithering sound of the satin moving upward on the skin of her narrow thighs. Her panties were on. The hair had vanished as if it had never existed. She put her hand inside the garment for a moment, arranging something, getting comfortable. The red satin bulged and moved. She withdrew her hand. Then came the small slap of elastic as she let go.

"Hold it right there!"

A man's voice barked from the door. I stiffened. Cold and prickling, I turned to see a burly man standing in the doorway. It was the superintendent of the building, the night man. He was wearing a gun, but he wasn't holding it. In his hand was a riot stick.

"What are you doing here?" He came into the office, looking around to see if I was alone.

"I had some work to do." Slowly, I relaxed. "It's my office, you know. I'm Mason Elliott."

The super didn't know me. We'd never met. He was still suspicious. I smiled and showed him my key.

"You should close the door, Mr. Elliott," he growled. His menacing voice didn't change in tone even when he accepted who I was. I could see the man practicing at his home in front of the mirror, like an actor rehearsing his part.

He looked at the pair of red panties in my hand. He looked at me. Christ, I thought, had he seen me holding them to my face?

"You're not expecting anyone, are you?" He glanced toward the half-open door of the inner office. He must have thought I was there with a woman or waiting for one.

"No, no. I'm alone."

The super left, disappointed that he hadn't caught a criminal red-handed. In a sense, he had surprised a criminal, a Peeping Tom, a sexual pervert, not red-handed but red-pantied.

I pulled out the sofa in my office. It opened into a springy bed. I decided to sleep here. In the morning I would confront her.

I turned out all but a single lamp beside the sofa. This night I was almost afraid of the dark. Having no pajamas or a change of clothes for the next day, I thought about Barbara. I'd have to go home tomorrow. I'd have to talk to her once more, try to explain. But how could I? What would I say? That this new secretary of mine retyped Alexis's letter and put it in my jacket pocket so that my girlfriend would find it and . . .

And what? Setting aside the mystery of why she had done it, the effect had been to drive a wedge of jealousy between Barbara and myself.

I drifted toward sleep. The last thing I remembered was the image of Ursula bending, picking up cigarettes, turning to me, knowing I was there in the mirror . . .

"Christ!" I sat up in the creaking sofabed, startled into waking by a dream. She was standing beside me.

"Would you care for some coffee?"

She wasn't quite Ursula. She wore a white dress and a gloriously sympathetic lipstick-free smile, a fresh-faced angel from a chidren's story. I smiled too.

"Thank you, nurse." I started on the coffee. She went back to her desk in the outer office and carefully pulled the door almost shut. Presumably, that was to allow me to dress or do whatever I had to do in private. It was as if she had discreetly pulled a screen around her patient's bed.

Once again I was at a loss with her. I got out of the bed, realizing that I had no fresh clothes. I had to see Barbara. I heard the phone ringing. Ursula answered it. I could hear her saying, "I'm sorry, Mr. Elliott's not arrived yet." Was she expecting an explanation of how I had come to spend the night in the office?

The room was stuffy. I opened the window onto the alley. There was my black BMW. The boy from the garage was cleaning it. I looked at my watch. It was eight forty-five. A new day, hotter and potentially more confused than the old one. I went into her office.

Ursula looked up from her list making. She reached across to her desk and gave me a plastic-covered coat hanger with a pair of cleaned pants and a packet of three freshly laundered shirts.

"I took the liberty of picking them up," she said sweetly. "I found the tickets in your desk."

I now remembered that Alexis had taken them in to the cleaners a couple of weeks, or centuries, ago.

"I paid for them out of petty cash," she said.

"Just what I need." I coughed.

"When you've changed, I'll make the bed."

"You don't have to do that," I said awkwardly.

"It's a pleasure." Then she said, "Your mother just called. She wants you to take a meeting with her. Urgently, she said."

"Take a meeting?"

"That's the way she put it."

We both smiled. That was Felicity, seizing every opportunity to sneer at me. Just what I needed right now, a sickening confrontation with my mother. But that wasn't all. Now came the stinger to the whole embarrassing scene.

Ursula's red panties were lying next to the lilac word processor, like the evidence of an office party. I must have left them there. Or she had deliberately moved them from somewhere for me to see. It all seemed like a conspiracy between Ursula and Felicity. I ignored the panties.

Taking a shirt from the package, I crept back into my office. I had to pass her twice more on my way to and from the bathroom at the end of the hall. I had a shit, a shave, and a wash. I could see her smiling at me.

When I left my office, the domain that was no longer solely mine, Ursula seemed to be in full charge of my life. She sat comfortably at her desk. The red panties were gone, fuck knows where. I was certain I hadn't seen the last of them. She was visibly happy. Her raven hair shone like black car metal in a thick beam of morning light. Her smiling lips glistened with fresh, bright red makeup. She had changed again.

# 12

# GRIDLOCK

The ultimate driving machine wouldn't start. The kid who'd been cleaning my car had moved to another vehicle. Pedro got twenty-five bucks a week from me for cleaning the car every Monday, Wednesday, and Friday. I think he was from Guatemala. His auntie had cleaned Barbara's shop for about a year until Barbara fired her for stealing. Sometime later Barbara told me that she had come into the shop early one morning to find Pedro's auntie on the office floor with the head of a black delivery man between her legs. Barbara could be quite prudish. After five minutes of frustration, I gave up on the car.

I got into a station wagon/taxi on the street beside the Regent Beverly Wilshire. The driver was a woman of about thirty with blond hair dyed dark red. Beside her sat her partner, a German shepherd that seemed to be asleep.

"Don't be nervous; she won't bite," said the woman in a husky tone. "Where to?"

I told her. She had no idea where it was. Like so many L.A. cab drivers, she didn't know the city, just parts of it. She was a good, sensible driver though.

We headed straight into a traffic jam on Santa Monica. The car fumes were oppressive. I wound my window up. Soon I found myself sweating.

"The air-conditioning's kaput," she said, looking at me in the mirror.

We were in a gridlock. Cars were locked in lines, West and East against South and North. The city designed or at least imagined for automobile freedom was truly a victim of its own desires. L.A. was running late.

I wondered why Felicity wanted to see me. It had only been a couple of days since I'd seen her. I wasn't looking forward to another similar encounter, but it was a good opportunity to ask her for the title deeds of the apartment for the bank.

It took almost an hour to get to the apartment building. I paid the driver. As I got out of the taxi, I saw that the German shepherd hadn't moved. I realized the animal was stuffed; its eyes were glass.

I could hear the music coming from Felicity's apartment. It was Liszt and loud. I was concerned. The front door was open. I closed it as I came in. Something was wrong. Then I saw my mother lying on the floor in her black housecoat. She was lying quite still as if she'd been shot. I bent down beside her.

"Mother, what's the matter?" Was this it? Was this the inevitable day I would find my mother dead?

Slowly Felicity reached out for a glass of vodka on the carpet near her.

"What's happened?"

When she spoke, Felicity's voice was different, lower toned and breathy. She looked as if she'd been drinking for days.

"Barbara came to see me," she said.

"Barbara?"

"She told me what a shit you've been. That doesn't surprise me. You've always been a shit. Like your father."

"Why did she come to see you?" I was puzzled and angry too. It was unlike Barbara to run to anyone, least of all Felicity.

"She wants you back, Christ knows why. I'd have thought she'd be pleased to see the back of you. I was elated as fuck when your father walked out. I'd been trying to get rid of him for years."

Felicity was at her worst, but there was something quite new in her attack. My father, the lost, the hated; I couldn't remember when she last talked in any detail about her relationship with him. She constantly referred disparagingly to me as being like him but now she launched into a memoir, obviously prompted by what Barbara had said to her.

"I only saw him once after he left me. That was in England. The asshole wanted to borrow money."

Shit. This wasn't going to be the ideal occasion to discuss the deeds of the apartment.

"You know, Mason, there was another child after you."

"What do you mean, another child?"

"I mean I had another fucking baby. As if you weren't enough."

Felicity was very drunk and when she got drunk she imagined things. So while this revelation was startling in itself, it was not necessarily true.

"Anyway, you were enough so I gave him the other one. Fuck it, if he was responsible for her, he fucking well ought to look after her."

She was crazy now, pouring the vodka into the glass so it spilled. I tried to get the bottle away from her. She punched me in the shoulder quite hard. I wanted to get out. Fuck her and fuck the deeds.

"At least you've never asked me for money," she said. "Have a drink."

"What did Barbara say to you exactly?" I wanted to get away from the unreal past. It was Barbara who interested me, not my father whom I didn't even remember and hardly ever thought about.

"She said you've been fucking women all over town. I told her my son couldn't fuck anything, not even a dead sheep."

"Thank you."

"But she said she loved you and wanted you back. I told her throwing you out was the smartest thing she'd ever done and my opinion of her had gone up several notches."

"Why are you telling me this?"

"I just want you to fucking know that you are universally despised."

I had to go. Felicity was out of her gourd. The vodka spilled down her chin. I felt sick, as sick as her.

"Don't call me at the office. Don't waste my fucking time with this shit."

She called me back from the door.

"Mason. One thing. I don't want to see you again. Never. You fucking hear me?"

"Loud and clear." I slammed the door.

60

As I hunted for a taxi to take me back to the office, I tried to imagine my mother as a child. I couldn't.

There was a young guy dressed in soft black leather waiting in the outer office. Ursula was on the phone, making a list of notes, presumably for me. The man got up. He had lank black hair, dark eyebrows, and looked like a diver from *The Abyss,* but without his helmet.

"Mr. Elliott?" An oddly high voice.

"Yes."

The underwater man came toward me. He said nothing else before he slammed his fist into my guts. I doubled up, not in agony but breathless. I fell backward onto the couch.

"I'm going to beat the shit out of you."

The man had a wild look in his eyes. He attacked again. I raised my right foot and kicked as hard as I could. I felt the impact of my shoe against his left thigh. He yelled, then came at me again.

"Fuck you! Fuck you!" He was screaming. "You fucked my girl."

"What the fuck are you talking about?" I tripped him and he fell heavily beside me on the couch. "What girl? What are you talking about?"

"You scumbag. I'm talking about Alexis."

The guy got his arm around my neck. I gripped his leather jacket. My fingers slipped squeakily on the black skin.

Suddenly, his arm relaxed. I couldn't see why. He slipped away from me. Then I could see what had happened. Ursula's white hand was gripping his crotch from behind. He couldn't breathe. I was lying back on the couch as she literally pulled him back by his balls. I just watched as her hand tightened, her nails sticking into the fine black leather of his pants. The guy yelled and writhed in her grasp. To an observer it must have looked comic.

Ursula brought her right leg sharply across the back of his knees. She let go of his pants as he fell. She quickly knelt beside him on the office floor and bent over him. For a crazy moment it looked as if she was going to kiss him. Ursula was pressing the thumb and forefinger of her right hand into his neck. The guy's eyes rolled, he screamed without much sound. His feet twitched as if he was dying.

"Ursula!" I got off the couch, still winded from the fight. She pressed his neck until he passed out. Then she stood up. She pulled her skirt straight.

"I didn't know who he was. He said his name was Rodney Alderton and that he had an appointment with you."

"We'd better call the police."

"I've done that. They're on their way."

"Where did you learn to fight like that?"

"Self-defense class."

"Very impressive." I looked at the man on the floor.

"He'll be fine in a few minutes," she said.

"I've never seen the guy before. Obviously he's the boyfriend of my ex-secretary, Alexis, but I've no idea—"

"Mr. Elliott, I'm not interested in your affairs before I came to work for you."

Jesus, this was the woman who had revamped Alexis's letter and contrived to get Barbara to read it, and here she was acting like none of this was her business.

The office door opened and two Beverly Hills cops came in.

"What happened?"

Ursula explained her part of the story. I explained mine, but with one omission. I didn't mention the letter.

While we were talking, Rodney began to stir. He coughed and tried to get up. Ursula went to answer the phone.

"Do you want to make a charge?"

I hesitated. "Well, I—"

"No, I meant him," said the black cop.

"I don't want anything," Rodney said, his voice thick with phlegm.

"Still, we'll have to make a report," the cop said.

"I want to get out of here," Rodney said to the cops, who glanced at each other.

"We've got your address. I suggest you two guys stay away from each other."

The cops looked frequently at Ursula with long stares. Did they suspect her of something? Was it possible that Ursula had somehow got hold of Rodney and lied to him? Was this woman behind everything that happened to me?

The cops left; so did Rodney. Ursula went back to work.

"I took the liberty of making an appointment here at four-thirty with Paul Jaspers and Joe . . . to discuss *La Belle Dame Sans Merci.*"

"Oh, fine, but I've got a meeting at Universal at two. Will that leave enough time? My car's died on me. You'd better arrange a taxi."

"There's no need. I called the garage. They sent a man over to fix your car. It's working perfectly."

"Thank you," I said limply. How did she know the BMW had broken? I hadn't come back to the office to tell her. She must have seen me trying to start it from the window. But there was no window to the alley in the outer office. It didn't matter. Ursula saw everything, knew everything, controlled everything.

"How was your mother?" She sounded concerned.

"She was fine, thank you." I had to stop saying thank you. "And thank you for your help with that madman."

"You're welcome, Mr. Elliott. So shall I confirm the four-thirty meeting?"

"Definitely." At least I could be definite about that.

# 13

# THE HANDSOME MAN WITHOUT PITY

Leaving the Universal lot, I ran into Os, almost literally ran into him. Os was a Sunday driver.

"I could kill my fucking agent," Os said.

"Why don't you? It would simplify a lot of things."

"Agreed."

"What are you doing here?"

"Shit, I'm trying to repair the damage done by Larry. He's about to blow a deal. We've been trading calls all morning. I think he's dodging me, fuck knows why. I pay his salary. So, I'm here to talk to the producers myself."

"Can I help?"

"No. I'll handle this. One day we'll be partners, buddy. Rest assured about that."

"Well," I said, "you know where I am. What's happening with Sophie?"

Os replied, "How's that secretary of yours? She's a real find. What's her name?"

"Ursula."

"Yeah. Weird name, great body."

"Hands off." I was almost serious.

"Oh, it's like that, huh?"

"No. It's not like that, huh."

"So give my best to Barbara. Ha ha!"

"Asshole."

Driving back, I wondered if there could be a part for Os in Joe Ransom's project. Could he play the guy Paul Jaspers had in mind, the man who discovers he needs to be dominated? Interesting casting, against type. Os would be too expensive for Joe's low-budget project, but on the other hand if the script was that good, he might be persuaded. This was way down the line. The first battle would be getting Joe to accept Paul's Macbeth story.

I didn't recognize her immediately, the girl who was talking to Ursula when I came into the office. The lemony smell mixed with a faint smoky aftermath. Had she decided to smoke out of nerves or frustration? Or was it a small act of rebellion? I had told her she could smoke anytime she wanted, so perhaps the office was becoming an extension of her home, wherever that was.

"Silvia Glass, Mason Elliott." Ursula introduced the girl in what seemed to me a tone of some pride. Now I knew. She was the smiling photograph from the casting lady in New York. I had been right. She did look like Barbara. And like the girl in the hotel hall.

I shook her hand, a surprising contact. On this warm day in my office, with its less-than-adequate air-conditioning, Silvia's right hand was as cold as fruit from the fridge. Seeing these two women side-by-side was a chilling reminder of the woman in black and her sensual victim.

"Come in and we'll talk for a bit." There was still a half hour before the scheduled meeting with Joe and Paul. Ursula's face seemed to be smiling with satisfaction as I closed the door to the outer office. Did they know each other?

Silvia talked freely about herself and her enthusiasm for boxing, although I had the impression that some of what she said was fabricated. Maybe she was a good actress after all.

So in my new mood of acceptance, I told her that I was prepared to take her on as a client for a six-month trial period. She was pleased but I could see that she expected nothing less. Then I could hear voices from the outer office. Paul or Joe had arrived for the meeting. I stood up. Silvia held out her hand. This time it was not cold to the touch but slightly warm, slightly damp. Did this mean she had been nervous or that she had lied? Silvia Glass tightened her hand just enough to send fifteen volts of sex to my brain, a tingle of thank you. As I saw her out, she gave me her phone number in L.A.

"It's only temporary," she said, waving at Ursula, who was chatting with Paul.

"Let's just talk for a minute before Joe gets here," I said to Paul.

Ursula asked, "Would you like coffee now, Mr. Elliott, or shall I wait for Mr. Ransom?"

"We'll wait," I said. "What did you think of Silvia?"

"Interesting."

"I've taken her on."

"Good. We won't regret it." She made it sound like it was her idea.

Paul and I went into my office. And what did she mean "we"? Ursula was starting to talk as if she was my partner.

"If your new secretary could act," Paul said, "she'd be perfect as Lulu."

I could have told Paul she was perfect without acting.

"Listen, when you pitch your story, for God's sake don't make it sound too downbeat."

"Lulu isn't downbeat."

"Not to you, kiddo. You're forgetting where you are. This isn't Berlin."

"I'll make it sound just great. Trust me."

Paul turned out to be as good as his word. Joe was hooked by Paul as much as by his story.

"I like the domination thing, but I think he has to kill her in the end."

"But that's not logical," Paul said. "She's helped him find himself and also she's done great things for his business. Why would he kill her?"

"Because she's bad, that's why." Joe turned to Ursula, who was there taking notes. Joe had been turning to Ursula quite a bit during the meeting. He was intrigued by her, like so many other people.

"What do you think?"

"It's not for me to say, Mr. Ransom."

"I'm asking you." Joe swallowed a pill and drained his coffee cup.

Ursula looked at me for guidance.

"Go ahead. Speak."

She glanced nervously at Paul. He nodded. We were all there waiting for the woman's point of view.

"Well, suppose she was telling the story, narrating it, then we'd learn a lot about why she wants him. We know what fascinates him about her, but what is it that she sees in him?"

"Interesting," said Joe. We waited.

Ursula went on, without nerves. "We're treating her as if she's the femme fatale. But perhaps she sees him as the male equivalent of that, a sort of homme fatale."

"That's brilliant," Paul said. I could see also that Joe was almost sold.

"Maybe we could translate the French title *La Belle Dame Sans Merci*. What would that be for a guy?"

Paul said, "It would be *The Handsome Man Without Pity*."

"What's wrong with Ursula's *Homme Fatale*?" I asked.

"Maybe," said Joe.

"Yes, but in French you wouldn't have the *e* at the end of *fatale*. It would read *Homme Fatal*."

"Let me think about it," said Joe. "But the concept's right." He looked at Ursula. "The only question is, what is it that the woman sees in the guy that makes her do all those things? After all, she arranges a murder. You got to have a hell of a motive for that and it can't be money. It has to be something in him."

"Maybe he's just beautiful," Ursula said. "But I'm not the writer." Strangely, she was looking not at Joe or Paul but at me. I felt uncomfortable without knowing quite why. What did she mean "beautiful"?

"I'll get something down on paper," said Paul. "Give me a couple of days."

The meeting broke up with everybody happy. Ursula had done her stuff brilliantly. She went back to her office talking to Paul. After we'd discussed Paul's deal, Joe stayed with me for a moment.

"That girl," said Joe. "What did you say her name was?"

"Ursula. Ursula Baxter."

"Really. Hmmn."

"What do you mean 'really'?" Didn't Joe believe me? Or didn't he believe her?

"What I meant was, we know her as Gala, don't we?"

"Gala?"

"Don't play coy with me."

"Wait a minute." I was shaking inside my head. "What are you talking about? You know her?"

Joe stopped smiling. "Ursula Baxter is Gala. Obviously that's not her real name. Her name never appeared on the credits."

"Gala? What the fuck are you talking about? What credits?"

"You've never seen the movie *Gala*? It's a hard-core porn pic. That girl played Gala. Don't look so shocked, Mason. Good choice of yours. Your secretary's a porn queen. If she's as good in the office as she is in bed, you'll be more than satisfied. I'm impressed.' Joe took out a pill. "Got a glass of water?"

# 14

# GALA

Joe Ransom had to be mistaken, had to be. While Ursula was in the bathroom I signed the letters of the day. My hand was unsteady. Things blurred. I recalled Os's violent reaction years ago when he found out his girlfriend had been in a soft-core movie. I felt that jealousy now. But Ursula wasn't a girlfriend. She was an obsession.

I had to see this film. I began to imagine the scenes. For the rest of the day, when I looked at Ursula I saw moments from *Gala*. As she typed, I saw her thin fingers massaging the cock of some faceless man. I saw her blouse being opened. I saw a mouth at her nipples. When she licked a stamp I saw her tongue flicking at a tight scrotum. When she blew her nose into a Kleenex she blew my mind as well. The soft white paper wiped the blown sperm from her lips and chin. It was just insanity.

The frozen photographs of my earlier fantasies were now moving pictures. Elegant, posed images became quivering, rough incitements to orgasm. There was no mystery now. It was all exposure. No artfulness, just blatant sexual excitement. In these fantasies Ursula lost her character and I lost mine. We didn't know or care who we were. We had no names, played no roles. When I managed to think about it, I saw that in reality there was no "we." "We" didn't exist. It was all me. It was me who didn't exist. She was solid, the bitch.

Joe Ransom's house surprised me. Up in Nichols Canyon in the Hollywood Hills I was somehow expecting a modest modern house, the sort of insubstantial place a third-division movie producer would own. When I pulled off the road into the short driveway, I entered a perfect Mediterranean world. Joe's house was maybe the prettiest little Italian villa I had ever seen. Creepers and flowers climbed the old brick walls.

The single-storyed stuccoed house was decorated with shut-ters and huge flowerpots. The pale walls that were not lat-ticed were dappled with shadows from avocado trees. It was entrancing. Barbara would've loved it.

As I approached the oak door, the door itself opened as if inviting me in. A girl in a white dress stood there. She had long red hair, couldn't have been more than eighteen. Joe appeared behind her.

"Come right in, Mason. She's just leaving."

I smiled at the girl. She somehow went with the house. I hardly registered the fact that Joe didn't attempt to intro-duce us.

"See you later," Joe said to the girl.

I went inside, then glanced back to her. I couldn't help myself. As I did she turned and suddenly ran back toward the house, toward me, toward Joe. She threw her arms around his neck and kissed him. Her tongue went as deep as it could into his mouth. I was a little embarrassed and went into the hall, leaving them.

A few moments later Joe closed the door. The girl in white was gone.

"Mustn't let them get to you, though," Joe said.

He had invited me to see *Gala*. I had called him that night after the revelation, hoping to trace the movie. Joe told me he had a pirate cassette. He wasn't prepared to lend it to me but I would be welcome to watch it at his place. My rela-tionship with Joe had become apparently closer after our meeting. He had liked Paul and was looking forward to get-ting started on our project.

Joe sat me down in his den and took a cassette from a wall of tapes.

"You're quite a collector."

"I get ideas from them. I don't read much anymore but I get a kick out of watching these things."

From the titles of the cassettes in the library I could see that Joe's was primarily a collection of erotic films. It was obvious now that his mission as a producer was to contribute to the field. *La Belle Dame Sans Merci,* or *Homme Fatale,* or whatever it would finally be called, would soon be on these shelves.

Joe inserted the cassette and moved a vase of yellow

roses from the cane table that stood between me, on the sofa, and the big-screen Mitsubishi that was to be my companion for the next hour or so.

"I'll leave you to it. I'm going to make some calls. I'll look in again in an hour. As far as I can remember it's under an hour, the running time."

People tell you that pornography is an empty experience, an emptying experience, if you like. It makes you want to come, so you jerk yourself off. And that's it until the next time. That's the theory, and maybe it's true. But when you know the person you're watching, if she is in some way close to you, then the effect is very different. It goes way beyond the realm of sexual excitement. Watching *Gala,* alone in Joe's den, took me into a territory I hardly knew existed, full of fear and anguish. Through these images of sexual encounters I was rocked into a state of panic I hadn't known since I was a child living with Felicity in her wasteland of sex.

*Gala* was way beyond my expectations or previous fantasies. The story was simple. Gala was a woman who lived alone with her two cats in a house on the beach. She did nothing except lay about or wander around with very few clothes on. People passing on the beach—men and occasionally women—would notice her and venture up the wooden steps into her domain. Gala said nothing but acted seductively and then made love to each of her uninvited guests, who then left.

The sexual acts were very graphic. The first man was out walking his dog on the beach: The dog sat on the verandah while Gala undid the man's pants and massaged his cock with shaving foam. The sequence consisted of shots of an erect penis moving in and out of Gala's foam-covered hands. It ended with her washing the thing in a bowl of water and then drying it with a hair dryer. Somehow I had expected her to get a razor and shave the guy's pubic hair. There were very few shots of Gala's face and I still doubted that it was Ursula. I watched her fingers very carefully. They were certainly like Ursula's but I couldn't bring myself to accept that it was her. I forced myself to believe that while the wide shots could be Ursula, the close-ups had to be someone else.

But of course they weren't. In the next sequence two young men playing Frisbee were ensnared. As Gala sucked

70

one cock and then the other I felt as if I were toppling off a high building. To see that beautiful mouth taking their arching cocks down into her throat brought the first foul taste of vomit into my own mouth. That mouth, those lips were mine. Mine. This section of the movie ended with the two guys jerking each other off and together sending their sperm onto Gala's tummy. They were trying to get it all into her navel.

At this point I froze the frame using the remote and grasped a bottle of mineral water that was standing on a lacquered table beside the television. There was no glass, so I drank from the bottle. The sparkling water got rid of the taste of vomit but the bottle in my mouth pushed my erection to its limit inside my pants. If Joe had come in I would have been embarrassed.

I sat down, crossed my legs, and watched the third sequence. The traditional figure of the traveling salesman arrived at the door. He was selling books on erotic art through the ages. As Ursula looked through the reproductions, the salesman, who was bald, took off his clothes. The guy had the longest cock I have ever seen. It dangled almost to his knees. Ursula rubbed and licked it to get it hard. It must have been fifteen inches long but it wouldn't become truly erect. The man's cock stiffened as she slapped it back and forth across her small breasts. The scene was grotesquely funny. I was sure you were supposed to laugh but I couldn't. I watched Ursula's breasts. They were exactly as I had imagined, not quite belonging to her body. They were like swollen glands that had grown out of her ribs. They made her look as if she had a disease, yet they were delicate and in danger of being bruised by this guy's floppy stick. She finally brought him off without touching his cock at all but by playing with his balls. She squeezed them with both hands until the salesman ejaculated. Sperm dribbled out of him, but his penis never became properly hard. I concluded that that size never really does. It just pointed downward at forty-five degrees. After he left she wiped the floor with a handful of Kleenex.

As Gala sat alone examining the book left by the salesman, I felt numb watching her. Had Ursula really done all these things, serviced all these men, and why? Had she done it for the money? From what little I knew of this field, I was pretty certain they didn't pay that much. Finally seeing Ur-

71

sula's body naked, I realized it was hardly the shape associated with hard-core movies. She was in no conventional way voluptuous. She was thin, almost angular, more attractive with clothes on. For me, Ursula's black hair and red clothes were Ursula. Until now. Now I wondered how my reactions to her would change from here on. I knew I would never get these pictures out of my mind. I knew that every time I saw her from now on I would see her as Gala.

From close-ups of the erotic plates in the book, the film cut to shots of Gala masturbating. This sequence had a quite different effect on me. I was no longer watching her with men, feeling violently jealous or physically sickened. Now I was alone with her, watching. As she folded back the layers of skin and hair around her vagina, my sexual excitement increased. When she licked her fingers as if each was a penis, I was overcome with a splash of happiness. I had an orgasm, not sudden or electric as when I masturbated, but soft and slow, like running in warm water. The feeling wasn't just in my cock and at the root of my spine but all through me like a wonderful drug injection taking effect. For a while I didn't look at the TV screen at all. There was a new screen in my mind and on it were projected extraordinary images of desire and satisfaction. Memories of waking and drifting back into sleep as a child, of being picked up and held gently. I couldn't hear anything. The absence of sound was an absence of fear. The sickness vanished. I was alone at long last. But with Ursula inside me. This woman was in my body. When I moved, she moved. When she breathed, so did I.

When I came to and focused again on the TV screen, there was a girl with Gala. I don't know where she came from. I must have missed it. The girl put down some groceries. She had probably been to the supermarket. I tried to concentrate. Gala was wearing a red silk robe. She approached the girl and kissed her on the mouth. The girl ran her hands over the silk, stroking Gala through the material. My old consciousness returned and I recognized the girl. I leaned forward on Joe's sofa as if to get closer, to see better.

There was no doubt in my mind: This girl was the girl from the hotel in New Mexico. This was the girl Ursula had pulled along the hall. It was her. The same face and hair, same swimmer's physique. Everything. I wasn't imagining it and it couldn't have been coincidence, not the two of them together. The woman in black, now in red, and her blond victim.

The girl slid down to her knees, her fingers sliding, scraping the silk gown. Ursula looked down as the girl slowly undid the knot of her black sash. The girl's hands opened the gown at the waist. Ursula's body looked different. Her skin seemed softer, her flesh fuller. It was the lighting of the film. The sun was beginning to set across the ocean outside. The house was suffused in yellow and gold. The bland harshness of the earlier daylight was replaced by a romantic glow. The men had gone.

The girl pushed her blond head between Gala's thighs. Ursula closed her eyes. She waited. The girl's tongue licked the dark pubic hair. Her hands stroked Gala's tense legs. Ursula reached down and gripped the blond hair. Then she too knelt down. They kissed and curled around each other.

Lying on the rug, the two women undressed each other in the sunset light. Gala pulled the girl's panties off, carefully as if fearful that they might tear. She held them to her face and took several deep breaths. The girl put her tongue into Ursula's left ear, causing her to shiver. Gala's legs parted slightly as she bent forward to hold the girl's right breast in her hand. She pressed her lips to the nipple.

Then came a shot of a man's face, none too clear at the window, looking in on the scene. Neither of the women saw him. But I did and I didn't like him. I knew he was going to spoil everything. This was my fantasy. It belonged to me alone.

The women stood up, kissing. They held the kiss as they walked together, arms around each other, to the bathroom. The girl sank back into the bathwater. Ursula began to soap her shining body.

I couldn't believe what I was seeing. What was happening was exactly what I had imagined. They were together in the fucking bath. This was really spooky. I pressed the remote to freeze the picture and then started it again just to make sure I wasn't imagining what was on the screen. I wasn't. I had actually seen this before in my mind. It wasn't exactly the same as my invention. Of course not. Otherwise I would have been crazy. As the scene progressed, Ursula

73

and the girl made love in and then out of the bath. Eventually, they went to the bedroom and fell asleep with their hands between each other's legs. So there was no death of the girl, no murder. But then, how could there be? Hadn't I myself seen the aftermath of the death or murder in New Mexico?

When she made *Gala,* Ursula must have been having an affair with this girl. It was simple. Detective Elliott. I hadn't exactly solved anything, but I had discovered something. I was thrilled and was about to turn the movie off, thinking it was over, when I received a shock that jolted me with a thousand volts.

The man who had been watching the two women at sunset was now quietly breaking into the house. The camera followed him into the bedroom where they were asleep. Up until now the guy was in shadow. Gala's bedroom was lit by candles. As he moved into the flickering light, I recognized his face.

"No!" I shouted. "No! That's not possible!"

Shattered, I fumbled with the remote, rewound and watched him again. Not fucking possible. The man was me. I believed it.

# 15

# ECHOES OF MURDER

My heart was beating in my ears. The man watched Gala. Slowly she stirred, aware of his presence. She looked at him and smiled. Ursula's smile was a miracle. I had never seen it like that before. Her smile when she woke me after my night in the office was sweet and fresh. This was something else again. She was pleased to see me. I mean, she was pleased to see this man in her room. She disentangled herself from the girl without waking her. The girl turned over on her back, her breasts moving. She put one hand to her left nipple and let it rest there.

Ursula moved toward the man. He pulled off his light-weight jacket. She took it from him, smelled it, and placed it carefully on a chair. Nothing was said. No one said anything in this movie. Except me. I was talking to myself, my attention split between Ursula's naked body in candlelight and the guy who was me.

She began to undress him. The fucking camera moved away from him flickering in the light and focused obsessively, stupidly on the ritual process of her fingers unbuttoning, unzipping, unhooking, pulling aside, parting the clothes from the man. She slipped her hand through the opening into his boxer shorts. Her hand moved inside the material. His face was not shown during this. But his reactions were mine. I squirmed with pleasure.

Now the man's clothes lay in a heap on the bedroom floor. He lay near them on a fur rug. Gala bent over him, kissing his nipples, sucking them more like a child with hunger than a woman with lust. His face was still tantalizingly indistinct. That's to say indistinct to me. For the male spectator for whom this movie was produced, it couldn't have mattered less. They wanted to see Gala, not some anonymous jock. And see Gala we did.

She opened herself to this man as to no other guy in the film. She showed him the inside of her mouth, but she wouldn't let me kiss her. She opened her cunt with both hands inches from his face but she slapped his fingers away when he moved them toward her. She leaned over to lick his erect cock.

Now I knew it wasn't me. This cock was uncircumcised. She drew the skin back from the hidden head, rolling it downward. Her perfect mouth closed over the twitching glans of his penis. Of course it wasn't me, but why was the man's face so similar to mine? Just an accidental resemblance? Obviously. But the chain of our encounters, from the hotel hallway to watching this movie, had to be beyond any coincidence. While she worked on him with devotion, not letting the man touch her, the girl on the bed masturbated in her sleep.

The man finally came with a long dying cry. I didn't. Something else happened to me. Again, it was something that hadn't happened since childhood. I wept.

75

"Enjoy the movie?" Joe put his head around the door as I was rewinding the cassette.

"It's garbage," I said dumbly, coughing away my emotion.

"What do you think of your secretary now?"

I drove back to the office and didn't even notice the dismal traffic. All I could think of was that she had made me cry and I had no idea why.

Ursula was on the phone when I came in. I couldn't look at her for more than a glance at a time. The images that came into my mind were overpowering. It was worse than I had imagined. Every gesture, every look of hers recalled Gala. I had an inkling now of my inadvertent effect on Alexis. That pathetic letter at the beginning of it all had become a document of my life. *La belle dame sans merci.* Ursula probably cared no more for me than I did for Alexis.

As I walked into my office, I almost tripped over my own suitcases. Ursula appeared in the doorway.

"Barbara came by. She brought them. She said if you want to call her she's in most evenings."

"Thank you, Ursula." I almost said "Gala."

She could see something was up with me. I expect she assumed it was to do with Barbara.

"Is there anything I can get you?"

"No. Thank you. But I think I'll leave an hour early tonight. There's something I have to do."

"Don't worry. You look tired. I'll lock up."

That smile again. I had to know what it was about. Fuck. That was it! Ursula's smile. Her utmost pleasure. That's what made me cry.

It was absurd, of course, a boss following his secretary home. When Ursula started her job she gave me a home phone number but not an address. I didn't think anything of it at the time. She said she was staying at a friend's house for the time being while she, the friend, was away in Europe. I now realized she had given me a Beverly Hills number.

I left early on Friday, around four-thirty, and hung out at the coffee shop across the street. I took the precaution of driving my car away from the office and parking it in the subterranean lot of a nearby supermarket. I had to admit to myself that for a man who was so curious about this woman I had done no basic research into her life. I wasn't much of a detective. I was happy enough imagining things, inventing scenes, re-creating events. The constant presence of Ursula in my life, her physical proximity during the day, had been stimulus enough.

She came out of the office at five-thirty and set off along the street toward Wilshire. I left the coffee shop and followed her on the other side of the street. The offices were emptying and the comparatively crowded streets gave me the necessary cover. Ursula crossed Wilshire and went to the taxi stand next to the Beverly Wilshire hotel. This was going to be tricky. How could I get a taxi to follow her without Ursula seeing me?

I waited to see where her taxi was headed. I had to take a risk. I crossed Wilshire and went to the taxi stand just as her taxi turned west. I prayed she hadn't seen me. Luckily, the heavy traffic helped. I climbed into a taxi and we turned west, following Ursula. There were two cars between us. The traffic hardly moved. The gridlock I usually cursed was now my ally.

The progress was slow. I followed Ursula west down Wilshire all the way to Santa Monica right into the setting sun. Stopping, going on, stopping and going on again into increasingly purple light was like a dream journey. The eeriness increased suddenly as Ursula's taxi stopped outside Barbara's jewelry shop. I felt a twinge of fascinated panic when she got out of the taxi and went to the entrance of the shop. She tried the door but the place was closed for the day. Barbara had gone. Ursula got back into her taxi, which drove north through Santa Monica toward Venice.

The light was fading fast now. What had Ursula said to Barbara? Obviously, they hadn't arranged to meet this evening, otherwise Barbara would have been at the shop. Ursula wanted to tell her something, but what? Perhaps it was about Felicity. No, that couldn't be. Barbara must have talked about me. But what had she said? She must also have told her where the shop was.

"Pop in any time. I've some very pretty things." I could hear Barbara saying it. It was a mystery, the whole thing. Yet nothing that was now happening was as disturbing as the images of Ursula's opening legs, the fur, the widening slit, the bald man's fingers pulling at the sticky flesh. The experience of watching *Gala* was a crazed invitation to some excess, to a mindless trip into the dark. I pulled at my pants, resettled in the back of the taxi. The half erection was uncomfortable.

We drove down Main Street in Venice, that weird wasteland inhabited by artists and criminals where the struggling easel painter met the doomed drug dealer.

Ursula's taxi turned west again and stopped outside Rebecca's, a fashionable bar and restaurant serving margaritas and nouvelle Mexican cuisine. She got out of the taxi, paid the driver, and went inside, pushing her way through an informal gathering of Armani lounge lizards deciding how to waste their evening.

I decided to keep my taxi, however long she took. You simply don't find passing taxis in Venice and if Ursula ordered a taxi later from the bar I wouldn't be able to follow her. So I waited across the street. I could see my driver starting to get worried. He kept looking at me in the rearview mirror. I gave him a hundred-dollar bill on account. That made the poor man happy. He started to read a book on opera.

After fifteen minutes I wanted to go back to smoking. My patience was strained. Whether I was doing the right thing or not, I got out of the taxi and went into Rebecca's. I knew it would be crowded. A couple of hundred people had walked in while I'd been sitting outside. So I had plenty of cover. If she happened to see me, it would be a coincidence. I had my story ready.

Rebecca's was a zoo. The noise was deafening, music and voices without Dolby C reduction. I'd been to Rebecca's two or three times but I'd never seen the place crowded like this. It was going to take ten minutes to find her. I had to be careful. I couldn't see her right away and it was possible I'd bump into her without intending to. The way to find her was to climb up to the raised restaurant section and look down through the wash of green and orange light. I found a spot and watched.

There were at least three women to every man, would-be actresses, pretend artists, people in the music business, perhaps even an agent or two. Like my life right now,

Rebecca's was dominated by women. Two arguing women pushed past me. A pair of tits brushed my jacket. No apology. I retaliated by deliberately looking down the front of her dress. That was a mistake. It got me thinking about *Gala.* Then I saw her.

She was sitting at one of the few tables for noneaters talking to a bearded man of about fifty. He was talking. She was listening. There were some papers between them but it was impossible to see or hear anything. Ursula nodded frequently. She seemed to be taking advice from this man, who looked like an architect or a designer of some kind. She smoked constantly. The office must be torture for her. Then she leaned across the table and touched his hand, held his hand, gripped it. Now she was upset. What had he told her? Whatever, it was serious.

The man left the table probably to go to the men's room. While he was gone she took a sip of his drink. Hers was finished. Suddenly, she looked in my direction. I turned quickly away, pretending to be with a chattering group next to me. She couldn't possibly have seen me. I prayed.

When I looked again, the man was on his way back to the table. He sat down. She pointed to a gigantic crocodile suspended above them. They seemed to be discussing the decor of Rebecca's, pointing to the wild objects around the bar. There were papier-mâché masks and skulls and artifacts suggesting a carnival of death.

Ursula finally got up to make a phone call. This I guessed was for a taxi. It was my cue to get outside. As I watched her weave her way to the phone, she looked pale, frail, even deathly. In the livid green light she looked like a ghost. I thought of her nakedness in *Gala,* her sexual excess, her waiting for people, her body a mask even more than her face. Having seen almost every crevice of her folding skin, I still knew nothing about her. After all, *Gala* was only a movie.

The taxi came. She said good-bye to her friend, kissing him on both cheeks in the French manner. She carried with her the papers they had been discussing inside. My driver put down his book and we set off on the second part of the night journey.

"Do you mind if I play some opera?"

"Not at all," I said.

"I like this one a lot," said the driver. And to the strains of Verdi we drove after Ursula toward Sunset Boulevard. The dark trail led away from the ocean. We drove east on Sunset back toward Beverly Hills. Ursula turned up Benedict Canyon.

"Don't get too close," I told the driver.

Off the main street a following car at night is pretty easy to spot. We were now on La Cielo. Strange. Os used to have a house on this street, but he moved away. He couldn't stand the constant sightseers who came to gawk. They weren't gawking at him, of course, and that was maybe the real reason he moved away. They were gawking at the house next door where Sharon Tate and her friends had been murdered by the Manson family.

Ursula went into a driveway at the far end of the winding road, two hundred yards from the murder house. She got out, paid the driver, and opened the gate herself. I got my driver simply to drive past as if we were on our way somewhere else. Ursula didn't turn when the taxi's headlights picked her out clearly as she walked up the short drive. I gave my driver twenty bucks over the hundred.

"You couldn't pay me to live up here," he said in gratitude. "This is a scary area."

Now I was on my own. I didn't know how I would get a taxi but I didn't care. My breathing seemed noisy as I walked up to the house. I was on dangerous ground. Prowlers in Beverly Hills were usually taken for thieves by the security patrols, and the police were inclined to shoot first and not bother with questions at all.

The house was surprisingly large, built in the Twenties Spanish style. There was a wooded area at the back. The small swimming pool was empty. The place was desolate but not overgrown. It was clearly looked after, but without much interest; this was the sort of house that belonged to old people in Beverly Hills, and that local realtors kept their eyes on, waiting for the owners to die.

As an owl hooted in the hills, a light came on in one of the ground-floor rooms. I moved toward it across a patch of lawn. The outside of the house was not lit up, which was good and bad. Good because I wouldn't easily be seen, and bad because I couldn't easily see.

I approached the window. Through net curtains I glimpsed Ursula moving around. She was in a dressing gown. It looked like a man's dressing gown. She was opening a cupboard. The room was probably a guest room, sparsely furnished, seldom slept in. This then was not Ursula's bedroom, but I had the strong impression by the way she walked around that this was her house, even if she didn't live in it alone.

From the cupboard she took what seemed to be leather clothing. She dumped it all on the bed, and disappeared from sight. When she returned, she was wearing only the red panties from the office and black socks. They were new, surprising. It was a peculiar shock. Ursula was almost naked but it wasn't on film and it wasn't in my imagination. To begin with it had no effect. Strangely, it wasn't until Ursula started to put on the black leather clothes that I became aroused.

First came the pants. They were fairly tight and she had quite a struggle getting into them. Maybe she'd taken a bath and her skin was still damp. She almost lost the battle, half fell over, steadying herself with the side of the bed. I had never seen or even imagined Ursula in pants before. She sat on the bed, almost facing me. I stepped back a couple of paces. She firmly pulled the pants on over her hips and stood up, pulling at them in the crotch, smoothing the leather over her thighs. She turned her back to me. I could hear the scraping zipper go up. Then she bent and wriggled her narrow bottom to get comfortable. This was more erotic than anything in the movie. Because it was real and it was unconscious and it was awkward.

Next came the jacket. She pulled it on, one raised arm at a time. Up went the zipper. Her breasts disappeared. This was the last sight of Ursula's pale skin. When she put the black leather gloves on, I realized I had been watching a striptease in reverse. She had now taken herself from me and I was left only with my memory.

Lastly, Ursula struggled into a pair of leather boots. She got them on, stamped her feet to fit them tightly, and left the room. The light went off.

Nothing happened for two minutes. I was lost. I walked away from the window, around the other side of the dark house. Then I heard the unmistakable sound of a garage door winding back. I walked stealthily in the direction of the sound. Had someone arrived? I hadn't heard a car.

As I groped my way toward some shielded view of the garage, I started to imagine why she had dressed in leather at all. I imagined she might be like the Jane Fonda character in *Klute,* going out at night to visit rich clients for whom she would pretend sex, become a fantasy for them, and find or lose herself.

Then I heard the sound like a machine gun of a motorcycle starting. As I came into sight of the garage, I saw Ursula, helmeted now, like an angel of death, drive out of the garage on a bike. She drove down the drive and out onto the road. It was sudden, violent, and sexless. No one could tell it was a woman astride the machine. She turned on the road and drove off. The gunfire of the engine faded with the glimmering light of her single headlight.

There was silence of a kind. Animals, night birds, and the far distant traffic made an eerie soundtrack. My decision was instantaneous. I had to get into the house. The garage door was still open. I walked confidently toward it. It was my house too, I told myself. I had a right to go in. I wanted to see the interior of the house with the same erotic desire I wanted to see Ursula.

I entered the darkness of the garage. There was a car in there, a red Honda Civic. At the rear of the garage there was a door that had to lead into the house. I prayed it wasn't locked. I tried the handle. It was stiff, seldom used. Then slowly it turned. And I went inside. Far away there was a woman's cry, screams followed by silence. A reaction to rape, a discovery of infidelity, the beginning of labor pains. Something female. Or maybe it was a far cry from the past, of the mad murders that made La Cielo notorious.

# 16

# NIGHT WITHOUT SLEEP

I turned on the light at the kitchen door. Maybe it was dangerous, but I had to. I ought to be sure there was no functioning alarm system. Then I realized that I would already have broken the circuit by coming in from the garage. And if Ursula had put the alarm on, she would surely have locked the kitchen door and closed up the garage. That in itself was slightly odd, that she hadn't locked the house at all.

The kitchen was surprisingly spare. It seemed to have none of the usual high-tech equipment or gadgetry that are emblematic of Beverly Hills homes. In fact, it didn't look as if anyone had cooked a meal there for months. There was no kitchen smell.

The main hall was underfurnished. A large oak table, four heavy chairs, a dilapidated red leather sofa, and a wide worn Islamic rug covered the Mexican terra cotta–tiled floor. It looked as if whoever lived here once had moved away, leaving only a skeleton of furniture, not enough even to rent the place. The only light in the atrium came from a huge iron candelabrum with six flickering white candles, each four inches thick. There was a hickory smell of burnt logs that emanated from the open fireplace. But nothing was burning now. The fire had been out for days, maybe weeks.

I climbed the creaking wooden stairs and looked back. The house belonged in the past. It was a set for a Victorian tale, a long way from the kind of place I had imagined for Ursula. I had seen her in a glossy designer apartment, overly tidy, crazy clean, something like Helman's photographs. Since watching *Gala* I had had flashes of seeing her in that house at the beach. I shouldn't have been surprised though by anything I might uncover about Ursula.

The four rooms upstairs were brown and empty. I turned the lights on, and off again quickly, just to see. Naked bulbs.

One room had an unmade bed and nothing else. The others were musty and hollow. I could see now why she hadn't bothered with an alarm. There was nothing to take. All the clues were in the master bedroom. I was led there, along the hall, by the smell of verbena.

The largest upstairs room was, like the atrium, lit by giant candles. The lemony smell seemed to be coming like incense from the candle smoke. This was Ursula's bedroom. It was religious, like a small church. I was standing facing the altar, the place where she went to bed, where she woke up, the vestry where she showered. This was her own church, where she put on and took off her clothes. Over there, through that doorway, she peed and shat. There she made up those elegant lips, facing an icon that was a reflected image of herself. The mystery was right here, and it was alive.

Far from being orderly, her bedroom looked like the inside of a handbag. It was dense with pieces of furniture, large and small, equally for giants and dwarfs. The door of the tall armoire was hanging open as if someone had made a sudden escape from inside. The armoire itself was full of clothes, things for every occasion, party dresses, ball gowns, pant suits, even a wedding dress, all cream lace and satin. Who was she married to? Was he living with her? No, there were no men's clothes. Jumpers and undergarments were strewn over chairs, on the unmade bed, on the triple-mirrored dressing table, and under it on the floor. I got the sense that not one but ten women lived here.

There were piles of books, some in shelves, some on the bed, and on the floor. I could see what looked like the complete works of D. H. Lawrence, volumes of Balzac, and on the bedside table an open copy of *The Lost Girl*. There were no new books, no modern stuff that I could see. And the classics were all in old editions.

On a small table cluttered with antique perfume bottles, jewelry, and makeup jars, I saw a brass ring. I picked it up, turned it round in my hand. Shit. I knew this ring. It was Barbara's. As a matter of fact, I bought it for her birthday a year ago. I bought it from her. I paid for it, then gave it to her.

How could it be here? Maybe Ursula had happened to buy it in the shop. No, that was impossible. Barbara never sold duplicates. This was getting scary, way beyond coincidence. I wondered if there were any more surprises.

I saw a black laquer box. I picked it up. I tried to open it, but it was securely locked, the only thing in the house that was. I put it back. I could see clearly my fingerprints on the shiny surface. But then my prints must be all over the house by now.

On a writing table was a sheaf of papers. They looked like maps. I held one of them up to the candlelight. It looked like a map of the universe. It had her name on it at the top: Ursula Baxter. I examined it and realized it was an astrological chart. These signs and numbers and circles and bisecting lines represented her destiny. Or fate. Whatever you want to call it. I put the thing down.

I knew I ought to get out. Now. I felt it. Yet I was drawn to the place, fascinated.

I went to the bed. It gave off a smell, her smell, not the verbena. I wanted to get into the bed, to lie where she had lain, to be with her, mixing limbs. I felt hot. Under the pillow I discovered a leatherbound book. I opened it. It wasn't printed but handwritten. It seemed to be a journal.

I started to read. Her handwriting was like an architect's, more formal than her note-taking style in the office, bigger letters, more confident:

> I learned the other day that Japanese women invented the novel. It was in the fourteenth century. The women were literate. Their husbands more often than not weren't. These books were like journals, diaries. While the men were away fighting clan wars and killing each other the women wrote down their own thoughts after doing the household accounts. They told tales, Monogatari they were called, of their childhood, adolescence, first loves, hopes and unhappiness with their lot. The tone of these writings was resigned, sometimes amused, always tolerant of their fate. By the time their husbands came home, if they had not been killed, they had hidden their little books. As a matter of fact, they concealed them each night pointlessly, from their maids who couldn't read, but above all from

themselves, by putting the folded pages under their pillows. That's how these female tales came to be called Pillow Books.

The phone rang loudly. I stopped reading. Ursula's voice on the machine came over loud and clear: "I'm in the bath right now so I can't pick up your call. Please leave your message after the tone. I can't promise to ring you back immediately, but I know you'll understand and be patient. Goodbye for now." Her voice was very Californian. In different circumstances I might not have recognized it. It could have belonged to someone else. I had a vague idea the message was directed at someone specific, not at just anyone who happened to call. Ursula was expecting a call. She was expecting a visitor. I had to get out of there. But not before the beep. A man's voice bellowed into the machine.

"Hey, kid, I want to see you. Call me when you pick up. You know that bath sounds real inviting. I'll be waiting for your call." Then the man hung up. There was silence, then the sound of the tape winding inside the machine. Maybe the guy wouldn't wait. He'd just come right over.

Having imagined I was alone with her while I was reading Ursula's journal, I had now heard the sound of someone else in her life. The voice on the phone, was it the guy she was with at Rebecca's? Or was it one of those jocks or weirdos from *Gala*? One of the candles flickered and went out. It caught my eye. I saw a large black moth fluttering its wings violently. The moth entered a flame. The flame engulfed the moth. I would swear I heard the cry of death. That was my cue. I left the bedroom. It was like a perfume factory. I was sure my clothes would stink of verbena for days. At least Barbara wouldn't smell it. I wouldn't be seeing Barbara. But she might smell it, Ursula. Then she'd know I'd been here. But then wasn't it true that you couldn't smell your own scent on someone else when you're wearing it yourself? There, I was thinking like a criminal again.

I went down the wooden stairs two at a time. I took the risk. I tried the front door. Two turns of the latch and the door swung open with a heavy creak. Wait a minute! How was I going to get back? This house was miles from the office or my apartment. Of course, I'd thought about it before. I just hadn't bothered to figure it out.

I went to the phone in the kitchen. There was a directory beside it. I found the number of the Beverly Hills Cab Co. I ordered a taxi to pick me up, not at this house, of course, but at the corner of La Cielo and Benedict. That was about a five-minute walk. The taxi would be there in ten minutes, they said. I took one last look around downstairs. The phone rang again. I was out of the place before the machine picked up.

I hurried along the dark curving street. The moon had come out now to light my way. A car came along. I thought of ducking down or pretending to walk into the drive of the house I was passing. But that was the Manson house of murder. I got to the corner of Benedict Canyon and waited. Cars passed. I prayed that I wouldn't be seen by a security patrol or the police. I thought up a story. My car had broken down . . . but then they might want to see my car. No, much better, my car had been stolen as I was visiting someone. Then whom was I visiting? It isn't that easy to make up alibis that hold water. Finally, finally the taxi came. I got in. I was safe. Ursula hadn't yet returned.

On the drive to my office, my mind was awash with questions. That ring of Barbara's bothered me most. How did Ursula come to have it? What had she and Barbara talked about when I was with Felicity and Barbara was delivering my bags to the office? There had to be a reasonable explanation. Mystery was all very well, but it had to stop somewhere and reason would have to take charge.

The taxi radio was loud. It interrupted my thoughts. It also brought back a memory. The voice of the man who called Ursula. I had been thinking of what the guy was saying. But now for some reason I recalled a telephone conversation I had in my car the morning after Barbara and I returned from New Mexico. I had woken Os up. He told me his dream about the woman who seemed to me to have been the same dark-haired woman I had seen in the mirror of the hotel hallway. Ursula. But that voice on her machine, it was the same voice. It was Os. It was impossible. But it was Os.

When I got to the office, I paced about. I couldn't sleep. I was dog tired but sleep simply wouldn't come. I thought of

Paul's Macbeth story of *La Belle Dame Sans Merci,* "Macbeth has murdered sleep." But I wasn't Macbeth. I hadn't murdered anyone. I dozed on the couch. I was awake the whole night but with my eyes shut.

I was still wide awake when there was a ring of the doorbell. It startled me. I came to out of a reverie of her. The phone had rung twice already, but that had been a distant bell and a light flashing on my desk phone. The fax machine had pumped out a couple of messages, one of them from Mike Adorno in New Mexico. His movie, *Ghost Town,* was nearly through shooting and he was tired and happy and he had something interesting to tell me about a death in the hotel where I'd been staying. That was it, signed with "Love to Barbara and my favorite agent—Mike."

I got up off the couch and went to the door to the outer office. It was the cops, one in uniform, one not, and neither had I seen before. It had to be about that crazy boyfriend of Alexis. He was pressing charges. Maybe something worse than that. Alexis. She was pregnant and was trying to nail me with a paternity suit.

"Mr. Elliott?"

"Yes."

"Mr. Mason Elliott?"

"Yes."

"May we come in? We're police officers."

"What's happened?"

"We have . . . not good news, I'm afraid."

"Come in."

It was something to do with Ursula. She'd been killed. Some maniac had cut her up.

"Felicity Elliott is your mother, isn't she, sir?"

"Yes. She is." I knew it. She was out of her skull. She fell.

"I regret to have to inform you that your mother is dead."

"She had a fall." I was right.

"What?"

"I mean, did she fall?"

"I guess so, Mr. Elliott. She was murdered."

"Murdered?"

"Why did you say she fell?"

88

"I guessed. I don't know."

"When did you last see your mother?"

I couldn't think of that line as funny. My memory jammed.

"It was two days ago . . . no three . . . let me think . . ."

The cops watched me as if I was their prime suspect.

"We need you to identify the body."

"Where is she?"

"In her apartment. She was killed there. Or so we believe."

"I'll come with you." I knew I was saying something but not what I meant to. For a few seconds I went deaf. I might have said, "I'll come quietly, I'll confess." But I didn't.

I looked around the office. What was I looking for? Something to take? My toilet bag. It was absurd. I left the office, my office, with these cops and I felt guilty, guilty as hell.

As I walked between the two guys down the echoing passage, I might as well have been on my way down Death Row.

"Ursula, I want you. Now. With me." I suddenly looked at the cops as we reached the door to the street. They didn't react. They hadn't heard me. I hadn't spoken. I felt criminal and lost. Somewhere inside me I must have wanted to kill her.

The cops were all over the apartment. Felicity's body was lying in exactly the same position I had found her. I bent down beside her.

"Don't touch the body please."

I wanted to cry, but I couldn't. There was too much pain in my head, memories of Felicity's abuse of me, as a child, as a man. That was over now. My mother looked as if she was asleep.

"How was she killed?" I couldn't see any marks on her or signs of violence.

"We'll have to wait for the autopsy. But it looks as if she was asphyxiated."

"Asphyxiated?"

"Smothered."

The police photographer took a flash shot of a bed pillow.

"Who could have done it?"

"It looks like an intruder. But nothing seems to have been stolen. Your mother had over a thousand dollars in her purse. There are signs of struggle, but there was no break-in. She may have known her murderer."

"I have no idea . . . I mean, I don't know." I was dizzy. I had to sit down.

"Don't sit in that chair, sir. We don't want to disturb anything. This must be a terrible shock to you, but I have to ask you about your mother's friends. If you could give me a list of people she knew."

"I don't know who her friends were. I mean, she didn't seem to have many friends."

"We're especially interested in her women friends."

"Women friends? Why?"

"We don't know yet for sure, but it's beginning to look as if your mother's murderer was female."

"I don't believe it," I said. I was panicked now.

"Why don't you believe it? Women have been known to murder other women."

"Why do you think it was a woman?" My voice was croaking.

"Can't you smell the perfume?" The detective looked at me as if I was a moron.

I sniffed. Of course I could smell it now. It was like a musky men's cologne.

"One of our detectives has identified the perfume."

"Maybe it's my mother's."

"No. We've been through the whole apartment. She had several bottles of perfume, but not this one."

I sniffed again. It wasn't the lemony smell. It wasn't her. But I knew the perfume from somewhere. I realized I knew it very well. It was Barbara's. But that was impossible.

Then I saw something that shook me to the center. Lying on the coffee table was a postcard, addressed-side visible. It had Barbara's name and our address on it. I didn't dare look too closely. I didn't have to. The perfume said everything. It was definitely Barbara's scent. I had introduced her to it. Barbara had been here, not Ursula. She had had a fight with Felicity two days ago. That was what had set my mother on her binge. Whatever they had said had led to this. Barbara had killed Felicity.

90

"I can't stay in here," I told the chief detective.

"I understand. But soon we will have to talk."

The police dropped me back at the office. Ursula was there looking fresh as a daisy, now dressed in white. She knew something was up. I looked like rat shit.

"Good news," she said to cheer me up. "Silvia's been offered a job. A good one, a second lead in a picture called *Zen Bowler,* subtitled *You Are the Ball.* Isn't that wonderful?"

"Yes," I said. "My mother's dead."

I told Ursula what had happened. But not my suspicions.

Barbara. Had she really done it? Now I thought about it all, the evidence was only circumstantial. Yes, she had had a fight with my mother but that didn't mean she had come back in the middle of the night to kill her. It had to be someone else.

I couldn't remember much about the next few hours. I was light-headed. My sleepless night was taking a heavy toll. My eyes kept closing. The police called again. I talked to them. I said nothing. Of course, I knew nothing. They were persistent in their theory of the murderess. Otherwise, I dodged everyone. Ursula was my cushion. She took all the calls for the rest of the day, which seemed more like night to me.

Once again, she was a different woman, warm, almost affectionate. She wanted to minister to me. She insisted that I eat. It was the last thing I wanted to do, but in the end I gave in. I needed to be with someone. And after all, hadn't I thought, dreamed for so long of being with her?

We went to a Mexican place she knew in Venice. She drove. She ate, my food as well as hers. She joked. She picked up the check. She drove me home to her place. That was the strangest part, being taken openly to the place I had spied on, secretly invaded only the night before. What I had done furtively she now offered me, and with enthusiasm. Felicity's death had somehow had the effect of opening doors.

I was too tired to appreciate fully this piece of magic. My eyes kept closing as she drove up Benedict to La Cielo. I dozed. And when I woke, we were there, at the entrance to the house of danger. I followed her up the stairs in a dream. I

91

sat in a chair in her bedroom. I was enveloped by the flickering candlelight. I was parched, dehydrated. While she went to get some water, I remembered the moth burned in the flames.

Then I was on her bed, or was it in her bed? It all had the quality of a grotesque fairy tale. Would I sleep for a hundred years? She leaned over me. I was with the woman who had occupied all my thoughts for days or weeks. My mother was dead, maybe murdered by my girlfriend. I simply couldn't focus. I needed sleep.

All thoughts of making love to this woman vanished. I had fucked her so often in my mind, but now I'd had it. Strange, I felt relieved. The death of Felicity had shocked me but now I felt as if a great weight was being lifted. It seemed to me as if I had been under hypnosis for years, in a thrall. Now I was light, lightened.

While I could still think, I asked her again if she had been to Artesia, New Mexico, to the Sierra Hotel, last Sunday. . . . She said no with a look on her face that suggested I was delirious. Maybe I was.

She began to take off my clothes. After all this, it was quite unsensual. It was just one person helping another. Her bedroom seemed tidier now in the last of the daylight. She took off my shoes and socks. I was wearing only my undershorts. I sank back onto the bed.

Next to my face was a small red satin pillow. It gave off a strange scent of its own. There was also a regular pillow that had been embroidered, probably when it was the fashion to embroider pillows with little sayings, but this had a heavy saying on it: "Life must be lived forwards but can only be understood backwards." Ursula bent over and smoothed my forehead. Then she kissed me, softly and lovingly. It was the most beautiful kiss I had ever received. It went on and on like the sea and I slowly drifted into sleep. The last thing I think I remember was Ursula's voice saying quietly, "It's going to be all right now. I'm with you. We're together at last. You're mine."

# PART
# TWO

# 17

# THE BEHOLDER

My fascination with Mason Elliott began with an image, a moving picture. I had arranged to meet with two people by the pool on the roof of the Bel Age hotel in West Hollywood. It was around six o'clock in the evening. The last people were leaving the poolside. To the accompaniment of hotel Muzak the attendant was picking up the wet towels and clearing away the drained cocktail glasses. I was sitting at a table, smoking, reading a book of poems, waiting.

I didn't see him get into the pool. My first sight of him was as he swam underwater. The sun was going down. Two thirds of the pool was in light, one third in shadow. His body glided below the rippling blue surface of the water. His skin was pale in the sunlight and became darker in the shadow. The man appeared to stay underwater for several minutes. I became nervous. I glanced at my watch. I must have been stretching time as I watched, perhaps to prolong the picture in my mind. The image was calm. I was anxious.

His head finally broke the surface. He pushed back his dark hair and stood up in the shallows, the water just above his navel. He had a simple, straight body, not especially muscular, softly tanned. It gave me a feeling of surprising delicacy. From his lean face I guessed he was in his thirties, although his body looked younger. He seemed preoccupied as he climbed out of the pool. He didn't look in my direction. Why should he? He walked over to the chair where he had left his robe. Nice legs, narrow thighs, small bottom visible under his white swimming shorts that stuck wetly to his skin. The dark hair on his legs and back made a grained-wood pattern. There was no hint of aggression.

In fact, there was nothing obviously remarkable about the guy. Yet he had an upright, unself-conscious beauty. Beauty? There was no narcissism. He was alone, unaware of himself or of anyone watching him. He didn't give the impression of belonging to anyone. He didn't look like anyone's partner. When he closed the long black toweling robe around his body, he looked suddenly different. He became taller. He became aloof. He looked out across the hazy landscape of the city. In my mind, there was a definite mystery about him now. I saw him as a traveler who had just arrived from a far-off place. He was here, surveying a new land.

At no time did he look at me. That was just as well because he would have caught me staring at him. I didn't feel any specific sexual desire, just a faint interest.

A blond girl appeared in a yellow dress. She came up to him. He recognized her. Girlfriend, I thought. But they didn't kiss. They clearly knew each other from somewhere. She was an L.A. girl, I could tell, not coming from here myself. So perhaps he wasn't a visitor after all. He was from here. Then why was he staying at the hotel? The girl moved on toward a table. She picked up her dark glasses, which she must have forgotten, waved again at the man, and hurried away.

I hadn't been able to hear what they had said. The sound of their voices across the pool was blocked by an overlay of taped music from the speakers near the bar. I was aware though that his voice was quite deep, surprising coming from that face. After the girl had gone he stood for a few moments, looking again at nothing in particular. Again, his image for me had changed. The sun had moved and now he looked lost, abandoned, tied only to his own dark shadow, which seemed like an extension of his black robe.

My friends were here. They saw me and called out. It seemed as if the arrival of Alain and Annabel had suddenly made the man conscious of something he had to do. His mood was broken. So was mine. He walked quickly away, toward the elevator. It was as if they had scared him. By the time they sat down at my table, he'd gone.

Alain Jussieu was a successful French director of commercials who had come to Los Angeles at around the time I did, seven years ago. He had directed a skin flick called *Gala* in which I played the heroine. He was sitting with his girlfriend, Annabel, who was a friend of mine. I'd met her on a modeling assignment. Annabel had become Alain's slave, literally it seemed to me. She would do anything for him. Among the things he had wanted her to do was to play a lesbian who would make love with me in one of the episodes in *Gala*. She did.

One evening a year or so ago Alain had proposed to me that I play Gala in his projected movie. He discovered through Annabel that although I wasn't an actress I was an attractive girl with modeling experience and very few inhibitions. Annabel, a pretty and fleshy blonde who had sporting aspirations, was quite shy with people. She had adopted me as her role model for open-mindedness and fearless honesty. Imagine. This evening she looked pale and there were beads of sweat on her forehead. She wasn't well.

At the time Alain didn't have to talk me into doing *Gala*. My motive for agreeing to the film hadn't been money. I had plenty of money after Brian, my husband, died. My motive was disobedience. It was like a great big dare. I'd always wondered what it would feel like to do those things in front of a lot of people. We did them in private, so what was the difference? It was a test of my courage. Most women wouldn't do it. We're a frightened lot. I took the test. I passed. Straight A.

There had of course been other motives for doing the film. While we were shooting, I was aware of performing something socially unacceptable, forbidden. There was an excitement in that. I could see my now-grown-up school friends saying, "How could she do it? I've never even done those things in private." Against society, against convention, against good literary taste. I've always been a reader. I wondered what Charlotte Brontë would make of it. *Jane Eyre* was my favorite novel. I wanted to read the scene where she fucks Rochester when he's blind. That would have made a great ending.

Then there was my father. I wanted to show my father a thing or two about sex for its own sake. Sadly, he was dead before I did the movie, but he'd have been impressed. That was something he hadn't been while he was alive. In order to impress him I was prepared to hurt myself, degrade myself if you like. There's always been that in me.

"We're thinking of doing a follow-up," Alain said.

"Not with me."

"Why not? Annabel wants to do it."

I turned to Annabel. She didn't want to do it. She looked as if she had just received some fearful news.

"If I were Annabel, I wouldn't do it."

"But you were so good." He was getting angry.

"Look, Alain. I did it. I can't say I enjoyed it, but I wanted to do it. It's done. It's history."

"So your answer's no?"

"Yes. It's no."

Annabel looked relieved. We talked on for a short while. The shadows were lengthening visibly. Lights were coming on across the city. It was changing for the night. Suddenly, I hated being here. I just wanted to go, to be gone. I didn't want to be reminded of *Gala*.

As I drove home, the image of the nameless man by the pool drifted to my consciousness, uninvited. There were several images really: his body moving underwater, the appearance of his face emerging, unself-consciously offering itself for appreciation, his standing figure, dressed in black, unaffectedly staring out across the hazy city. Had he been trying to remember a face or trying to decide a course of action? Probably neither. It was just me and my guessing games.

I couldn't help wondering about the shape of his life. Was he married? Did he have children? What was his job? I'm not that good at figuring other people's jobs, people I don't know. I invariably get them wrong, because I invent people's worlds for myself. It was an unrealistic habit, I knew, but that didn't stop me. So I went on.

There was something vaguely artistic about him, but he didn't look like a painter or a writer. His casual acknowledgment of the girl by the pool revealed nothing. I was finding it harder than usual to invent for this man. His air of self-containment was undeniably attractive. But I couldn't easily imagine him with a woman.

Why was I thinking about him at all? The fact was that at this low point in my life I had no one to talk to, no one I wanted to think about. I was slightly lonely, slightly bored. So I let this man occupy my thoughts for a while. No harm in that.

Seeing Alain and Annabel had depressed me. Just thinking about someone outside myself raised my spirits. An early impression of the man returned. There was something beautiful about him.

To describe a woman as beautiful right away conjures a picture of her. Whether she has dark or fair hair, blue eyes or brown, whether her figure is slim or fleshy, the word instantly conveys a harmony of features, a naturalness, a balance.

To describe a man as beautiful is almost confusing. It's such an improbable adjective unless you're describing a perfect naked figure. To call a man beautiful implies a certain mindlessness. To call a woman beautiful implies an ideal. The beauty of the man by the pool, in my eyes at least, was his containment, his mystery. Perhaps that's close to it. To find a man beautiful is to invest him with mystery.

At home I went to bed to read again a book of poems by Anne Morrow, the wife of Lindbergh the aviator. It was a book I really loved. There were three lines which to me were completely beautiful:

> Him that I love
> I wish to be free—
> Even from me.

Why were they beautiful? Because they described something wished for but unattainable. I had two lives, like most people. One life was what you did and what was done to you. The other was what you dreamed about and never happened.

# 18

# THE LISTENER

The second time I saw Mason Elliott was in the bar of the Regency Beverly Wilshire hotel. I had been shopping for shoes. Usually that cheers me up. This time it hadn't. I didn't feel like going home in the middle of the day, so I had slipped into the hotel bar. It was spacious and comfortable. I could sit quietly alone in the window opposite the main entrance of the hotel and read in good light and look around at the purposeful clientele and not be bothered by men trying to pick me up.

It was the deep voice that drew my attention to his table, that resonant, vibrating tone. Two weeks or more had passed since I had been entranced by the man at the Bel Age pool. Provoked now, my memory of the scene was clear as the water in the pool. In that time I hadn't consciously thought about the man. Now he was sitting at the next table. As the silent, underwater image of his body had introduced him before, this time he came to me through the sound of his voice. I could now listen to him as well as watch.

"There was this guy who needed a heart transplant. His doctor had located just two potential donors. One was a twenty-three-year-old decathlon athlete. The other was a seventy-six-year-old lawyer.

'This is your choice,' the doctor told the guy.

'I'll take the lawyer,' he said. 'The seventy-six-year-old lawyer? Are you crazy? For God's sake, why?' The guy replies, 'I want a heart that hasn't been used.'"

I laughed, probably out loud. The man with his deeply serious voice was funny. The beautiful man of mystery had a sense of humor. I had to turn and look at him.

He was dressed in a gray Italian suit, white shirt, emerald silk tie. His dark hair framed his head differently now that it was dry and combed. It was longer, heavier than I had remembered. Superficially he looked like a successful executive. But everything else about him worked against that stereotype. The self-containment was no longer evident. He was talking to a young man who looked like an actor but who, I discovered by listening to the conversation, was a writer. So my man was involved with art. I had been right.

"Mason, I'm stuck," the young man said. "I'm fifty pages in and I've lost my way."

"Write the ending."

The man's name was Mason. A strong name, I thought, but somewhat artificial, one of those transposed last names. Hardly his fault though. Mason. Okay.

The young man said, "I have the ending. There's a chase on foot in a department store. It's like a comic version of a car chase. His shoes come off, his jacket gets ripped—"

"Fine, but write it. I guarantee it'll clear your block."

"How?"

"Don't ask me how. I know it works. Even if you find you want to change it later. It doesn't matter. The important thing is to know where you're going. Write everything down, every scene you can. Don't wait. Don't be afraid of doing things out of sequence. It'll all fit in the end. You'll be surprised."

That struck a chord with me. I had always been interested in writing. It went with my reading. In my early twenties I started a diary. It was a way of controlling pain and unhappiness. Writing things down, reading them back, gave me a sense of continuity. What this man was saying was great advice. If I ever got down to writing a novel, I'd remember it. Write what you can. Get the ending written.

A waiter came up to their table.

"Mr. Elliott, there's a call for you, your secretary."

I watched as he stood up and followed the waiter to the phone at the bar. I realized the young man was looking at me. I pretended to return to my book.

So his name was Mason Elliott. He wasn't a guest in the hotel. He hadn't been staying at the Bel Age either. He lived and worked here in L.A. Good.

When he returned to the table I waited for more. More of the voice. More of the look. More information. More surprise. But I was disappointed.

"Paul, I have go," he said. "Alexis just got a fax. I have to reply right away." He put a twenty-dollar bill on the table.

"Hey, I'll get this," Paul, the writer, said.

"The agent pays. Your turn'll come when I get you an assignment."

"Thanks, Mason."

So he was an agent. I watched him leave the bar, watched him all the way to the door, waited and watched him through the window as he came out of the hotel entrance, and watched him stride away. He didn't ask the valet for a car, so I guessed he must work nearby in Beverly Hills. And that was it. He was gone. I smiled again at the joke. I'd try to remember it. I returned to my reading. I didn't notice the young writer leave. When I looked around again, two women were sitting at the table.

I went upstairs to my bedroom. I pulled the drapes closed, locking out the remains of the daylight. I lit my candles. I was intensely restless. I took off my dress. I went into the bathroom and turned on the water in the tub. I looked at myself in the mirror. I took off my underclothes and stared at my body. Somehow the body wasn't mine. It was in the way of my feeling. I felt sick looking at my flesh. I put on a terrycloth bathrobe to cover it. It was Brian's robe. It belonged to his ghost.

Brian Baxter was a sweet, sweet guy. When I first came out to Los Angeles, it was on a modeling job. I got more work, some fat commercials, and stayed on. At that time I seemed to fit a popular photographic image. And with the work came the men. But it was over as quickly as it began. What you don't care about doesn't last. Within three years I was down to catalog work, underwear mostly. Even that became sporadic. I needed money.

I took a typing course, started a book, the usual autobiographical rubbish, and ended up naturally enough as a secretary. That's how I met Mr. Baxter and eventually came to live in this house.

I'd been working as a secretary to the manager of a chemical company in the San Fernando Valley. In those days I lived in Tarzana. My boss had a friend whose name was Brian Baxter. Brian, who was forty-five, couldn't keep his hands off me. I was used to that. The surprise was that he was a very pleasant man. He was generous and a bit of a snob. He loved my "educated" accent. He adored my narrow bottom. He wanted to make me happy, more than he wanted to be happy himself. He was the good man.

He loved to hear me talk and talk. When I ran out of things to say, he had me read to him. I used to read him to sleep. He admired D. H. Lawrence. He liked to believe I'd been called Ursula after the heroine of *The Rainbow* and *Women in Love*. The truth was my father named me after the first girl he ever fucked.

Brian's first heart attack occurred while I was reading to him. He was falling asleep when it happened. I was terrified. At that time I was half-living with him in this house on La Cielo. I was so frightened of his dying that I wanted to leave him. I suppose I didn't want to be responsible for his death. I saw him dying as we made love.

Instead of leaving him, I became Mrs. Baxter. It was Laszlo Ronay who in a way persuaded me to marry him. Laszlo was an astrologer who had come to this country via Australia after the Hungarian uprising in 1956. Like so many unhappy people, I looked for solace and guidance in the stars. Laszlo had been very accurate about me in the past. He had predicted that my modeling career would be short-lived. He had predicted an upheaval in my life and a complete change of direction at the time I was seeing Brian; I concluded that our marriage was, if not inevitable, then certainly the way to go. I did not for one second think that it was Brian who would go, that it was his death and not our marriage that was the great change of direction Laszlo predicted.

Within a year Brian was dead. He had a heart attack while we were making love one night. He struggled out of bed and collapsed in the bathroom. Waiting for the paramedics, I covered him in the bathrobe I now wore. Afterward, when I thought about him, I missed him. I missed his love. I missed his gentle hands on my bottom, stroking it, opening it, feeling his way in, looking for something, a simple and not too painful pleasure. Poor Brian. Rich me. He left me his money and his house. But poor me too. Any love there had been in my life died with him.

A few months after he became a ghost, I went on a sexual rampage. For a long time I was every man's dream of a nymphomaniac. I must have slept with well over two hundred men. It seemed like two thousand. Sometimes I had four or five in a week. When I thought about what I was doing, I was scared. I just couldn't seem to control my lust. When I wasn't fucking I read books. I didn't need to work for a living. I told my diary, the Pillow Book, I was fucking for fun. In fact it was more like a regular job. My Filofax was full of assignments.

I tried not to sleep with the same guy twice. I found I lost interest the second time around. Sex fascinated me because I could have an orgasm very easily, very quickly. But while premature ejaculation in men irritates women, instant orgasm in women excites and fascinates men. For me, the act of sex was never a means to an end. I wasn't trying to ensnare anyone. The activity justified itself. It was like constant power. I didn't look to sex as a way to find love. They were unconnected. Sex was pure desire. The goal wasn't some kind of fulfillment. It was the continuation of desire itself. I wanted to be permanently in a state of wanting. As soon as I got it, I wanted it again. It was there all the time.

Like everybody else, I suppose I thought fearfully about AIDS, but apart from avoiding drug addicts and gays, I didn't insist on making it all safe. I wasn't looking for danger. I myself was dangerous. I could get all the romance I wanted from novels. But books were useless when it came to sex. For that you needed men. And maybe women.

I tried that too. I liked holding another woman's breasts. I liked kissing lips that had been made up. I liked opening thighs and finding my own shape in someone else. But I found I didn't like the girls themselves. So I didn't pursue them. Whereas with the men I didn't care whether I liked them or not. I didn't need to have any opinions about their personalities. Men were objective.

The making of *Gala* was the climax of my sexual odyssey, the last act. The movie was shot in ten days. I didn't expect to get any pleasure out of doing it. Having coldly to perform the same actions two or three times for the different camera positions gave the enterprise a dreamlike, ritualistic character. Most of it was shot without sound. With a man's dick in my mouth, all I could hear was the whirring camera motor and Alain calling out instructions. It wasn't fun and I wasn't free. After the first day I began to pray for it all to end.

When I saw the movie cut together, with its added grunts, groans, and gasps on the soundtrack, I felt completely used. The woman on the screen wasn't me. I had insisted on wearing a red-brown–haired wig over my naturally short black hair. I suppose I didn't want to be recognized. But the reason I gave to myself was that it made me look more desirable to men, less like a predatory vamp. I have always believed that my appearance, my face especially, was off-putting. My allure, though enticing, was somehow repellent. You would have to penetrate the mask to see the real Ursula beneath. Wanting Ursula was easy. Understanding Ursula was hard. Loving Ursula might be impossible. My husband was the one exception.

Brian's appeal to me was that he resembled not my real father but the father I would have liked. I was quite conscious of that. He fulfilled the romantic fantasies of my teenage years at boarding school, away from my father's house in Portland, Maine.

My father was a womanizer in the grand manner. I went through a stage of being disgusted by his outrageous behavior and it was only in my late teens that I began to see him as an innocent man. Because he thought only about sex, my father had no pretensions when it came to women. He never lied to them. He never made false promises. He had no evil designs on their lives. If he hurt them, it was only in bed.

When I came home from school on vacations, I expected to find one or two girls around the house. One girl I liked especially lasted quite a while. Her name was Audrey Johns. She had been an art school model and she really fell for him. She couldn't have been much older than me. I think she was the daughter of a business associate.

Audrey and I became friends. She would take me clothes shopping with her. She had a passion for buying underwear, which she would later wear around the apartment. In retrospect, I think my father, whose name was Richard but who insisted on being called Dick, would have liked to have taken us both to bed with him. But he didn't have the nerve to ask me. He certainly made sure I was around the house while he was fucking Audrey.

I tried to avoid them when they embarked on their sessions. I would go out of the apartment even though I had nowhere really to go. I'd come home at three in the morning, having wandered the streets of Portland for hours, only to find them screwing in my bedroom. I don't know why Audrey finally left, but one day she just wasn't there anymore. My father never spoke about her again. And I never saw her again. I think something terrible must have happened, and he had fallen in love with her. Sometimes with strangers I have used her name as my own in memory of her. I have been Audrey Johns when it suited me.

After *Gala,* I was finished with the flesh. In the next few months I became a recluse. The lonely lady in her mansion. I had no desire except to read. I went out infrequently. When I did, it was to buy books and eat Mexican food. From my childhood, Mexican food had seemed exotic. It wasn't to be had in Portland. But here in Los Angeles I could indulge myself in the fantasy of living in a country of escape and danger. An imaginary Mexico of wild *pistoleros,* vivacious whores, brass and guitar music, and sleeping till noon in deeply shadowed rooms baked in the heat of the day. It was the stuff of fiction.

I sat down with my journal, my Pillow Book, and picked up my pen. Thinking about the ghosts of my father and my husband, I concocted a little tale of reincarnation . . . how one man after he was dead became reincarnated in another man and how the heroine, that was me, fell in love with the second guy, believing him to be the first. . . . But she was deluded because the new man was in fact completely different, and had nothing in common with the dead man, although she couldn't see it. . . . She was a victim of her own imagination. . . . Now, how would that end? The ending. I stopped writing. I didn't have an ending.

"The important thing is to know where you're going. . . . Write the ending." Mason Elliott's voice came back to me. I could hear the certainty in its deep tone. I began to think about him again. He had crossed my path twice now. The first time he had helped ease my depressed mood. This time he'd given me good advice. Mason Elliott was not only beautiful, he was useful. Could anyone ask for more?

# 19

# MORE

I can't say at what point exactly I needed to know more about Mason Elliott. It was a slow discovery. A dawning of want. In the weeks after seeing him in the bar of the Beverly Wilshire I found myself looking around for him. When I went to a restaurant or a bar I would glance about to see if he was there. I caught myself listening to conversations hoping to hear his distinctive voice. Bored with my own company, uninterested in seeing people, I realized I missed him. It was absurd. I was aware of that. I didn't even know the man. I lived on the memory of those images and the sound of his voice. He must have his own life. He had absolutely no need to see me. It was not in my nature to chase a man. I'd never had to.

One afternoon I had been looking at the latest novels in Book Soup, a bookstore in West Hollywood, and when I came out of the shop I realized I was standing in the shadow of the Bel Age hotel. I went inside the lobby and took the elevator to the roof. Did I seriously expect him to be there? Of course not.

I sat in the same chair as before, but the pool area seemed different. It was crowded. Two children were splashing and yelling in the water, drowning out the piped-in music. An uneven row of artificially relaxed, supine bodies dripping with sun oil were without sensuality because they were still and bored. My memory of Mason Elliott was a memory in movement, which I could run back and forth like videotape, slowing it down to watch a gesture repeated and out of the repetition discover something new and different. Was I merely entertaining myself in a private game of self-stimulation? I got up and stood where he had stood looking out at the city. I saw nothing. It was too early in the afternoon. I needed the light at the end of the day, the beginning of sunset. I needed the moving shadows. I hung around the pool for an hour, lost.

I was beginning to see myself in a new light. As a retired woman. My entire life seemed over. Things present were receding into a past time. I was no longer in step with myself. When I sat down to a Mexican dinner and looked at the familiar menu, I had the impression that I had already eaten. I was no longer hungry. Looking at a freshly poured drink, I felt as if I'd just finished it, drunk without having drunk. I started a new novel and after a few pages I imagined that I'd read the whole thing. I turned to the last chapter, something I never do, just to get rid of the book. Retired, I had no tasks left. Except him. Like a school project, Mason Elliott, his life and times, was to be my sole theme for the long summer vacation.

I called Laszlo Ronay, not to check on my future because I didn't feel I had one, but to ask a simple question.

"How would I go about contacting someone I've seen a couple of times but don't know?"

"You know their name?"

"Yes."

"Look them up in the book."

"No, I mean contact in the sense of spiritual contact."

"Oh, I see. Well, when did they die?"

"They're alive."

"Are you crazy?"

"You know I'm crazy," I said. Just how crazy was evident in my referring to "him" as "they."

"You want to be with someone without actually being in their presence, is that it?"

"Yes."

"Can I ask why you want to do this?"

"I'm not sure why."

"I don't know how I can help. Do you want to follow them?"

"No," I said. That was a lie and I knew it. That was exactly what I wanted to do. And Laszlo couldn't help me. I was becoming afraid.

Sitting in the bar of the Regent Beverly Wilshire at the same table as before, I could see and hear him. Silently, I told myself the lawyer joke. "I want a heart that hasn't been used." When I took that punchline away from the joke and considered it in isolation, it became a line of verse. And quite beautiful. Worthy of Anne Morrow Lindbergh. That was what I wanted, a heart that hadn't been used. Was it his?

The bar was my waiting room. He was out there, on a street, in an office, in a restaurant, at the beach, at home, in bed, sick, or with a woman. A woman. Someone *that* beautiful must have a woman. What kind of woman would she be?

What was his type? He wouldn't have a type. He would want a woman for herself. He wouldn't give a damn what she looked like. She would be someone who fit with him.

For the first time a specifically sexual feeling was aroused in me. For a woman as resolutely sexual as I had been, it was strange that this sensation hadn't occurred before now. Why was that? It was hard to figure. But then, this whole thing was hard to figure. I felt my body tense. It was unmistakably a feeling of panic, the panic that accompanies the beginning of physical desire.

I could see Mason Elliott lying asleep on a bed at dawn. He was sprawled naked on top of the soft covers. As I drew back the blinds to let in the first light of day, his body became illuminated. As I watched, the flesh seemed to give off a light of its own.

I paid the check at the bar and left. I have no recollection where I went or who I met for the rest of that day. It was as if I had had an illumination, a conversion. I had faith. I was in contact with him. For several days after that we were together. We wandered around Beverly Hills. But it was the streets that moved. We marked time. We drove down to Venice and sat on the beach. We were the center. Other people played around us. We hardly spoke. No question-and-answer sessions. No exchanged tales of uneasy childhood or difficulties with parents. None of that biographical stuff. We didn't need history or analogy. We were together in spirit. And because of that we exhausted ourselves in bed, on the beach, and still needed more. I took him for a ride on my bike. He loved it. And I loved him. It was so simple. We understood each other completely. We were happy. But as with all happiness, the days were numbered, like the pages of a book.

Sometimes, when I most wanted him, he wasn't there. I couldn't seem to summon his presence. I'd lost my power. I couldn't find him. His absence was depressing. Then it became painful. I ached. I spent hours in bed waiting. Two or three times he came to visit. That was wonderful. But I couldn't bear his leaving. That knowledge ruined our time together, the thought that he would soon leave.

I had no idea where to find him now. He knew where I was but I didn't know where he lived or where he went when he left me. While that had been our unspoken pact, no checking up, no big questions, no little traps, I just couldn't take it anymore. I smelt of jealousy and it was an unpleasant scent. I had to get rid of it.

After days like nights of sleepless torture, I recalled Laszlo's first response to my question about how to make contact. "Look them up in the book," he had said. I hadn't done it then. I lacked the courage. I had made contact another way, but now I had lost that contact.

The Beverly Hills directory contained several Elliotts. There were different spellings. Eliots with one *l* and one *t*. Elliots with two *l*'s and one *t*. I shook with impatience. Then I found it. Out of this available list of names and addresses, of men and women and their work, came one name and one address that had for me the enigmatic force of lines from a poem waiting to be interpreted. Mason Elliott and Associates, Talent Agency, 409 North Camden Drive, Beverly Hills.

I was coming out of my retirement to stop thinking and begin to act. I could hear my heart beating in my ears.

# 20

# ALEXIS

I started with his office. On and off for two days I watched him come and go. I pretended to window-shop across the street from the front entrance. Then I realized that Mason parked his car in the alleyway in back of the building. It was easier for me to watch from there. I managed to get a picture of him through the windshield of my car. Nights at home I would look at the photograph. It wasn't enough. I had to get closer to him. So I had the photo blown up. Full face. Now we were equal.

Next I targeted Mason's secretary, Alexis. I hung around one afternoon waiting for him to leave. I wanted to get in and see the place, feel the atmosphere, be where he worked, look at what he looked at, to smell his smell. The smell was important to me. I had always been fascinated by smells. Perfumes, the smell of places, of people, provoked my strongest memories. Sounds had never meant so much to me. I tended to cut them out. And music was my blind spot.

The first time I walked down the ground-floor passageway to his office I was intoxicated. It was an old building, only two floors and a remnant of what you might call old Beverly Hills. I couldn't honestly say that I could smell Mason as I went in, but I smelled what he smelled, and that was enough. For the time being. The hallway was faintly musty, an old brick smell, not especially romantic but evocative of the past. It could be my future.

I knocked and entered Mason's office. Alexis was sitting in the outer office. In her mid-twenties, she had a pleasant, wide-open manner. I guessed that she had the same welcoming smile for everyone, famous or unknown, who might come through the door. I liked her.

My story was that I was a would-be actress in town looking for representation. I told Alexis I was a model from New England. I was wearing my wig. I took my glasses off.

"Mr. Elliott doesn't represent models," Alexis said politely, "but if you leave your CV I'll see that he reads it."

I couldn't find a good reason to stay longer. The door to his own office was tantalizingly open. I could see a framed photograph of a client I didn't recognize that was hanging above a fish tank. Alexis smiled at me, waiting for me to leave. So I did. I had no choice.

I began to follow Alexis when she left the office in the evenings. I discovered where she lived, who her boyfriend was, and where he lived. I knew where she bought her groceries, where she shopped for clothes, and where she wanted to shop for clothes but couldn't afford to. I knew everything about Alexis, except that she was hopelessly in love with Mason.

One day I contrived to bump into her during lunchtime at a croissant and sandwich place. She was by herself. The place was crowded with secretaries. I managed to sit opposite her.

I told her I hadn't heard from her boss. She said Mr. Elliott would like some photographs to go with my résumé. That was one thing I daren't give him.

"What's he like—Mr. Elliott?"

"A very nice man. A hard worker!"

Not the kind of thing I wanted to hear.

"You know him quite well, I imagine." I was fishing.

"I've been with him two years."

"From what I hear he doesn't seem like your typical agent."

"He has integrity."

"Is he a family man?"

"Why do you ask that?" Alexis's tone changed. I had touched a spot. Be careful.

"No reason really. I can never imagine an agent with a family. I guess I'm a bit naive."

"He's not married."

I had to let it go at that.

The next time I saw Alexis was genuinely by accident. I had been buying books down on Sunset at Book Soup. On my way home I stopped for a Japanese meal at the Imperial

Gardens, a stone's throw from the Bel Age hotel. The restaurant had a special menu in Japanese that offered dishes that weren't on the main menu in English. Brian had taught me what they were. He was an eggplant fanatic and the Imperial Gardens has a delicious baked eggplant with finely ground spiced beef. I was eating that when Mason and Alexis came into the restaurant. She didn't see me, thank God. Without my wig and glasses, I didn't think Alexis would recognize me, not at a distance. I spent the next hour and a half watching them. They sat several tables away. I couldn't hear a word that was said, but the scene was fascinating.

For most of the time Mason seemed to be talking about office matters. I imagined a discussion of work, clients, money, the things of the day. He drank water with his sushi. He ate carefully, slowly, almost delicately. The man had natural grace. But it was Alexis and her behavior that revealed so much. To begin with, they looked like lovers. My heart pounded.

Alexis ate almost nothing. She drank a bottle of wine herself. She was often silent while he talked. She watched him. She regarded him with a look that was impossible to misinterpret. Alexis was in love with Mason. It was two looks in one. The first was a smile of adoration, youthful, uncritical. The second was its mirror opposite, an expression of hopelessness. There was a silent desperation in her hand movements, in the way she pushed her fair hair back frequently even though it wasn't covering her face. But they weren't lovers. It was a one-way affair.

The two faces of her love were brought about, it was obvious to me, by Mason's fundamental indifference to her. At no time during the meal did he touch her. His smiles in her direction were office smiles, a boss taking his secretary out to dinner, probably after a long day. There was no more to it than that. I was relieved. Now Alexis was on the brink of tears. My own reactions were split.

I was jealous. She was where I wanted to be, next to him. Yet when I looked at her as she was now, how could I be jealous? The girl was lost. Why didn't she tell him the truth? She was in love with him.

After a while I could see he was getting bored. He'd given her dinner, thanked her, and that was it. I turned away

113

as they left, Alexis, her eyes clouded by tears, couldn't see five yards in front of her. He looked straight past me. If only he knew he was going to want me one day.

The next time I encountered Alexis was in a bar. I knew where she went after work. She was not alone. When I got there she was having a fight with her boyfriend, Rodney. I guessed it was probably about Mason. So many love affairs were one-way streets. Alexis didn't want to sleep with Rodney while dreaming all the while of Mason. All Rodney could see was that she didn't seem to want him anymore the way he wanted her. I watched the fight. It gave me a lucky break.

Rodney, the violent little bastard, hit Alexis, slapped her face. Quite a few people in the bar saw it. In the midst of a rumble of bad feeling, Rodney left, squeaking in his tight leather outfit. I'd get him for that one day.

As Rodney went, so did the thick mask of makeup on Alexis's skin. The pancake, the rouge, the lipstick, even the mascara vanished in seconds, absorbed by the invisible sponge of emotion. I sat down in Rodney's chair facing her. She realized I'd seen what had happened. In our previous encounters Alexis had had the upper hand, advising me what to do, how to go about things. Now I had been a witness to her humiliation. For the first time I had the advantage.

"I don't know what to do," she said.

"Do the right thing," I said.

Alexis smiled. "I wish I knew what that was." She fumbled in her purse for makeup. "I know I look awful."

"I saw a movie on cable. The guy said: 'There comes a time in every man's life when he has to give up his principles, and do what's right.'" I didn't think she got it.

"We still didn't get your photos."

"I'm having them redone," I said.

"I'm so sick and tired of men, I can't tell you. The trouble is what I want I can't have. And what's on offer I don't want. I suppose you think that's obvious."

"What's obvious is that that guy's no good."

"No, it's me that's no good." Alexis forced a laugh.

"You've got a good job, working for someone you like. That's half the battle, isn't it?"

"Half? Sister, that is the battle."

114

"You've lost me."

"I"m a cliché. A dumb, stupid cliché. I'm in love with my boss."

"But he doesn't love you."

"You guessed it. Double cliché."

"Then leave."

"I can't do that."

"Why not?"

"I love him."

"And the guy who hit you?"

"That's my boyfriend, wouldn't you know. He loves me."

"Then give them both up," I said.

"Good idea."

"If he doesn't want you, you should leave. Leave them both. Start again."

"You're probably right," Alexis said.

I could see in her face the seeds were sown. I was only telling her what she already knew. I didn't want to hurt this girl. I liked her. But even a wildly romantic woman like me has to be practical. So I became practical in a wildly romantic way. I became reckless.

# 21

# THE RING

I followed Mason home. To begin with, I didn't realize the house in the Palisades where he lived wasn't his own. It belonged to his girlfriend, Barbara Kovak. I discovered later from Alexis that she owned a jewelry store and that they had lived together for more than a year. Mason had settled down with Barbara after a succession of girlfriends. Alexis had found out he had a reputation as a seducer. This intrigued me. I hadn't seen it in him. Maybe it wasn't there anymore. After all, I'd had my share of that game and it wasn't in me anymore. Maybe we were ready for each other.

Barbara would sometimes come into the office at the end of the day and they would go home together. Other times Mason would drive home alone. I tried to imagine their relationship. I started to watch their house at night. I became a voyeur, a voyeuse, something I had never been before. I had always thought of that as exclusively a male province. But of course there was no such thing. Essentially, people were people, regardless of gender. If types or groups existed at all, they cut across the boundaries of sex. I, for example, belonged to that group who liked to hunt and discover and not wait passively at home.

I started to park my bike two hundred yards from the house itself. I'd simply watch and wait. It was actually a pretty spot. A piece of country far from the city. Slowly, I got bolder. I found a hiding spot from which I could spy on them properly. Flowers bloomed while I waited. But watching at night was difficult. I became frustrated. Three or four times I hid in the tall shrub that separated their place from the house next door.

Sometimes I took greater risks. After they had come home, I would go in close to the house. They both had to be there, otherwise one of them arriving home might see me. I would glimpse them moving around inside. It was a diminishing thrill. I could never really attain my goal and see into their bedroom. Even if the light was on, it didn't help much. Barbara's bedroom windows were protected by stupid bamboo blinds. In my own house I never bothered with that sort of thing.

Then I tried a different approach. I would go to bed early and get up at five in the morning. I took the car, which was less conspicuous than the Triumph, to the Canyon. I parked and watched the house from before dawn. I was occasionally rewarded by seeing them in the kitchen, which had a screen door that Barbara liked to open on warm mornings while she fixed breakfast.

I was intrigued by Barbara. I wanted to know more about her in order to know more about him. On with the wig and glasses. I went as a customer to her little jewelry shop in Santa Monica. It was called Pandora's Box. I opened it. Nothing could stop my careful recklessness.

Then Barbara came up to me, smiling, hopeful that I would buy something.

"Can I help?"

"I was just looking at the wonderful things you've got here."

"Thank you. What are you looking for? A ring? A brooch? A necklace?"

"Something I can feel sentimental about."

"Is it for yourself?"

"In a way. Someone I know wants to buy me a piece of jewelry but I'm going to choose it myself. It'll save taking it back."

"Good for you," said Barbara, sensing a kindred spirit. "Men are selfish when they buy things. They buy what they want, not what we like."

"Not only in jewelry."

"You're absolutely right." Barbara smiled. It was her best feature. She had dimples you could put your little finger in. That's the first lesson of charm school: Perfect your smile. Probably the first lesson for a salesperson too. I looked at Barbara's hands. She was wearing eight rings. I counted them.

"That's a wonderful ring you're wearing," I said.

"Which one?"

I took Barbara's left hand in my right. I touched the ring. I felt a sharp frisson. This woman's hand had touched Mason, his hair, his clothes, his skin.

"Have you got another one like this?"

"I'm afraid not. All our pieces are originals."

"Shame. I really like it." I held her hand as long as I could before she took it back. Slowly, Barbara removed the ring from her wedding finger by putting the finger to her mouth and licking it.

"If you like it that much, I could sell it to you."

"Oh no. It's yours. I couldn't possibly do that."

"To tell you the truth, I sometimes wear my jewelry as a kind of advertisement. People see a piece they like and ask about it. It's better than a catalog."

She got the ring off and handed it to me. It was still warm. I tried the ring on one finger, then another. I examined my hand in the shop's adjustable mirror. Barbara watched me. It was an easy sale. She charged me sixty bucks

117

for this chunky piece of brass. She could see how much I wanted it and probably added twenty to the price.

"As a matter of fact, the guy I live with really likes that ring," Barbara said.

I shivered. I came to the shop to see Barbara, to get a feeling of the woman who was so close to Mason. Now I had her ring on my finger, a ring he had touched.

"I hope the guy who's buying it for you likes it too." Barbara was sincere. I paid cash. When she asked for my address for the receipt, I gave her a fictitious one. I used the name Audrey Johns.

After the sale was completed, I leaned forward and impetuously kissed her on the cheek, a fleeting thank you, perhaps a tease. I felt the soft blond hair of her cheek on my lips. As he must have. My hand brushed her hip at the point where the flesh went from hard to soft. She didn't seem to notice.

"Come again," Barbara said, smiling.

"I will," I said.

I realized that my plan would take time. I just had to be patient, patient, patient. To me, the city of Los Angeles had become a gigantic waiting room. I found an unexpected sensuality in the delay.

Now I lay back in my bath and with the help of some soap removed the ring from my finger. I sank down. I examined the ring. I kissed it. I pressed it to my left breast. I pushed it into the flesh. I fitted it over the hard nipple, but it wouldn't stay there. I hunted for the ring beneath the soapy water. I found it under my bottom. Where else? I scraped the brass ring over my belly. I tried to stretch my navel open to get the ring inside. That didn't work. I pushed it between my legs, but not too far. I didn't want to lose it.

The bath wasn't working. I wanted Mason. Nothing else would do. I got out of the water. I put the ring back on my finger. You belong to me, I thought.

I dried myself in Brian's bathrobe. I lay back on my bed, damp, tired by the hot bath. I fingered the new trophy on my hand. I unwrapped a picture of Mason with a group of movie morons that I'd found and cut out of *The Hollywood Reporter*. He looked so young.

I couldn't stand it any longer. Where was my little pillow? I opened the robe and pushed my red satin pillow gently between my legs. The satin was always cold, oblivious to room temperatures. But like a cold-blooded serpent it warmed instantly to flesh temperature. The pillow was about eighteen inches square. I had bought it with my pocket money in a flea market in Portland. Two corners of the pillow were rounded and the other two were rectangular. Sometimes I would push the relatively sharp corner into my cunt. Other times, I would stroke myself with the rounded edge. One was a thrust, the other a stroke. Right now I needed a stroke. Who knows why? The rules of obsession are never clear.

I wanted to come quickly now, but it was interminably slow. I forgot the brass ring. I forgot the photo clipping, all the fetishes. Instead, I summoned his face, his presence. I would make him come to me. I would make him come. It was inevitable. There was no way out for either of us. There was only a way in.

Suddenly, it started. Mason. In seconds there was a new stain on my beloved pillow. It spread like a contagion over the residue of the others. It was the happiness that is the promise of happiness. All of me rolled over. I felt him on top of me, not crushing my body but melting it. He himself ran down my sides. God, I wanted this man.

# 22

# HOOKED

The first impression would be everything. Make or break. Before Mason, I had never wanted or needed to devise a plan to get a man to notice me. Now I was scared that my appearance alone wouldn't be enough. If Barbara was really his type, I might repel him. I had to attract him irrevocably. However desirable I thought I looked, there was no guarantee Mason would respond. I believed he would, of course.

This was not a problem for which the solution could be found in the pages of *Cosmopolitan*. I had to figure a plan that couldn't fail, something like the perfect crime. They do exist, not usually in the movies or books but in life. It was like writing a story for myself. I thought up and discarded many approaches. One had been to create a situation in which I could save him physically from something and make him grateful. Another was to collapse in the street in front of him, or better, in his office. Then he would look after me. The trouble was that these plans would not guarantee his continuing fascination.

I needed to devise a situation in which he would want to know more about me, want to see more of me. He had to be thrown into a state of mind in which he would want to come looking for me. After reading scores of mystery stories and seeing movies like *Dangerous Liaisons*, I came up with my own staged drama. In this scenario I wouldn't speak to him at all. I certainly wouldn't touch him. There would be no contact other than sight. He would see me doing something that would set his mind racing, that would get him hooked.

No man can resist an image of two woman together in a sensual situation. Freud said the reason men were sexually aroused by seeing two women together was that it appealed to their latent homosexuality. Nice idea. But if it was true, it ought to follow that women seeing two men together would be equally stimulated. That wasn't true. However, my father loved being with two girls at the same time. And the most successful erotic scene in *Gala* was where I had made love to Annabel. Everyone agreed about that. So, I would not be alone when I presented myself to Mason. I would be with another woman.

Now for the scene itself. It would have to be mysterious, ambiguous. It had to be capable of interpretation, even misinterpretation. Something sensual was needed, but it mustn't be simple voyeurism. That wouldn't necessarily solve the problem of needing to stimulate Mason's desire to know more about me. Reading a Patricia Highsmith book gave me the clue. A crime. If you were witness to a crime, you were hooked. You had to find out more.

So I would let him observe what he would imagine was a criminal act with sexual overtones between two women, myself and someone else. But there must be no chance of his preferring that someone else to me. It was tricky. I needed a friend I could count on.

Annabel had moved twice since *Gala*. She was no longer living with Alain. She had her own apartment now. It took me two days to track her down. She sounded pleased to hear from me. She was living in West Hollywood. She told me that Alain came and went. I didn't want to meet him. He was going to be out during that afternoon. We made a date.

I drove over to her apartment building on Crescent Heights. Annabel's apartment was on the second floor. I rang the bell. In a bathrobe, she opened the door. There was something wrong. Annabel looked as if she had been crying, more unhappy now than when I had seen her last at the Bel Age, on the day that had changed the course of my life.

"What's the matter?"

"Nothing. Nothing. I was just getting into the tub."

I followed her to the bathroom. I sat on the toilet seat as she got into the tub. Annabel was shaking.

"Now tell me, Annabel, what is wrong?"

"I don't want to do that movie. I don't want to."

"Then don't."

"He's making me do it. You don't know what happened after *Gala*. He didn't tell you."

"You tell me."

"A lot of bad things happened. I mean, I didn't think anyone would really recognize me. From those movies no one remembers the faces."

"Hopefully," I said.

"Alain decided that after our scene together I had a real career ahead of me. He'd always wanted to make proper films. His favorite was *Room With a View*. *Gala* was fairly successful, as you know, and I thought he would get the chance to do something with some class. What happened was he went on to make another porno movie. I think he got a lot of money from an Iranian here in L.A. He wanted me to star in it, to become like you. I really didn't want to. He would never show me the script, so I had no idea what I was getting into. I guess I was naive. It was really horrible, much worse than *Gala*. I didn't mind taking my clothes off and stuff, although my girlfriends told me not to. Nobody was doing that now, they said. I had no idea what Alain wanted me to do."

"I can guess, but tell me."

121

"It was disgusting. He wanted me to lie there while some Arab shat on me. I mean shat! This guy drank like a whole pot of espresso. Then he climbed on top of me. I can't tell you. I was sick. The stuff came all over me. I started to vomit. When I tried to get up, they held me down while this fucking animal dumped on me again. I can't tell you. I could smell it for days. I don't know how many baths I took; it didn't go away, the smell." She rubbed her arm as if it itched.

"Why didn't you just get up and leave?"

"Good question. Alain made me stay. He told me I was wonderful. I had the makings of a big star, he said. Now look at me. The whole experience was shit."

"Why didn't you quit? Leave Alain?"

"He threatened to kill me. What could I do? I'm scared, Ursula, really scared. I really don't understand what he wants. I can see now that he must hate women. Why, I don't know. What do they all get out of it? I mean, you fuck a girl, and then you can boast about it to your friends, I can see that. But you shit in someone's mouth and who're you going to tell?"

As I listened to Annabel's grotesque tale, I couldn't help but imagine myself in that situation. I would never have agreed to what she did. But then, what would happen if I had to do that sick stuff to get Mason? Would I do it?

Annabel started to cry. I put my arms around her. She was like my little sister. I hugged her to me. I felt her tears on my own cheeks.

Annabel sat in the bath, quivering with fear. I soaped her back, massaged her shoulders, and told her something of my plan. It was hardly the ideal moment, but I had to get on with it. I explained that I needed her to enact a little scene for me, no nudity, no sex, nothing like that, just be with me. I couldn't tell her when and I couldn't tell her where. Annabel wasn't really paying attention. She couldn't concentrate. She became interested in the five hundred dollars a day I offered her.

"So how many days?"

"One, maybe two. I don't know yet."

"I could use a grand," she said.

"It's a deal."

Annabel cheered up. I gave her a kiss and told her I'd be in touch in a while.

"I really could use the money," she said again.

"I'll give you five hundred now."

"Thank you. You're a good woman. Not like me."

Now it was my turn to cry.

I took Santa Monica going back into Beverly Hills. Not too brilliant, but quicker than Sunset. God, the place was sleazy. There were times when the town looked like a make-shift hell. Something around fifteen on the Richter scale would settle it once and for all. Maybe Mason and I would leave here one day. Go to Mexico.

Annabel was perfect for what I wanted, but I was worried about her. I was sure she was on something, perhaps smack, the way she kept rubbing her arms. She needed money badly. She didn't ask me exactly what I wanted her to do. Poor Annabel. We can all get hooked. Money, drugs, sex, work even, it doesn't matter what. Any god will do.

I was on my way to meet Alexis for a drink. We had arranged it for six-thirty. I still needed something from her. Like Annabel, she was integral to my plan. She was like Annabel in another way too. Mason was a drug for Alexis. I had to get her off him. She had to face the withdrawal.

Women are not naturally slaves, but they, I mean we, are drawn to the state of slavery as an easy way out of emotional contradiction. Slavery is not a natural condition. We know that. Men know that. But it is a way station. Slavery for a woman is a kind of adolescence. We had to go though it. But through it like purgatory. And out the other side.

Alexis wasn't there. At quarter of seven I got nervous. I had the horrible, crazy idea that she would bring Mason with her. I was on my feet about to leave when she came in. She was alone. She seemed in good spirits and pleased to see me. But I thought she'd been crying. She wanted to talk. I was pleased. I thought she wanted to talk about herself and Mason. Alexis wanted to talk about Mason's mother, Felicity.

I was disappointed. While everything about Mason interested me, I didn't really want to hear about his mother. But as I listened to Alexis I began to think that Mason's mother was some kind of old Mrs. Bates figure out of *Psycho*. Alexis must have been exaggerating and yet she knew what she was talking about. What she was saying was that any woman who was interested in Mason would have to face Felicity. Alexis was on her third glass of Chardonnay. She made a remark that stuck in my mind. She said: "Felicity is a razor blade. You know she's dangerous but you don't realize right away that you've been cut."

The wine did its work and Alexis went to the toilet, carrying her purse, but she left her bag beside her chair. I looked inside and took the office keys. I had to get inside the place, not to steal but just to be there. She came back and we talked for about half an hour, mostly about what bad luck she'd had with men. I wanted to tell her, but didn't, that luck played a very small part in these things. You had to work at your life. Luck, as someone said, was nothing more than the residue of effort.

Another glass of Chardonnay and it was back to her leaving Mason.

"You're right. I've got to go."

"Well, give him a month's notice anyway." I figured that would be enough time to get my plan together.

"Why? No, when I go I'll just go."

"That's not very fair."

"Has he been fair?"

"He doesn't know how you feel."

"I'm not so sure about that. He acts like he doesn't know. But maybe he does. Men can be pretty cruel, you know."

Before she left to meet the obnoxious Rodney, Alexis left me one marvelous and tantalizing clue: "One of his clients, an actor named Mike Adorno, has gotten a job on a movie in New Mexico. I know Mason intends to go visit him on the shoot. Maybe that's when I should go."

"When does the film start?"

"In two weeks."

"How long is the shoot?"

"Eight weeks, I think. Why are you interested?"

"No reason."

"Come on, Audrey, you were thinking there might be a part for you in it." Alexis smiled and winked. And that was the last I saw of her.

# 23

# PRESENCE

My nocturnal visits to the office gave me plenty of useful background information. The most fascinating stuff came from the messages on the answering machine, rather than from letters, memos, or faxes. For the first time I heard the voices in Mason's life. Barbara was an open book. The actor Os Yates was interesting. He was the one person I'd "heard of," having seen a couple of his movies.

The most striking and appalling voice I heard during my playback sessions was the sound of his mother, Felicity. Alexis had not exaggerated one bit. I had never heard a woman, an old woman at that, use such concentrated filthy language. It was incredible to hear her talking to her son like that. Some of what she said was funny. I laughed out loud once or twice. Her diction was so defiantly sexual and her gravelly voice so bitterly offensive, I found an unexpected sensuality in the performance. I could clearly imagine a woman whose past was filled with sexual adventure. Perhaps Mason's childhood had not been so very different from my own.

One night I discovered in his diary Alexis's reminder note of the date for his trip to New Mexico. It was three weeks away. She had written down the flight number and the address and phone number of the Sierra Hotel in Artesia, where he would be staying for one Saturday night. I was thrilled. I would have him alone and far away from L.A. So the time and the location for my little drama were fixed. I now knew where I was going.

And Annabel was coming with me. I saw her twice again before the day. She had become more cheerful. She was looking forward to getting away. I gave her more money. I fixed a hair appointment for her. I told her if she was going to be a proper actress, which was her heart's desire, she

125

would have to look the part. As a matter of fact the style of Barbara's haircut suited her. And Annabel liked it too. She felt different, better.

I became a working girl again. I got myself a job, having applied to the employment agency Alexis came from. If I was to take Alexis's place, I would need a good reference. I knew Alexis would take my advice and leave Mason within the next few weeks. When she did eventually quit, Mason would be shocked. He would call Fast Finders in a panic. I would be there, ready to apply.

My current job was with a legal firm and was horrendous. But I had a gift which they admired: I was a whiz typist and a brilliant speller. After a week I wanted to leave, but I stuck it out. I was in prison but I'd be paroled quite soon.

I would go home after work, bathe, masturbate, and then drive over to the Palisades to catch even a glimpse of my man.

I really wanted to burn the fucking house down with a flame thrower, and then save Mason from the inferno at the last moment, leaving Barbara to perish. I had visions that when the fire department arrived, the place would be completely gutted, just smoke drifting across the canyon, and the burned-out shells of the refrigerator and the BMW. All they would find would be lumps of melted brass jewelry. No bones, just ash. Barbara and Mason would be pronounced dead and gone. Meanwhile, I would be living happily with Mason in a hotel in Acapulco for the rest of our lives. For now I had to be content spending a couple of hours every so often at night, swiveling slowly round in Mason's chair at the office, my legs pressed together, listening to the distant city sounds of wailing ambulances and police sirens.

In a small pharmacy on Melrose near my office I found a bottle of a perfume called Presence. I was astonished. They had three bottles. I bought them all. Presence. It was a sign.

This perfume had enormous significance for me. It was my father's favorite. He gave Presence to all his girls, Audrey included. The associations of this scent were a mix of nostalgia and a sweet sickness I've always associated with sex. The scent of Presence filled my mind like a crowded dream. For a while it had been impossible for me to kiss someone without smelling this perfume from the past. I smelled it when it wasn't being worn. Presence overpowered all other body smells. It was sensuality itself.

I read about a theory of sex which suggested that human sexuality was a disease. People were the only animals that had no definite mating season. Men and women wanted to fuck all year round. Apparently something happened in our evolution that corrupted the strict rules of sexual attraction. Now there was no form, no discipline to the sexual impulse. It had acquired the unrestrained madness of an open season. According to this theory, the disappearance of seasons for sex came about as man developed his imagination, the main thing that differentiates him from other animals. We have an ability to imagine the future, instead of just responding to an eternal past of coded instinct. Our growing appreciation of a chance-riddled present pervaded by sudden stimuli was a parallel to new and special sexual response. This response no longer required the actual presence of the object of our desire. We could arouse ourselves, alone. Some animals were known to masturbate, but never without the presence of the desired mate. This theory was mixed up in my mind with the opening of a bottle of Presence. The perfume was no longer manufactured. It had not finally been a success. But now I had three bottles of the lemony scent. That ought to be enough.

I was lying awake one night dreaming of Mason, imagining him with me in bed, feeling his skin against mine, when the scent of Presence wafted upward from the bed. The perfume smell grew with his erection and became dense as a cloud as he entered me. I came instantly, and shook for several minutes.

In the afterglow I saw how to use Presence in my plan. On the Thursday before Mason was due to leave for Albuquerque, New Mexico, I managed to break into his car at lunchtime when he and Alexis were out of the office. On the floor of the backseat I dropped a Kleenex soaked in Presence. He probably wouldn't notice the white ball with all the magazines, but he would be aware of the smell. It would mean nothing to him yet. But when he came back from New Mexico, it would be another story. I was planting the seed, or spraying the aroma, that would flower, or cloud, in his memory and in his nose later on. That was called forward planning. Sex and the imagination.

It was sweltering when Annabel and I arrived in Albuquerque. I had two days in hand before Mason was due to be in Artesia, which was a two- to three-hour drive south, almost to the Texas border. I had decided to spend one night at the Hilton and drive the next day. Annabel was happy to be out of L.A. and away from Alain, though she phoned him twice the first day. She didn't tell me what tale she had concocted to explain her absence. I didn't ask.

I knew I was going to stupendous, if not downright ridiculous, lengths of effort, plotting, and disguise to grab this man. I could simply have gone up to him and confessed my feelings, but I was afraid of taking my chances. I was afraid of chance, period. I couldn't face rejection. Not from this man. My route to Mason was circuitous, and dangerous too, but ultimately certain. I had been very successful so far and I saw no reason to alter my tactics. It was exciting, this urban chase. I was the hunter. The prey, bless him, didn't even know he was the prey.

I still felt sort of lightweight, lightheaded. One margarita at the bar and I was practically drunk. Annabel said it was the heat, well over ninety degrees, that and the height of Albuquerque, five thousand feet, that produced my headiness. But I knew it was Mason.

By early evening she was feeling fairly relaxed. She had spent an enervating hour by the pool. I stayed in my room and read *Villette*. We had a Mexican dinner in the old town, a mixture of Spanish-mission and frontier-post architectures. Two scoops of guacamole and I was full. Annabel ate half my combination plate as well as her own dinner.

We went back to the Hilton and watched *The Getaway* on television in my room. Annabel hated it. She hated the violence. She called it obscene and went to bed in her own room about halfway through. I thought it was great. Maybe it happened to suit my mood, but I loved Ali MacGraw doing all those things for Steve McQueen. I had read that in real life McQueen had at the time left his wife and family for her.

Good for him. The ending of the film was wonderful. They got away with it. That was the way things ought to be.

The next day on the drive south from Albuquerque I hit a dog on the highway. I couldn't help it. The animal appeared from nowhere. I swerved to avoid it, honking my horn, but the poor thing reacted by jumping the wrong way, into the car. There was a horrible thud. Annabel screamed. I pulled over. The dog wasn't dead. He was whimpering.

"Do something!" Annabel screamed.

"What can I do?"

"Get it to a hospital."

"How can I? Where?"

I looked around. There were a few cars racing past on the highway but not a town in sight. It was the middle of the desert. We might as well have been on the moon. I pulled the dog to the side of the road. A passing truck honked at the awkward way I'd stopped the car. Annabel was getting more upset. I had no alternative but to continue. It was a bad thing to have happened. I looked down at the twitching dog. He was quiet now in his agony. If I had been Ali Mac-Graw, I would have taken out my gun and put the animal out of his misery. It would have been the right thing to do, and Annabel would've understood.

The Sierra Hotel was the only hotel in Artesia, so it wasn't difficult to find. I discovered that the movie company had already shot some scenes there in the hotel, but that the cast and crew were staying in motels nearby. That was a big relief. Mason would be alone and not surrounded by people.

Having installed Annabel in her room, I went downstairs to question the guy on the desk about Mason's booking. He would be staying one floor above mine. So I would have an escape route if necessary down the stairs. The elevator looked old and unreliable.

"Elliott. That's correct," said the desk guy. "They're expected late this afternoon."

"They?"

"Mr. and Mrs. Elliott."

# 24

# THE HALLWAY

**S**tay calm, my girl, stay calm," I told myself. I left the lobby and climbed the stairs. Mr. and Mrs. It must be Barbara. Unless of course Mason had decided to bring his mother. No, that was absurd. It was Barbara and unwelcome news for me.

As I climbed the creaking stairs, the heat became more intense. I seldom sweat. My father told me not sweating was a sign of being uninhibited. I reached the third floor and turned into the hallway. I stopped and stared at it. This was where I would stage my scene with Annabel.

I looked at myself in the old mirror beside me, speckled like the back of an aged hand. This was the woman Mason would see. This was the woman who would soon belong to him.

Annabel hadn't locked her door. I found her lying on the bed in her underwear. It was incredibly hot. The air-conditioning unit was noisy and ineffective. I saw that Annabel's skin was shiny with sweat. She was lying on her right side apparently asleep, except her eyes were wide open. I bent down beside her. I was worried that she might have had heat stroke.

"Are you all right?"

"I'm fine," she said almost inaudibly. "Just fine." Her eyes didn't blink. On an instinct, I went into the cramped bathroom. Her clothes were in the tub. The contents of her handbag had been poured into the wash basin. She had obviously turned out her purse, looking for something. I found it on the table beside her bed. The hypodermic.

Shit, this is all I need! I thought. Maybe I was being unsympathetic, but it could spell disaster.

As it turned out, Annabel was completely cooperative. The smack, if that's what it was, had produced a state of mind that suited my purpose perfectly. Annabel would now do what I wanted without argument. I had become worried by her possible resistance, especially after the incident with the dog on the highway.

I left her and went to my own room. From my overnight bag I took some sheets of writing paper and a ballpoint pen, both anonymous drugstore items. It would have been stylish to write my first message to Mason on my own writing paper and using my own fountain pen with my distinctive brown ink. Stylish but stupid.

I wrote, "I saw you." Then I wrote on another sheet, "I know you saw me." That was nice. It had a veiled threat in it. Then I wrote, "Please forget what you saw." No, that was too ambiguous. I wrote, "You saw me. I saw you." Silly, that one. I tried a couple more versions, then I settled for "I know you saw me." I toyed with the idea of "I know you saw us." And then, "We know you saw us." No, I must leave Annabel out of this altogether. The best one was definitely the second: "I know you saw me." I wrote it out again carefully in capital letters without my characteristic slanting handwriting. Then I put it in an envelope and sealed it. I wrote "Mr. Elliott" on it. That was good. I did it once again, neater and squarer, and then put the letter inside the envelope and sealed it. I tore up all the others.

At five in the afternoon while Annabel slept, Mason arrived with Barbara. I watched them from the window of a cafe down the street. Barbara seemed happy. Mason seemed bored. She tugged at his arm like a child, I thought. She had obviously been looking forward to the trip. I decided then to leave them until the next day. Sunday. Tonight, obviously, they would go to dinner with Mason's client and some of the movie people. Sunday would be good, perhaps when he came out of his room to get the newspapers, or something like that. I could relax tonight.

I didn't though. I had a shitty night. I took a risk and went out to dinner with Annabel. She called Alain before we left and again when we got back. I checked out the little cantina carefully. I didn't want to end up in the same place as Mason and his party.

At dinner I told Annabel how I planned to stage our scene the next day.

"Is this all for someone you love?" she asked suddenly.

"Why?" I was surprised. Her question came out of left field.

"I can't imagine anyone going to all this trouble otherwise."

"No, you're right."

"Good," she said. "I hope it works."

"It will."

But was it really love? Can you love someone you've never actually met? What I felt was probably closer to a fan's obsession for a star.

My original timing was a bit off. After sleeping fitfully, plagued by nightmares in which Mason was fucking Barbara while I watched through a two-way mirror, I finally fell into a deep slumber. When I awoke, it was eleven in the morning. I went to see Annabel. She was crying on the phone to Alain. Eventually, unable to speak through her sobs, she hung up.

"I shouldn't have left him. I shouldn't."

I consoled Annabel, got her dressed, and went to check on Mason's key. The key was hanging above the front desk. They'd gone out. Shit. But their hired car was in the parking lot behind the hotel. So they'd only gone for a walk. I went back to my room, had a bath, put on my black dress, and doused myself with Presence. By lunchtime I was ready. While I was shaking with nerves, Annabel was relaxed again. She'd given herself a shot.

Mason and Barbara came back to the hotel at one-thirty. They'd had lunch or a drink somewhere. From my vantage point across the street I could see in her expression that Barbara was ready for bed. I could see by Mason's expression that he wasn't. It was stinking hot again. I wondered how anyone could live in this climate, let alone fuck in it.

At around two-thirty Annabel and I were ready in the hallway. The hotel was quiet and empty. A train rumbled past, a long, long Santa Fe freight train. I got Annabel to lie down on the carpet. She did exactly as I directed. I practiced pulling her along. It was harder than I thought. I got better at it. I prayed that Mason and not Barbara would come out of the room. My arms ached. We rested.

I took a chance. I went to their door. I listened. I could

hear only the sound of the television. I returned to Annabel and pointed to the filthy carpet. She lay down again. We both waited. Annabel yawned. The whole thing seemed completely crazy.

I arranged our positions so that when Mason came out of the room he would see us in the old mirror. When Mason came out. . . . Suppose he didn't come out? It was all taking forever. If it went on much longer, someone else would see us, a chambermaid or another guest. In my worst fantasy, perhaps a cop would appear from nowhere, for no reason, to destroy us.

Then it happened. After what had seemed like a week, the door opened and Mason appeared. I only heard him because I had my back to him, but I felt his presence. I whispered to Annabel, "Now." And our strange, planned ritual began.

I pulled Annabel by the upper arms, slowly but evenly along the rough carpeted floor. It was physically hard. She was a deadweight. I could imagine Mason watching us in the mirror. I wondered if he would come up to us, ask if he could help, get a doctor or whatever. I hoped it looked like a murder, with me disposing of the body. He'd never forget that.

Now came the all-important moment. I glanced up from Annabel to the mirror. Mason was there. A ghost behind the mottled screen of blemishes in the mirror's surface. It was only a glance. I couldn't really see his eyes. I looked down again and continued to pull Annabel with all my strength.

Then I heard a door close. I knew Mason had gone back into his room. I counted to five and straightened up. Cautiously, I turned to look. The hallway was empty. It was over.

"It's done," I said to Annabel.

Annabel didn't answer. She lay at my feet inert, her eyes closed.

"Annabel!" I felt a surge of panic. I bent down. I was scared. Had this staged scene suddenly become real? Was she actually dead? Had I killed her? Annabel was breathing but unconscious. I tried to bring her around. I couldn't. I lifted her up from the waist. This was horrible. A woman's accented voice said, "Can I help? What's happened?" An aging Mexican Indian maid was standing a few feet away, looking at me.

"My friend's fainted," I said. The maid didn't seem to understand. "Fainted." I repeated it. "Don't worry, she'll be all right when I get her to her room."

Annabel began to move. She opened her eyes. She was nauseous. I got her to her feet. The maid watched without apparent suspicion as if this were an everyday occurrence. Using all my aching strength, I helped Annabel, who hadn't uttered a word, down the stairs to her room. I looked back for the maid. She had disappeared.

I put Annabel on her bed. I was still scared. I hadn't thought of Mason for five minutes. Shit! The note.

I left Annabel and ran back to my room, took the envelope, and raced downstairs to the reception desk. There was no one there. I put the envelope on the desk. Then I went outside.

I wasn't sure what to do. I went down the street and into a cafe. I was sweating. Was Annabel all right? I was concerned. I ought to go back and look after her. I couldn't risk Mason seeing me. I wondered what would happen to the note. I found a window seat in the bar. Leaning forward and craning my aching neck, I could just see the entrance of the hotel. I wanted a beer. But it was Sunday and New Mexico was dry on Sundays. Then I saw Mason come out of the hotel, the letter in his hand. He appeared worried. He looked around for a few moments before going back inside. What had he thought about what he had seen? Would he tell Barbara? Unlikely. Call the police? The hotel manager? No, he'd keep it to himself. But he wouldn't forget.

I waited in the cafe, drinking a coffee I didn't want. I was worrying about Annabel. She'd performed wonderfully but she was sick. I knew that. I had to get her back to L.A. soon.

Mason and Barbara eventually came out of the hotel. They walked in the opposite direction, out of sight. Mason looked around once. I left the bar and hurried back to the hotel, up to Annabel's room. She was asleep on the bathroom floor. I woke her. She started to moan.

"I want a child. I want a baby. I want to be a child. I want to be a baby."

I tried to console her. She was delirious. It crossed my mind that Annabel might be pregnant.

"We're going back to L.A.," I told her. "Let's get dressed."

"I need a bath," she said.

She pulled off her clothes. She came up to me naked, put her arms around me, kissed my neck.

What could I do? After her bath, during which I got my things together, I found her back in bed all wet. She hadn't dried herself. Annabel was adamant. She was not going back. I couldn't persuade or move her. But I had to leave. I had to be back in Los Angeles. The next day, Monday, was crucial to my plan. I had done what I came to do. Now I had to leave. With Annabel or without her.

I found out that Mason and Barbara had already checked out. The only thing I could do was leave Annabel where she was. I gave her a thousand dollars and put it with her plane ticket from Albuquerque to L.A. She would have to hire a car. I needed ours.

"I'll call you in L.A.," I said and kissed her good-bye. Annabel kissed the money, kissed me, and said, "I'm going to have a baby."

Perhaps I should have forced her to come with me. Twenty miles out of Artesia on the highway driving back to Albuquerque, I stopped the car. I wondered if I should turn back. I was pleased with my scene in the hall. Mason was hooked. He had to be. But somehow Annabel's state had gotten to me too. I felt responsible for her. She was picking up the tab for my experiment. Don't be sentimental, I told myself, no one else is. I put the car into gear and drove on.

I remembered the spot on the highway where I had run over that poor dog. I slowed. The animal was still there, but now he was clearly dead. Half his stomach had been eaten away, perhaps by another animal, more likely by a vulture. I drove on.

Just outside Albuquerque, as the traffic became heavier, I noticed a three-legged dog limping across the road between the cars. Drivers honked their horns but the dog was not to be hurried. It was a bitch. I wondered if she was related to the dead dog. She went at her own speed, a mongrel survivor. Survival was everything, wasn't it? I had read in a nature magazine that vultures were now an endangered species. Conservationists were putting meat out for them on the rocks of the snowy high Sierras where they used to nest.

135

# 25

# BETWEEN US

He did what I had prayed for and called Fast Finders the moment Alexis left him. Without that call I wouldn't have known what to do. I would have had to rethink my entire plan. Bless him.

I could hear his voice on the phone as I knocked on the outer office door. I trembled with anticipation. I was worried that my own voice, if it trembled too, would give me away. I knew my appearance would shock him. I had the advantage, but I didn't want to abuse it. Demure. That's what I told myself I had to be, and stay that way right through the interview. I shook out my body to relax, and entered.

It was more like an audition than an interview. I was an actress who knew the moment she walked into the room that she'd gotten the part. He tried his best to disguise his shock at seeing me facing him in his own office. My response was split. On one hand there was the thrill of finally seeing and talking to Mason Elliott, just being with the man. And on the other was my nervousness in guessing his reaction to me.

The perfume got to him. He smelled me like an animal. The glasses, however, confused him. I had decided to buy a pair of glasses to plant some necessary doubt in his mind. I didn't want to look exactly as I had in the hotel hallway, just close to it.

He couldn't help himself. He had to ask if I'd ever been to New Mexico. I told him a bit of the truth. I had been in Taos once. For the rest, I lied. One day I knew I'd have to tell him the truth. But not yet. I had influence over him now. I could see that in his confusion. I felt a prick of sadism. I tried to counter it by being amiable, even a little funny, to go beyond demure. After all, he had a sense of humor, and he'd appreciate it. Avoid any female stereotyping.

As he talked about his work, his admirable way with his

136

clients, he seemed to acquire a fresh solidity. He was no longer just a figure in my imagination. Quite suddenly he became a person. Despite my anxiety, I was reassured. He was a living being. I wanted desperately to touch him. He was in his shirtsleeves and I could feel his skin beneath the pale blue cotton. I could see the body of the man in the pool. I noticed that he had hung his jacket over the back of his chair. For no particular reason that seemed important.

My early impression of Mason Elliott's self-containment was confirmed at close range. I was relieved that he had no associates, that he was alone. Maybe he didn't need help in his work, but I felt an overpowering desire to give him more confidence. I almost regretted my whole subterfuge.

When he called me Miss Baxter, I didn't correct him. I didn't want to explain anything about my past. Perhaps I never would. My fantasies about us had been cleaner, purer, without explanations. For me certainly, this was a new life. I resented the fact that the longed-for purity had somehow not been sustained in my dreams. Could it be maintained in practical life?

"Just let me touch you," I wanted to say. But I had to wait until we shook hands as I left the office. We studied each other. It wasn't fair. I knew so much. He knew so little. But he would want to know more. And we would have plenty of time.

As we spoke I began to wonder what he thought about Ursula Baxter, not the woman in the hotel. He looked at my legs. I crossed and uncrossed them for him. I would love to have taken off my skirt then and there. Did he feel my rising desire? The feeling of panic from the hotel came back. I was getting sticky. I kept my right hand open. I didn't want my first physical contact with him to be a sweaty palm.

When we said good-bye I felt a surge of helpless sex as we shook hands. This was what I had been waiting for. The pact was sealed as our skins touched. Now I didn't care whether my hand was dripping with sweat. My scalp was itching and I was beginning to get damp between my legs. I had to get out of there before I said or did something dumb.

"I hope to see you again," I said. I don't think it sounded like an invitation. I couldn't really hear my own voice. I could only hear his.

137

"I hope so too."

I tried desperately to walk in a straight line down the passage from his office to the street. I think I made it.

It was late that night when I let myself into the office. I don't really know why I went. I had the job. I knew it. Why take any risks? As usual I went through the correspondence on the word processor. I found Alexis's letter. It was terribly sad. What would happen if Barbara were to read it? All that was needed were a couple of changes. A small rewrite. After several attempts in rough I signed a passable signature, "Alexis."

I was surprised that Alexis called me at home to tell me what she had done. She was calling from her home back east, where she said she intended to stay for a while. She told me she had left Rodney, at least for a few weeks. Then she told me she had written a letter to Mason, resigning and giving her reasons. Good for her. Good for me. When we finished our conversation I called Annabel's apartment. She wasn't there. The machine with Alain's voice answered. I hung up without leaving a message. I was worried.

My first day was wonderful. During the morning, he seemed on edge. By lunchtime, I thought I had put him at his ease, as far as it was possible with the memory of the woman hauling another along the hall of a small hotel in Artesia, New Mexico. I reminded myself that he probably still wasn't sure it was me. I was sure, though, that he hadn't told Barbara, the hotel manager, or the police about the incident. That was between us.

I called Annabel again during the lunch break. The machine answered. Again, I didn't talk.

I was reading the screenplay Mason had given me called *Who're We Gonna Get?* when Os Yates came into the office.

"Hey, you're not Alexis."

"I'm Ursula."

"What happened to Alexis?"

"She left."

"Boy, things sure change fast in this town. Would you tell the mastermind I'm here."

"Certainly. Please take a seat." I told Mason that Oswald Yates was here to see him.

"Not Oswald, Os. Oswald was an assassin. I'm an actor. The only people I assassinate are directors. But that's mercy killing."

I didn't care for Os. He was coarse. But I had a strong feeling he was important to Mason. That made him important to me. As he went into the office, he turned in the doorway and gave me a wink. I smiled politely. The door closed, but I could hear Os's loud voice as if he'd been sitting next to me.

After he left, Mason took time to explain who Os Yates was. I had seen a couple of his movies. It was obvious now that he was crucial to us. Mason explained about Os's agent, Larry Campbell. I'd heard bad things about Larry before this. I supposed everybody in town had. Mason wanted Os as a client. Larry Campbell stood between him and Os. It was that simple.

I liked Paul Jaspers as instinctively as I disliked Os Yates. Perhaps because I recognized him from the bar at the Beverly Wilshire. I saw him as an ally in some way. He had an attractive lost look. I could see that he used it in his life to great effect. Mason treated him like a younger brother, affectionately, protectively. Paul had the observation and calculation of a writer.

While he was talking to Mason, I got a call from Barbara. Mason had said "no calls," so I took the message. I wasn't concerned that she might recognize my voice. How could she? Voices went with faces and I had worn a wig when I went to her shop. Barbara sounded anxious, but I didn't tell him that. I simply gave him the message. He must have told her about Alexis leaving, but certainly not why. Eventually, Barbara would want to meet me, I felt sure.

I'd been dying for a cigarette all afternoon but I promised myself I wouldn't smoke in the office. I knew Mason wouldn't like it. However, I did take a cigarette out and played with it without lighting the thing. Accidentally, I knocked the box on the floor. The cigarettes went everywhere. I was bending down picking them up when Mason came up behind me. He didn't say anything for a moment. I knew he was there staring at my back. I stayed very still so he could have a good, long look. This was the biggest thrill of the day. I could just feel the heat in him, restrained and silent.

"Good night, Mr. Elliott," I said as formally as I could at the end of the day. He was probably miserable, but I left the office happy. At about four in the afternoon I had found the moment of opportunity I'd been looking for. His jacket had been hanging over the back of his chair, waiting for me. I put Alexis's revised letter in one of the pockets, carefully folded, a paper bomb that would detonate itself only when read by the person for whom it was intended. Had I become a terrorist? Of course not. I was a freedom fighter.

# 26

# HELP

Mason was embarrassed when he saw me waiting outside the office. He had forgotten to give me the keys. I lied about how long I'd been there. Ten minutes, I said. I didn't want him to know I'd been waiting for more than half an hour, in a state of exquisite torture. We went into the office like a couple going into a hotel room.

I was happy. He was wearing a suit. A beautiful suit. So the jacket was at home, with Barbara, ready for the cleaners. Had she already gone through the pockets?

Mason stared at me for a long time. Was he reading my thoughts? I hoped not. I wanted him to read my feelings like a book but never my thoughts.

"Does this black dress depress you?" I asked as innocently as I could. He shook his head. I was rewarded by his sweetness. This man was going to give me anything I wanted. And he would get everything in return.

"Smoke if you want to. I mean it."

Well, I'd worked for it, hard and long. As he left, for a meeting at his bank, I whispered, "Good luck."

While he was out I went through the mail, answered the phone, took messages. Then she called, Felicity.

"Where the fuck is he?" She was one person who didn't miss Alexis. Her voice was truly startling. It was frightening.

Alexis had been dead right about her. This was a monster. Of course, I had heard that voice before on the answering machine when I was alone in the office at night. But it had been nothing like this. She hung up before I could even reply. It must have been a good two minutes before I could do anything. I went on hearing her voice.

A Federal Express package arrived from a casting agent in New York. I wasn't sure what the office policy was. Should I open it and put the contents on Mason's desk, or should I simply put the unopened package on his desk? Open it. Don't think about it.

The package contained three photos of a girl named Silvia Glass, and a videocassette of her work. She had been a photographic model and had done some commercials and a walk-on in a small independent movie. Perhaps I was imagining it, but Silvia looked very much like Barbara and also like Annabel, after I'd fixed her hair.

This girl had the smile of success on her face. She had the tough-vulnerable look so beloved by movie producers, like a young Kathleen Turner. Silvia could have been a swimmer. I was intrigued to read "boxing" in her résumé of interests. I found her attractive. However, I wasn't sure Mason would go for her. Too much like Barbara. I added Silvia to my list of persuasions. I would definitely try to get Mason to take her on.

Mike Adorno called. He was the actor Mason had gone to see in Artesia. This gave me a twinge of nerves. Again, I felt guilty about Annabel. But what could I do now? I should've brought her back with me. I promised Mike I would give Mason the message about his per diems when he returned. In fact, I was able to fix it in the meantime.

"Where's Alexis?" Mike was curious. I told him the official story. Problems at home. I had the feeling he really wanted to talk to her. He was obviously used to talking to Alexis. He didn't trust me.

When Mason came in I was talking to Laszlo, arranging to see him later. I hurried the conversation to a close. From the look on his face I got the definite impression that Mason thought I was talking to a boyfriend. That wasn't the impression I wanted to give. Apart from the fact that it wasn't true, it wasn't my intention to make him jealous of me. I wanted to help him.

He was impressed when he discovered all the things I'd accomplished while he was at the bank. That was another nice aspect of his character: Mason had no false pride. He was pleased with my initiative, not jealous of it. Jealousy was Barbara's department.

Her performance when she crashed into the office was wonderful. There was another woman inside her who exploded like the little alien that came out of the astronaut's body in the movie. And like that creature, this real and jealous woman grew alarmingly in front of our eyes. Great.

The dust settled. Barbara had gone. I could see that Mason, despite his cool, felt he owed me an explanation. That was the last thing I wanted. Above all, I didn't want him ever to get into the habit of confession. We didn't need to justify anything. There was to be no crying on shoulders, no pleading for understanding, under any circumstances. But he said nothing to me. That was very cool. I was pleased. It was as if he had read me properly. An encouraging sign.

I recognized the guy the moment he came in. It was Rodney. I knew why he had come. Alexis must have told him about her feelings for her boss, probably on the phone from her home. She'd made a mistake. She'd fallen too quickly into the pit of confession, and blurted out her burning secret. Freud said no human being can keep a secret. Well, he would say that, wouldn't he? He was everyone's policeman, after all.

I tried to get rid of Rodney. He said he would be happy to wait all day if necessary. It was a personal matter, he said. I could see what was coming, but I had no way of warning Mason.

When he eventually came in, it happened very quickly. I hadn't wanted to interfere. It was like a rerun of the scene with Barbara and it was not one of my making. The trouble was I felt a sudden surge of protectiveness toward Mason. He was my man. I grabbed Rodney by the balls and put a stop to him. Maybe I was paying him back for the way he'd treated Alexis. On both counts I had to admit it was very satisfying. Mason was aware of my desire to be helpful, but I don't think he'd expected me to go this far. There was something surprisingly erotic in wanting to help. It was a disguised seduction. And what I'd done was in line with precisely what I intended to do, save him step by step.

After his trip to Universal, happily driving the car I'd had fixed, Mason seemed calm and controlled. It told me a lot about him, the way he took this series of shocks and bounced back. He was a natural survivor and without aggression.

The discussion that afternoon about *La Belle Dame Sans Merci* was a case in point. I sensed he was worried that Paul Jaspers would seem too intellectual to Joe Ransom, the producer. But I knew Paul was a skillful game player, maybe cleverer than Mason realized. When I was called into the meeting, Paul seemed to me to be in need of a little help. I gave it to him. Just a suggestion or two from me that effectively showed that Paul Jaspers was open to criticism. Joe Ransom picked that up immediately. Paul got the job.

Talking about the homme fatale, the woman's angle, and so on, I was of course thinking about Mason. The truth was I found him irresistible, the more so since he didn't know it yet. Why was his ignorance such a charge? Would my feeling for him change after he realized it? There was still a chance he'd reject me. Don't think about that. Just enjoy his presence.

Joe Ransom was the kind of man whose presence I couldn't enjoy. I had the oddest feeling during the meeting that he thought he knew me from somewhere. He said nothing to me but I was sure he wanted to. There was something creepy about him. If push came to shove, I'd rather have spent an evening with Os Yates than Joe Ransom. When he looked at me with a hint of suspicion, I smiled back as if he was the most delightful person I'd met all week.

I had time to kill before seeing Laszlo. When I left the office, I went to a bookshop to browse. I often did that in the evenings when I worked at the law firm. It was relaxing after the tensions of the office day.

I met Laszlo in a cafe. While I was with him, I was thinking all the time of Mason, wondering where he was at the moment. He must be unhappy. I wanted to be with him.

"Something's happened to you." Laszlo broke my train of reflection.

"What do you mean?" What was he referring to? Any number of things. It had been an eventful day.

"I don't know."

"A good thing or a bad thing?"

"That's up to you. Whatever it is, my dear, it could go either way."

Help, I thought.

# 27

# BARBARA'S BRUISES

I took a cab home. I was still very worried about Annabel. I called her. The damned machine again. I had a brainstorm. I called the Sierra Hotel in Artesia. She could still be there. As I reached for a candle to light my cigarette, I felt a pain shoot up my arm. I dropped the unlighted cigarette. The candle wobbled. Shit. I'd twisted my arm when I put Rodney out of action. Now I was paying for my machisma.

"She's not taking any calls. I got a note here. No calls," said the girl on the desk at the hotel.

"How would I get in touch with her?"

"I have no idea."

I didn't want to leave a message with my name.

"No message," I said. Annabel had probably locked herself in her room with her drugs. She wasn't going to come out until she'd used them up or wanted more. I was afraid for her, really afraid.

I wrote in my Pillow Book, "This woman is the nearest thing to a born victim. I don't believe in born victims or born anything else, but there are times when I can't help wondering about it. No. A woman can always fight back. Look at Barbara. She didn't collapse in a heap when she read the letter. And I'd thought of her as a sort of victim when I first met her. The Jane Eyre in all of us doesn't give in." I was tired. I stopped writing. Where are you now, Mason? I need you.

It turned out that the poor guy had spent the night in the office. When I got in at eight-fifteen with his laundry I'd picked up, I found him asleep on the sofa bed. He didn't wake. Asleep, he looked like a fallen angel, arms folded like wings. There was no anguish on his face, which was a mask of peace. He hadn't gone back to Barbara's. He hadn't anywhere to go.

On the far side of the sofa lying on the floor were my red panties. My heart stopped. I was happy, and appalled too. He had found them, held them, taken them to bed with him. Perhaps he'd masturbated with them, perhaps into them. I tiptoed around the bed, then quickly bent down and picked them up. My leg joints clicked as I went down, like distant cracks from a fired pistol. Mason stirred slightly but didn't wake. I took the panties and retreated to my office. I closed the door and examined them, it. There were no marks on it, them. I was disappointed.

What should I do with them? I wondered. Mason had fallen asleep before putting them back in the packet, in the desk drawer. If I put them back, he'd remember when he woke that he hadn't done it, so I must have. I could put them back where I found them, pretending that I hadn't seen them. But I wanted him to know that I'd seen them. So I compromised. I put them neatly beside the word processor. They'd be there for him to see later. He would wonder if he had in fact left them there himself in some dreamy state before going to bed. Or he might just think I had found them by the bed and moved them while he was asleep as an indication that I knew, and wanted him to know it. There was no end to the tactics, real or imagined, that desire could conjure.

I went out into the hall, came into the office for a second time, and started over again. This time I made some coffee and brought it to him as he slept. I was his maid. I watched over him for a few moments before he woke. His first expression was fear, then pleasure at seeing me. He called me "Nurse." Maybe that's what he needed.

I could see in his face that he still distrusted me. I couldn't blame him. I'd set it all up. It hurt to see him worrying. But he was vulnerable and that encouraged me. I left him to get dressed.

The phone rang. It was Felicity. She said the funniest thing. She wanted to "take a meeting" urgently with her son. This time there was no foul language. She just said what she had to in her gravelly voice and hung up. Without a smile, I passed the message on to Mason. He smiled.

When he saw my red panties by the word processor, his smile vanished. When he eventually left to visit his mother, wearing one of the shirts I'd picked up, I went about my business, his business, answering the phone and making a neat list to aid my capricious memory.

Midmorning, Barbara came into the office in cold anger. She was lugging two suitcases. I got up from my desk to help her.

"He's not here," I said.

"Good. I don't want to talk to him."

Barbara paused for a moment, to catch her breath. She looked me straight in the eye.

"I know I'm going to be lost without him."

This was an unexpected admission. That long look at me had been a test of trust. Barbara wanted to talk. She decided she could trust me.

"I understand," I said. I wasn't being ironic.

"I know I'll want him back."

I could see the mother in Barbara. Was there a mother lurking in me? I didn't think so. That was my strength. He had a mother. He could treat me as an equal, as a woman who had come into his life without association. Together we were a clean slate.

"I've just been to see his mother," Barbara said. "If you work here, you won't be able to avoid Felicity. She's truly crazy."

"So I gather." I stiffened.

"Personally, I can't stand the bitch. I've tried to get Mason to cut her out of his life."

"It doesn't work that way, does it? As long as she's there—"

"I went to tell her just to leave Mason alone. Every time he visits her, it has a bad effect on him, just terrible. She undermines him. Frankly, I wish she was dead."

"Be careful. That kind of wish can come true."

"It'd be no more than she deserves. She's killing him.

146

Or trying to. He'd be happier without her for one thing. So would I. We often fight over her. Sometimes I can see Felicity in Mason. It's like there's another person inside him."

Now I had to meet Felicity. I had to find out for myself what of her was in Mason.

"A couple of years back, just before I really got to know him, Mason went through a bad patch. It was because of her, I know it."

"What kind of bad patch?"

"He'd become angry, and sometimes violent, for no good reason, it seemed. People thought it was coke or booze, but it wasn't. There was a time he lost clients over it. He went into therapy for a while."

This was an eye-opener for me. In my eyes Mason wasn't a violent man. His calm, his lack of neurosis, was one of his most appealing features.

"I still don't understand why you went to see her."

"I told you. To get her to leave him alone."

"Oh yes."

Barbara gave me another of her long hard looks.

"You're very bright. To be honest with you, I went to see her because of this business."

"You told her about Alexis?"

"Did he tell you about what happened?"

"No."

"The truth is, I need someone to talk to. Most of our friends are, well, Mason's friends too. I don't want to talk to them. Talking to my own friends would make me look stupid. I can hear them—'How come you didn't know? You say it's been going on for months.' You know the sort of thing. I can't handle that. I probably shouldn't have told Felicity. But I did, I'm afraid. She screamed and ranted. She said it was my fault. I was wrong for him, stuff like that. I told her to shove it. I swore at her. I've got quite a temper myself. I guess you know that. So anyway, we had a big fight. And I mean a fight. Fists. She hit me, actually hit. All I'd done was take a swing at her. Didn't connect. But that bitch hit me really hard. You don't believe me."

"Of course I believe you."

"Take a look."

Barbara undid her blouse and showed me two livid

147

bruises above her left breast. I got a strange feeling, seeing Barbara's exposed skin. Not that I wanted to touch her. But I could see Mason's lips kissing her skin where the bruises were. I could see his mouth move down toward her wide nipple, which was visible to me through the material of her bra. I turned away.

"Not very pleasant, is it?" Barbara pulled her blouse closed.

"He may come back to you," I said, like an asshole.

"I don't know. I guess I hope so. Right now I don't want him." Tears came to Barbara's eyes, but she refused to cry. "I don't know what to do. How can I make him love me again? You can't make them, can you? Shit. I'm my own worst enemy. I know that. We all are, I guess."

The phone rang. I picked it up. Someone looking for Mason. I watched Barbara. She took her purse and went out of the office to the bathroom. I got off the call. I stood up. Something drew me to her shopping bag. I really don't know what it was. I went over to the couch where she'd left it. I looked into the shopping bag. I don't know what I expected to find. In retrospect I must have had some obscure intention but at the time I didn't know it.

Among her things I selected a spray of Guerlain perfume, Samsara. And I took a postcard without even looking at who it was from or what the message was. It was a picture of Las Vegas at night. I put the two things into my own handbag and closed it.

I was on another call when Barbara came back into the office. She waited for me to finish. She put her purse into her shopping bag.

"I hope you didn't mind me talking to you."

"Of course not." I smiled.

"And I'm sorry for those things I said to you before. I didn't mean them. It was very rude. Forgive me?"

"Yes."

"You do? Really?"

"You're forgiven. I understand. I'd have done the same."

"You never know what you'll do until something happens. Here's my card. I've got a little shop in Santa Monica.

Drop in anytime. Or give me a call. I think we're going to be friends. You don't mind, do you, if I want to talk to you again?"

"Not at all." I now had two of Barbara's business cards.

"Thank you, Ursula." Barbara leaned forward and kissed me on the cheek.

"Don't use me in your fight with Mason," I said. I meant it.

"I won't. You're not Alexis, I know that. She was a tramp from day one."

Barbara left but everything she'd said and done remained. I felt my mind had been squeezed. Something had happened to my feelings for Mason. They had become denser. There was an element of contradiction that wasn't there before. I had felt I knew him. Maybe I didn't. A phrase of Barbara's stuck in my mind: "You can't make them, can you?"

I had to concede there was more to Barbara than I had guessed. She was no bimbo. She had things to say and there were things to be said for her. She could be a serious block to me. She wasn't just a girlfriend. She was a full-fledged wife.

I was beginning to feel like a witch. I had to have things of hers, to control her in some mysterious way. I already had her ring. Now I had her perfume and her postcard. I was building a small collection. Freud, that policeman of our dreams, would probably have said these were token thefts. I really wanted to steal her man.

I had a wild fantasy. I imagined that the bruises she showed me weren't from a fight with Felicity. They were the marks of a fight with Mason. She had lied. It was he who hit her, not his mother. In one of the bouts of violence she'd spoken about, he had attacked her, out of frustration perhaps. Was it too fanciful? I could see the bruises on Barbara's breast, like stains, purple and yellow, flecked with small brown indentations, stains on a cream-colored hotel wall, ambiguous, mysterious, and open to endless interpretation. The bruises weren't bruises at all; they were ink blots of the kind used in psychiatric tests. What you saw in them revealed not what they were but who you were.

# 28

# MUMMY

Something had happened. After the meeting with Paul Jaspers and Joe Ransom, Mason had become preoccupied. He would look at me for a few seconds at a time, without saying anything. I had no idea what he was thinking. I was scared of losing Mason before I had even held him in my arms. He had walked out of the office that morning without telling me where he was going or when he would be back. And that was the first time.

The way he looked at me when he came back was so odd, as if suddenly he didn't know me. After he'd gone I had the feeling that he'd perhaps met someone who knew me, or knew something about me. He was distressed and I felt sure that it was because of me. Whatever it was, I knew now that I had to act, and quickly, to help him. I had teased him, intrigued him, haunted him long enough. It wasn't fair anymore. What had excited him about me before seemed now to be depressing him.

Quite irrationally I imagined that he'd somehow located Annabel and was seeing her. Whatever or whoever it was, he appeared tortured. He was suffering. He mustn't suffer. I had to stop it. Barbara had given me the clue. She hadn't meant to. But the thought now implanted in my head was making me shake.

After work I went to the Beverly Wilshire hotel and caught a taxi. I felt too nervous to drive myself all the way to Venice to the place I had arranged to meet Laszlo. He had prepared a new chart for me. There were things I urgently needed to know.

I sat in a slow-moving jam for twenty minutes listening to voices in my head mixed with the driver's radio. The driver didn't look old enough to hold a license, but he was listening to a music program of songs from the Forties. "If love goes wrong, nothing goes right . . ." It was one of those catchy tunes you found yourself humming without knowing why at completely inappropriate moments. But this song was on target. Voices in my head were saying: "Do it! Do it now! It's all for love!" The song was saying: "If you don't do it nothing will go right."

There was another voice talking at the same time. A warning voice, of course. "There's still time to get out of all this." I heard it, but I ignored it. "This thing will destroy you." Yes, yes, yes. I know, I said in reply. But I was too unhappy to worry about trivial matters such as my destruction.

The cab took me to Venice. I had a special affection for Venice, California. I'm not sure why. Perhaps it was the idea of the pier that no longer existed. It had been undermined in a violent storm some years ago. The remains were removed because it was dangerous and the authorities had decided not to restore it. The sign warning you that the pier was dangerous was still there, even though the pier wasn't.

Venice, where Laszlo lived, was home to many astrologers, clairvoyants, palm readers, and tarot freaks in the same way as one or two of the coastal towns of Maine. There was something in the presence of the ocean that encouraged thoughts about fate, or destiny, as lady travelers of the last century called it.

I wasn't crazy about Rebecca's at all. The guacamole wasn't bad, but the place was too damned loud. There were just too many people. I'd been there twice before, once with Laszlo, once with someone else.

"What's up?" Laszlo asked.

"That's what I was going to ask you."

"You look more nervous than the last time I saw you."

"I am. What about my chart?"

He handed me the chart. It was impossible to study in this atmosphere. I needed quiet.

"Tell me," I said. "Is it good or bad?"

"You know I can't answer that. It's up to you."

I knew what it was, of course.

He smiled his nervous smile and got up. He went to the toilet. I finished my margarita. I lit a cigarette. I took a sip of his drink. Then I saw I still had a cigarette burning in the ashtray. Talk about nervous. I smoked them both in turn. Cigarettes. They were so unsatisfying. But maybe that was their attraction, constant promise, perpetual desire, unfulfilled.

I looked at the chart in front of me. I had the sense someone was looking at me. I wouldn't turn around. Why give them the satisfaction? Again, I wondered about Mason. What had upset him?

When Laszlo came back, I left our table to call for a cab. I fought my way to the phone. People, people. They were demonstrative but ineffectual.

People did not take charge of their lives. They let themselves be. Most of the men and women around were quite capable of ruthlessness in their business affairs and in their professional lives, but when it came to their emotions they were perpetually indecisive.

The taxi was on its way. I went back to the table. People don't act on their desires. Those who do are called perverts. Love may be vague, but sex is always specific, exact. Sex is satisfying only when you get what you want. Love makes you curious about other people. Sex makes you curious about yourself.

Someone was watching me. Who the fuck was watching me? It was making me very uneasy. I kissed Laszlo good-bye. I hoped it wouldn't be for the last time.

It was a scary ride home. Nothing happened. Not on the road anyway. It was all in my head. I went upstairs, got undressed, showered, and came down to the guest bedroom. I took my leathers from the cupboard and climbed into them. It wasn't that easy. Maybe I had put on some weight since I last rode the bike. One day I would take Mason for a ride on my Triumph.

For some reason I had the feeling I was still being watched. Don't get paranoid.

My bike couldn't wait to be on the road. It started the first time. I knew exactly what I had to do. I needed to get on with it. Now.

It took just over half an hour to get to Felicity's apartment building. I kept my speed down. I didn't want to be stopped by the cops. I parked the bike on a lot a hundred yards from the building. I carried a document case that had come with the bike. There was nothing inside, but it made me look like a man delivering a message. I kept my helmet on when I went inside.

I passed one person, an old man who seemed drunk, before I reached Felicity's door. I let him get out of sight before I pressed the bell. I waited. Even through my helmet and visor I could smell the bad drains and the dankness that came with inadequate plumbing and outdated air-conditioning.

There was no answer. Just the sound of the building, a muffled ship's sound. I was anxious. Had I mistimed it? Had she gone out? Then what? Just wait around, or go back home and restart the whole thing later, or on another night? I couldn't bear it. I rang the bell again. Come on, woman. Open the door. You're going to have to in the end.

I heard a sound. I took off my helmet. I didn't want to scare her. She had to open the door. It happened. Through the gap held in place by a brass chain we looked at each other. Felicity had the face of a crazy woman, or perhaps it was just the chiaroscuro lighting. I gave her my very sweetest smile. She looked angry and defensive. I searched for Mason in the features of her face.

"Mrs. Elliott?"

"What do you want?" The mouth belonged to Mason.

"I just want to talk to you for a moment."

"So talk," said the wicked witch.

"Not through the door. It's personal." I smiled again. It worked. She fumbled, seemingly drunkenly, with the chain. It took a while. I kept smiling inoffensively. She opened the door. I waited. I didn't want to push my way in and alarm her.

She was wearing a black silk dress. She was made up as if she was either expecting a gentleman caller or prepared to go out to find one. She was vain, and reminded me of photographs of Jean Rhys, the great writer of decaying gentility and hopelessness.

She stood back but didn't say anything. I assumed the gesture meant "come in." I did. Watching me, she slowly closed the door. I got the flash feeling that she would have liked to have left it open.

"Who are you?" She was trying to hide her fear. She had a gesture for that, touching the pale brown spots on the back of her right hand with the fingers of her left. I could see myself thirty years from now, except that I wasn't nervous about growing old. I knew I wasn't going to make it.

"There's no point telling you my name because it wouldn't mean anything."

"What do you want then?"

"I just want to talk."

"What about?"

"Girl talk, you know."

"Give me a clue." She smiled. Her tone changed. What was she thinking? There was something about Felicity I liked. No, not liked. I admired her manner. She reminded me of Mason the way she quickly accepted something of which she was uncertain or suspicious. Mason had accepted my arrival in the office even though he must have imagined that I was dangerous. Felicity wasn't afraid of me.

"Like a drink?" she asked.

She sort of pushed me into the living room. I sat on a sofa engulfed by the sound of classical music. I'm no expert, but it sounded like mournful chamber music.

She brought me a vodka with ice in a thick red Mexican glass. She put an ice bucket beside it.

"You like to drink, don't you?"

"Why do you say that?" It was true.

"My husband was a drinker. He didn't bother with ice. In fact, he was a fucking alcoholic. He told me once that real drinkers don't like ice because it makes the drink cold and then it takes longer to hit the bloodstream."

"I don't think that's true."

"Maybe not. He was a fucking liar."

"Then what did you see in him?"

"That's a weird fucking question."

"I'm interested in what people see in each other."

She accepted this bizarre to-and-fro conversation as if we'd had it before.

"In the beginning I liked him because he said very little. He hardly spoke, you understand. When he wanted something he didn't ask for it, he just fucking took it."

"Like Peter Rabbit."

"Who?"

"Beatrix Potter."

154

"Oh yes. I used to read that shit to my son. I don't think he understood it. He's a moron, my son."

"I haven't got any children."

"You've got a great body, though."

Felicity reached forward and squeezed my breasts. That I didn't expect. I wasn't going to be unnerved.

"I had tits like yours. They're the best. Not that flabby sort men seem to like."

"What about your husband? You were saying he just took things. What did he take?"

"For one thing he took me. He'd ram me up against some fucking wall. One night we were having dinner. He got up, pulled me to my feet, and bent me forward over the chair I was sitting in. He lifted my skirt, tore my panties, and started to shove it in."

"You obviously liked that." This was getting preposterous, a Dickensian encounter gone wrong.

"As a matter of fact, I did. The thing was, we were in a restaurant." Felicity suddenly laughed, a throaty, gurgling laugh, the kind you expect from some faded movie queen remembering the great days. I laughed too; it was funny.

"Has that ever happened to you?" She wanted to know.

"Yes. Well, something like that. But I wasn't in love with him like you."

"It didn't last. My husband was the kind of man who liked doing that kind of stuff with hordes of women. I learned a lot from him. He freed me up, you know."

"It sounds cruel."

"Men and women are cruel. It's natural."

"Not with the guy I'm with, it isn't. He's not cruel at all. That's why I love him."

"There's something wrong with him."

"You're right. There is something wrong with him. His mother."

"Sounds like my son. The wimp."

"So you were cruel to your son."

"That's what he thinks."

The music stopped. Felicity got up and went over to the cassette deck. She put the same piece on again.

"What's the music?" I asked.

"It's Schubert. Don't you know it? It's the most famous fucking thing he wrote. *Death and the Maiden.*"

"I don't know anything about music."

"Poor you. Now, isn't it about time you told me why the fuck you're here? Why don't you take your glasses off?"

"I suppose I'm here to tell you something about myself and also something about—"

"About my son."

I stiffened. This woman was psychic.

She said, "You think I'm psychic? You're the second woman who's come to talk about my son. You may even know the other one. She's the bimbo he lives with."

"I've met her."

"So who are you? You're the secretary who left him. Bimbo Barbara told me about you."

"No, that was Alexis. I'm the woman who replaced her. I work for Mason."

"Why do you all come to see me? Do you want to ask me for his hand in marriage?" She laughed again, the raucous sound. This time I didn't find it so infectious.

"What the fuck do you all see in him?"

"I can't talk for the others, but I see someone who's apart from most men. He's not a control freak. He doesn't try to dominate the people around him."

"He's a wimp, that's why."

"He's a decent man. You've done your best to crush him ever since he was born. You've ridiculed everything sensitive in him. You've tried to rob him of his independence. You've kept him in a cage like some animal. You torture him when you feel like it. What you've done is worse than murder."

I shouldn't have said that word, *murder*. My anger and revulsion with the woman were so intense at that moment that I let it out.

"You can't see the shit for the trees. You're sorry for him, that's all. Never feel sorry for a man. They'll fuck you over as soon as look at you."

"For God's sake, stop talking about him as if he was your ex-lover or something. He's your son."

"Men are all the same."

"Like women are all the same, is that what you mean?"

156

"Pretty much. He came round here himself whining like the little wimp he is. I threw him out. And that's what I'm going to do with you."

"No, you're not."

She didn't hear me. The woman was truly sick. She probably needed help, lots of therapy, but that wasn't my problem. I was going to put her beyond therapy.

"He used to call me mummy, that fucking feeble English expression. He must have got it from his father. He was born in England. Mummy. As far as I'm concerned, a mummy is a pile of bones wrapped up in bandages inside a pyramid."

"That's very apt," I said. "You are a mummy. Dead inside and out. Don't worry, we'll get you a pyramid."

"We? You and Mason. You stupid fuck. You don't get it, do you? Mason is not the guy you think. He's not decent. He's an asshole. He wouldn't fucking begin to understand you. Or what you're talking about. You won't keep him. You'll get him. I can see that in your eyes. You've got the cruelty. But you're going to meet your fucking match with Mason. You just don't get it, do you? When it comes to cruelty, you ain't in his league. He's in another class, girl. Mason doesn't care about people. He just takes every fucking thing he's offered. Like his father. He did that as a child. He still does it. He's still a child. He'll never grow up. He takes but he never gives. So he's fucking dangerous. You don't understand. But you will if you stay with him. He doesn't fucking understand you. He never fucking will. Mason'll destroy you if you let him. So watch out."

I'd had enough. I got up. She laughed at me. I picked up a cushion. It was a large pillow covered in faded damask. Felicity watched me. I came toward her. She started to get up. I pushed her back. She knew what I was going to do.

"You can't kill me. You haven't got the balls."

I pressed the cushion into her sneering expression. She started to struggle. Her face disappeared into the soft damask. I pressed home, not violently—I held my anger in check—but firmly. Her arms struck out. She made dull gurgling sounds. Her thin legs flicked this way and that. It was like smothering some mutant insect. I pressed harder and harder. I don't know how long it took to silence her for good. All I thought was "Mason will be free now."

After a while Felicity stopped struggling. I felt a strong sense of pleasure in what I had done, the feeling that comes after you've done some difficult thing, the thing you've been putting off for too long.

I waited a few minutes before pulling the cushion away. I wondered what her face would look like. I expected a grotesque mask of death, like those carnival masks from the real Venice. I slowly removed the cushion. The curtain rose. Her face in death was a shock. I would never forget it.

Felicity's face was a mask of peace. Her eyes were shut. There was the hint of a smile on her lips. It wasn't the smile of scorn I expected. It was a smile of relief. The thing was over. The battle she must have had with life, and all her life, was lost. But in her expression it was won. Had the monster defeated me after all? Of course she hadn't. She was gone. That was all there was to it. Mason was free to be with me.

I removed Barbara's postcard from the zippered pocket of my jacket and put it on the table near Felicity. I took Barbara's perfume spray and went around the room with it, spraying into the air. The smell had to last for hours in case she wasn't found for a while. It was a small revenge against Barbara. I don't mind admitting that. I knew the cops would pick up the clues. They'd question her eventually. It would come out that she'd had a fight with Felicity. I didn't imagine for one moment that the police would arrest her. After all, Barbara would have an alibi for where she was right now. All I wanted was to give her a jolt. She deserved it.

I left the apartment, didn't even look around. I felt no conventional remorse. I had done a necessary good deed. I wasn't afraid. Technically, I had committed murder. So what? If I had a criminal mind, it was probably the dark side of my romantic nature. Desire can never deceive you.

I rode home feeling relieved and exhilarated. Murder isn't necessarily bad, not if it produces something good, as this one would. I did wonder, though, if I would sleep or not. I put the bike away and went into the house through the garage door into the kitchen. I switched on the light, went to the refrigerator, and took out a beer. I drank from the bottle. Oh Mason, if you only knew. What would you think? I'll never tell you, my love.

Then I noticed something odd. Beside the kitchen

phone, the directory was lying open. I hadn't made any calls from the kitchen. I was suddenly nervous. Someone had been in my house. I ran upstairs to the bedroom.

Nothing in the place seemed touched. It was scary. I never locked my house. It was my superstition. I believed that if I left the house unlocked I'd be less likely to be robbed. There wasn't much to steal anyway and I carried no insurance. I guess I took that from my father. He didn't believe in insurance. He never locked up anything. Except me.

I went downstairs. Who would have come in without taking anything? Why would they make a call? And if they did, why leave traces? It didn't make sense. I took off my leathers and put them away in the guest room downstairs. My panties came off inside my leather pants. I left them. I had many similar pairs. Then I knew.

It was Mason. Mason must have been in my house. Why he'd made a phone call I couldn't guess. But he'd been there looking for me. He must want to know about me. I was happy. He was a sweetheart. I showered and climbed into bed. He'd soon be there with me. Come quickly, Mason.

I considered writing about this night in my Pillow Book. It was a dangerous thing to do. I knew that. Why tempt fate? I was very tired. I'll write in the morning, I told myself. I'll be fresher then. I left the candles. They'd be out by morning. I liked the smell of the dying smoke.

## 29

# SLEEP OF THE DEAD

I skipped down the passage to our office. I danced past the psychoanalyst's room. I put my brilliant key in the wonderful lock and gave it a tumultuous turn. It didn't turn. I tried again. I tried twice before I realized that the door was unlocked. All I had to do was turn the handle and go in.

I immediately guessed what had happened. Someone had found Felicity's body. They'd called the police. The police had located Mason. They'd taken him to identify his mummy. In his shocked state he'd forgotten to lock the office. Thank God. I had had fears that Felicity might have stayed there for days before she was discovered. The phone rang.

"Is Mr. Elliott there? This is Louise Sheppard's office."

"Mr. Elliott is out of the office right now. I'm Ursula, Mr. Elliott's assistant. Can I help?"

"Let me put Louise on."

I waited. I wondered when Mason would come back, probably not for a couple of hours. On came Louise, a pleasant, slightly husky voice. She was the producer of *Zen Bowler*. Silvia had gone to see her for a part in the movie. Louise wanted to know when she could speak to Mason. She sounded quite excited. "If he calls in for messages, is there anything I can tell him?" I asked.

"You could tell him we were very impressed with Silvia. We'd like to see her again and in the meantime we'd like to talk numbers. If you could tell him that."

"I'll tell him. Do you think we could see a script?"

"We're in the process of rewriting. It should take another week or so, but that won't delay the start which is, let's see, seven weeks from Monday."

"I understand."

"My director's in love with this girl. She's so fresh, and she's got the athletic thing we're looking for. Where did you find her?"

"Mr. Elliott discovered her. He thought she was wonderful and took her on immediately."

"We were both bowled over, I have to tell you."

I laughed. I couldn't help it.

"Why are you laughing?"

"Bowled over. *Zen Bowler*."

"Yes, yes, I see. Congratulate Mason for us. To be frank, I'd never thought of him as an actress's agent. I've always thought of him as representing mostly men."

Well, Mason, I thought to myself, it's all going to change now. You're going to be hot.

I suddenly realized I hadn't picked up my own messages at home from last night. I dialed myself. I heard Os Yates's voice on the machine. He sounded in good spirits, too good spirits. Perhaps I should have changed my message about being in the bath. Os didn't need encouragement. He was a groper. Even his voice on the phone groped me. He wanted to talk to Mason. But if he couldn't do that he wanted to screw Mason's secretary. He was a name. We could use him on our books. We had to get him away from Larry Campbell.

For the first time I felt this office was my domain too. It didn't just belong to Mason. I had never seen myself enjoying office life. But this wasn't office life. There was no staff, just Mason and me. It would be our life.

I was sitting at Mason's desk when I returned Os's call. He was very apologetic, even embarrassed. I was surprised.

"I tied one on last night. I couldn't find Mason so I called you. Sorry about the message. I didn't really mean to come on to you like that."

"How did you get my number?"

Os didn't answer that. He said, "Maybe you should change your message on the machine. That thing about being in the bath, dangerous stuff. In the wrong ears."

He was right, and now I was embarrassed. It was stupid. I couldn't think why I'd ever recorded it. There had to be a weakness in me somewhere, a need to provoke. To seduce?

"Mason still isn't here. Can I give him a message?"

"Not really. I guess I just wanted to talk. I had a hell of a day yesterday. That man's driving me crazy."

"What man?"

"Larry. My agent. You know what he did? He threatened me, indirectly that is. Larry wouldn't threaten me personally. He's only five three, for Christ's sake. He's been telling people around town that if he hears that I've been bad-mouthing him, he'll sue me."

"For what?" Out here in California everybody loved to sue. It was a way of life. If you weren't suing, you weren't happy.

"For breach of contract, kiddo. There's a clause in there somewhere that says we mustn't say bad things about each other. I could kill the fucker. I tell you, I've had it up to here."

"I'm sorry about it."

"Okay, so look, tell your boss when he gets in that I called. And again, I apologize for last night."

"There's no need."

"I want to make it up to you. How about dinner Thursday?"

"Mr. Yates." I tried to sound prim.

"Okay, okay, I'm going."

He went. Now I liked Os a little better. Larry Campbell was shaping up like another Felicity. The sound of the fax machine attracted my attention and I crossed the room to check the message. I banged my foot into one of Mason's suitcases.

The fax was from Mike Adorno in Artesia. It read: "Thanks for your help with the per diems. I'm a rich man now. But here's an interesting tidbit. There was a girl found dead in the hotel you stayed at. The cops suspect what is laughingly called foul play. Did you see her? Did you know her? Did you do it? She's been dead two days. It's given us something to talk about when we get bored. See you in a couple of weeks. Love to Barbara and my favorite agent—Mike."

So Annabel was dead. I felt sick to my stomach. I called the hotel, but at the last minute when the deskman answered I couldn't think of the right question so I hung up. All my worst fears had come true. Poor Annabel. She hadn't had a chance. And I hadn't helped. I gave her the money for the drugs. Except Mike's note said "foul play." Did somebody really kill her? Maybe Alain had found out where she was.

162

The truth was I'd done it. One way or another I'd pushed her toward her own death. It was spooky remembering pulling her along that hallway as if she'd been dead already. I needed a drink. I gulped down the burning vodka. That was two women I'd killed. I shook from head to foot.

When Mason came back into the office, he looked shattered. I had recovered somewhat and was on my guard. I launched into the good news about Silvia and then handed him the fax from Mike. He glanced at it.

"My mother's dead," he said in a dead voice. I acted shocked, asked what I could do. Nothing.

"Was it a heart attack?"

"She was murdered."

"That's terrible. Why? Who would have done it?"

"Who knows? She's dead. I saw her dead."

"I'm so sorry. I can't believe it."

"The really horrible thing is the last time I saw her she said, 'I don't want to see you again.'"

There had been something psychic about the old witch. I wondered if she had been expecting it, expecting me.

"I don't know what to do next. I suppose I ought to think about the funeral."

"What about your father? Shouldn't you tell him?"

"I haven't seen him for twenty-five years. They split up when I was a kid. For all I know he's dead too. Whatever has to be done I'll do myself."

He was close to tears. I wanted desperately to hug him, kiss him, take him and comfort him. That would come. I'd have to wait.

"I know what that's like," I said. "When my father died, I was his only child. I did everything."

"What happened to your mother?"

"I don't know. I never knew her."

During the rest of the day Mason tried to work. He made the necessary calls, but he couldn't concentrate. I answered the ones I could and left the others. I told people that Mason had suffered a family tragedy. I didn't say what. Maybe he didn't want to tell people. It's one thing to say that your mother has died. It's another to say she was murdered. Later he said, "Maybe she asked for it."

We didn't eat lunch. The police called again, twice. I

163

didn't hear what they said. Mason left the office for an hour to talk to them. When he came back he looked exhausted.

"You ought to eat something."

"I'm not hungry, but you should go out for a while."

"I'll stay here."

By five o'clock he looked so terrible I couldn't stand it. I decided to take charge.

"Come on. You're going to eat whether you like it or not."

To my surprise, he didn't protest. He didn't want to talk but he didn't want to be alone either. I locked the office.

"Would you mind driving?" he asked.

"Of course not. Where shall we go?"

"Somewhere outside. I don't want to sit in a restaurant."

I tried to think of somewhere open at five in the afternoon. I remembered a Mexican place in Venice that had a patio and was open all day. I'd been there once with Laszlo. It was another long drive at that hour of the day. Mason didn't seem to mind. He opened the windows. I desperately wanted a cigarette, but I was strong.

After ten minutes of silence I knew he wanted to talk. He glanced at me two or three times. I waited. I guessed he wanted to tell me he'd come to see me last night, that he'd been inside my house while I was out killing his mother. It was funny-grotesque. I did the deed. Mason had the guilt. We were sitting in the restaurant garden when he came out with it.

"I don't want to be alone tonight. I can't be with Barbara."

"You don't have to explain. You're welcome to stay with me."

"I suppose I could go to a hotel."

"Don't be silly. I'm happy . . . to do anything I can."

"Last night. I didn't sleep at all. I guess maybe I knew something was happening. I don't know."

This was better than I could have hoped. After all the suspicions I'd created around myself, he'd come to trust me. I was thrilled, but it wasn't the hard thrill of danger like last night. This was a soft thrill, a thrill of anticipation. I crossed my legs and pressed them together. I put down my margarita. I hoped he wouldn't see how unsteady my hand really was. I reached out and touched his knuckles.

164

"I'm pleased to help." To say the least.

Mason smiled for the first time today. I had done it. Well, almost. He seemed relieved and started to eat. He even sipped his beer. I watched him as I smoked. Now I felt like a mother, not his mother of course, just a mother watching her child eat and drink after having been sick. Someone I never thought I'd be. I wanted to pick him up and to hold him in my arms, put his head between my breasts, nuzzle him, even as he ate his chicken enchilada. Funny-grotesque.

Now I was ravenous. If I couldn't eat him, I'd finish off the plate of guacamole instead and the salsa and the whole bowl of tortilla chips. I smiled to myself and ordered another drink.

"You like to drink," he said.

"I like margaritas." My smile broadened.

"What are you smiling at?"

"Nothing really."

"Tell me."

"I came across this guy once by the pool at the Château Marmont. It was very early in the morning. He was sitting alone drinking. Six A.M. I laughed. I couldn't help it. He didn't think it was funny, this guy. He said, 'I'd rather have a bottle in front of me than a frontal lobotomy.'" I laughed again now, thinking about it.

"What were you doing at the Château?" Mason asked. He sounded serious. My little joke had misfired. Mason was jealous.

"Seeing someone. It was a long time ago," I said defensively. He smiled. I could see he'd forgotten Felicity at least for a moment. We'd made a start.

"I've heard that pun before," he said.

"Yes, well it wasn't all that fresh then. I remember I told some friends a few days later, and they said it was a very old joke. But what the hell, you know. It was new to me."

I thought it was time to go. I waved at the waiter, scrawling "I love you" up in the air, which he read as "Check please."

"I'm sorry. I'm not at my brightest tonight."

"No more jokes, I promise."

"No. I like jokes. I'll tell you a good one tomorrow. A producer joke. Then you can tell me you've heard it before."

We were both smiling again.

"Let me get this," he said when the check came.

"No, please let me."

"No. Come on." He was insistent. I wasn't going to fight over something this trivial. And yet perhaps it wasn't so trivial. I saw this as a test of macho. To be a male, did he have to pay? I held the check. He was going to pull it from my fingers. Then he looked at me, right into my eyes. It was a look of incredible sadness. I had to let the check go.

But Mason didn't take it. Instead, he stood up.

"You get it," he said. He spoke it like an order, but I knew he'd given in. I loved the man.

Mason dozed in his car as I drove us along the snake of Sunset Boulevard to La Cielo. It was dark now. I glanced at his face from time to time in the headlights of passing cars. This was no baby beside me. He was like a sleeping soldier.

When we turned into my driveway, Mason was still asleep. What was he dreaming? Was this madness? Were we both insane?

I switched off the engine, took out the key, and waited for him to wake. I didn't want to give him a start. He'd had enough. I waited for a few minutes. I couldn't let him sleep here. I wanted to wake him with a kiss. My courage failed me. I put my hand on his forehead. The bone beneath the skin was hot as a radiator. I pressed. The heat from his head made the palm of my hand sweat. He awoke. I took my hand away.

"We're here," I said.

He opened his eyes fully. He rubbed them. I wished I could have done that for him. He smiled, stretched, and got out of the car. He walked to the front door.

I took his arm as we climbed the steps. He was quite unsteady, between sleeping and waking. He accepted my hand, gripping the joint of his elbow. I recalled with pleasure, without irony, that he had called me "Nurse" when I found him in the office asleep one morning.

I led him up to my room. He stood quite still while I lit some candles. I cleared a velvet-covered chair of my underclothes and sat him down.

"I'm so fucking exhausted, I can't think," he said.

"Then don't. Let me."

166

"You're a doll."

I didn't like that. I excused him because of his tiredness. I shouldn't take every remark of his so seriously.

"Would you like a drink?"

"Have you got a mineral water?"

"Club soda."

"Great."

"I'll get it."

It was torture. I had to leave him for a few moments. I left the room. I ran along the passage. I leapt down the stairs. Even with my high heels I had no fear of falling. I raced into the kitchen, opened the fridge, scared for a moment that there was no club soda. Fuck! There wasn't. Wait. I knew I had some somewhere. I'd had a case delivered weeks ago with all kinds of stuff from Gelsons. In the garage!

I went into the garage and pulled out two liter bottles of club soda. I came back into the kitchen. I took a glass from the cupboard. In my nervous state I dropped the fucking thing. The glass shattered on the tiled floor. Shit. I couldn't stop to sweep it up now. I took another glass. I poured some. It wasn't really cold. Shit. I opened the fridge again, the freezer section, and struggled to pull out an ice tray. My fingers stuck to the ice-powdered aluminum. Using all my force, I smashed the metal tray into the sink. Some ancient ice cubes were dislodged. I took three, no four, and put them into the glass of soda. The fizzy water overflowed. I tipped some out to avoid spilling any more. I left the chaos of the kitchen and the burning neon lights and headed upstairs with the drink.

Mason wasn't in the chair anymore. He was on the bed, lying facedown, asleep.

I put the glass down on the bedside table and went into the bathroom. While the tub was filling, I undressed in the bedroom. I was naked as I watched him. I resisted any temptation to go to him. Later. Maybe.

I turned to look at my candlelit body in the mirror. This was the way he would see me. Over my shoulder in the mirror image I saw Mason on my bed. He stirred, groaned. I fled to the bathroom, leaving the door ajar.

I got into the tub. He didn't wake. I was pleased. I didn't want him to see me in the bath, some wet woman at a disadvantage. I stood up. "I'm no doll. You'll see." With my favorite violet towel I firmly rubbed away the drops of water that were resting in my pubic hair. Then I dried the rest of me. By the time I'd finished, my hair was damp again.

I came back into the bedroom wearing a scarlet cotton-toweling robe. Then I had a shock. Mason was awake. He had found the water and was drinking it.

"I shouldn't sleep here. This is your room. Put me in the guest room or something."

"No. Stay where you are. Please."

"Ursula. There's something I have to know. Were you in New Mexico, in Artesia last Sunday?"

"No, why? You asked me that before."

"All right. I'm glad it wasn't you. God, I'm tired." Mason sank back on the pillows. I had to lie to him. He'd had enough for one day. I blew out the candles.

"Leave one or two," he said sleepily.

I left three. His eyes closed and he went into a deep sleep, like hypnosis. I watched him for a while from my rocking chair, then I must have fallen asleep myself.

When I woke, I saw that it was three-thirty. The bedclothes were all on the floor. Mason must have had a fight with himself. I knew that struggle very well. I went over to the bed to straighten the covers. I made a decision. I started slowly and carefully to undress him. I was sure he wouldn't wake. I took off his socks, undid his black leather belt, unbuttoned his pants. My heart was thumping as I eased them down his legs. Mason was lying on his side. I tugged to get the cloth free from under his hip. In my pulling, his briefs came down partway too. For a moment I didn't stop. I didn't look.

I pulled the pants away completely. I put them over a chair. Then I turned back to him. The upper part of his penis was visible in the candlelight. I put my hand out toward his white briefs. I touched the cloth. I looked up to his face before bending down on my hands and knees beside the bed. I reached forward and with both hands moved the white cotton aside. Slowly I pulled his briefs down to his knees. His penis lay asleep between his legs. The tip rolled onto the sheet as he moved slightly in his sleep. I stopped breathing.

I stretched after a few moments and pulled his briefs clear of his ankles. As I leaned across from my kneeling position, my robe touched his penis. I threw the briefs with the trousers. I opened my coarse robe and leaned forward so my left nipple touched his penis. I pressed the tit against his inert flesh and just breathed out.

I didn't care now whether he woke by chance or not. I wasn't going to wake him, not deliberately. I didn't even think of arousing him. I didn't want to see his penis hard. Not now, not tonight. I only wanted to look at him, hold him, but lightly. I lifted his penis in my hands. It was heavy. I did not kiss it. I stared at his dark pubic hair as if I'd never seen a man's pubic hair before. I moved his penis and touched his balls with the palms of my hands. I didn't want to use my fingers. I didn't want my nails anywhere near him. His balls felt strange to my palms. I was dying to lift them but I didn't. I took my hands away and clasped them tightly between my own legs.

I leaned over close to his genitals and breathed onto them. My neck ached. My lips were close to his skin, but they touched nothing. His penis, his hair, his balls were under my microscope. Every part of him looked enormous, not like a man at all but part of some great beast. My eyes were hurting. I could hardly keep the surface of his skin in focus. Tears of pain came. I couldn't stop them. I breathed more heavily. His hair moved. A tear fell off my cheek onto him. Then I really started to cry. I couldn't stop. I sat up and took deep breaths of air, gaining control.

Now I undid the buttons of his shirt one by one, starting at the navel, working my way up. I opened his shirt. The hair on his chest and abdomen looked as if it had just been combed. It was like wood grain. I undid the buttons at the cuffs and took off his shirt. I pulled it free of his body weight and up behind his head. I was careful not to let the material touch his face. He mustn't wake now, as he was completely naked.

I took my robe off. I couldn't be dressed next to him. I stood up and looked down at the man. I wasn't going to touch him again tonight, I decided. I touched myself instead. I looked at his forehead and touched my own. I looked at his eyes and closed mine. I looked at his mouth and put two fingers into my own. I looked at his nipples and stroked my own with my wet fingers. I looked at his penis and parted the lips of my cunt. I stroked the inside, silky and wet, but I didn't feel my own flesh, I felt his. I pushed my hand deeper into myself. What I felt wasn't his hard cock inside me but his soft penis there filling me with flesh without pushing or rubbing, just there.

The smell was overpowering. Even Presence, the real and imagined perfume, faded before this. It was the scent of nature, of growth, of the world. I had never smelled this before. It was him and him alone.

When I withdrew my wet fingers, I saw they were covered with blood. It was impossible. My period wasn't due. But the blood was real. This man was my new moon. Something moved in the room. I jumped. A shadow. I swung round with a gasp of fear. Someone had come to take him away. No, it was one of the candles that had flickered and died. Smoke rose like incense.

I bent down beside Mason and softly dripped my blood onto his belly around the navel. I got some more and dripped it onto his chest. Now he was mine. I kept my promise to myself. I didn't touch him. I covered him up, lay down on the fur rug beside the bed, and sped into sleep.

# 30

# HUNGER

Watching Mason sleep was almost becoming a way of life. He seemed to sleep forever. He was dreaming, but what about? Me or his mother? When would someone invent a machine to record your dreams? How would it play back? It would have to go straight into the brain to the dream screen there, perhaps entering by a probe through the ear. I looked at Mason's ears, examining them. What could you tell about a man from the shape of his ears, everything or nothing? I had heard that the earlobes of criminals were all of a certain shape. Did I have those criminal ears?

Eight o'clock and he was still asleep. I'd made a pot of coffee but it was cold now. I ran a bath for Mason for when he would awake. I went to make some more coffee. I found a few aging rice cakes that would have to do for toast. For some reason a couple of lines were running through my head. I could hear my own voice in my ears, "If I should die before I wake, I beg of thee my soul to take. If I should die before I wake, I beg of thee my soul to take. If I should die before I wake . . ."

When I got back upstairs Mason had woken up and had gone into the bathroom. The door was open, but only two inches. I could hear water sounds but I didn't go in.

"Are you all right?" I called through the door.

"Fine, thank you. I'm not taking your bath, am I?"

"No, it's for you. You'll find towels and things there."

I wondered what Mason would make of the blood marks on his body. He came out of the bathroom eventually, but made no mention of it. He was wearing my red cotton robe.

"How do I look?" He was in a good mood. We laughed.

He drank the coffee, wisely ignored the rice cakes, and said this to me: "A man goes into a butcher's shop to get a pound of brains. The butcher says to him, 'We have writers' brains at five dollars a pound, or producers' brains at fifteen dollars a pound.' The man is amazed. 'How come producers' brains cost three times writers' brains?' The butcher says, 'Do you realize how many producers we have to slaughter for a pound of brains?'"

I laughed. Mason smiled.

"I told you I'd get my sense of humor back after a good night's sleep."

He couldn't have timed the joke better. All the tiredness, dizzyness, and breathless pain of the night before vanished. I pulled back the curtains. There it was, another warm, sunny day in L.A.

I left him to get dressed and invented work for myself downstairs. In the kitchen I suddenly felt violently hungry. I opened a can of tuna and ate it with a fork straight from the can.

It was ten o'clock and we went to the office together. Mason drove. The traffic was heavier than ever and we stopped frequently. Mason showed no signs of frustration. He was preoccupied, probably not with me but with his mother's death. I still had no feelings of regret or remorse. I had done it for him. I knew that if I were discovered I'd be sent to prison for life, most of my life. My terror was that I would be parted from him. If that happened, I'd kill myself. But whatever happened to me in the next weeks, Mason would be free of Felicity forever. And that made me happy. I felt calm. My only real unease was the thought of Mason's reaction if or when he discovered the truth.

There was a brief report of the discovery of the murder in the L.A. *Times*. Mason read it. He handed me the paper without comment. I scoured it for anything about Annabel. There was nothing. It was too far away.

During the morning Sophie Richer came into the office to see Mason. I didn't know who she was.

"I'm a friend of Oswald Yates," she said. "Is Mr. Elliott in?"

"Yes, he is, but he's on the phone."

"Can I wait? It's important."

"When he's off the phone, I'll tell him you're here."

Sophie was the classic Parisienne. I envied her. From her thick blond hair to her worldly manner and charming accent. I guessed she was twenty-two, twenty-three years old. Sophie was nervous.

Mason told me to send her in. I was jealous. There was no way I could hear what was said in his office, not with the door shut. Sophie reappeared twenty minutes later. Mason kissed her good-bye on both cheeks and told her not to worry.

"She's concerned about Os," he confided in me.

"What's happened?"

"Nothing new. Os is going crazy with his agent. She's scared of what Larry Campbell might do. I was in a restaurant the other day talking to Joe Ransom. There was a fight at another table. Larry insulted her. She threw a drink at him and walked out. It's all building to something, I know that."

"Does she want you to take her on, as a client?"

"I guess so."

"Don't."

"Why not?"

"Get Os first."

"Interesting. What do you mean?"

172

"Exactly that. Don't sign her until you've signed Os."

"That could be two years away. I thought you were in favor of new actresses."

"I am. But this girl isn't just an actress. She's Os's girlfriend. That's different. It could look as if you're using her to get to Os."

"You're right. It could."

"Perhaps Os sent her."

There was a long pause. It was a tactic Mason hadn't considered. It was in my devious mind.

"I don't think that's at all likely. Do you?"

The office door opened and Silvia Glass came in. She went straight up to Mason and gave him a kiss on the cheek. He gave her a hug.

"Thank you. Thank you," she said. She was jubilant.

Mason looked over Silvia's shoulder toward me. He smiled and nodded, as if to say to me, "Thank you, you were right about her." He took Silvia into his office and closed the door.

In a few days it seemed as if I had gone from the new face in the office to the permanent fixture, from being on approval to someone whose approval was sought.

Suddenly, I was inside Mason's skin. I could feel as he did, a man surrounded, enveloped, absorbed, even trapped by women, lots of new women. It was as if meeting me had brought them all into his life. Perhaps it reminded him of the old days when he had an army of girlfriends, before Barbara.

Half an hour later Barbara called Mason in a panic. I could guess why. Her voice was wobbly. I didn't try to listen in on their conversation. Mason and Silvia came out of the office after a few minutes. He told me he had to go to the police station with Barbara. I didn't ask why. I could see in his face that he thought she might have killed Felicity.

When he got back around lunchtime, Barbara wasn't with him. It occurred to me that this affair might bring them together emotionally. That worried me.

"They're holding Barbara," he told me. He was nervous now.

"They don't think she did it, do they? That's ridiculous."

"I don't know what they think. They're questioning her.

173

Apparently they found some things of hers in my mother's apartment. Barbara went to see her. They had a fight. Now I guess Barbara's a suspect. But they haven't charged her or anything."

"I'm sure they'll let her go," I said. Of course they'd let her go, I told myself. She didn't do it. She must have an alibi.

Mason spent the afternoon making funeral arrangements. It was difficult because the police wouldn't release Felicity's body until the autopsy was complete. He showed no sign of emotion during those hours. I was impressed but also alarmed. I could see he was bottling it all up.

At about three-thirty a ten-page fax came in, a contract. I put it on his desk. He looked up at me. There were tears streaming down his face.

"Sorry," he said.

"What for?" I resisted touching him.

Barbara called. The police had let her go.

"Thank God," said Mason. He wanted to see her. For some reason Barbara didn't want to see him. I could imagine how she felt, but I couldn't feel sorry for her.

She called again an hour later. They talked for a while. He shut his door. I didn't hear what was said. I felt excluded. I was miserable. Then Mason left the office to see her. My worst fear. At five-thirty he called and told me I could go home. He'd see me in the morning. He didn't ask about his messages. I was distraught.

After I left the office I had three margaritas at the Red Pepper and ate two bowls of guacamole and tortilla chips. I had been so close to him. Now I seemed so far away. As Barbara said, "You can't make them, can you." Maybe now she was getting her way. Maybe right now in her doll's house she was making him.

At home around eight I took a bath. I was bleeding badly. I was miserable. I went to bed and read for a while. I tried to write in my Pillow Book, but the words wouldn't go down on paper. I thought for the first time in a long time about Brian.

He used to ask me things about my past life. I liked to tell him about my spell as a near-prostitute. One night he said, "Ursula, that's not right. You've changed your story. That wasn't what you said before." I laughed. "Novels get rewritten," I said. "So why not lives?"

I woke from a fitful sleep. There was someone in the house. I shouldn't be so cavalier about not locking the place. I thought about the house down the road, the Manson house. Strange that it should be known as the killer's house, rather than the house of the owner and the victim.

I sat up. I was scared. I had a gun. I'd never used it. It was Brian's. I took it from the drawer and walked to the open door of my bedroom. I could hear a noise, definitely. I looked at the gun. Was I about to commit another murder? I didn't even know whether the safety was on or off. I took a deep breath, pulled my robe around me, and went downstairs to meet my fate.

I was shaking. Apart from the candles in the hall there were no lights on. I went into the kitchen. I turned on the lights. Nothing. The door to the garage was closed, but unlocked of course. How could I have been so stupid? I left the lights on, crossed the hall, and went to the guest room.

I heard someone moving about in the room. I immediately thought, It's the cops. Someone had seen the delivery person in leathers. Now they had found the costume. I'd be arrested, tried, convicted, and that would be the end of the story. Well, Ursula, go in and face it. You've failed, girl. That's all there is to it. No point lying about it. Face it, get it over with. Join Charles Manson. No apologies. Treat it as a victory.

The door was ajar. I pushed it open. My gun was lowered; I didn't want some trigger-happy cop to shoot me dead. There was someone lying on the bed, a long shape in the dim light. It was a man. He lay still. I couldn't see his face. His body was covered by an Indian car rug. From the hills around the house came the cry of an owl.

The man moved. I saw enough of his head. It was Mason. He must have heard me come in, but he didn't turn around. I sighed.

"I was worried about you," I said.

There was a long pause before he replied without turning to face me.

"I should've called you," he said. "But I didn't really think you'd mind."

Either Barbara had thrown him out, or he'd just left her. She wouldn't do that. He'd just left her. I was relieved, happy.

"It's okay. But you gave me a scare."

"I'm sorry." He sat up and turned to me.

"Do you want to sleep upstairs in a proper bed?"

"No. I'm fine here. I'm not in the way, am I?"

"Of course not."

"I mean, you haven't got anyone—"

"No. Absolutely not. We're alone." I smiled.

Mason lay back. I took this as a signal for me to leave.

"See you in the morning," I said. "If there's anything you want, just shout."

I left. I wanted to kiss him good night, but I resisted the impulse. I didn't know how long I could go on resisting those impulses. Be patient. Mason had come to see me. He had been to the house before. He knew it was unlocked. Coming to me was a big step for him. His ordered life had been blown apart. It would take a while before all the pieces went back together. I got into bed with my pillow.

It was three o'clock when I woke slowly out of a deep sleep. Mason was getting into bed beside me.

"I couldn't sleep," he said.

I slipped my hand under his head and pulled him toward me. I settled his head between my neck and left breast. I smiled and thought to myself that for a man who's trying to sleep this was hardly the ideal course, getting into bed with me. He knew what I was thinking.

"This isn't going to improve my reputation as a seducer of secretaries."

I laughed, but I didn't like being called a secretary. Then I thought of Barbara. I absolutely didn't want to, but I couldn't help myself. To dispel the thought I leaned over his face and slowly and carefully kissed Mason on the lips, very lightly brushing them, breathing through my nose so he'd feel a tiny rush of air on his cheek.

I waited for his tongue. It wasn't long in coming. He licked my lips. His tongue seemed slightly coarse, perhaps because my lips were dry. I squeezed my cheeks, summoned some spittle, and wet his tongue for him. Our tongues touched inside his mouth, inside mine, until it was hard to breathe.

"How long is it since you've been in bed with a man?" he whispered.

"What a funny question. Do you really want to know?"

"It's none of my business."

"About seven or eight months."

"That's a long time."

"Not for me. I'm choosy."

"Are you choosing me?"

"Absolutely."

He put his hands on my breasts, resting his palms on my nipples. How strange that he should like that feeling. I had always wanted a man to do that, but no one ever had.

"Are they the way you expected?" This was an unfair question. I regretted it. So what? I had no intention of being fair about anything.

"Yes. Exactly."

He sat up and pulled the bedclothes back in order to see me. I was wearing red panties. I was a little nervous about my bleeding. It wasn't ideal. But then he had caused it. How could I ever tell him that? Mason looked at me. He touched the panties.

"You moved them, didn't you? In the office that morning."

"Yes, I did."

"Why?"

"I wanted you to know I'd seen them. They were beside your bed."

"Christ."

"Don't be embarrassed. I thought it was wonderful."

"Is that why you're wearing them?"

"Yes." I lied.

"They're very sexy."

I personally don't think anything in the world is more erotic than a simple naked body. The true mysteries are in the shapes and the folds of flesh and in the hair and movements of the body, not in the clothes.

He kissed me again, returning both hands to press on my breasts. He sucked my tongue and I could taste the hunger growing.

177

"I wanted you from the first time I saw you," he said.
"Me too."

Neither of us meant the moment when I walked into his office. I certainly didn't, and though he seemed to accept that I had not been in Artesia in that hotel hallway, I still thought that that was what he meant by "the first time."

I stroked the hair on his chest. My hand went to his navel. I licked the soft hair that grew around the scar of his birth. He pressed my face into it. He breathed deeply. I heard his tummy rumble from the depths of his intestines.

I moved my head down toward his briefs. I pushed my tongue into the cotton. I felt his penis begin to move. I prodded his genitals through his briefs. For a moment I looked up toward his face in the flickering candlelight. He was watching me, propped up now on a pillow. My mouth found the toughening head of his cock. I licked the cotton, making it damp and then wet. Under the cotton his flesh changed shape, grew and twitched. I made no attempt to take off his briefs.

Something snapped inside his head like elastic. I felt it. I felt the pop go all the way down his body. After the small shudder, he put a hand on the material of my underwear. I knew he'd been trying to avoid that, but he couldn't help himself now. He was losing the first stage of control. I could feel the mixture of curiosity and panic when for a few moments everything sensual seems possible.

Two fingers traced the outline of my vagina. He felt the folds. With the sides of his fingers, he squeezed the damp curled hair and the softening flesh. As he pushed into the satin I felt the liquid flowing, my pulse beating. He moved his legs in response. His left knee bent and rose up, passing my cheek. I opened my mouth wide and let the head of his penis inside. His briefs were soaking. I kept my hands to myself. It was a matter of pride.

He couldn't bear it. He needed something to hold, something to take the strain. He chose my hand. He put my three middle fingers in his mouth and sucked them. He held two of them for a moment with his teeth, quite lightly. I moved the free finger inside his mouth, massaging the gums behind his teeth.

Then it was my turn. I wanted to open his briefs with

my tongue. I found the slit and tried to find a way in. But I'd left it too late. The cotton was too wet. The opening in the material had stuck. His cock was so tense that the cotton was stretched tightly, too tightly for me to get inside with my tongue alone. I had to use my hand. Shame, but there it was. I'd lost a small skirmish. His fingers were now pushing into me through the wet satin. My hips moved involuntarily.

I whispered, "Take them off. Please."

He had a problem. I could sense it. He was being told what to do. He didn't like it. I knew that because it was something I too hated in bed. Being told what to do was an admission of the man's failure to get me to do what he wanted. He shouldn't have to ask. He took my hand out of his mouth.

"Please," I repeated as quietly as I could.

He brought his hand down to the other and started to pull the elastic of my panties. I put my hand on his. He had misunderstood.

"Not mine, yours."

Was I being cruel? Was this a kind of revenge, treating him the way I had so often been treated? I waited. He had no alternative. He took his hands away from my body. I sat back slightly to watch the sweet, awkward struggle.

Mason reached down under his own buttocks and began to pull the wet cotton away. He had to bend his legs, lift his bottom, tug the briefs away from his hard cock, and pull them down his thighs, over his knees, along the calves to his ankles and pull them over his feet. And all of it while I just watched in the candlelight. I wasn't going to help him at all. I think he must have known that. The operation left him in an exposed position, an almost comic attitude, his legs bent and high up.

As the briefs cleared his feet, I moved my head down to his penis. Any embarrassment he may have felt was relieved immediately. I licked the slippery sides of his penis, selecting little folds of his skin to suck tightly between my lips. Conventionally, his hands went to my head. He didn't try to manipulate my head, just stroked my hair.

I put my tongue to the hole at the tip. My left hand stroked upward from his balls. Slowly, I let my fingers curl around the hard flesh. I moved down with my mouth and upward with my hand. I felt the pumping blood in the outstanding vein. I did everything very slowly. We were underwater or in a dream together. I was sure he wanted me to go faster. His whole body became tense, a single, complex erection. I wanted him to feel what I felt, passion and love and not just a sexual effect. To me it wasn't simply sexual. It was an act of adoration for which I had waited a very long time. I had killed to make it possible.

When he came, leaping in my mouth, he shuddered and twisted as if he wanted to get away. I was softly shattered. I swallowed some of his sperm but not all. I kept some in my mouth, mixed with saliva so that when he relaxed and I kissed him I was able to tongue it back into his mouth.

Nothing was said for a long while. We just lay there looking at each other. Then he decided to repay me. Gratitude and revenge together. He ran his hands down to the red panties and began to pull them down my legs. I don't know whether he saw the blood or not in the candlelight.

"I'm bleeding a bit."

He didn't reply. Perhaps he hadn't heard. I wasn't going to repeat it. He spread my legs wide, stroked my pubic hair, and opened the lips. He moved his hand into me. He found the tampon string. He showed no surprise, no distaste. He pulled gently, then gripped the sticky thing and removed it. I didn't know what to do. He did. He leaned over to a box of Kleenex and put the tampon into a handful of tissues. Once again, Mason had done something no man had ever done to me before.

He touched my sex. He stroked my clitoris with the head of his cock, back and forth. I tried to watch, but I couldn't keep my eyes open. I was awash with nothingness. There was a quiet, throbbing electricity. I didn't see or hear anything. I know I made some sounds, but God knows what they were, groans or cries or sighs; it was one long response. As I started to come he moved farther inside me. My womb and the inside of my mouth contracted together. He didn't seem to be thrusting at all. He was simply expanding inside me. I felt like a heavy drift of snow. I lost consciousness for a while.

When I came to, Mason was bending over me. He was at my sex inserting a fresh tampon he must have found in the bathroom. I kissed him over and over again. He held me on top of him. We relaxed into sleep.

When I awoke he was inside me again. When he came, I came. We went on. When there seemed to be nothing left in him, I found more. When I was closed and dry, a small gesture, licking me under the arms, produced a new flood. We slept again in the dampness of our skins.

It was nine in the morning when I drew the curtains back to let in the light. As I stood at the window, I felt his hand between my legs. I took his fingers and kissed them. He gripped my buttocks and slid down to his knees. He put his tongue between my opening legs. I stood helplessly.

For the first time I wondered what we had done. Were we going to pay for this? I cast out the Puritan thoughts. We. We. I realized I was thinking and wondering about us, and no longer about me alone. Then the reality of the outside world entered our bedroom with the sunlight. Together we thought of the same things, Felicity, the funeral, the demands of the office. The only thing I didn't wonder about as we drove to the office was who had murdered his mother.

# 31

# THE TWO OF US

Felicity's funeral was to be on Wednesday morning at Forest Lawn. She had reserved her plot years ago. Mason didn't know. She had wanted to be buried standing up, but the funeral authorities refused to dig a hole deep enough to take a coffin on its end. The police had now agreed to release the body. They were finished with it. Mason went to pick it up.

While he was gone, Barbara came into the office. She looked terrible. She confided in me that the police suspected her. She had an alibi of course, but she was still concerned that they continued to suspect her.

"That's their job," I said. "The cops live for their suspicions. They're only happy when they suspect someone."

"I don't understand how my perfume got into the apartment. And apparently there was a postcard addressed to me as well. I couldn't have left it there. Not possible. You remember, I had them when I came here to bring Mason's cases."

"I don't remember seeing them."

"No, I know. I don't mean you saw them. I mean I had them here when we talked. They were in my purse. I only noticed the perfume was missing the next day. I could've left it somewhere, I suppose. But the postcard . . ."

"How's he bearing up?"

"Nowadays you see more of him than I do. I don't know. It's horrible to say it, but I think he's relieved."

"Relieved?"

"She was destroying him. And he knew it."

"He seems pretty shocked."

"He is. But I'm telling you, Ursula, whoever did it, did him a big, big favor."

"Are you two getting back together?"

Barbara gave me one of her long, hard looks.

"We haven't talked about it much. I guess I blew the Alexis business all out of proportion. Right now, everything's Felicity. We'll have to wait, the two of us."

"First things first. Or in this instance, last things first."

Barbara didn't even smile.

"Mason has a wild theory about who killed her."

"Oh?" A moment of panic.

"I probably shouldn't tell you, if he hasn't. But Mason thinks it was suicide."

"How could it be?" The panic went. Now I wondered if the love of my life had gone nuts.

"A kind of suicide. He thinks Felicity had wanted to die for years. She was getting old, couldn't face it, was very lonely, and had a kind of death wish. He could be right about that. She was pretty destructive."

"But how could she have killed herself? She was smothered, wasn't she? You can't smother yourself, can you?"

"Wait. Mason's theory is that she hired someone to do it. She couldn't do it herself so she got someone else."

"That's crazy. Who?"

"A hit man. She paid some contract killer to do it. That's Mason's theory, but don't tell him I told you."

Mason shouldn't have become an agent, I thought to myself. He should have been a writer.

"Did he tell that to the police?"

"I don't know."

"I hope not."

"But I'm still scared. Real scared," Barbara said.

"What of?"

The long hard look came again. "I can't tell you."

Did she suspect me? No. Too improbable. As far as she was concerned, I didn't have a motive. It flashed through my mind that Barbara's scary thought was that Mason had killed Felicity. It wasn't so crazy, not from Barbara's point of view. The policeman would have put Mason at the top of the list of suspects. It was pretty classical, after all. Oedipus lives.

"I guess he'll have money now that she's gone. Unless she left it all to her cat or something."

I smiled. On her way out of the office she turned to me.

"Coming to the funeral? It's on Wednesday." She smiled. Now that was really sick. And funny.

"I don't think so. Someone's got to mind the store."

When Mason got back he asked me if I would go to the funeral. I was the wrong person for that kind of support.

"The next, the only funeral I'm ever going to," I said, "will be my own."

Was that too curt after the intimacy of the night before and this morning too? A strange awkwardness had arisen between us. My house, my bed, was one place; his office, his desk, that was another. They would merge eventually, but for now they were separate territories. The experience had been so intense. It was as if we'd committed a crime and couldn't quite look each other in the eye afterward.

Later in the day I offered Mason the keys to my house.

"You're not leaving?" He was devastated, thinking they were the office keys.

"My house keys." I smiled. "Not that I ever lock the doors."

Mason sighed with relief. "Sorry. I'm very slow today."

I looked at him long and hard, the way Barbara looked at me when she was about to reveal something.

"Please take them. If you don't want to stay over, fine, I understand. But you can if you want to."

He took the keys. He was hooked. They were the keys to me and, if he but knew it, to Mason. His hand closed over them. We each had a key now, the two of us. He put the keys into his jacket pocket. Barbara wouldn't find those.

By ten o'clock that night we reached an agreement. We never wanted to fuck again. It had been enough for a lifetime. I was sore inside and out. It hurt to pee. My breasts were covered with red marks. My lightest kiss on his cock made him wince. His merest caress between my legs was agony. We had reached the point where we didn't dare touch each other.

Midnight, and neither of us could sleep. I went to get a book and started to read.

"What is it?" he asked, leaning his head on my shoulder, jealous of my self-absorption.

"I'll read it to you."

I read him the story by Guy de Maupassant in which a man whose wife has recently died visits her grave. While he's there he sees a woman a little way off crying over a grave. He goes over to her. She's just lost her husband, she tells him. She is destitute. He takes pity on her, takes her home, gives her money, starts to fall in love with her. After a few months she leaves him, taking a lot of his money. He is devastated. Eventually he gets over it. One day, when he's putting flowers once again on his wife's grave, he sees the same woman in the distance. Now she's crying over another grave. It's raining. As he watches, a man goes up to her, just as he did. They talk for a while. Then the two of them leave together under his umbrella. The end.

"It's nice. But what's the moral? Sounds like it should have a moral," Mason said when I'd finished reading.

"Just don't go picking up girls at Forest Lawn before, during, or after your mother's funeral."

He laughed. Mason really laughed. I was pleased. It was completely involuntary. He was like a child. They were all children when they laughed. I kissed him. It was ridiculous. I wanted him again.

The next morning when we got into the office the sad funeral march had begun.

"I don't have the right clothes for this," he said.

184

I told him that when I went to my father's funeral I looked like a clown. "I hoped that if he could see me, he'd laugh. So go happy, not mournful."

"You believe in an afterlife?"

"I have a funny feeling sometimes that I'm in it now."

On the day of the funeral Mason wore a dark suit, a white shirt, and a scarlet tie. That was a small victory for me. Was it in memory of my panties? I hoped so.

That night I didn't move toward him in bed. He hadn't said a word about the funeral after he got back from Forest Lawn. Nothing. I woke up around two o'clock. I looked at Mason in the candlelight. He was turned away from me. I went back to sleep eventually. Around five I woke again. He was down the bed, his mouth sucking my nipple like a thumb.

It was the strangest week of my life, full of ecstasy and awkward moments. At night there was sex. In the daytime it was all about death.

# 32

# THE WIND

On Thursday Os called. He sounded miserable when he spoke to me. I didn't hear what he said to Mason, but whatever it was it didn't help the gloom. Only I could do that.

Friday evening when Mason signed my paycheck I told him I had someone to see. He looked disappointed, or suspicious, but he didn't question me. At six I went into Century City.

A warm wind drove across the concrete and marble plaza. It made the place feel completely artificial. If the wind was the Santa Ana, then it was supposed to bring disaster in its wake. It would certainly bring disaster to Larry Campbell. That much was certain. I waited beneath his office building. It was going-home time. I was the only unmoving figure in the rectangle of shadows.

I got a fit of sneezing standing there. I couldn't stop. The wind must have been full of dust. I imagined myself, seen from the top of the building, the tiny form of a waiting woman who had been stood up by someone, or was simply lost in herself. I wanted to see the man. Nothing more.

The sun had gone but the wind remained when the tiny form of Larry Campbell emerged from the building. He really was small; Sophie had described him perfectly. He wore a gray suit, white shirt, dark tie, quite unremarkable in every way. I started to walk after him, looking for an opportunity to cross his path. I wanted to see his eyes.

He approached a waiting, chauffeur-driven Mercedes. I picked my moment and walked past him as the chauffeur opened the door. I turned and looked straight at him. His eyes were as dark as mine. I had to admit they were riveting in a way. His hair was thinning. Larry Campbell looked like a short, black-eyed demon. He smiled a preset smile at me and got into the car. He hardly had to bend. The car drove away. His look to me had said, "Whatever it is you want, I can't help you."

When I got home Mason was on the phone in the kitchen, talking, I guessed, to Barbara. From what I could gather, without staying in the kitchen, the police no longer suspected her and they seemed to have no other leads. I noticed he had bought a VCR machine. It was on the kitchen table. He moved his lips to blow me a kiss as I passed. It was domesticity of a kind.

Half an hour later I was in the tub. Mason came in. He bent over and kissed me lovingly on and in the lips.

"The thing I don't understand about you is how you can stay mysterious when you're completely naked."

"I don't think I'm mysterious to everyone. It's just you."

"I don't believe that."

"To me you seem mysterious, but you can't think of yourself that way."

Mason pulled up his shirt sleeve and put his hand into the bath. Under water, he stroked me between the legs.

"Where did you get that ring beside the bed? The brass one. It looks like one of Barbara's."

I thought fast. "Brian gave it to me."

"He must've got it from Barbara's shop."

"It's possible," I said, "but he didn't tell me."

He pushed his fingers into me. I squirmed, splashing.

"Let me get out," I said, "and you can do it to me when I'm dry."

"I want you wet."

Mason bent down, put one arm under my knees and the other above my hips, and lifted me out of the water. He was surprisingly strong. His fingers dug into my flesh, gripping my skin so I wouldn't slip away. He took his mermaid to her bed and put her down dripping wet onto the covers. He tickled my ribs and pulled off his sopping shirt.

I noticed that he had set up the television, which I never watched, and the new VCR at the end of the bed. I undid his shoes and pulled off his socks. I sucked his toes as he unzipped his pants. When he was naked I bit his shoulder. He moved away to the end of the bed, moving like a swimmer out of water and switched on the television and the VCR.

The moment before the image appeared on the screen I knew what we were going to watch. I was afraid of this, but Mason was in good spirits, as if he'd been drinking, which he hadn't. How long had he known about *Gala*? From the beginning, whenever that was?

"Close your eyes," he said. It was an order I obeyed.

Mason arranged me on the bed between him and the screen. He draped me in front of him face downward. He sat cross-legged and stroked my body. My face was buried in the bedclothes, my arms straight by my sides, palms down. I looked up at him from time to time, but not at the screen. He turned the sound up loud and we began.

"What sort of men appear in these films?" he asked.

"All sorts. Sometimes they're friends of the producer who do it for a lark, out-of-work actors, male models, sometimes just oversexed men with ego problems."

Mason's hands moved down from massaging my shoulder blades to the base of my spine. He pressed. I sank into the bed. I tried to imagine him.

"The guy with the huge cock?"

"I think he was a bookseller or an antiques dealer or something. He was in demand for these movies. You can imagine."

"I can't. Tell me what it was like, that thing in your mouth."

"It was like a lump of warm rubber. I didn't think of it as anything else. It wasn't erotic at all."

"Not like this." Mason took my hand and put it around his hard penis. I squeezed.

"Of course not. I want you." I started to move my fingers up and down, pulling at the skin.

"Why did you make the film?"

"Lots of reasons. But not for money. I guess I wanted to shock."

"Who?"

"Perhaps my father, or his memory anyway."

"I don't know if my father's dead or not. I don't miss him."

"Of course you do. Just as I miss my mother."

Mason moved a hand under my thighs, feeling his way inside me. Involuntarily, I moved.

"Do you ever wonder what kind of mother you'd make?"

"No."

"I thought all women did."

"I suppose all women do sometimes. But I want my life to be with a man, not a child."

"You're not a feminist."

"I'm not a theorist."

With his other hand Mason felt his way between my buttocks. He pushed a finger into me. He moved his two fingers like points of a blunt compass toward each other. One finger moved in a clockwise direction, deeper, the other in an anti-clockwise direction. I held my breath as they touched that tough wall of sinew between. There was no way through. Physically you can only go so far. Then fantasy takes over. Fantasy leads to sex, and then sex leads to fantasy again.

"Does it hurt?"

"No. It feels firm."

As I spoke, the firmness, the grip inside, gave way to a rush of liquid. I cried out.

"Hold me!"

My mind went blank and I started to shake. Mason must have had difficulty holding his fingers together, one feeling the other through the strong wall. I became overcome with pure violence. My strength was invincible. It was beyond pleasure. I felt I was making something, God knows what. I thrashed and fumed. Mason lost his grip. It was impossible to hold me. In those moments I could break the world in half.

I have no idea how long it went on, this violence. My eyes were shut. I think I ground my teeth. My thighs opened and shut, my spine arched to its fullest. I was madness.

Slowly my power weakened. I opened my eyes. Tears were pouring down my cheeks. I went on twitching, I know. I felt Mason's hands on my flesh. I couldn't tell which part. The inside of my thighs grew cool with the damp. The liquid was beginning to dry. I looked up at Mason. I thought I saw some obscure fear in his eyes. I kissed him. I wanted to suck his tongue clean out of his throat.

*Gala* was going on. Neither of us was looking at it now. But the groans and moans from the screen were an aural aphrodisiac. It didn't matter that they were fake. Mason began to suck my left breast. He pulled the whole thing into his mouth, his tongue circling the nipple.

After a few moments he withdrew his lips. He was gasping. He lay on his back and drew me into a kneeling position, my knees on either side of his legs, which were together, his long raised penis pointing upward at nothing in particular. For all its precise physiology, desire was such an abstract thing.

He moved his lips toward my hanging breasts and began again to suck them in turn. He pushed my torso gently from side to side to make my breasts swing slightly. They seemed to grow fuller in his mouth. No, not *seemed,* they did grow. I tried to guess what he was thinking. This woman is the best lay I've ever had. This woman will do anything. Was he comparing me to Barbara? Was he thinking at all of his mother? This is great but what does she really want? Who is this woman?

I took his penis in one hand, moved my hips to get the head into me, while still keeping my breasts close enough to his face so that he could continue to suck. His penis pushed the outer lips inward. I moved him against my clitoris, back and forth. There was a wonderful warmth but I was too wet to get that sharp punctured feeling that would make me come. Perhaps I wouldn't come for a while. Nothing could follow what happened before.

I decided to concentrate on him. I moved up and down slowly. It worked. His sucking of my breasts became slower, as if he was tired. But he wasn't tired. He was just starting to give in. That was what the woman wanted, submission. Submission of him, submission of herself, submission without power.

So far we had said nothing. After his questions and my answers we had stopped trying to speak. The sound of the movie irritated me. I groped for the remote control to switch it off. I couldn't find the right button without turning away and looking, so I pressed everything. The sound got louder for a moment or two. Then I must have found the right one because there was a sudden silence and the pale light from the screen vanished. Outside, I could hear the Santa Ana wind blowing through the canyon.

As I spread his legs wide apart, I began to talk to him.

"I'm going to make you come as you've never come before. It won't take very long. Not long at all." I watched his face while I talked. He didn't reply. He didn't have to. He would soon be beyond words. He looked at me with the smile of a happy boy.

"While you're inside me I'm going to use two hands on your balls. Don't be afraid. If I squeeze you, it won't hurt. Breathe normally. Don't hold your breath, whatever you do."

I put my two hands underneath his sac as I moved up and down very slowly. I pressed the testicles together. As I felt him take in breath, I moved them apart.

"With two hands I will make you believe that there are two women with you, two women who want you. These two women aren't fighting over you. We both want you equally."

With one hand I traced the cord of skin stitching that joins the testicle sac to the body. Why a man's balls aren't contained in a single piece of skin is a mystery. It is the only part of a man's body that appears artificially joined. There is no equivalent in a woman's body.

With the other hand I held his penis as I slid it in and out. I varied the pressure of my grip so it became a kind of pulsing ring. The effect on Mason was exactly what I imagined. He alternately relaxed and tensed. His balls drew themselves together as they were sucked to the root of his cock. Their softness disappeared. They became hard as wood.

"Now I'm going to tighten my grip. So is she. Neither of us can stop. We're together. We are all mouth. We're turning ourselves inside out for you."

Mason started to moan. His head moved from side to side. His eyes were still open but he couldn't see a thing.

"Louder," I said, "louder."

His groans became louder.

"Faster," I said, "faster."

As he quickened his movements, I slowed mine. It was irresistible. He was close. I moved my hand from his balls. They had no more feeling. I wormed my hand under his bottom and quickened my movement on his penis. It was covered in foam. My index finger found the knot of his anus. It was wet from my liquid.

"You're there," I whispered.

I pushed my finger slowly into him. He gave a cry. His bottom left the surface of the bed. I lifted my thighs up with him, then brought them together. At the same time I slid my finger in. I slammed my thighs down onto his penis, crushing my own hand between our pubic bones. The joints of my finger clicked as if they had broken.

Mason roared like a beast from the jungle. He shook with growling and started to come. I did not really feel his semen spurt into me, I was far too wet, but I knew it was happening. He occupied my soft cage like a snake gone wild, spitting itself to death.

Sometime in the night I left him sleeping and went downstairs. I stood outside my house naked, feeling the warm gurgling wind on my damp skin. We would soon be free.

# 33

# CAMPBELL'S SOUP

Larry Campbell had to be up to something, something
secret. For a man who was so perpetually angry, who
so consistently hovered on violence, I thought he must have
a private world. Violence comes from somewhere. So I
waited and watched to find out what or where it was. Or
maybe who. A person can become a world. Like Mason for
me.

I was parked across from Larry Campbell's Tudor-style
house on Alpine Drive, a conventional street of overpaid law-
yers and psychiatrists at the east end of Beverly Hills. It was
late Saturday afternoon when Larry Campbell came out of
his house and went to the garage. He was soberly dressed.
Out of the garage came a white VW Rabbit with Larry
Campbell at the wheel. Hard to believe that he would drive
something so modest, so sensible.

I didn't expect to discover his secret so quickly. I assumed he had been sent to Gelsons to pick up some forgotten
item for the weekend dinner table.

He turned out of his house and headed north toward
Sunset and the hills, away from Century City and Gelsons.
There is an undeniable excitement following someone in a
car. With every turn in the road, wondering where they were
going, guessing what they were thinking, imagining the place
and the person they are on their way to; it was a living mystery, a narrative in action. Everybody else's life was a fiction,
by turns fascinating and dull.

I speculated that Larry Campbell was going to meet a
man, a young man, possibly a client, with whom he was having a homosexual affair. Or maybe he was going to meet a
blackmailer, someone who had once followed him like me,
and learned his dark secret. Larry Campbell was on his way
to pay the guy off, or to dispose of him. No one would be

surprised to learn that he'd killed someone. He was probably a Scorpio, vindictive, vengeful, with a memory of past injuries as long as life. I read somewhere that most Scorpios are murderers or remarkably victims of murder. It was the same identity.

He stopped at a minimall. Of all things, he went into a flower shop. He came out with what looked like a single flower in a cellophane wrapper. He got back into his car and drove on. I had been wrong about Larry Campbell. Armed with his flower, he was going to meet a woman.

The white Rabbit took Coldwater over the hill and down with the sinking sun into the San Fernando Valley. My Honda followed the Rabbit like Alice. Was it a magic world he entered when he finally parked his car outside a motel in Van Nuys? I couldn't see if someone opened the door, but he disappeared into room seventeen. I found myself a shaded spot on the parking lot. The blinds were down. There was nothing to see. I had to imagine it all, but I had exhausted my scenarios about Larry Campbell. My mind drifted back to Mason.

Did all Hollywood agents have secret lives? Did Mason? Was he right now somewhere, seeing someone, doing something I knew nothing about, would never know? Agents knew hundreds of people, they knew so many secrets, they knew so much in fact and rumor, too much perhaps. Agents, Mason had told me, were the bloodstream of Hollywood, running through the veins and arteries of Tinseltown, keeping the tanned, overweight body going. Surely, like blood, they must carry diseases as well as oxygen. Then I knew what Mason's secret life was. I was his secret life.

Just over an hour later the door to room seventeen opened. Larry Campbell emerged into the golden light. He looked exactly the same as when he went in. He gave the same cursory, not-too-worried look around, headed for his car, and drove away. This time I didn't follow the white Rabbit.

I had to wait ten minutes before a tall, elegant woman about thirty came out of room seventeen. She was dressed in a blue suit and carried an alligator handbag. I couldn't discern much more from where I sat at the wheel of my car.

The woman went to the motel office, out of my sight, presumably to return the key and pay. I waited. She didn't reappear. I got out of the car to go and look.

Then I heard a door slam. An engine started. From the other side of the motel a car appeared. I watched as it came toward me. I got back behind the wheel as the woman sped past in a green Alfa Romeo. I'd have my work cut out following her in that.

When I turned onto the wide road, I had already lost her. Or thought I had. The Alfa passed two streets away, between the motel and a gas station, going in the opposite direction from me. I spun my Honda around and set off to track her in the light of the setting sun. I could really have used my Triumph for this.

Once I got on her trail, I clung to it. The woman drove fast and I had to hold my foot on the gas to keep up at all.

We reached an apartment building in Sherman Oaks. It was a recently built, expensive-looking place with silver-gray windows you couldn't see into but which reflected the sunset landscape brilliantly. It represented another Los Angeles, non–show biz, a combination of city and suburb where people would work from their houses, each apartment being an office as well as a home, operating through the fax machine and computer terminals. It was a surprising place for this woman to be living.

I let the Alfa go into the evening darkness of the subterranean parking lot. I waited before following. I re-made up my face in the car mirror, probably not too well in the available light. I opened my hatbox and took out the wig I had worn for *Gala*. But now I was the user, not the used. I put my glasses on and took my new black Italian cashmere coat from the backseat; I was ready for my performance, my impersonation.

I parked my car underground in one of the spaces reserved for visitors. The green Alfa was in 11D. I pulled my coat around me, arranged my double string of pearls, and rode the elevator to the eleventh floor. I went up to the front door of 11D and rang the bell. It took a while for the woman to open her door after checking the video-screen image of me and wondering who I was. She had changed her clothes, or at least the ones I could see. She now wore a pale green dress and still looked the image of a businesswoman.

"Excuse me for troubling you on the weekend," I said, "but I have to talk to you." I tried to seem both rich and helpless. Not an easy task, but irresistible if you pull it off.

"What is it?" She looked at me suspiciously, but after my encounter with Felicity at her door I was getting fairly confident about persuading women to let me into their apartments.

"I want to talk about Larry Campbell."

Her face was an icy mask.

"Who are you, a cop?"

"No, no." I tried to look embarrassed.

"A private eye?"

"Do I look like a private eye?"

"They got women private eyes. I heard that."

Now I knew she was a prostitute. "I'm an acquaintance of Mr. Campbell."

"You're his wife."

"No, I'm not. I'll tell you who I am and what I want, and how much I'm prepared to pay."

She invited me in. From the outside of the building and from the woman's clean-cut appearance I had imagined something antiseptic. I had been wrong. The place looked lived in, not a crazy quilt like my bedroom, but lived in by more than one person.

"My name's Audrey something-or-other," I told her.

"Mine's Rita," she said. "Rita Hayworth."

We both smiled. Without being asked, I sat down on a chesterfield. I had the feeling Rita liked me.

"I'm really a friend of Mrs. Campbell," I said. "She knows her husband has been seeing you. She doesn't know who you are, of course."

"But you intend to tell her."

"I don't. Mrs. Campbell isn't interested in who; she's only interested in why."

"This has nothing to do with me."

"Yes and no, wouldn't you say?"

"It's purely a transaction between Mr. Campbell and me."

"Yes, from your point of view."

"That's the only point of view I care about."

"Please hear me out. I don't know how she found out.

195

She probably just guessed. As you can imagine, her first instinct was to confront him, to get him to stop. But she doesn't want to risk losing him."

Rita said nothing. I could see she understood. Through my tone of voice I'd made it plain that I understood the other view, the girlfriend, mistress, whore, that side of things. Rita just listened.

"I suggested to Mrs. Campbell that she try another tactic. You see, what she really wants to know, to understand, if you like, is what is missing in her relationship with Larry. She wants to find out why he feels the need for . . . another relationship. She loves him, you see."

"Are you asking me to give him up as a client?"

"I want to know what you do for him when you meet. What is the sexual practice he gets from you."

"That's something his wife should ask him, isn't it?"

"Mrs. Campbell doesn't want to do that. I guess she's nervous. But I'm not nervous and I want to help."

"How exactly? You're aware that Mr. Campbell pays me a substantial fee for my services."

"Now here's what I suggest." I must have sounded like an agent for Mrs. Larry Campbell. In fact, I was being an agent for an agent. I was trying to cut the deal for Mason. And eventually for Os Yates. "I quite understand that you wouldn't want to disclose the secrets of your meetings with Mr. Campbell to a complete stranger. So to avoid compromising you in any way, I myself want to take your place."

"What do you mean?"

"I want to replace you at your next encounter with Mr. Campbell. I'll be there instead of you. Whatever you do for him, I'll do."

Rita smiled. "That's the wildest thing I ever heard."

"Naturally, I'll pay you. How much do you get a session?"

"Five hundred."

"Good. I'll give you two thousand."

"Two thousand?"

"I'll give it to you now. I need to know the place of your meeting and the time. Is it always the same place?"

"No. We use different motels each time. I set it up and pay for the room."

196

"Fine. All I want is for you to give me the date of the next meeting, and I'll be there."

"And me?"

"You'll be off sick that day."

Now Rita laughed. While she was laughing I opened my purse and counted out twenty hundred-dollar bills. While I was doing that, a woman came into the apartment. She was in her fifties and carried a miniature poodle. Rita didn't introduce us. I nodded at the woman. Her face looked enough like Rita's for me to conclude that she was her mother.

"I'll call you during the week," I said. "And you can let me know the details."

"This is really crazy."

Rita gave me her card. She was intrigued.

"This is the name I use. Crane. I'm usually in most mornings."

I held out my hand, said good-bye, and thanked her. Rita looked doubtful but I knew the two thousand dollars would overcome that. It was all quite businesslike.

As I drove back over Coldwater, I thought about my use of money. Without money to pay people like Annabel and now Rita, I wouldn't have been able to pursue my love for Mason, not in the way I had chosen, not in this foolproof way. Love and money had a special link for me. I was using my money as a tool, not as a source of attraction. I felt quite moral about it.

I was pleased with the ingenuity of my deal with Rita. I was pleased that the first stage had been accomplished so smoothly. I had been burning to ask what she actually did for Larry Campbell. Would it be really horrible? I couldn't imagine it would be anything I hadn't done before. And she hadn't objected that I might not be up to the assignment. I liked Rita, or whatever her name was. She was somehow on my side.

From time to time I was struck by the essential difference between life in Portland and life in Los Angeles. There was no sense of community out here. People lived very separate lives. They merged for one thing, the deal. If you made a deal, you made a friend. For a while, anyway. When I thought about the manner in which I'd gone about my love for Mason, it seemed typical of Los Angeles. The strategy,

197

the tactics, it was an artificial way to get what you wanted. But there was nothing artificial about what I wanted.

Mason was on the phone when I got back home. He was refusing an invitation from someone to share their fun Saturday night. I sat on his knee. He finished the call. We kissed for twenty minutes. Neither of us had the slightest desire to see anyone other than each other. We were like children, living between ecstasy and unease.

We got up to the bedroom, undressing each other as we climbed. I saw that my dressing mirror had been moved. It was now at the end of the bed, angled downward a few degrees, so that when we were on the bed we could see ourselves. Mason had arranged it. I didn't say anything. It disturbed me.

Did he need to see himself while he was making love to me? Did he want to see double? I remembered a phrase of a girl who worked at the law office. "Double it and you got it," she used to say about everything.

I was now aware that the TV was on. I turned to look. He was watching the scene in *Gala* where I got off the bed, leaving Annabel to go to my demon lover.

"Switch it off." The candle flames beside the bed flickered to an angle of forty-five degrees in the draught from my mouth. One of them went out in a snake of smoke. Had I shouted? Mason switched off the TV.

"Where did you hear about the cassette?"

"Joe Ransom."

So Joe had recognized me. Shit. I hadn't liked Joe the first time I saw him. But that couldn't be helped now. Secrets were ceasing to be secrets day by day. Mason looked away from the mirror.

"Tell me. What did you think of me when you first saw me?" Mason held my head between his hands. He wasn't going to let go of me until he had an answer that satisfied him. Was he going back to the hotel hallway? Did he want me to tell him that I'd been there? I had already denied that. I had to lay this ghost to rest once and for all.

"When I first saw you? The first time I saw you was on the roof of the Bel Age. You were swimming."

He remembered the day and whom he had been with. He didn't remember seeing me. I told him more about other times I had watched him, followed him. It took on the tone of a confession. Mason was visibly affected. I hoped I had dispelled his questioning thoughts about the hotel in Artesia.

People think of confession as an admission of guilt. But it can also be a valuable weapon. Confession seems admirable to the person hearing it, a victory for the listener. In reality, confession weakens the person who hears it. It undermines his desire to unearth something more. It takes away his appetite for punishment, because he feels a complicity with the person who's reached the point where he needs to confess.

Mason was awash with fresh emotions that he couldn't control.

I lay back, breathing deeply. I looked at us in the mirror. A naked couple, reflective, belonging together in the frame like a painting. Yet, like two studies for naked forms, we were separate, as if the artist hadn't quite worked out the relationship between us.

"What do you want from me really?" Mason asked.

"I want to share your life."

"Is my life that interesting?"

"It is to me."

"Am I that interesting?"

"To me."

"We're kind of bound together now, aren't we?"

"I hope so."

"I don't understand you, Ursula."

"I'm simple, Mason."

"I have a feeling you might be expecting too much."

"That's for me to decide."

"You decide a lot of stuff."

"Sorry."

"Don't be. It's useful. Right now I'm not at my most decisive."

"I know that. I want to help you."

"I think you might be too subtle for me."

I suddenly remembered what Felicity had told me about Mason, "He'll never fucking understand you."

"The more I fuck you, the more I need you," said Mason. "But it's like one step forward and two steps back. I don't know."

"Thank you."

199

"Don't be hurt. You know what I mean."

"No, I don't." I was angry with him. But I wasn't sure why. So I said, "Shall we stop it all now?"

"What!" He was panicked. "What do you mean?"

"Finish it. End it now. Say good-bye." I propped myself up on one elbow. I waited.

Now there was a pause, a long one. Like an idiot, I had given him a way out. He put out his hand and touched my breast.

"Come here," he said.

With a sigh of relief, I came. He had let me off the hook.

# 34

# ALIBIS

It was Sunday. I got up early and washed my bike. I transformed this middle-class chore into a ritual cleansing. Ever since I read *Zen and the Art of Motorcycle Maintenance*, I viewed my Triumph as a Way instead of a Means of getting about. With true zeal I applied the bristles of the toothbrush to the spokes. As I cleaned the machine, I imagined I was wiping fingerprints from a murder weapon.

Mason was intrigued by the bike, by my interest in it. For him, there was something incongruous in the relationship between a frail woman and a heavy piece of machinery. Perhaps if I had had huge tits and big buns it would've seemed consistent.

"I'll take you for a ride one day," I said.

"I want to go now."

"I haven't got a helmet for you."

"That doesn't matter. I won't come off."

I felt like his protector.

"It's dangerous. If there was an accident I'd be responsible." Responsible? Was this me talking?

Midmorning, we set off, Mason without a helmet. I'd have let him use mine but it didn't fit.

To begin with I was very cautious. I didn't want to break the speed limit. This was not the moment to get pulled over by the cops. I was cautious too because of my precious passenger, his arms around me, his head behind mine.

A motorcycle weaves through traffic. It was in the nature of the beast to overtake, accelerate, and go where automobiles can't follow. My Triumph was more animal than machine. It was an extension of me. No, not just an extension; it was an expression of something inside me, someone inside me who would only escape the cage of everyday life by charging forward. You can't reverse a bike. It was all forward rush. At one point on the freeway heading north I let rip. I couldn't help myself. Mason clutched me tighter for a while. As he got used to the speed, he gradually relaxed his grip until at 120 mph he seemed almost comfortable.

I drove for about twenty minutes and suggested we stop somewhere in the Valley for a cup of coffee. Mason wouldn't hear of it. He didn't want me to stop. He was hooked. I kept well within the limit of fifty-five on the way back.

Just as we entered Beverly Hills a raccoon ran across the road. I avoided him easily.

"That was close," Mason called out. He was thinking like the driver of a car.

I could see the three-legged dog on the New Mexico highway. It brought back miserable memories of Annabel. If only Annabel had been more like Rita and not so fucked up. I would call Rita when we got back.

I didn't though. Mason was high from his ride and wanted to make love immediately. He didn't give me the time to get completely undressed. I left his semen on my jacket. It dried quickly, like correcting fluid. Making love after the ride had for me the unexpected intensity of a dream. It was an extension of the fast-slow progress of the journey. Mason became my mech-animal beast, that creature inside me.

"Next time we'll drive at night," I said. "It's different."

Monday. Minutes after we arrived at the office there was a call for Mason. The police wanted to see him. He didn't know why. Somehow he had thought it was all over.

"They've probably got a lead and they want to tell you about it."

"I think it's something else."

"What?"

"I think they want to talk to me about where I was the night my mother was killed."

"What makes you think that?" Now I caught his nervousness.

"They asked me before. And I told them I was working here at the office, and that then I went out for a meal and came back here and slept here."

"So what's the problem then?" I knew the problem, of course. He had lied.

"The trouble is I wasn't with anyone. There's no one I can go to to prove where I was."

"That's absurd. They surely don't suspect you."

"Maybe not, but maybe they think I know who did it."

"I don't understand. What motive could you have?"

"I suppose you could say money."

"Money?"

"My mother left quite a bit of money."

"It must be something else."

"I did a dumb thing. I told them that my mother was a little crazy and that in my opinion it was possible that she had gotten someone to do it."

"Do you believe that?" I was still perplexed even though Barbara had told me about Mason's theory. "I thought they said a woman did it."

"They did. But I think that was a kind of smoke screen. They suspected Barbara, you know. Now they're apparently working on some other theory."

"Why don't you use me?"

"You? What are you talking about?"

"If you can't prove where you were, and you need an alibi, use me. Say that you were with me."

"I couldn't do that."

"Why not? Because you didn't tell them before? Well, you can say you didn't want to reveal that part of your life. You could say you didn't want Barbara to know, especially after that business with Alexis. Or you could say you didn't want to compromise me."

Mason rubbed his forehead. "I couldn't do that," he said again. There was a small hesitation in his response. So I took the plunge.

202

"Mason, I know where you were that night."

"What?" He turned to stone.

"You were at my house."

He stared at me. He thought of denying it for a moment, but what would be the point?

"How did you know? Did you see me?"

"No, I didn't. I guessed. You made a phone call in the kitchen. I knew someone had been in the house. When you came back to sleep in the guest room, I knew you'd been there before."

"I should have told you."

"Look, it doesn't matter now. We're together now. That stuff's all in the past. Why don't you tell the cops you were with me?"

"That's not really the truth."

"What's the truth, for God's sake? It could've been true. You wanted to be with me."

"Yes."

"And I wanted to be with you. A couple of nights later it was the truth. What's the difference?"

"I don't want to involve you."

"I am involved."

I took Mason in my arms. He put his arms tightly around me. He gripped my bottom as if my flesh was a rock face he was clinging to, high above the abyss.

"Who cares what people think, my darling? Sleeping with a woman from the office may not be kosher but it isn't murder, is it?"

While Mason was with the police I called Rita. She didn't yet know the time or venue of her next encounter with Larry Campbell. It would probably be next weekend, she said. I told her I'd call her again in a couple of days. I was getting anxious. I wanted the whole thing over and done with.

Would Mason use me as his alibi? If the police scared him enough, he would. Otherwise, it would be the last resort. He wouldn't want to change his previous story. I didn't doubt his commitment to me. He didn't try to hide his feelings. He didn't mind being seen with me outside the office. But no one had put him on the spot yet.

I knew I was putting myself in danger. I too would have to lie about where I was that night. Maybe I should sell the Triumph and not be sentimental about a hunk of machinery that could bring about the end of everything.

While Mason was still at police headquarters, Mike Adorno came into the office. He was a jolly man in his thirties with a nice sense of humor.

"Welcome to the nuthouse," he said. "Where's my secret agent?"

"He should be back in an hour or so."

"So don't tell me where he is."

"Can I help?"

"Sure. Get me a job. No, I'm just kidding. Look, I just popped in to say hello. I got this news item here that'll interest Mason."

Mike produced a newspaper clipping. He showed it to me. The headline read WOMAN'S MYSTERY DEATH.

A woman identified as Annabel Hart was discovered dead today in her room at the Sierra Hotel in Artesia, N.M. A quantity of drugs was found in her possession. Police are anxious to talk to anyone who knew Ms. Hart or visited her. It is understood that she was traveling from Los Angeles in the company of another woman who has since disappeared. This woman registered in the hotel under the name of Audrey Johns and is described by the management of the Sierra Hotel as very slim, dark haired, late twenties. Local police are anxious to talk to anyone who saw this woman or knows of her present whereabouts.

Mike said, "Mason stayed at the Sierra with Barbara. He might have seen this mystery woman. It's obvious, isn't it, the fuzz suspects her of murder?"

"I don't know," I said. "Is it obvious?"

"Are you all right?"

"Yes, I'm fine." I evidently wasn't covering my emotion very well.

The phone saved me from further conversation with Mike. While I was talking he made a photocopy of the clipping.

"Give this to Mason when he gets back." Mike scribbled a message on the copy and left with a cheery wave. I got off the phone and looked at the message, "Did you see this girl, Audrey Johns?" Once again, I put the message from Mike on Mason's desk with the mail and the messages. Last time he hadn't responded to the fax. This time the newspaper description was a fair picture of me. But we were past that stage now, weren't we? Mason no longer needed to speculate about the mystery woman in black. He had me, the real thing.

"I didn't use you as an alibi," Mason told me when he got back. "I stuck to my original story. Fuck 'em. They can believe what the fuck they like."

"I don't think they really suspect you," I said. I was pleased with the way he'd handled it. Yet if he had used me for an alibi, I would've had one also. Strange.

He looked at the newspaper item. He looked up at me. He kissed me gently, still holding the photocopy. I didn't know what he was really thinking. There was nothing suspicious or accusatory in his tone. And the kiss was delicate.

We began to live as if we were married. I don't know if I liked it or not, but I couldn't stop it. After the office we'd have supper somewhere on the way home. I refused to cook any meals at all. I wasn't that married. We'd go to bed around nine, our drinks usually unfinished. When we came to, it was four-thirty or five in the morning. Our days and nights became restructured. Whether Mason found this congenial or not I don't know, but he adapted to it. I bought him an English Filofax refill. It had blank pages instead of days set out by the hour, starting at eight and ending at six. It was open-ended. You could start your day before your first breakfast meeting at eight. And there was no end to it but the next day.

My week was spent preparing for my encounter with Larry Campbell. That wasn't going to appear in any diary. Rita didn't want to talk on the phone, so we arranged to meet. Her reason was simple. She wanted more money. I gave her another fifteen hundred. I enjoyed parting with the cash.

Rita told me what I'd have to do. "It's not that difficult really. You just have to have the right manner, very cool. He does most of the business to himself."

205

"Is he violent?"

"Not with me."

"What do I need to take?"

"Wear a little black dress. No underwear. Are you on the rag?"

"Not at the moment."

"Good. Because that's a no-no."

I was becoming more and more intrigued. My apprehension about the whole project had been injected with a growing excitement. This would be the last of my pieces of staged theater. It would be performed without any rehearsal or runthroughs.

"I've got the black swimsuit."

"One-piece?"

"As you told me. Any special kind of orchid?"

"No. Just make sure it's a single bloom in a clear plastic box. Make sure you can open it easily. If you fumble with it, it could wreck the whole thing."

"I won't fumble," I said.


# 35

# AN EXISTENTIAL WOMAN

The assignation was Friday late afternoon. On Wednesday I told Mason that I was taking him out for a surprise on Friday, so we'd close the office in the afternoon. To begin with, he resisted it. We were busy and he was in good spirits. The deal with Silvia for *Zen Bowler* had been cut. Mike was up for a third lead in a big comedy at Paramount with Arnold Schwarzenegger. Os Yates's girlfriend, Sophie, had formally approached us for representation. I didn't believe in her as an actress and I was still worried about her closeness to Os. But Joe Ransom expressed interest in her for a movie of which he was executive producer and which was scheduled to start in six weeks. So she would probably be working. My target was still Os Yates. I knew that when we represented him, the agency would change for the bigger and the better.

Larry Campbell had selected a motel similar to the one where he met Rita. It was about five miles farther up the freeway. Rita had made the reservation. I wore my neatest black silk dress. We got there around four-thirty.

"What is this? A dirty weekend?" Mason was mystified.

"Not exactly."

"Who's the orchid for?"

"You'll see. It's a surprise."

"You look like you're dressed for a funeral."

We went into the motel room. I drew the blinds. I explained that someone would be coming to see me in half an hour, and that Mason would be an observer. There was a closet in the motel room with louvered doors. I told him that he was to go into the cupboard, close the doors, and just watch.

"Watch what?" he wanted to know.

"Think of it as a little play."

"Do I know this person who's coming?"

"Yes you do. But not well."

"This is crazy."

"Remember, you mustn't make a sound. You're invisible. But whatever you think, don't come out."

I put on my black gloves and switched on the TV. I could see Mason was becoming impatient.

"Don't touch anything," I said. The room must be covered in a thousand fingerprints but I didn't want his to be conspicuous. At ten to five I ushered him into the closet. I thought I heard a car pull up outside.

"Not a sound, my darling. And don't come out, whatever happens. Stay put. Promise."

A few moments later a shadow passed across the blinds. I glanced toward Mason. He couldn't be seen behind the slats. There was a knock, two knocks.

I opened the door. Larry Campbell stood there, smiling with an orchid wrapped in cellophane. When he saw me, his face fell.

"Where's Mrs. Crane?" He looked around suspiciously.

"She's sick. She's got the flu."

"I don't think this is going to work." He was on the point of leaving.

I had to keep him somehow. I knew it would be wrong to touch him, to try to hold him. I didn't want to sound desperate.

"I have the swimsuit."

Larry still wasn't convinced. "You're not wearing it."

"No. Of course not."

"If it's not right, I won't pay."

"I understand."

"I'll simply leave."

"It will be fine."

I waited. It was touch and go for a few moments. Then he made up his mind. He closed the door behind him. Mrs. Crane didn't tell me how much smiling was permitted. Knowing what I was supposed to do, I decided not to smile unless he did.

"This is for you." Larry handed me his orchid. He didn't smile. I produced my orchid. I put his orchid on a table. I opened the box and took out mine. I smelled it, looked at him, and dropped it on the floor. I had considered throwing it onto the bed but this seemed a classier rejection. I knew from Rita, Mrs. Crane that is, that I would have a certain license. Larry wasn't an absolute stickler for detail. He looked at my orchid. Then he looked at his, still in its box.

"What's wrong with my orchid?" he wanted to know.

"I don't accept presents."

"You shouldn't have done that." He looked at the orchid on the floor.

"I don't like the perfume." I dug the tip of my high heel into the flesh of the orchid. At no time did I glance toward the closet. I wondered what Mason could make of this. I hoped he wouldn't get the giggles.

Larry bent down. He picked up the orchid. He handed me the ruined bloom.

"Eat it."

Shit. I hadn't expected this. I hoped the thing wasn't poisonous. I put the flower into my mouth and started to chew it. I didn't quite know whether to appear to enjoy it or not. I decided not to react either way. I chewed it. It wasn't too bad. I swallowed some of the flesh quite mechanically and without expression.

"Why do you reject everything I give you?"

I stopped eating the orchid and dropped the uneaten part.

"It's you I reject. Your manner is abrasive. One minute you give me a present, the next you insult me."

Larry took off his jacket.

"Kiss my shirt."

I walked toward him. I saw the embroidered initials *L.C.C.* I wondered what his middle name was. I bent at the knees and kissed his initials. I could feel the muscles of his chest grow tense at the pressure of my lips. I waited in that position. I felt him looking down at me. Was I accepted yet?

I had to forget Mason was watching.

"Undress me."

I stood up and started on the buttons of his shirt. He moved away. What was wrong? Was it the black silk gloves? Rita had told me to wear them.

"You're not dressed," Larry said. He must mean the bathing costume. Okay, but where should I change into it? In the bathroom or in front of him? Rita hadn't told me that. I decided on the bathroom. I turned away, praying I hadn't lost him, hadn't ruined his fantasy.

I picked up the swimsuit from the bed and went into the bathroom. I didn't close the door. I undressed and redressed just out of his sight. As I pulled the strap up at the top around my neck, I caught sight of Larry Campbell reflected in the mirror of the medicine cabinet. Had he moved to watch me?

When I approached Larry Campbell again, he seemed to be in exactly the same position as before. I returned to undressing him. I didn't hurry it. Don't fumble.

"Can't you feel the strength?" Larry asked.

I assumed it was a rhetorical question.

"Everyone bends to my will," he went on. "I'm a powerful man. That's why people are attracted to me."

I bent down and undid his shoelaces. I remembered reading that the first thing a prostitute looked at when she approached a potential client was his shoes. Larry Campbell's shoes were custom-made.

"People are afraid of me. They cower in my presence. And that's as it should be. I'm a lion tamer. I crack the whip. Sometimes just a look will bring them to heel. They're scum and they know it. They need the discipline. You know what I need in return?"

209

He lifted one leg, then the other, as I pulled his pants down and clear away. I decided to fold them neatly.

"I need devotion. It's my curse. I am cursed, you know; I have this strong need to be obeyed. Obeyed with love, with devotion."

Now all that remained were Larry Campbell's Ralph Lauren undershorts. This fantasy was so different from *Gala*. That was fake. This was authentic. He reached forward and put his hands around the back of my neck. I tried not to show alarm. I was scared. But this was too early for me to make my move. I would have to catch him totally off guard to be sure of success. Larry Campbell undid the clip of the strap and eased the top of the suit down to my waist. He was careful not to touch my skin.

He took his hands away and looked at me. I remained still. I could feel my nipples harden. God knows why, I had no desire for this man. Perhaps it was because he hadn't touched me. For Larry Campbell the essence of passion was not to touch. I realized he had no intention of trying to possess me. He wanted to possess himself.

I could see his penis moving under his shorts. He looked down at himself. He waited. It was my move.

I started to pull his shorts down his legs. I bent my knees. By the time I'd got them down to his ankles, his cock was extended. The tip touched my shoulder. Larry Campbell, small though he was, was hung like a bull. His testicles were like eggs. He started to finger his cock. From my crouching position I could see that this was the perfect moment. He was offering himself to me.

"I want to make it real. I wish them dead. They must die so I can live."

Suddenly, I pictured Larry Campbell's wife and children smiling.

"Why am I like this?" He rubbed his cock with long strokes. "Why am I who I am?" He rubbed harder. "Move closer."

I obeyed. My face was six inches from his penis. I knew he didn't want me to take him in my mouth. It was obvious he wanted to spurt over my face. I looked up. I saw he had closed his eyes. Now! It was now!

I clenched my right fist. My muscles tightened. I brought my fist upward with all my force. I slammed into his testicles as they were climbing up in their sac.

Larry Campbell uttered a great howl and collapsed sideways, falling heavily. I prayed I had knocked him out. He lay still. His mouth was gasping for air. I leaned over him.

I heard Mason open the closet door.

"Christ, Ursula, what have you done?"

I was going to take Larry Campbell's jacket, fold it, and cover his face while he was still unconscious. But I'd failed. He wasn't unconscious. He suddenly grabbed my hair and his hands went to my throat. Even in his gasping agony Larry Campbell had a steel grip. I was suffocating. He was going to kill me.

Mason gripped his hands and tried to pull him away. It was hard. Larry Campbell had the strength of a man who will not die, the strength of a newborn baby who can lift himself up with one hand. That infantile strength was quickly lost. You spent the rest of your life trying to get it back. That's what was happening to Larry Campbell. He was going backward.

Mason wrenched one of his hands away from my neck. I gasped for air. I put both hands to Larry Campbell's Adam's apple and pressed them together as I had been taught in self-defense class.

Twenty seconds later Larry Campbell was dead. The curse on him was finally lifted. I felt no sorrow, no pity, nothing. I did what I set out to do.

Mason stood up. For a long while he didn't look at me. He stared down at Larry Campbell. I pulled off my bathing suit. I rubbed my aching neck. I started for the bathroom to pick up my skirt. Mason caught my arm. He was breathing hard. For a second, I thought he was going to hit me. He watched me getting dressed for a few moments, then went into the bedroom. When I came out I saw that he had picked up my crushed orchid and the box it came in. I got all my things together.

"Don't touch anything," I said.

He looked shocked. It was natural. But he'd get over it. He had to.

I thought about Rita. The police would suspect her, but

then how would they find out about her? These assignations were not the kind of meetings Larry Campbell would put in his diary. If Rita read about Larry Campbell's death, if she did, she wouldn't want to get involved. And if she did go to the cops, all she could tell them was a tale about a red-haired woman who was a friend of Larry Campbell's wife. That trail would only lead to Larry Campbell's wife, a dead end because she would have an alibi and wouldn't know any red-haired women.

I looked out of the window, across the parking lot. A car was leaving. Then it all seemed deserted. I turned back to Mason. He was looking down, staring down, at the body of Larry Campbell, the second dead person he had seen in the past two weeks. I wiped the room key with my nail polish remover and threw it down beside Larry Campbell's body.

"Come on," I said. "We're out of here."

Mason nodded but he kept on staring down at Larry.

"Come on," I said again. I left the room and went to get the car. I got in. I turned the car around. Mason still hadn't come out of the room. I backed up to the door. He finally appeared. His right hand was covered in a handkerchief. He closed the door of the motel room and came over. He didn't look around. He didn't seem nervous. I opened the passenger door for him. He got in and slammed the door.

We left the motel parking lot. I still kept looking around. Mason was watching me. We were on the entrance ramp to the San Diego Freeway when he spoke.

"Stop the car."

"What is it?"

"Stop the car."

I stopped the car. Mason leaned over and took me in his arms. He gave me the most loving kiss I have ever had from a man. I moved away from him and took his hands in mine. I kissed the fingers in turn.

I had made a reservation at the Casa Vega on Ventura Boulevard. It was the perfect spot. They'd be unlikely to remember that we were a few minutes late, and even so, so what? We'd spend the evening there, have some margaritas and guacamole, and leave.

The Casa Vega was wonderfully dark. The bar was a coven of locals shrouded in cigarette smoke. The waitress,

Maria of course, showed us to a booth. No one seemed to take any special notice. We looked like a couple escaping from home, from wives and husbands. The place was so unfashionable, there was almost no chance of being seen by anyone Mason knew. And if we were, so what? We were establishing an alibi. If necessary.

After the first margarita from the pitcher, Mason got up. He took my hand. He wanted to show me something. He drew me to the toilet. We went into the ladies room, bolted the door, and undressed each other from the waist down. With our underclothes around our ankles we tore into each other. When we had finished I found myself laughing, not in derision but with sheer pleasure. For the first time our sex together was funny.

At dinner, Mason seemed relaxed. He drank more than usual. I got buzzed. We didn't mention Larry Campbell at any time. I paid for dinner. Mason drove us back to Beverly Hills.

At home I lit the fire in the hall. Neither of us wanted to go upstairs to bed. He wanted to talk, about anything amusing. He wanted to entertain me. I wanted to be entertained. He recounted an anecdote. "Billy Wilder once suggested to Sam Goldwyn, I think, that he make a movie about Oedipus. 'You mean that Greek guy who married his mother?' Sam said incredulously. 'But I've got a switch,' said Wilder. 'The guy marries this woman, then finds out she's not his mother. Then he kills himself.'"

I laughed. The silly story reminded me of something our drama teacher told us at school. I told Mason about it. The flames from the logs leaped high in the fireplace. I hadn't lit a fire in a long time.

"Our teacher said that in his opinion the Sophocles *Oedipus* wasn't really a tragedy, not in the way people thought. He said that Oedipus knew all along that he had killed his father. He knew that he had married his mother. He knew everything. He did everything deliberately. He just thought he could get away with it. He believed he could defeat the gods, and cheat his fate. The tragedy, according to my teacher, was that people always thought they could beat the system, like gamblers."

"That's not exactly a joke," Mason said.

"I know. It was just something I remembered."

"This is a night for jokes," he said.

"You're right," I said. "This is no time to be existential."

I threw my wig and the black silk gloves into the flames. It was the end of the masquerade.

We finally got into bed, God knows when. I was drunk by then. Mason still seemed sober. He switched on the television.

"Not *Gala* again," I said.

"No, no. That's past. It doesn't exist anymore."

He selected a channel that was rerunning an episode of "Hawaii Five-O." Someone had been murdered. We watched the screen. Larry Campbell just didn't exist anymore.

Mason made love to me as I slumbered. It was love, misty, not clear. Things dissolved. Then they faded.

The last thing I remember as I drifted into sleep was the TV voice of Jack Lord addressing his sidekick, James McArthur. That was quite clear: "Book him, Dan-o," said McGarrett. "Murder One."

# PART THREE

# 36

# AFTERWARD

You hear about men's hair turning white in the course of a single night. Well, checking the mirror the morning after Larry Campbell's death, I saw that my hair had stayed the same. It was very dark and wavy like everything else in my head.

It took me days, weeks, just to accept what had happened. During that time my life seemed to have changed gear completely. To begin with, I thought simply, I'm an accomplice to murder. Murder. It was murder, for Christ's sake.

The morning after, Ursula was more cheerful than I had ever seen her. Her wry humor was transformed into smiling lightheartedness.

"What shall I wear? The red? The black? No, something new. What do you think of this?" She held up a lavender dress I hadn't seen before.

She was blooming. She put on the radio, which she'd never done before, and danced to the music as she dressed. It was like the first morning of a honeymoon. I smiled with her but I was numb. I went along with her mood. I danced with her in the bedroom.

I was dizzy with apprehension. I had the impression she had bought the lavender dress for this very occasion.

Why the fuck hadn't I stopped her in the motel room? Why? I had had the chance. Why didn't I act? I just let her do it. More than that. I went along with her. I caught sight of us in the mirror as we danced. It was madness. We were like tabloid killers exulting over our crime.

We stopped off on the way to the office at the Beverly Hills Hotel. Ursula wanted a real California breakfast: pineapple, berries, papaya, herb tea, among the flowers on the patio. It was perfect. Strange fruit, bitter tea. We were on our way to death row.

217

"Wait a minute," I said. I put down my forkful of bleeding red berries. "Today is Saturday. Why are we going to the office?"

"You're right." She laughed out loud. "Aren't we silly? We've got the whole day in front of us. It's great. What shall we do?"

I thought, We could turn ourselves in. Get it over with. Some black humor seemed appropriate, but I said nothing. I felt sure her ridiculously happy mood would change when the truth struck her. Meantime, stay cool and wait.

I said, "You decide what to do."

She thought for a while. "I'd like to swim. Where shall we go?"

"You have a pool, don't you?"

"It's filthy, the water. The pool man's stopped coming. I want to go somewhere nice."

We could go to the Bel Age hotel, I thought. Occasionally I went there myself to cool off.

We drove into West Hollywood. The valet took my car and we walked into the lobby. Ursula was still in high spirits. She put her arm around my waist.

"Damn. I forgot my shorts," I said.

"Don't worry. I'll buy you a pair."

She took my hand and led me to the hotel shop. She chose a pair of white shorts, paid for them, and gave them to me with a kiss.

I changed in the men's room and came out onto the roof. There were four or five people around the pool. I looked for Ursula. She was already in the water, swimming below the surface. She wore a dark one-piece swimsuit. I eased myself down. I shivered. She swam toward me. As she broke the surface next to me, I realized that the black suit was the one she had worn in the motel. The black costume of murder. She put her pale thin arms around me.

"I feel so fresh."

What was she trying to do, wash away her guilt, our guilt?

She turned over on her back and floated away. I watched her. A terrible thought occurred to me. Swim after her, pull her down, hold her under, drown her. It would be so easy,

218

except that people were watching. I swam toward her, feeling like a murderer. She had made me feel that way.

"Why did you put that suit on?"

"It suits me," she said. "Don't you like me in black?"

"Don't make jokes."

"I'll take it off if you like."

She stood up in the shallow end of the pool and started to undo the back.

"Ursula!" I plunged toward her.

When I reached her, she pulled the suit down to her waist. Her small breasts and dark nipples shone in the sunlight.

"Are you crazy?" I knew everyone around the pool must have been watching.

"Don't be embarrassed."

"I'm not embarrassed." And it was true. I wasn't. Perhaps I ought to have been. But the truth was, I was suddenly proud that she was with me, that she didn't care about other people. How many women would undress in public just to show how much they wanted you?

I took her head in my hands and kissed her open mouth. Her skin squeaked against mine. She put her hand into the back of my white shorts and squeezed my bottom underwater.

"I want you so much," she whispered. "Let's find somewhere."

"We could get a room here in the hotel."

"No, not in a hotel. Somewhere else."

I now felt foolish for suggesting that. We had had enough of hotels, motel rooms. I reached down and, in full view of the poolside, I drew the black material up, covered her breasts carefully, turned her around, and did up the short zipper at the back. I put my arms around her thighs and lifted her up into my arms. I waded through the water waist high and climbed the tiled steps carrying her, with her arms tight around my neck. I turned at the sound of clapping. It came from two laughing men beside the pool.

She didn't want to go home. I didn't want to go to the office. There was no bed in my old apartment. So I took her to Felicity's apartment. I told myself it was just the nearest

219

place. Ursula didn't ask me where we were going. She watched me unlocking the array of seven locks on the door. She said nothing. We went in, me leading the way into the murder room.

The apartment had been cleaned. It was tidy. It looked different now. I had to look at the place on the floor where I had seen her lying dead. Her? Did I think of Felicity now as her, as a woman who used to live here?

Ursula went to the refrigerator and looked inside. She discovered two bottles of Stoli. It was as if she was in a hotel room raiding the minibar. She held up the bottle.

"Want one?"

"No."

She poured herself a half wineglass of vodka. Then she took off her shoes and put them in the refrigerator, pushing the door closed with the heel of her right foot. I followed her into the bedroom.

"You know, don't you, I'd do anything for you. Anything." She swallowed the vodka at a gulp.

"Anything?"

"Everything."

"Do you masturbate?"

"When I think of you."

"Show me."

"That was Gala. I'm not Gala."

"You said anything."

She looked at me, then suddenly threw herself onto the bed. She bounced face down. I thought she was going to cry. I went to the bed, my mother's bed, and knelt down. I put out my hand to touch her shoulder. I stopped my hand in midair. Her left hand was moving. She began to stroke her thighs with her palm. I watched. She was like a mechanical doll or a programmed ballet dancer. Only her arm and hand moved. Otherwise, her whole body was still.

She pressed her fingers into the material of her lavender dress. She moved them in small circles. I waited for her legs to move. They didn't. She opened her eyes and looked at me. I wanted to undress her, but I knew that if I touched her now, it would change the mood, break the spell. She was doing what I had asked. She must finish it herself.

For a time it seemed as if she didn't belong to me or to

220

anyone except herself. Her finger movements changed. She was opening her lips beneath the silk of her dress. Watching her, my body tensed. I resisted touching myself. I wanted to kiss her moving fingers. I would wait.

There seemed a great distance between us. We were in our own worlds, joined by sensuality, separated by a criminal act. How could we stay together now? Impossible. We didn't fit. Nothing fit. It was all so lonely.

She watched me intently as she began to come. I thought she smiled. Then I saw tears form in her eyes. Her mouth opened slightly. For the first time I could hear her breathing. A distant cry came from her lips. Her legs moved apart, then closed. She twisted suddenly onto her right side, away from me. I couldn't see her face as her body shook. She began to convulse. She threw herself back again to face me. Her face seemed contorted with pain. She cried out. She took her hand and thrust the fingers into her mouth. Her teeth bit into the bone. She lurched. She grappled with what seemed like invisible ropes tying her to the bed. I was watching a woman dying.

It was quite different from our sex together. Her last agonizing throes, like an epileptic fit, scared me. She had never come like that with me. Her body twisted inside the soft lavender dress, jacked violently across my mother's bed. She could not break loose. She was dying under torture. And I was her tormentor. Having thought of myself as her victim yesterday, I now saw myself as her nemesis. What she had done for me I had somehow made her do.

I suddenly felt a savage pain in my head. That twisting female form in front of me was a projection of my own desperation. I gritted my teeth as she started to shout. Her cries of sex were coming from me. There was a pop in my head; a blood vessel seemed to explode. Cords of restraint snapped in my body, in my thighs, in my shoulders.

She was quivering as I climbed onto the bed and pulled up her dress. Her chalk white panties were soaking. Underneath the material her black hair was like a bruise. I wrenched the panties away, down her thighs. I didn't pull them off. The pain in my head was intense. There was no time to take off my pants. I wanted her sex in my mouth.

I sucked and spat. I pushed her legs apart, wide, wider.

221

My mouth, my nose, my chin, all ran with her liquid. I put my hands under her and clenched her buttocks. As I sucked her clitoris, I pushed two fingers of my right hand into her from behind.

Her pelvis began to rotate moving my hand upward, clear of the bedcover. She started to come again. She closed her thighs, sharply trapping my hand. Far away, as if in another place, I too began to come. My penis, held tightly in my pants, ached for freedom. Her gasping orgasm became mine. We were apart together. I shouted into her thighs, a muffled ecstasy. God, I love you.

Afterward, as she licked my face, and the pain had gone, I remembered I had said that. But was it a true confession to her, something I had never before admitted, or was it a different statement of fact? Could it be that it was not her I loved, but myself?

# 37

# THE SLAP

Ursula handed me the *Times*, pointing to a brief report headed AGENT FOUND DEAD. She made no comment and went on with her phone call as if the item was no more significant than a piece of ephemeral gossip in the *Hollywood Reporter.* It was a piece simply stating that the body of Larry Campbell had been discovered in the motel room and that police were investigating the case. I still had the paper in my hand when Os came into the office.

"Well, what do you know?" Os also had the paper, folded open at the same page.

"Terrible thing," I said.

"For who? Listen, kiddo, you've got yourself a new client."

Os tried not to smile as he held out his hand to me. We shook hands. He turned to Ursula.

"What about a drink?"

"You're not thinking of celebrating a man's death, are you?" I said.

"I most certainly am." Os suddenly put his arms around me. He hugged me and gave me a kiss.

When Ursula brought the Bollinger from the fridge, Os kissed her too.

"There's going to be a lot of happy people around town this morning," Os said.

"Was he really that bad a guy?" Ursula asked.

"He was a monster."

"He had courage though. From what I hear he didn't give a damn about anyone."

Ursula sounded as if she meant what she said. Did she regret what she had done? No. There was a decisive tone to her conversation. So how the fuck could she say that? Talk about masks. This new one was harder to penetrate than any before.

"I wonder who did it," Os said. "What was Larry doing in that motel room?"

"What does anyone do in a motel room?" she said.

"You don't know that." She had to quit talking like this. It was all very well to be bold, but this was dangerous. Something could slip out. What would Os say if he knew? Would he go to the cops?

As she bent down to pour more champagne into my glass, I saw those small pale breasts through the opening of her black dress, just as I had in the mirror of the hotel passage in what now seemed like an earlier existence. Inexplicably, my heart melted. Before, my cock had hardened in response to the same sight. It was a surge of affection, soft memory, a sadness, a new sensation for me.

"I hope they don't catch the guy," Os said. "Do you realize that only thirteen or fourteen percent of all murders committed in this town are solved? That's pretty damn good odds for the murderer, don't you think?"

Os saw the pain in my face.

"Hey, Mason. I didn't mean to say that. I'm sorry. After your mom and everything. I'm sorry."

"That's all right, Os. I'm starting to get over it now."

Os finished his drink, got up, shook hands with me once more, and left, waving at Ursula and blowing her a kiss on his way out.

At the end of the day I drove home, following her car. Home? It was hardly my home. Yet it was the only place to go. The only place I wanted to go.

When I got upstairs she was waiting for me, naked. She kissed me hungrily, lovingly. She wanted me. She was irresistible, as always. We started to make love standing up. I felt strong, physically powerful. There was this creature in my arms, all love. No anger now. All that had gone. As she licked and sucked and clung to me, I felt like a giant with a miniature woman climbing up me.

We lay on the bed. She pulled off my socks. She stroked and kissed my foot.

We had a great time, our sex in silence. The only thing that was different from before was that she didn't reach an orgasm. I came. She didn't.

We had made a kind of peace between us, which was just as well because the next two weeks in the office were the most exciting I had known. When word got around that Os had joined Mason Elliott and Associates, I received a dozen calls from potential clients. I was in demand. I was getting hot. Having been around for years, I was suddenly the new kid in town. And it had come from the murder.

"I'd like to go away for the weekend," Ursula announced.

"Where?"

"Let me think of somewhere. I'll fix it. It'll be a surprise."

Another surprise, I thought. But she was in such a sunny mood that I didn't oppose it. What I really wanted was just to rest up for a couple of days. I was exhausted. I didn't need a trip.

It was lunchtime Saturday when we arrived at the airport. When we got to the Delta desk and she produced the tickets, I had a flash. I knew where she was taking me. I grabbed my ticket and looked at it. Albuquerque.

"We're not going!"

"Don't be silly."

"You lied to me!"

"What are you talking about?"

"We're going back."

I pulled my bag off the weighing machine and walked away across the concourse. She called after me. I didn't turn around. I was dizzy. I found her car in the short-term lot.

"I'll drive."

"No, it's my car."

"I said I'll drive. Give me the keys."

In silence she opened her purse and gave me the keys. I opened the driver's door and got in. I slammed the door. I leaned across and opened the door for her. I started the Honda and moved off before she had closed the passenger door.

"Be careful," she said.

For all my outward determination, I was unsure how to deal with this. I wasn't going to start in on it now, not in the car. I'd let her have it when we got back to the house. I glanced at her once or twice on the way. She was looking at me, waiting, I thought, for the explosion.

Why hadn't she told me everything before? It was senseless. Of course she'd been in New Mexico. Of course she'd been in the hotel. She'd watched me, followed me, burrowed into my life. She'd set a trap for me. I'd taken the bait, swallowed it whole. The outcome was murder. I still had difficulty saying that word, even silently to myself.

I left the bag in the trunk of the car. She followed me into the house like a dog. A bitch. I started in the hall.

"How long had you been following me? Before New Mexico."

"Weeks. I saw you first at the Bel Age pool. You were swimming. Then I saw you again in the bar of the Beverly Wilshire."

"What did you want?"

"I just wanted you."

"That's crazy."

"Is it? Haven't you ever seen someone and wished you knew them?"

"I've never done what you did."

225

"You should be flattered that a woman wanted you that much."

"Flattered? I feel like I've been used."

"Oh dear. Used? Abused? You poor man. It's all right for a man to pursue a woman, isn't it? But if a woman goes after a man, she's crazy. She's sick. She's an abuser."

"Don't talk crap."

"You're angry because your pride's been hurt. Your ridiculous male pride."

She started up the stairs. Now I was following her. We went into the bedroom.

"Kiss me," she said.

"Go fuck yourself." I could feel the blood draining from my face. Involuntarily, I clenched my fists.

"Do you want to hit me?"

Yes, I thought, I do. But I've never hit a woman in my life.

"If you want to, I think you should."

She started to take off her clothes. She pulled them off quickly. It was as if she was getting ready to fuck. She stepped out of her panties, pushing them away with her left foot. She came close to me, her arms at her sides. She looked into my eyes, and waited.

"Hit me."

"Now you're being absurd."

"Am I?"

In a sudden movement of her arm she slapped the flat palm of her hand into my chest.

"Don't try to provoke me. It won't work."

"I have provoked you. Be honest."

"Honest? Boy, you're the paragon of honesty, aren't you?"

"If you want me to apologize for what I've done, you can forget it. But if you want to punish me, that's okay."

"I just want to know why. That's all. That's it."

"No deal. I don't have to explain."

"Look, Ursula—"

She lashed out, striking me in the abdomen. I gasped. I hit her across her left shoulder. She swayed.

"That's better," she whispered. "Now, go for it."

"Stop it." Cold and angry blood was filling my brain. "Stop it now." I was aware that I was really talking to myself.

"Kiss me."

She moved her face toward mine. I slapped her. With all my strength I hit her face. She fell sideways to the bed. Her body slipped off the edge of the bed onto the floor. She lay completely still.

I couldn't believe that I had really hit her. It had seemed like someone else using my hand, my strength. I slid down onto the fur rug beside the bed where she lay.

For a moment I thought that she was dead, that I had killed her. I leaned over her face. Her eyes were closed. Then I saw the pulsing throb of blood in the veins of her neck. She was alive. I breathed deeply. I had no idea how hard I had struck her face. The face that had haunted me. In that moment of violence I had lost all sense of myself.

Ursula opened her eyes and looked up at me. She said nothing. She looked at me as if I were someone she'd never seen before. A complete stranger who, like the king's son in the fairy tale, had woken the sleeping princess. But with an angry slap, not a gentle kiss.

Ursula got up. Her face was distorted in pain. She quietly crossed the bedroom and went into the bathroom. For the first time since I had known her, she closed the door on me.

I sat in a chair and waited. I felt dizzy, as if I had been struck, not her. I saw myself in the long mirror. The bathroom door opened. Ursula appeared draped in a long violet towel. She had put some cream on her face.

"You'd better go," she said. Her voice was calm.

I couldn't read her expression. Apologize. I couldn't. The violence was still in me. She went back into the bathroom and closed the door. I went downstairs. I left her house. I would never see her again.

In the bright sunlight I went crawling back to the womb of the apartment of my childhood. To an earlier mirror, an earlier bedroom.

In my briefcase I carried Felicity's Last Will and Testament. That murder too had changed my life. I knew she had some money, but until I visited her attorney's office I hadn't

227

realized the extent of it. I had imagined that the act of formally drawing up a will would have been alien to my mother's temperament. I half-anticipated that her final gesture, if any, would be another fuck you, Mason. No will, no money, fend for your fucking self.

Her attorney, a predictably Dickensian figure with an anachronistic office in an old downtown building, was quite precise. She owned stocks that were worth in the region of $400,000. A case of her jewelry had been lodged at her bank. The valuation for insurance purposes was $268,300. She had $23,000 in her current account and $200,000 on deposit. Her apartment would fetch around $450,000. The place where I now sat could be put on the market for $290,000. So, with one and a half million coming my way, I was a rich man. And the office was thriving. The office.

I sat at my desk. I tried to read but I couldn't concentrate. I moved to sit at Ursula's desk. What would it be like now, without her? I looked at her pack of cigarettes, the book she had brought to the office, *The Lost Girl* by D. H. Lawrence. I remembered her reading some of that to me one night in bed.

In her desk drawer I found her hairbrush and a comb, some lipstick, and a bottle of perfume called Presence. I had never known its name. That lemony scent I had followed. And her name? Was it really "Baxter"? From the start, what had I been looking for? Was it just sex? She had intrigued me, fascinated me, to the point of obsession. But what was the promise? And the price.

I thought about the police investigation. It had been bad enough with Felicity. Maybe I should go to them now. Confess everything. Tell them about her. Have it all over and done with. But somehow I couldn't do that. She had been incredible to me. When I needed it, she had looked after me. When I wanted affection, she had loved me. She had gone further. She had killed for me. She had done plenty for me. Now I was responsible for her. And I was also afraid of her. She had something on me. If someone asked me if I loved her, what would I say?

When I woke on the sofa bed on Sunday morning, she was there with my shaving things, fresh clothes, and a cup of coffee. She was dressed again in black. I woke to a dream of the past. The present reality was evident in her face, which was bruised on the left cheek. Later, she would explain it to people who asked as a bike accident.

She kissed me sweetly. She stroked my face. Inside, I winced. Was she trying to apologize for me? Saying I know you didn't really mean it. Nothing was said about the fight. It hadn't happened. It was as if there had maybe been an argument between us, a lovers' tiff, that was forgotten now, nobody's fault. By Monday we would be back in action on the phone with office business. Just like old times. It was unnerving.

She was in top form, intellectually that is, during my meeting with Paul Jaspers. We had both read his twenty-page treatment for the screenplay of *La Belle Dame Sans Merci*. We were discussing it before sending the pages over to Joe Ransom for his approval.

"So what do you think?" Paul looked at me, then to her.

"It's terrific," I said.

"Absolutely," she agreed. "Though I'd still like to learn more about her motives. She seems a little too destructive right now. Still a cliché of the femme fatale."

"I agree." As I spoke, I couldn't look at Ursula. She might have been talking about the two of us. I'm not a crazy killer, was what she was implying. Paul explained his intention.

"I thought I'd pretty much covered that area in her relationship with her sister. Her sister understands her because the same thing had happened to her once. But she backed off, the sister, whereas our heroine goes on to the bitter end."

Did Ursula have a sister somewhere? Why had I never asked? I knew so little about her. And here I was passing judgment. How could I know what was behind her actions? I could only judge her by her surface, the things she did.

"A French writer once said, *'Toutes les femmes sont fatales,'*" she said.

"Which means?" I asked her.

"Which means all woman are femme fatales," Paul

translated. "So, given the right circumstances, the right chemistry, if you like, every woman can have that power over her man."

"How about men?"

"Men too, I guess," Paul said.

"Hommes fatals," Ursula said.

# 38

# ON THE BEACH

This was the fourth week since Larry Campbell. I had started to think of my life that way. Before Larry Campbell, after Larry Campbell. To begin with I had read the *Times* every day, looking for information about the progress of the police investigation. There had been a flurry of theories at the beginning. After the second week, the investigation was no longer reported. I relied on talking with Os for clues. The latest thing was that Larry Campbell had been mixed up with the Mob. Maybe he had.

Ursula wasn't interested in the rumors. She didn't read the paper. She didn't ask about it. For her, the matter seemed to be over and done with. She was incredible.

There were some tense moments between us, but no out-and-out fights. Mostly it was a state of underlying unease. When she caught me looking at her, wondering about her thoughts, she became angry. "Stop staring at my bruise."

Sometimes she was touchy. "Don't you like this dress?"

Sometimes she was querulous. "You look as if you want to say something. What?"

There was one question I was curious to ask her. How had she discovered Larry Campbell's secret life? Obviously, he had been in the habit of visiting prostitutes to satisfy his bizarre needs. But how did she know that? She didn't offer the smallest hint.

I had begun to look at the property pages in the *Times*. I needed a place of my own and now I could comfortably afford it. I suppose I needed time off from her, although I would never have admitted it openly. One property in particular attracted me. I called the realtor and went out to see it.

I didn't have to go inside the house to know it was what I wanted, a small shack right on the beach north of Malibu Colony. It had wooden steps leading up from the beach to a deck, a large panoramic window reflecting the Pacific Ocean, a private beach, and a view of a secluded bay.

I followed the real estate lady up the sand-dusted steps, looking around as I went.

"The asking price is six thirty," she said.

"I guess I could make an offer."

"They've already come down twenty," she said sweetly. She had narrow legs that made her look very tall. She unlocked and opened the sliding window. The house reminded me of somewhere. I had been in scores of houses and apartments along the coast but this particular house set up a particular echo. I couldn't place it.

"There are two bedrooms. The master has an en suite bathroom. The other is quite small, but it would make a neat den. Then there's the kitchen and a separate toilet. It's very compact, easy to maintain."

She didn't have to sell me. I knew I didn't want to look any further.

"Is it just for you?"

"How do you mean?"

"I guess I mean do you have a partner?" she said.

"No, no. I'm alone."

"I believe you can get permission to build on another floor, but I'm not quite sure about that."

I didn't care about that. I liked everything just the way it was. Suddenly, looking at the bedroom, which was dark because of the closed blinds, I knew where I'd seen the place before. It was identical to the house in *Gala*. That was it. Even out here I couldn't escape her.

We went outside again. A man was walking his German shepherd along the beach. That could be me in a couple of weeks.

"You know what would go brilliantly with the house?" said the lady, reading my thoughts. "An Akita."

"A what?"

"An Akita."

"I'm very happy with my BMW."

She looked at me as if I was a moron. "An Akita is a dog. A Japanese guard dog."

"One thing at a time," I said.

"Absolutely. That's my motto too. However, if you decide you want one, I know the guy who breeds them."

I decided then and there to make an offer of six ten. I would put four hundred down and get a mortgage for the rest. The bank had already agreed to give me a bridging loan until the probate of Felicity's will. I felt good about it all. Almost free.

On the way back to town along the Pacific Coast Highway I stopped off at Don the Beachcomber's. I wanted to celebrate. By myself. It was midafternoon. The weekday lunch crowd had gone. I sat in the long window overlooking the rocky beach. The tide was coming in fast here. Not like my little bay. That's how I thought of it now. I looked down on a wave as it crashed. A Hawaiian waiter stood beside me, waiting.

"I'll have an alcohol-free mai-tai and a plate of rumaki."

The waiter in the flowered shirt grunted, and left for the dark area of the bar where some serious drinkers were holed up watching a ball game.

Wave upon wave crashed below me. Boom! The sound was loud, seductive. Beyond the surging foam was a broken line of surfers. It was "Hawaii Five-O." It was that night after Larry Campbell. I was back in bed with her.

I had never fucked a sleeping woman before. A strange sensation, but no stranger than the events that preceded it. She was dry, but pliant like a human doll, life-sized, evenly warm. It was, I supposed, a male fantasy of domination. But that wasn't what I felt. When I moved her limbs, arranged her body for myself, entered her, it was as if I was doing it to a dead woman. The word was *necrophilia*.

As I made love to her, she flopped about. Occasionally, she moved. Her muscles tightened slightly before relaxing again. I wasn't trying to animate her. I did nothing to her asleep that I hadn't done before while she was awake. It felt vaguely pornographic. At orgasm I imagined I had killed her. Only my imagination. Afterward, I turned her over and just

232

looked at her body. Never before had I thought a woman's body was so wonderful. I kissed every part of her, from the soles of her feet to her armpits. I was Frankenstein. I had built this monster.

"Mr. Elliott?"

I looked up. The Hawaiian waiter had come back to my table.

"Yes?"

"There's a call for you."

"For me?" How could there be?

"You can take it at the bar."

I followed his orange and purple shirt away from the waves into the pool of darkness. No one could possibly know I was here. I myself hadn't known until half an hour ago. I picked up the phone.

"Hello."

"Mr. Elliott. You're not going to get away with it." The man's voice was muffled, as if he held a handkerchief over his mouth.

"Who is this?"

"You'll find out one day soon." I could hardly hear with the roar of the ball game crowd on TV.

"What are you talking about? Who is this?"

There was a click. The voice had gone, but the panic it had induced in me stayed and grew. Who could it have been? How did they know I was there? It had to be about Larry Campbell. Had I been seen at that motel, seen and recognized? I shivered.

The voice had sounded melodramatic. There was a heavy threat in it. But what threat? No one would call me if they were thinking of going to the cops. It had to be blackmail. Shit. Put it out of your mind, I told myself. You must put it out of your mind. If it's serious, they'll call again. So forget it. Think of something else.

As I drove back to the office I realized I had to tell Ursula about the house at the beach. I didn't know how she was going to take it. It meant I would soon be living in my own house. In her present state of mind I was afraid she would think I was leaving her. In a way I was. I wasn't going to ask her to come and live with me. We would still see each other all the time, I would tell her.

233

She was at her desk when I got to the office. She didn't look up. I was wondering whether she had had a call like mine. This was not the moment to ask. In front of her were the realtor's photographs of the beach house and the purchase details. Ursula got up and closed the door to the passage.

"Why didn't you tell me?" Her voice was cold and calm.

"I was going to tell you when I made the final decision."

"You've already made the decision, Mason. Why aren't you honest with me?"

"Wait a minute. Were you honest with me, about Artesia?"

"I wanted you. Now you don't want me."

"I'm just buying a house. I need a place of my own. I've been a gypsy long enough. I'm selling the apartments and—"

"—why so far away? It's over an hour's drive to here."

"Look, I won't be there all the time."

Her cold manner suddenly caved in to sorrow. "I'll miss you."

"We see each other all day in the office. We sleep together every night. You can't ask for much more."

"I'm not asking for anything. I want you to be happy, that's all." Her voice cracked.

"I'll be happy."

"With or without me?" Was she going to cry?

"I'm not leaving you."

"Why are you guilty?"

"I'm not guilty."

"Look, you didn't do it. I did it. If it ever came to court, I'd tell them you had nothing to do with it."

"I was there, Ursula. I saw it. I was there."

"I wish I hadn't taken you."

"Why did you? You could have done it without me."

"I took you because I love you. I wanted to show you how much I loved you. Don't you understand that?"

"I understand." Intellectually, I understood. But emotionally I still couldn't handle it.

"If you hadn't been there, Mason, I'd be dead. Do you realize that? If you hadn't been there he would have killed me."

Ursula made no attempt to answer the ringing phones. Nor did I. This was a crisis. We were close to the heart of the matter.

"So I owe you, Mason. You saved my life."

It was true, but it wasn't quite the way I saw it, or wanted to.

"I love you. I know you don't like to think about that. It seems to make you guilty."

It was true. I did feel guilty. Why?

"It's all for you. Everything I do."

I folded her in my arms and held her. She was quivering like a bird. Her life was in my hands. For a while I forgot about the muffled voice on the phone.

# 39

# LIES, ALL LIES

Two days later Ursula contracted a stomach bug and left the office early to go home. I hadn't told her that Barbara had called while she had been out at lunch. Barbara wanted to see me. She sounded lonely and lost. So I worked late and then at around eight I drove out to the Palisades.

It was a strange feeling ringing the doorbell at a house where I'd lived for more than a year. Barbara was happy to see me.

"Where are you living now?"

"At the old apartment."

"Can you give me the number?"

How could I give her the number when the phone had been disconnected years ago. I must get it reconnected.

"You know, I can't remember it. I only go there to sleep. I'll call you tomorrow and give it to you."

"How are you coping?"

"Pretty well."

"And Ursula, how is she? I like her."

"Fine. She's very efficient." I had to find something to talk about where I didn't have to lie.

"I'm glad you came. I thought maybe you wouldn't, not after the way I behaved."

"You look tired."

"Things haven't been going too well. The shop's not making it."

"What's wrong?"

"I'm already behind a month with the rent. But really the stuff just isn't selling."

Barbara opened a bottle of wine. We sat in the kitchen as we used to in the evenings. In the weeks living with Ursula we never once sat in the kitchen.

"I know I overreacted about Alexis. I'm sorry."

"It wasn't true, that letter. I didn't have an affair with her. It was all in her mind."

Barbara nodded. "Would you consider . . . getting back together?"

I knew this was coming.

"Not right now."

What should I have said? The truth was I hadn't even missed her. But now I felt a wave of nostalgia. We'd had some good times together. I missed the comforts. Ursula left no room for ordinary life.

Barbara wanted me to stay. She kissed me, pressed her body against me, whispered in my ear.

"You're still the only guy for me."

Barbara was a good woman and didn't deserve this. While she was out of the room, I wrote her a check for five thousand dollars and pinned it to the board in the kitchen. Then I lied again. I said I had to meet someone for a late dinner.

Barbara hugged me at the door.

"I'll keep in touch," I said.

As I left I remembered that I hadn't told her about the house at the beach. Why not? I seemed to be on a binge of deception.

I drove back along Sunset. I thought again about that voice on the phone. There had been no more calls. It was a mystery. I knew there was going to be a payoff and that it wouldn't be pleasant.

The reflection of a headlight appeared in my rearview

mirror. I adjusted the mirror, and looked over my shoulder. A blinding, single beam. Not from the twin headlights of a car. This was a motorcycle.

It couldn't be her. Couldn't be. She was at home sick. I hadn't called earlier to see how she was. It could be her.

The headlight flooded the interior of my car as the bike came nearer. It was impossible to make out the rider. I put up my hand, flapping it downward to tell him to dip the lights. There was no response. My skin prickled. After a few moments the bike turned left. I saw nothing of the rider. It was dark again. So it wasn't her.

Had someone been following me? Was the voice on the phone the motorcycle rider? I turned up Benedict and onto La Cielo. I parked outside the house. There were no lights visible. I got out and went to the front door. I hesitated. I didn't go in. I had to check.

I went to the garage. I walked toward the bike, which was covered by a tarpaulin. Slowly I lifted the tarp. I touched the engine. The metal was warm. It had been her.

She must have been watching Barbara's house. She must have seen the last hug and kiss at the door. It had been innocent. But not to her. True or false, it wouldn't matter. The beach house again. Everything I did now became a criminal act.

She was in bed reading a book of poems. She looked up. I was waiting for it. She smiled and put down her book, marking a page with a business card.

"I'm feeling much better," she said.

"I'm glad."

"Come here and give me a kiss."

I kissed her. She put her arms around my neck and clung to me. Maybe I'd been wrong about the bike. Perhaps she had gone for a ride earlier in the evening. She did that sometimes. A ride seemed to help her clear her head, she told me. Maybe I was being overly suspicious, guilty without cause. After all, she would have had to race back along a lot of winding roads to beat me back to the house. And then get undressed and into bed.

Maybe I was imagining it all. I took my clothes off and got into bed. We slept.

I woke up choking. I opened my eyes. The bedroom was

237

full of smoke. Flames were licking at the drapes. I jumped out of bed. The room was on fire. I yelled at Ursula, who was apparently asleep. She opened her eyes but didn't move, didn't try to get up.

"Ursula!" I screamed at her. "What's the matter with you!"

I suddenly realized she wasn't naked. She had been naked when we had fallen asleep. Now she was wearing a long white dress. It was the wedding dress I had seen hanging in the closet and wondered about. The flames were growing like crazy plants. I looked around desperately. I tore blankets off the bed. I managed to put out a couple of small fires. It was nowhere near enough.

"Ursula, get up! For God's sake!"

I got hold of her arms and started to haul her out of the bed. She was a deadweight. She wasn't unconscious, but made no effort. She didn't want to be saved. She had to be saved.

I dragged her into the bathroom. There was no fire there. Maybe I should have pulled her out of the bedroom. I was panicked and all I could think of was that there was water in the bathroom and the door could be shut against the smoke and flames. I yelled at her to get in the bathtub. Hopeless. She didn't seem to hear.

It seemed too fucking slow. It took an age to drag her across the room, her white-clad body bringing the Oriental rug with her weight. I got a flash of the woman pulling the girl's body along that hotel passage. Everything seemed to be happening twice.

Finally I slammed the bathroom door, leaving her on the floor with the rug.

I remembered seeing a fire extinguisher in the garage on the wall above the bike. I tripped down the stairs, falling heavily. But I felt no pain. I only heard the cracking of my bones on the wood as I slipped and tumbled.

I raced to the kitchen. I wrenched open the door to the garage. Something broke around the lock. In my nostrils I could still smell the smoke from the bedroom. In my mind I saw the unstoppable progress of the fire, the drapes, the clothes, the bed.

I struggled with the heavy fire extinguisher. It was as old

as the house. It had never been used. Maybe it wouldn't work. I ripped the canister from its rusted clips on the brick wall. I went back into the kitchen fumbling with the heavy weapon. I desperately tried to extend the trumpet-shaped nozzle to a right angle. At the same time I was trying to read the instructions. Hopeless. I climbed the stairs two at a time, swearing at everything, at her, at myself.

In my head I could see the flames racing toward the bathroom eager to embrace Ursula, seeking her out, tracking her down. I kicked the bedroom door wide open. The inferno was enjoying itself. I choked in the smoke.

I pressed the lever on the canister. It was stiff. I put the thing on the floor, grappling with it. I had to kick the lever with the side of my naked foot. I didn't feel a thing. The extinguisher started to spurt with white foam. I struggled to pick it up, to aim it. It had a will of its own. It bucked wildly, making up for its lack of use in an uncontrollable spasm of release.

I started on the drapes. The roaring fluid attacked the flames. I choked. It appeared to be working, but I lost control of the thing for a moment. The canister spun around in my hands with its own force. I went with it. Through the smoke I saw the bathroom door was open. Open!

"Ursula!" I had gotten the canister under control. I sprayed the desk and the open wardrobe. I was enveloped in a thick mist of smoke and spray. Then I saw her.

She was standing by the window among the smoldering drapes, looking out. Her back was toward me. Even in my panic I could see that she hadn't been able to do up the line of silk-covered buttons at the back of the white dress. Like the drapes, I had covered her in white foam. There were no more flames.

I turned her around. She had a distant expression on her face, unconnected with what was happening. She was staring at something out of the window.

"Thank you." That was all she said, without looking at me.

I took her arm and sat her on the side of the foamy bed. I went back to the window and opened it to let the smoke out.

"Why didn't you stay in the bathroom?" I was still choking. She didn't answer. My questions were a waste of time. Ursula was somewhere else. I sat down next to her.

The white wedding dress was a shroud. She was silent.

I left her and started ineffectually to clear up the mess. I picked things up, moved them, wiped them, put them back somewhere else. From time to time I glanced at her. She got up from the bed and went back to the window.

I was living with a madwoman. A woman I didn't properly know or understand. A woman who had tried to kill us both, who would probably try again.

# 40

# THE HELMET

I was living a schizophrenic life. In the daylight hours she and I ran the office, efficiently and without argument. We were a great team. When darkness fell it was different. She was another woman. I was another man. We lived another life.

Ursula didn't come into the office for two days after the fire. She supervised the men who came in to clear up the bedroom. When she did appear, she was fine, cool as ever. But in those two days I needed a secretary. I hired a temp named Diana to answer the phones. The work load was heavier than I'd ever known it. I started at eight in the morning and seldom left before eight or nine at night.

Diana, who had once worked in Larry Campbell's office, occupied Ursula's desk. When Ursula returned we had to get another desk and put it into my office. The place had always been small. Now it was cramped. There was no privacy. That was the price I paid for being so busy. When Barbara called, Ursula heard everything I said. I became guarded about things I had no reason to be guarded about. I often sounded awkward on the phone without reason. When I wanted to call a meeting, there wasn't room. I went out more to meet people.

During office hours Ursula was unfailingly pleasant. She showed no sign of irritation or anger, no jealousy toward Diana, who was a secretary in the Alexis mold. At night though it was another matter.

She became insomniac. And that kept me awake too. She would read, take a bath, wander about the house. Our lovemaking altered. There were times when she couldn't bear to be touched. Other times she wanted sex for hours on end. I would take my cue from her. One night I woke to find her watching *Gala.* Could she have become nostalgic about a porn flick?

I had to talk to someone. But who? Not Os. Certainly not Barbara. When she had found the check, she called to tell me that she couldn't accept it. I told her I'd pay it directly into her account if she didn't. She was almost in tears. She had her own problems. I wanted to help her. I did help her. But she couldn't help me.

When I bumped into Kate from down the passage, I thought of talking to her. She was a professional, after all. But that would have sounded like "Doctor, I've got this friend . . ." Then I thought of Paul Jaspers. I wondered if I could trust him. He was kind of clever with female psychology. He would understand. He was already writing a version of my story in *La Belle Dame Sans Merci.* And he liked Ursula. They had always been on the same wavelength in our script conferences.

I arranged to meet Paul in a bar. I was very selective in what I told him. I stuck to my affair with Ursula and the fire.

"Leave her," Paul said simply. "Get rid of her. She's bad trouble, Mason."

I hadn't expected that. I suppose I had wanted a sympathetic solution. When he said it, I felt a rush of affection for Ursula. I couldn't just cast her out of my life. I wanted her, but not the way she was now.

"She's an obsessive. And her obsession seems to be you. Unless you're just as obsessed with her, it'll be pain all the way."

"I thought about letting her go. I couldn't do it."

"Maybe there's something else you're not telling me," Paul said. He was an acute kid.

"I'm not sure why she's so obsessed with me."

241

"It may not actually be you. Obsessives are involved in a pattern. They're drawn toward people who remind them of people in their past. Like guys who marry the same kind of girl over and over."

"I don't know much about her past. She doesn't talk."

"Let her go," Paul said firmly.

"Why? Do you want her?" I didn't know why I said that.

"She's very attractive in a sexy femme fatale sort of way."

I wondered whether to tell Paul about *Gala*. I wondered if Joe Ransom had said anything to him. I decided not to. I wasn't getting any closer to a solution.

"I've got a confession to make," Paul said after a couple of martinis.

"What? You know something about her?" Not another revelation. Or had he slept with her?

"Not about her. The other day I was driving along Highway One and I saw your car parked in the lot at Don the Beachcomber's."

"It was you on the phone."

"Yes."

"You little shit." I was angry.

"I know. I should've come in. I couldn't resist it."

"Just for that, you can pick up the tab." I had to smile. "In the future keep that sort of stuff for your scripts."

"Sorry about that. It's no way to treat your agent, is it?"

"I'm not in the mood for practical jokes at the moment."

"As your emotional agent, I've given you my advice. It's not much use, is it?"

"I wanted to know what you thought. And you told me."

"You told me once, I remember. 'Paul, you don't need an agent to get you things. You really need an agent to get you out of things.'"

In a way, I was thankful to Paul for his dumb practical joke. It reminded me not to be so jumpy. When I left the bar I felt lighter.

I bought Ursula a bunch of flowers. I took them home that night. I don't know what I was trying to say with them. It was strange. I had never given her anything before. No sentimental chocolates. No book. I wouldn't have dared guess her taste. No clothes, of course. And certainly no perfume.

I found her in the bathroom, making up in the mirror.

"Let's go out to dinner," she said. "I feel like going out."

She too was in a lighter mood. That was nice. Then I saw her made-up face as she turned to me, smiling.

The bruise from my slap, which had finally disappeared two weeks ago, was back. She had made up her face to reproduce the livid bruise on her cheek and temple.

"Why are you doing that?" I stood beside her, holding the bunch of flowers. What was she trying to say? That she hadn't forgotten, that she despised me, or what?

"Are those for me?" She ducked the question and took the flowers from my hand. She sniffed them.

"Are they orchids? How appropriate."

"They're lilies," I said. They were a stupid choice. They reminded her of the motel room and Larry Campbell.

"Thank you." She got to her feet and kissed me. "It's funny you should bring me something. I've got a present for you too."

She took me by the hand and led me to the bed. There was a gift-wrapped box on the covers.

"I hope you like it." She smiled sweetly. Nothing in her voice or manner conveyed the craziness of her action. I looked at the painted bruise on her face. I opened the present. I couldn't begin to guess what it was. It weighed about two pounds. Inside the wrapping that was a design of interlocking heads was a box about eighteen inches square. I opened it almost fearfully.

Inside the box was a shining, dark blue motorcycle helmet.

"Try it on. I think it's the right size. I measured your head while you were asleep."

I pulled away the polyethylene that covered it. She drew me to the mirror and helped me with the helmet. I felt numb.

"It fits perfectly." It did. I pressed it to my skull. She arranged the straps under my chin.

"Thank you," I said. This was madness.

She closed the tinted visor. I looked at myself. A spaceman in a striped suit. I felt a spasm of claustrophobia.

"Now we can go for a ride safely," she said. Her voice sounded a dull echo inside the helmet.

She insisted we go to dinner by bike. She had made a reservation at Casablanca, a Mexican restaurant on Lincoln Boulevard. I felt idiotic handing the hatcheck girl my helmet. Ursula ordered far too much food for us. I had no appetite.

During the meal she opened her purse and took out an envelope. It was addressed "To Whom It May Concern." It had been opened. I fished inside and took out the single sheet of paper on which was typed the message: "We saw you. We know what you did. We'll be in touch."

I was unnerved.

"When did you get this?" I heard myself say.

"Yesterday."

"Yesterday? Why didn't you tell me before?"

I looked at the note. It was typed on plain paper. Nothing distinctive about it. After the relief of the discovery of Paul's practical joke, all my fears were back in force. Someone had seen us. Someone at the motel. The Casablanca was crowded and hot. I was chilled. The breeze from the air-conditioners turned the sweat on my forehead to frost.

"Why did you keep it? You had it yesterday."

"Or maybe it was the day before," she said, as if she couldn't quite recall, it was all so long ago.

I slammed my fist down on the table. The plates jumped. Ursula didn't jump.

"I can't remember."

I looked around the restaurant. It was black and white and silver, decorated with stills from Bogart movies. It was meant to be cool in order to counter the spicy food. Diners looked at us, startled by the noise of my clenched fist on the table. Violence reared up in me. I grabbed her wrist. I was hurting her.

"You can't remember! How did you know it was meant for you? It might have been sent to me." Her craziness infected me. What did that mean, "To Whom It May Concern?" "Take that shit off your face."

I took her hand and brutally wiped it across her face, over the made-up bruise. I must have yelled at her, because the headwaiter came over to our table. I felt like hitting him too.

"If you guys want to fight," said Manuel, "and it looks like you do"—he nodded at the bruise on Ursula's face—"then fine. But not in here, *por favor*."

244

"We're leaving," I said.

"I'm paying," she said.

"As long as there's no fighting," he said.

"That's all right," said Ursula, as she opened her purse. "I can handle him."

She pulled out a pair of nail scissors with her right hand. She started to stab the points between the splayed fingers of her left hand.

"He loves me." Stab. "He loves me not." Stab. "He loves me." Stab. The twin points of the scissors cut the skin of her wedding finger below the center knuckle.

"Ursula!" I didn't want her to hurt herself.

"He loves me not."

I pulled the scissors from her grasp. She slapped my hand. The headwaiter brought the check. Blood dripped from her fingers onto the fifty-dollar bill. On the way out the hat-check girl reminded me of the hatcheck girl at the Casa Vega that night. I took my helmet. I gave her a dollar. I was through with Mexican restaurants. Was I through with Ursula?

We were crossing the parking lot. I didn't want to get on the bike. I was about to say so. She threw her arms around me and buried her face in my neck.

"Do you love me?"

"Yes."

"I love you. I love you so much I want to hurt you."

I wondered if I felt the same way. It seemed true for me too.

"Do you want to be rid of me?" she asked.

"Yes and no."

"I understand." She climbed onto the bike. "Let's go down to the beach."

"We ought to go home."

"I want to make love to you on the beach."

"It's a bit cold."

"I'll warm you up. I'm going to get sand in my cunt."

"You're nuts."

"Do you really think so?"

How could I not get on the bike? I was nervous, but to get a cab home now would be pathetic.

"Let's go," I said, as if it had all been my idea. And we went, huddled together, like lovers.

We got off Lincoln and went on Rose toward the beach in that no-man's-land between Santa Monica and Venice. I guessed she was headed to Venice Pier, or what was left of it. She had talked about it two or three times. She loved it, she had said, because it wasn't there anymore, except on the maps that they hadn't changed.

She turned right on Main Street and went north, away from Venice. I thought she might after all be going back home. I expected her to take a right at Sunset. But she went on, on to the Pacific Coast Highway.

"Where are we going?" I shouted in her ear.

She didn't answer. Maybe she hadn't heard. The lights were all green in her favor. There was no stopping her now. I knew where she was going. To Malibu. To my house on the beach. I knew it.

From inside my helmet I looked at the back of her helmet. Reflected in it, passing streetlights and the headlights of cars were like stars moving in an anarchic pattern. And in the center I saw the reflection of my own helmet.

I was claustrophobic. I wanted to take the thing off. For Christ's sake, stop this fucking bike, pull over and let's talk. I couldn't stand not being able to speak. I found it hard even to breathe. I pushed up the visor. The cold night air streamed onto my sweating face. I yelled at her. There was no response. I didn't want to tap her on the back in case she did something stupid with the bike.

She knew exactly where my house was. She knew the turn-off to the beach as if she'd driven it a thousand times. She'd probably been out here on her own. She could even have followed me. It made me dizzy, imagining what she might have done.

She stopped in back of the house. I got off the bike first. I waited. She settled the machine and started to walk toward the house. I called after her. She didn't answer. She hadn't raised her visor. She went around the house to the deck overlooking the cold ocean. She lifted the visor of her helmet.

"Aren't you going to invite me in?"

"I don't have the keys yet."

She lowered the visor. Before I knew what she was doing, she started to butt the glass door. Her helmet smacked again and again at the glass. I grabbed her around the waist and pulled her away.

"What the fuck do you think you're doing?"

She tried again. This time I used all my strength and wrenched her so violently that she fell over backward on the deck. I got down beside her and pulled off her helmet.

I expected her to struggle, but she didn't. The helmet was off. Her face was bathed in sweat, shining in the moonlight. Her black hair was plastered to her skull.

"What's the matter with you?" It was a dumb question. She didn't know the answer. She was gripped by some desire to hurt, to break, to destroy something. But that wasn't going to be me.

"I don't lock my house," she whispered. "You can come and go as you want."

She got to her feet. She looked at me. I had no idea what she was thinking. She turned away from me and started to take off her leathers.

"What are you doing? It's freezing." I tried to stop her. She pushed me away, but quite gently. She carefully removed her jacket. She took off her bra. She stood in her pants and boots. She walked to the wooden banister. Holding the rail with one hand, she lifted one leg to me.

"Help me take them off."

"Ursula. This is crazy."

"Help me. Please."

She was calm now. I looked across the deserted silvery beach, the white breakers in the distance, the half-moon on the ocean. I went to her, knelt before her, and tugged the boot off. She lowered her naked foot and raised the other leg.

"It's cold out here."

"We can't go inside, can we?"

I slowly pulled off the other boot, gripping the heel. I wanted to shake her, maybe even to hit her. But we'd been through that. I watched her, fascinated. She was from another planet. She lifted a leg again and started to take off her leather pants. I was inside one of my first fantasies about the woman in black. She threw the red panties at my face.

I watched as she walked naked down the sandy steps to

the beach below. I shouted at her to come back. She turned and waved. She ran across the beach, toward the ocean. I went after her. She stopped, waiting for me to catch up.

"Don't just stand there. Take your clothes off."

"You're not going to swim?"

"No, I'm not going to swim. I'm not crazy," she said.

She started to take off my jacket.

"Don't move. Let me undress you."

I shivered, because it was cold and because of what was happening, which struck me as grotesque. She knelt down, unzipped me, and pulled my pants down to my ankles. She nuzzled my briefs.

"I'll make a deal with you. I'm going to make love to you. If you don't come, you can leave me."

"What are you talking about?" My cock was soft.

She put her tongue into my navel, parting my shirt.

"That's what you want, isn't it? To leave me. Here's your chance. If I can't make you come, you don't have to see me ever again. We'll call it quits."

I had no answer. It was an insane challenge. In a crazy way it could be a way out. I was covered in goose bumps. Maybe I wouldn't come anyway. Would she really not see me again?

When she removed my shoes and socks, I was really shivering. The pale sand was like powdered ice. Then she set about me. She didn't ask me to lie down. She did everything standing up. She moved around me as if I were a statue she'd made. She kissed and stroked me. When she thought I was too cold, she hugged me, staying still for minutes at a time. I grew warmer. I became hard without her moving. There was a moment when we felt like one person.

There was nothing difficult about it. She stood on tiptoe and slid my cock into her. She clung to me, moving very slowly back and forth, circling round my cock. She made no attempt to go faster. The mechanical evenness of it all warmed me through and through. I forgot all about the deal. My mind emptied. I no longer felt cold.

When I came it was very slowly and it went on. Her fingers pressed into my flesh. She couldn't stay up on her toes any longer. She pulled me down with her. We might have

248

been in a warm bath. We splashed in the sand for a while, then lay still in each other's arms. At that moment I felt nothing but love for this woman.

"Oh, Mason."

I heard her voice against the sound of the surf. I had no recollection what time it was when we got back onto the bike.

I said, "Aren't you worried? About who sent the note?"

She said, "Whoever they are, we'll get them."

# 41

# ONLY CHILDREN

G et rid of her."

All night long, waking and slumbering, Paul Jaspers' instruction drummed in my head.

"She's bad trouble."

It was undeniable. But was she really trying to destroy me? Or just destroy herself? How could I have let it go this far? I watched her sleep, beautiful as always, peaceful in her expression, but inside her there was another woman.

She had washed the bruise off her face. I looked at her. It would be so simple to finish it now. Just kill her as she slept. Smother her with her favorite pillow. Simple. But for that you'd have to be a murderer.

I tried to sleep, to find peace. I longed to be in my house at the beach, alone, in freedom. But how could I be free when there was someone out there, maybe not far from where I now lay, who knew about Larry Campbell, who could finish the whole thing for both of us?

She woke when I brought her a cup of coffee.

"You don't have to come into the office if you don't feel like it."

"What do you mean?" She was still drowsy.

I modified it. "Come in later."

She said nothing for a few moments. Her silence was always hard to deal with. Silence was her way of lying. If you don't want to speak the truth, silence is the easiest way.

"It's such a pity," she said.

"What is?"

"What's happening to us."

I wanted to say something like, whose fault is that?

"We can't seem to stop it," she said. "It's like a virus."

"We'll get through it."

She took both my hands and pressed them to her breast. "Will we?"

How could I be angry? I was loved.

She didn't come into the office with me. She said she'd be along later.

The police called at around ten. The tingling and the sweat came back in a rush. The guilt. This could be it.

"We're holding a man who has confessed to your mother's murder."

I must have sighed with relief. When I thought of Felicity's murder it was so very far away, like the memory of a childhood trauma. It had no connection to my current anxiety. But having the police revive it drew that memory back into the mysterious and violent experience that now engulfed me.

Apparently the guy who had confessed had killed two other elderly women during the past year. He had sexually assaulted them, sodomizing them before suffocating them. What concerned the police was that Felicity had not been sexually assaulted before she died. I suddenly had a funny thought. Felicity would be angry if she thought that she had died without a sexual connection. In a life devoted to sex, it was an irony that she had been murdered in such a chaste way.

I was opening the mail when Os called. I had just done a very good deal for him. But that wasn't what he wanted to talk about.

"I just had a visit from the cops," he said. "They wanted to know where I was when Larry was killed."

"So you told them."

"I had to. Trouble is, I was with Sophie at her apartment. Now my wife's gone ape-shit. She's thrown me out."

"Wives," I said. "She'll get over it." I sounded confident. I wasn't though. In my sort-of-marriage to Ursula, she hadn't gotten over anything.

I called Diana into my office to dictate a couple of letters. Her face was blotched with tears.

"What's the matter?"

"Nothing." She sat down, her shorthand pad ready.

"No, tell me, please."

"I can't."

"Diana. Go on. Tell me. What is it?"

"I just had a call from Ursula." She looked away from me.

"From Ursula? What about?" My neck prickled.

"She accused me of . . . having an affair with you. Behind her back. She said we were sleeping together."

"She said what!"

"She was so angry. I don't think I can stay here. I think I should leave."

I grabbed the phone. I dialed her.

"What the fuck do you mean talking to Diana like that? You know it's not true. What's the matter with you?"

"I don't know it's not true. I don't know anything."

"Listen, you tell her right now, here and now, that you know it's a lie. You tell her. Right now. I'll put her on."

Diana didn't want to take the phone. I pushed it into her hands.

"Tell her!" I shouted at Ursula.

Diana listened. I didn't hear what Ursula said. After a few moments Diana said, "That's all right. I understand. Yes, I forgive you . . . I do . . . Yes . . . Good-bye, Ursula." Diana hung up.

"What did she say?"

"She apologized. She said she was under a lot of pressure. She didn't mean it."

"That's what she said?"

"I guess she's just unhappy," Diana said. "I know. I've been there myself."

My head was spinning. She'd been there before. I'd been there before. With Alexis and Barbara. Diana was calmer now. I was paranoid.

Ursula didn't come in all day. I didn't call her. When I got back to the house, she was out. Her bike was there. Her car was gone. Her absence was more oppressive than her

251

presence. I had wanted to confront her. To have it out with her once and for all. She cheated me by not being there.

I did something I had never done before, never thought of doing, never wanted to do. I went through all her things. I systematically looked into every drawer and cupboard and closet in the house. What was I looking for? Clues. Some indication of who she really was. Proof of something. Evidence for something. Once again, I was detective and criminal in one. I had no idea what I was looking for, so I didn't find it.

One drawer of the dressing table was locked. I knew that she kept her diary in there. Perhaps her "pillow book," as she called it, could provide me with the secret of Ursula Baxter. She had never shown me any of her writing or talked about it. On the other hand she hadn't locked the book up, not until recently.

I got into bed around eleven. I slept, waking only when she climbed into bed beside me. I didn't ask her where she had been. She kissed me good night, then sat up for a while reading. She studied the charts that recently seemed to obsess her. She didn't discuss their significance. Maybe these circles and signs were clues to her behavior. But I had never been interested in the occult. Things were crazy enough without that.

This was to be a night without sex. There were one in three of those now. The tensions of our life, our fears, had begun to drain us of desire. In the morning she was cuddled up next to me, her thumb in her mouth.

She came and went during the week. There were no more To Whom It May Concern notes. Or if there were, she had gotten hold of them and kept them to herself. I noticed an item in the *Times* about a call girl who had been pulled in by the police for questioning over the murder of Larry Campbell. The call girl wasn't named. Maybe it was through this woman that Ursula had gotten her fix on Larry Campbell. This woman could have written the note. I agonized over whether to show the item to Ursula. It would make things more complicated. I decided to hold off for the moment. Everything that happened now seemed like another blow to my concentration on office matters.

Ursula had always taken a special, personal interest in the *La Belle Dame Sans Merci* project, so when Paul came in to talk about Joe Ransom's notes on his treatment, she wanted to be there. There was a certain understanding, complicity between Ursula and Paul. The story attracted both of them as it disturbed me. Thinking now about Paul's violent denunciation of Ursula, it seemed overstated and pat. "Get rid of her!" She had touched a nerve in him, and it fascinated him. He must want her. They were talking to each other as if I weren't present.

"I'm not sure I like the thing about the sister anymore," Paul said. "Maybe the story should just be between the two of them. Two only children. Two people without family ties who have only each other."

"That's more romantic," she said. "If you don't have any siblings, there's a romantic feeling of being alone against the world, of making your own life, so when you find someone you want, it's overwhelming."

"But isn't that a compensation for early loneliness? You put all your emotional eggs into one basket."

"What's wrong with that?" Ursula said. There was a defiance in her tone, which I knew was directed at me. Paul was now in his element.

"My experience of only children is different. I had a girlfriend once who was an only child. She was very self-sufficient, so self-sufficient in fact that she was unable to give herself to anyone. I don't mean sexually. Emotionally. It was really hard for her to love someone. Maybe I'm a little bit that way myself."

Ursula smiled. "So why don't you model the guy on yourself?"

"We're in danger of making the guy seem weak," I said. "It seems like he's not deciding anything for himself. He's just reacting to her."

"I don't agree," she said.

"Nor do I," said Paul.

It was two against one.

"Let's see what Joe says. After all, he's paying."

By Friday afternoon I was looking forward to the weekend. By Friday evening I was dreading the weekend. What happened between three o'clock and seven o'clock was the arrival of the second note. "To Whom It May Concern." I picked it up with a pile of late mail dumped in the hallway just inside the street door. It was typed on a single sheet of plain paper. It read, "You are going to get away with it."

It had to be mistyped. Surely it should have read, "You are not going to get away with it." I stood in the hallway and read it over again. It was clear, but what the fuck did it mean? I folded it and put it away in my pants pocket.

I couldn't figure it out. Was it from the unnamed call girl? Why would she write that? Was it to tell me not to worry, the cops would never get to the truth? Or, don't worry, I'm not going to blackmail you. A spooky antithreat, a prediction of something that wasn't going to happen. I didn't show it to Ursula.

At eight o'clock we went to a preview of a new movie. Almost all the way through she held my hand. The film was a Touchstone comedy about a family where the pets take over the house. She enjoyed it. Afterward I refused to go to a Mexican restaurant. We agreed on the Imperial Gardens.

By coincidence we were seated at a table where I had had dinner with Alexis a few days before she quit. Ursula was in good spirits. She seemed to know the restaurant menu very well. She ordered some things that weren't on the English menu at all, Japanese specialties that only the Japanese knew about. As we left, the hostess asked us if we had enjoyed our meal. We said we had.

"You like this table," she said.

"It's fine," I said. I didn't really know what she meant.

"Madame insisted on it."

When I asked Ursula why she had insisted on that table, she said, "Sentimental reasons."

We drove home in our respective cars. Once again, I had no idea what was in her mind. Her secrets were no longer mysterious or exciting. They weren't seductive anymore. They distanced me from her. It seemed to me we had reached a point of no return. Or rather, I had reached that point.

We made love that night and it was as good as ever. Technically speaking. But I had lost the deep sensation of possession. At orgasm we were still separate people. Sexual attraction was failing us.

Saturday morning I went over to the real estate office to sign the papers and hand over the check for the beach house. It was a great moment. A door opened in my head right onto the ocean. Felicity's murder had made it possible. A sick thought, maybe, but it was a fact. Whoever killed her had given me this freedom. I put the house keys in my pocket. Two sets.

The real estate lady gave me the name and address of the guy who bred the Akitas. Maybe in my new life I'd get a dog. Man's best friend. Irrationally, I thought of the movie I'd seen the night before where the family dog takes charge of running the house, displacing the mother.

When I got back, her motorcycle was parked out front. She wanted us to go for a ride. She had her leathers on. She handed me my helmet.

"It'll do us both good."

"I don't really feel like it."

"Oh, come on."

"Maybe later."

"Look, I want to go now and I want you to come with me." She put her arms around me. "I love you so much."

"I love you too. I just don't want to go for a ride right now."

"You do? You really love me? Then come. You can drive if you like."

"Give me a break."

"I love you so much that I'm just not going to let you get away with not loving me back."

"You go."

She looked at me. A sad, sad look. She got onto the bike. She started the engine. She looked around at me, then accelerated away down the drive. What was it with her and that bike? As she turned out onto the road, I noticed that she'd left her helmet behind. It stood like a shining severed head on the gravel.

I ran to my car. I drove off after her. Turning onto Benedict, I narrowly missed an oncoming station wagon. I had to stop her. I could hear the explosive gunfire sound of her bike heading down the canyon toward Sunset.

A quarter of a mile away I heard the crash. When I

reached the six-road intersection at the Beverly Hills Hotel, I knew it was over. She was lying ten yards from the bike, which was still chugging on its side in front of a truck.

Four or five people got to her before me. She lay on the road, sprawled as if she'd been raped. Her face twisted in pain. I bent over her. She saw me.

"Now you can be free," she whispered.

I heard someone say, "It's crazy, these girls on bikes they can't control."

I leaned forward and kissed her. There was blood in her mouth. A cop pulled me back.

"You know her?"

"Yes," I lied. I didn't know her.

Her eyes closed. It was over, I thought.

# 42

# HAPPINESS

It's a miracle," the doctor at the clinic told me. "Somebody up there likes her."

Ursula had broken two small bones in her left hand. She had bruised her face, but not too badly. She had had stitches, but there was no prognosis for plastic surgery. The blood I tasted in her mouth had not come from a punctured lung but from her bitten tongue. She was bruised all over her body. Her breasts were unharmed. And that was it, physically.

She was in a state of shock. She had small memory losses. She could not, for example, remember why she rode off on her bike. She couldn't recall our scene in front of the house. She had no recollection of asking, demanding that I come with her. She believed that the accident had happened at night when she was on her way to visit someone.

"Who?" I asked her. "Who were you visiting?"

She looked at me through a collage of plasters and bandages.

"I don't know."

On another occasion, she said she had been coming back to the house after having visited someone. She was aware that her memory was faulty. To cover her embarrassment she concocted two versions. That was my reading of it.

I watched her while she dozed in her room at the clinic in Westwood. The TV was on, but silent. She was asleep, but awake. She seemed different now, not just because she was quieter, less talkative, or because of her appearance under a helmet of plasters, but essentially different in spirit. She seemed like a woman from another story, not ours. This was not the woman who had done what Ursula had done. This was a new person in my life. An invalid who needed looking after. There were moments when I felt I was the driver of the truck that she had hit, the man who was accidentally responsible for her state, her fate. The man who failed to kill her.

"Have I cut your balls off?" she said suddenly.

I laughed, but I didn't know what she meant. After three or four visits to the clinic, usually in the evening after closing the office, I began to understand. I was behaving differently, less forthcoming, less approachable. I probably looked different to her too, as she did to me. The truth was I felt like another person, too. A stranger. The fact of visiting her, arriving, staying a while, then leaving without her, all of that made me think of myself in the third person.

Not I, but he. He parked his car, not I parked my car. He held her hand, not I. He kissed her lightly, frightened of causing her more pain. He remembered the fight and its aftermath. He remembered seeing the bruise on her face develop, even during the course of a single afternoon. He saw the changing outline, the altering color, as if it was the result of something that had happened inside her head. Her fault. Her responsibility. It was her bruise. Not his. Not mine.

I was aware that this was an attempt to escape feelings of guilt, even though I wasn't guilty. Guilt, I knew from Felicity, is a commodity. People trade in it, transfer it, cash it in. Ursula's amnesia was the same thing, I guessed. She didn't want to say right out, "I tried to kill myself, you know."

Into the second week of her stay in the clinic I could see her accident had lifted a burden from my shoulders. Other

257

people were looking after her now. I had become an agent in a different sense. With a wise detachment I had become a go-between, going between her and me.

I felt an enormous tenderness toward her, and not only when I was at her bedside. I reached out to her when she was engulfed in silence. I talked to her about office matters whether her eyes were open or not. One by one the plasters and bandages came off. Every day there was another one gone. Eventually the stitches came out. The mask was removed.

There was nothing to report about the enquiry into Larry Campbell's murder, so I said nothing about it. She didn't ask. I brought what I thought were her favorite books, and she was pleased, greeting them like old friends. When I brought her the book of poems that had been covered in foam from the fire extinguisher, she kissed it on both covers.

But tenderness can be dangerous, I discovered. It can be like sticking your hand through the bars of a cage. With the best will in the world you can't be sure how the creature inside is going to react. One evening I brought her a plate of her beloved guacamole. She looked up at me.

"See anything of Barbara?" she asked.

"No. Why?" I was disturbed by the question. I hadn't seen Barbara. I had spoken with her a couple of times.

"What do you do for sex?"

"Nothing. What is this?"

"I'm teasing you. Lying here alone day after day your mind plays tricks. I invent things about you. What else have I got to do?"

"You'll be out of here soon."

"Yes, I will. But you know something? I'm not really looking forward to it."

My memories of her and me altered. Or maybe I chose to recall different things now that we were physically apart. I started to remember happier moments. I had now moved out to the beach. I had a mattress, a phone, a razor, and a cup and saucer. Away from the deathly house on La Cielo, I remembered a lot of the fun we had had, the jokes, the warm kisses, the long hugs, and above all her smiles. There had been many times when her pale mask had creased and cracked with amusement. Now that I thought about it, she

258

hadn't always been that still photograph out of Helman's book. On many occasions her black-and-white frozen face had moved and gone into color.

She was smiling when I walked into her room. It was her third week in the clinic. I had lost track of the days. She had written down the title of a book she wanted. *The Nowhere City* by Alison Lurie. It was out of print, she said, but I might find it somewhere, if not in paperback, then at Book City on Hollywood Boulevard. I didn't tell her that I was so busy I couldn't think of taking a couple of hours or more to find a book.

"If I can't get it, is there anything else you want?"

"A little happiness maybe."

"I'll see what I can do."

"That's what guys are for," she said, her eyes sparkling unexpectedly. "And you're my guy, whether you like it or not."

I took her hand and kissed it.

"Sometimes I think you're playing a game," she said.

"A game? What game?" What she had let us in for was hardly a game.

"A game where you don't have to do anything. You don't have to make any moves yourself. You just watch the other guy make all the mistakes."

"That's not fair," I said.

"What is?"

As I came out of her room I saw a man standing outside in the corridor holding a bunch of flowers. I'd seen him before but I couldn't place him. Fiftyish, balding, like a teacher or a scientist.

"How is she?" he asked. He had an accent. European.

"She's lucky. She's going to be all right."

"I'm a friend of hers, Laszlo Ronay."

Now I placed him. He was the guy she went to visit at Rebecca's weeks ago, before all this started. I had watched them together.

"How did you hear about the accident?"

"She called me."

I wanted to ask him what his connection was with her.

"She needs friends right now."

259

"She knew something like this was going to happen."

"How did she know?"

"I told her."

"You told her."

"She comes to me for consultations."

"You're a psychiatrist?"

"Clairvoyant."

Now it fit.

"I'm not so sure it was an accident," I said. This guy seemed to have some kind of power over her.

"You mean she tried to kill herself?"

"Maybe. It seems to me if you tell someone something's going to happen to them, and they believe you, there's a chance they'll make it happen themselves."

"You're saying I'm responsible?"

"I'm saying think about it, if you're a friend."

I left him and walked away. I could have asked him about her. He must know things. But I didn't like the man. Or was it that I didn't like the idea of someone else knowing her at all? I was jealous.

Watching the dawn come over the ocean was a new delight for me. The sun woke me in the mornings. I would walk out onto my deck and just look at the day before setting off for the office. I watched two girls in the early-morning light. They were walking across the empty beach laughing and kissing each other. I wondered what passions they had in their lives. They stopped at exactly the spot where Ursula and I had been that dark, cold night. They talked for a while before walking on. This image lingered with me during the day. Living with her, I had become so self-absorbed I had stopped looking at people around me or thinking about them. We had crowded everyone else out.

At night, lying on my mattress in the moonlight, listening to the ocean, I missed her. I missed her warmth. One night I missed it so badly I drove back to her house at three in the morning. I lay down on her bed, took deep breaths of her smell, her lingering perfume. I held her bathrobe as I prepared to sleep.

Then I saw the winking red light of her answering machine. There was a message on it, waiting to be listened to. I thought about Paul's practical joke, the muffled voice. I could see the strange, contradictory typed message: "You are going to get away with it." I wound back the cassette to listen. It was her voice I heard. There was a message not to her but from her.

It was no ordinary message and maybe it wasn't directed at me, but simply to whom it may concern. It was long. Like a story.

"My father liked cemeteries. When he took me anywhere as a child, on vacation or weekends we would always visit the cemetery nearby as if it had been a church or a museum. He felt that cemeteries were instructive. He loved looking for names he might recognize and he was fascinated by how long people lived. He was fond of telling me that husbands and wives frequently died within a year of each other. Whoever was left alive after the first death couldn't bear to remain on earth alone.

"Once, I remember we were in a cemetery perched on a cliff somewhere on the coast of Maine. I can't for the life of me remember the name of the place. I do remember there had been a terrible storm while we were having lunch in some old diner in the nearby fishing village. When the storm was over, we climbed the path up to the grassy cliff top. Black clouds, the remains of the storm, were sailing in a clear blue sky. The sun was stingingly bright. The mossy ground was wet from the rain, but the air was hot. Something had happened during lunch, a violent release in the sky. Those black clouds had had a duel. It was over now. The memory of that sky was later to connect in my mind with *Wuthering Heights* when I read it, and then by association with *Jane Eyre.* Of course, there were no sea and no cliffs on the Yorkshire moors, but there was a cemetery and that was enough for me.

"On that cliff top my father drew my attention to a grave with a peculiar statue on it. Two marble figures were entwined. There was no way of telling if it was a man and a woman. There was no sexual detail in the carving, no breasts, no penis. The inscription underneath was 'All for Love.' Two names, Alice and Henry, told you all you needed to know. Strangely, they died on the same day. My father said it was obvious that they had killed each other.

"Two men were digging a grave. We went to watch. The

261

black clouds were far away. My father put on his dark glasses. 'One day I'll be in a hole like that.' I suddenly wanted to cry. 'Don't worry, darling, it won't be for a long time yet.' He kissed me on the forehead. But the damage was done. When one day I got news of his death, they didn't want to tell me that he had died in bed with a girl. He'd apparently had a heart attack fucking. The girl was hysterical for days. Her husband had to be told, her parents too. She thought she would be tried for murder. I wanted to talk to her but her husband refused to let me.

"The death of my father meant that I now had no one in the world to go to. Even though I seldom went to him about anything, this hard fact reduced me to tears whenever I thought about it. I cursed him for leaving me. I cursed him for leaving my mother, whoever she was, wherever she was. And I cursed her for not being there to deal with his funeral.

"I knew he would've liked a stone similar to the one in the cemetery on the cliff overlooking the sea. I went to a stonemason and he did some sketches for me based on my poor drawing from memory. In the end I couldn't decide which way to go, what to order, or anything.

"The funeral itself was a mess from beginning to end. I wasn't up to all the arrangements. I went through his address book to find names to contact, but I had no way of knowing whom he liked or didn't, who mattered to him, or who would like to know. I couldn't bring myself to get in touch with any of his girls.

"Two men friends of my father and my father's daily woman were all who came to the graveside ceremony in a grim cemetery on a gray day in a dreary Portland suburb. I felt sick all the time. I had dyed my hair yellow, wore a wide red hat I'd once been to the races in, and put on my brightest party dress. I must have looked like one of his tarts.

"We all went to a bar afterwards and ordered a bottle of French champagne to go with the toasted sandwiches. The wine was warm. The barman said he'd have put it in the refrigerator if we'd given him enough notice. So we drank it with ice cubes stuck into tall flute glasses. I never saw any of them again. And I've never been to visit my father's grave with flowers or anything. I did order a stone, however, and had them put his name and the dates of his birth and death on it. When the stonemason asked for the text of the inscription, all I could think of on the phone was 'All for Love.'"

That was all. She must have written and recorded it while intending to commit suicide. I thought of my mother's wretched, friendless funeral at Forest Lawn. I thought of Ursula's funeral to come. I tried to imagine it. I missed my own father. I'm afraid I cried.

# 43

# A GOOD NIGHT'S SLEEP

P ut your hand on me." She took my hand and put the fingers in her mouth. She deliberately made them wet with her saliva.

"Just rub me." She moved my hand down the bedclothes. She pulled the covers away and moved her legs apart.

"Please. I can't seem to do it for myself. I need you."

I pushed my hand under her hospital gown. She reached down and drew up the clothing. I slid my palm along her thigh to her sex. When I touched her pubic hair she gasped as if I had pierced her skin. I stroked her the way I knew she liked it, putting my fingers deep inside her, then drawing them out slowly, twisting them around each other. It gave her the sensation that there was a creature inside her, not just a dumb prick. Not any guy, but the extension of a human being who understood her.

She started to cry. Tears poured out of her eyes as the liquid gathering inside her ran out like soap as I rubbed her. She gave a cry and started to shudder. I gripped her between her legs, steadying her as she shook. She said nothing. Her mouth opened, her lips moved, but no words came.

I wanted to get into bed with her. I wanted to hold her, make love to her, tell her how much I had missed her, how much I needed her. Whether I had the courage to do it and say it I won't ever know. There was a knock at the door. I removed my hand from under the covers. A nurse came in.

"Is she asleep?"

"Dozing," I said.

"You'd better leave." The nurse smiled at me. I kept my wet hand out of her sight. I picked up a newspaper from the bedside table and put it in front of me to hide my erection as I stood up.

She opened her eyes.

"Come back soon."

"I will."

I didn't kiss her. I left. The nurse opened the door for me. I was leaving her in prison.

The sun had set when I came out of the clinic. I felt horny. I sat in my car. It was still tight between my legs. I wanted a woman. I watched two nurses leave the clinic. They were laughing together. I wanted them. Now. I wanted to get out of the car, go up to them, talk them into coming home with me, then and there. Take them both home to bed, bury myself in their flesh, kiss two mouths together, feel four hands on me, take them apart, limb after limb, everything slippery.

I put the car into gear and headed off to the beach. As I passed the turnoff to the Palisades, I slowed. I waited for a gap in the traffic. I swung the car around in a forbidden U-turn and drove fast toward Barbara's house, toward Barbara. She might be out. I could have called. But what was the point? I was there now.

I parked in front of the house. I could see a light on in the kitchen. Good. She was in. I rang the bell. I waited.

A woman opened the door. Not Barbara. She had a glass of wine in her hand. I didn't recognize her.

"Is Barbara here?"

"She's in the kitchen. In the middle of cooking dinner."

"I just want to see her."

"Hey, wait a minute. Who are you?"

"I'm a friend."

I went past the woman into the kitchen. Barbara was straining some rice. There was a man with her. Maybe the husband or boyfriend of the woman at the door.

"Mason!" Barbara was surprised and pleased. "What is it?" Something in my expression alarmed her.

"I want to talk to you a minute."

264

"Well, okay. But I'm just—"

"Please."

She handed the rice to her friend. Before she could introduce me to her guests, I grabbed her arm and drew her out of the kitchen. I guided her to the bedroom.

"What's the matter, Mason? What's happened?"

I closed the bedroom door. I put my arms around her and kissed her. Her apprehension went as she started to respond to my tongue. I squeezed her breasts through her plastic apron.

"I want you."

"We can't."

"They can look after themselves for a bit."

"Someone might come in."

"Then they can watch."

I put my hand up Barbara's skirt. She started to take off her clothes. I unbuttoned my fly. She heaved my jacket off my shoulders. I lifted the apron over her head. She put her hand on my hard cock. This was too slow for both of us. We moved apart and took our own clothes off. We fell onto the bed, onto each other.

All thoughts of Ursula went from my head. Now I wanted Barbara. Just Barbara. I licked her blond pubic hair. I had got so used to dark hair I had forgotten the soft transparent fur. It was fresh, new to me. The smell of Barbara was so different from Ursula, like hazelnuts.

I was aware that she had lost weight in her thighs. Her stomach too seemed flatter, her navel more pronounced. Her breasts were still weighty but they stood out more prominently from her rib cage. I had an extraordinary feeling of newness, as if I were making love to her for the first time.

She was different. There was less calculation in her movements, more abandon. There were moments when she didn't seem to know what she was doing. She took my penis out of her mouth and took it down to her cunt. Then back to her mouth and then down to her cunt. Then back to her mouth as if she couldn't decide where she wanted to make me come.

Suddenly, without warning, she started herself. She pressed a nipple into my mouth and clung to me when she cried out. Before she finished, I turned her over on the bed-

265

spread and came into her from behind. Her head was pressed hard against the cushions at the top of the bed. As I came I saw her blond hair disappear as the cushions tumbled onto her head, covering it. I could hear her muffled cries of pleasure.

I was expecting someone to knock at the door. I don't know how long we'd been in the bedroom. No knock came.

"I can't just leave them," she said.

"I want you again."

"And I want you. But I can't. Maybe later. Can you stay for dinner?"

I smiled at the thought of us having fucked our brains out and then debating whether to stay for dinner.

"I must go to them."

Barbara lifted her sticky body off the bed and started to put her clothes on again hurriedly.

"Leave the bra off."

"All right."

I started to get dressed. Barbara left the bedroom, opening the door only enough to get through. She didn't want her friends to see into the bedroom, to see me.

After a few moments she came back into the bedroom. I was half dressed.

"They've gone," she said.

Barbara handed me a note. "We don't want to spoil your evening. Call you tomorrow."

"What must they think?"

"Do you care?"

"It's pretty rude, don't you think?"

"We can have dinner together after all."

Barbara laughed. "Let's eat."

We had dinner in the kitchen. We were silent. Neither of us quite knew what to say. Barbara wanted to say, Come back and live with me. I didn't know what I wanted. All I knew was I wanted to live at the beach.

Barbara started to clear away the dinner plates. I pulled her away and put my arm around her. We went back to bed and had each other for dessert.

After that I had the best night's sleep for as long as I could remember. When I woke I thought I was with Ursula. But it was Barbara who brought me the coffee in bed.

"Did you sleep well?"

"Great. Just great."

"I read somewhere that when a man's condemned to death, the night before his execution he sleeps like a baby."

"Is that so? I don't believe it."

"That's what I read. But we'll never know for sure, will we?"

"I hope not."

All my unease returned. I avoided making a date to see Barbara again. She didn't push it. I kissed her good-bye as I had so many times before.

"Be careful with me," she said, standing beside my car as I opened the door.

"I am careful. Maybe that's my failing. I'm too careful sometimes."

"I'm a very simple person. You know that. I believe things very easily. I'm not manipulative."

"You're saying I am?"

"In a way. You're a very dangerous man. You have an effect on me that I can't really control. I don't like that feeling, being out of control. I guess I'm very provincial."

I kissed her again, then got into the car, waved, and drove off. Barbara was right. But it's hard to be careful when you don't know quite what you want. As I turned onto the road I had a feeling I was being watched. Guilty again.

The office was instant nightmare. There was so much going on, so many calls to return, so many meetings to set up, so much paperwork. Diana was coping, but only just. I needed Ursula.

Around eleven Joe Ransom came by. I was surprised to see him. He was surprised that I was surprised. Apparently we had set up the meeting a week ago, but I had forgotten. That was something that almost never happened. I did not forget appointments. I wondered if there were others that I had forgotten since her accident. It pointed to how much I relied on her.

"I'm very pleased with the progress on *La Belle Dame*," he said. "Young Paul is a terrific writer."

Joe went on to talk details about the screenplay but I couldn't concentrate. He said he wanted to settle for the title *Without Pity.*

"I want it to sound like a suspense story," he said, "not a commercial for aftershave."

Joe was probably right.

"What happened to Gala?"

"She had an accident. But she's fine." I was angry.

"What, something got stuck somewhere?" Joe laughed. There was a pop in my head. I lashed out and hit him on the side of his face. It seemed as if he had hit me first. He fell backward. Right away I regretted it. But I couldn't stop myself.

Joe got up. He moved toward me. We were alone in my office. The door to the outer office where Diana was typing was shut, thank God. Shit. Not another fight. Joe put out his hand and patted my cheek. I flinched.

"I was out of line, Mason." He opened a tube from his pocket and put a pill in his mouth.

"You know, when I was in college I was in love with this girl. Or thought I was. I got into a fight with another guy over her. I ended up in the hospital. I swore then to never, never get into a fight over a woman. Pussy just ain't worth it. It can turn you upside down, inside out. But keep it on a fun level. Otherwise, before you know it, it gets out of hand. Afterward, you wonder what all the trouble was about. Ever looked at a woman five years after you were seeing her? You wonder what you saw in her? The rule is simple. The best fuck is the one you're having right now. Tomorrow it'll be someone else."

Joe was an asshole. If I told him the story of my relationship with Ursula, his hair would turn white. I could now see why Ursula hated him. She was right. I could see him through her eyes.

I felt a surge of sympathy for her. When I had hit her it had been out of frustration. When I hit Joe it was out of contempt.

After he left, I called the clinic. I wanted to say something nice, tell her I understood how she felt. The phone in her room rang and rang. I became impatient. Eventually, the switchboard operator came back on the line.

"She's not picking up," I said.

"Would you hold on one moment for the doctor?" she asked.

268

I felt a tingle down my back. What had happened? She'd tried it again. I knew it. She'd killed herself.

"This is Dr. Fleming."

"I'm Mason Elliott, Mrs. Baxter's employer." Why had I put it like that? That was a shitty way of putting it. But what could I say? I'm her lover, her partner in crime?

"Mrs. Baxter discharged herself last night. Around nine or nine-thirty. If you know where she might be, please get her to contact me, or someone in the office here. She hasn't settled her account."

# 44

# THE GUN

Nine o'clock last night. I'd been with Barbara. Nine-thirty. Ursula had discharged herself from the clinic. She'd gone home. Ten o'clock she'd called the beach house. She'd called the office. Eleven o'clock. She'd driven over to Barbara's. Some time during the night she'd seen us, maybe through the bedroom window. Or in the kitchen. I knew someone had been watching. Shit.

There had been no message from her on the office machine. I called her house. No answer. No machine message. No story about her father's death. Nothing.

When Diana innocently asked how Ursula was, I said fine, just fine. Os called, not about Ursula, but to give me an update on the Larry Campbell case. Apparently Larry's wife was now the number-one suspect. The new theory was that she had gone to the motel and killed him. Or alternatively she had found out about his liaison and hired someone to kill him. Strange. That had been a theory of mine about Felicity.

Around eleven I was talking to myself. Pacing around my office I fed the fish twice, refused all calls, and started to wonder if I should just go over to the house, see her, and face it. I knew she'd be there. She was probably waiting for me.

Fuck her. I had every right to see Barbara if I wanted to. Who the fuck was she to dictate terms? If she wanted to kill herself, well, okay. For a moment I regretted that she hadn't made it.

Diana came in with a parcel that had been delivered by messenger. What was it, a bomb? I opened it. It was a book, sent over from Book City. In a way it was a bomb. The book was *The Nowhere City* by Alison Lurie, the book she had asked me to get yesterday. Meanwhile, she had ordered it herself. What was she trying to say with it? Was it an invitation for me to take it to her? Or a warning of some kind? So much of what she did was in code. I decided to do nothing, but I hated not being able to lick this situation. It all came down to the fact that at some level I was sorry for her. It was a bad feeling.

During the afternoon I saw Kate in the parking lot.

"Why so sad?" she asked.

I hadn't wanted to talk to her before, but now I wanted a female ear. And with Kate I would get a therapist's voice too. I was hungry for clues to Ursula's behavior, perhaps some advice, even guesswork would do. Talking to Paul hadn't helped. On the spur of the moment I invited Kate to dinner.

"I'd like to talk to you about something."

She hesitated. She was wondering if this was a proposition.

"I've got a date," she said.

"Pity."

"But I can break it." She touched my arm.

We went to the Imperial Gardens. I didn't think about the irony of the choice until after we got there. It was still early. The table where I had sat with Ursula was free. I hesitated. It was tempting fate somehow. The Japanese hostess smiled at me. She probably remembered. What the hell. I shivered. The air-conditioning had been on all afternoon. I decided to be straight with Kate, without identifying Ursula. I gave her the bones of it.

"Now she's become erratic and I want to know how to deal with it. I can't seem to sit down and talk it through with her."

"It works like this. And believe me, it has nothing to do with her being female. Men react in exactly the same way when someone they love doesn't respond the way they want. Initially there's anger and even hatred which is directed at the other person. But that doesn't last long. The hatred is quickly transferred to a third party whether the jealousy is justified or not."

"Why? If there isn't anyone else? And she knows basically there isn't."

"She has to find someone else because if she went on hating you, the love-object if you like, it would be like admitting that you were unworthy of her love. And if that was the case it would reflect on her choice, on her. It would mean she had made a mistake. And love doesn't admit mistakes."

"So she looks for someone else."

"Exactly. It's fundamentally Oedipal."

"Oedipal? I thought that was to do with parents and children. Boys and their mothers."

"The pattern is the same. A girl with a very strong attachment to her father comes to see the mother as a rival. This becomes especially pronounced with second marriages, where the father's new wife becomes an object of hatred. So Mom in one form or another becomes the heavy and has to be attacked or gotten rid of. It's the same principle with love affairs."

It made sense. Thinking about Felicity, it made a lot of sense. Ursula would have hated her if she'd still been alive. For a moment, she had hated Diana. Now she would turn to Barbara. It was like a chain.

"What can you do about it?"

"One of two things. You can try to persuade her that her jealousy is without any foundation. Or you stop seeing her altogether, explaining why. Either way, it tends to be a lengthy process. And if you're not in love with her . . ."

"I am." Was I?

"That's something only you know."

I returned to the meal. Across the restaurant, the door

to one of the tatami rooms slid open. A man and a woman came out. They bent to put on their shoes. The man was Paul. The woman was Ursula.

How could she have known I'd be here? No one knew. Not even Diana. She was psychic. And what the hell was she doing with Paul?

"What is it?" Kate could see something had happened.

I was paralyzed. Paul saw me. He waved. She showed no reaction when she saw me. What did she think I was doing with Kate? She limped toward me.

Paul stopped at the table. He wasn't embarrassed in the least. I stared at her. Ursula smiled distantly as I introduced Kate to Paul. I felt hot. What had happened to the air-conditioning?

"Good food, isn't it?" She addressed Kate, ignoring me. Then she turned away and walked out without a word. She disappeared past the cashier, limping.

In a sweat I left Paul and Kate and ran off after her. The dining room was on the second floor. I pushed past a Japanese couple as I jumped down the stairs. The walls were lined with angled mirrors. I followed her disappearing reflection.

I caught up with her at street level opposite the bar.

I grabbed her by the shoulder. She whipped around and dug her teeth into the back of my hand. I yelled.

"Go on, hit me," she hissed.

"Why did you leave the clinic?"

"Where did you go last night?"

"That's my affair."

"Tramp."

I grabbed her shoulders. She opened her purse. She took out a gun. She shoved the barrel into my stomach.

"Let go. Or I'll blow you to pieces."

I let go. I knew she was crazy.

"Follow me," she said, "and I'll kill you."

She put the gun back in her purse and left the restaurant. People were looking out from the pink darkness of the bar. I don't know whether anyone saw the gun or not. I had seen it. And I wasn't going to follow her.

Where did she get the gun? Then I remembered the

night I'd gone into her house, to sleep in the guest room, and she'd come down looking for me, she'd had a gun in her hand.

Paul came down the mirrored stairs looking for us. There were two of him, two of me. More if you counted the reflection in the reflections.

"What did she say to you?" I had to know.

"She called up earlier in the day and asked me to come to dinner."

"So you said yes."

"Right. Is there anything wrong with that?"

"Not necessarily. What did she talk about?"

"She wanted to know if I knew any prostitutes."

"She what!"

"She said she was thinking of becoming a call girl."

"What did you say?"

"I said I didn't know any prostitutes and that she should be careful or she'd get AIDS."

Kate came down the stairs.

"Look, I don't care what's going on," she said, "but I'm going home. Thank you for dinner."

"Kate, I'm very sorry," I said.

She understood. "Good luck." She glanced at Paul. "I can see myself home."

I looked at Paul. "And she said nothing about me, huh?"

"Nothing."

I climbed into my car, inadvertently giving the kid who'd parked it a five-dollar bill. I drove west along Sunset. My car and my mind were both cruising. Other cars and ideas overtook me. Oedipus. The night of Larry Campbell's death I had told her Billy Wilder's Oedipus story. Hadn't she talked about how Oedipus knew what he was doing all the time? Had I known from the start what I was doing, what I was getting into?

I had been with Barbara. And I had cheated on Ursula. Even so, that word had been a smash in the face. *Tramp!* No one called a man a tramp. Kate might have said Ursula was really talking about herself. She had transferred to me how she saw herself. No. That wasn't right. She was incredibly faithful. I knew she hadn't slept with Paul or anyone else

273

since she'd met me. There were no men in her life. That foreign astrologer, he wasn't her lover. She didn't screw around. So how could I confront her? What with?

I didn't turn north on Benedict. I lost my resolve. I kept going along Sunset, cruising toward the ocean. When I got into my house I just wanted to sleep, to block everything out. I lay on my mattress listening to the ocean, nervous of the bad dreams to come. Even awake I couldn't control my thoughts. I couldn't seem to put them into order. There were a thousand loose ends. But they all joined in one place. Her. And me.

I was wakened from a deep sleep at seven by the phone screaming at me. I groped for it, knocked it over, finally got it to my ear.

It was Barbara in a terrible state. Her voice was trembling.

"I just had a call from the police."

"What's happened?" My mind went to Felicity's murder. My crazy thought that Barbara had killed her jumped back at me.

"The shop's been smashed up. It's in a terrible state."

"I'll be with you in half an hour. Stay there."

"What am I going to do?"

"Take it easy. I'm on my way."

I hung up. I showered but I didn't bother to shave. I could do that in the office. My hand was too shaky anyway.

Pandora's Box was wrecked. The mirrors were broken. Barbara was in tears. She hadn't paid the last insurance premium.

"The crazy thing is, nothing's been taken, not as far as I can see. Who would do this?"

I could smell the answer. The lemony scent.

I told her I'd call the insurance company. I'd make a case for her. She was only a couple of weeks behind and had never claimed before. I stayed with Barbara for about twenty minutes. She quieted down. I told her I'd call her in an hour or so from the office.

I drove as fast as I dared. This was it. I was going to let her have it. The doors were locked for the first time. All of them. I had left my key to her house at the beach.

I smashed in the kitchen door, using a wrench from the

274

garage. I cut my left hand on the glass. I started shouting for her as I came into the kitchen. I shouted all the way across the hall and up the stairs.

She was sitting on her bed, facing the mirror.

"Why did you do it?"

"You've gone back to her."

"That's not an answer."

"This could be the answer."

She pointed the gun at me.

"Don't be fucking stupid!"

She got off the bed. I watched her. She wasn't that certain of herself.

"I've killed before," she said. "One more won't matter."

I didn't know whether to believe this. The way she spoke, it sounded prepared.

"Were you with her last night?" Her voice trembled now.

"Where I was last night is my business." I was beginning to feel hatred.

"You're scared. Look at yourself." She turned to the mirror. "What do you see?"

"Give me the gun, Ursula."

I moved toward her. I held out my hand. I felt calm. She switched the gun to her left hand, farther away from me. She looked into the mirror.

"We met in a mirror," she said. "Are we going to part in a reflection?"

I thought of rushing her, grabbing the gun. I wasn't sorry for her now. Her gown was hanging open, untied. Still looking in the mirror, she put the barrel of the gun to her breast. She pushed it into the soft flesh. I could see her finger tightening on the trigger.

She moved the gun down to her navel, pushing it into the cavity. It was oddly erotic. She moved the barrel downward to her sex. She pushed the tip of it into her pubic hair. I didn't want to see this, but I couldn't look away. She started to push the gun in.

"Do you think people should have guns? What's your opinion about the gun laws? I read somewhere that the right to bear arms in this country is an emblem of the right to per-

sonal freedom. American society is an experiment in freedom. Take away the gun and you take away our freedom.
It's like calling off the experiment."

"Ursula." I couldn't let her go on. "Please give me the
gun. We'll work something out. Let's talk."

I sat on the bed. Any threat from me would make it
worse. She turned the barrel of the gun around in a small
circular movement.

"It's getting warm inside. It's funny, isn't it, how important sex is one minute and what a trivial pursuit the next?
It goes from being everything to nothing in a flash. Then back
to everything again. Then all of a sudden it's nothing."

Now I felt empty, without desire. She felt it too.

"I've been thinking a lot about the difference between
us. It's got nothing to do with sex, has it? It's not a question
of male or female. I do things most people only imagine
themselves doing." She turned to face me, close to tears. "I
feel freer when I follow my desires. You feel freer when you
don't. That's the difference between us."

"You can't do everything you want. Just as you can't
have everything you want."

"Do you get a charge out of stopping yourself? Does restraint make you feel good?"

"I think restraint means you're in control of yourself.
Otherwise it's chaos."

"In sex, restraint is the same as inhibition, isn't it? That's
not a good thing, sex with inhibition. Why doesn't the same
thing apply to the rest of life? It ought to. Sex isn't chaos, is
it? It's freedom!"

I knew she wanted me to say something. But what could
I say? I agree. I don't agree. You're right. You're wrong. She
needed help from me. I knew it. But I couldn't give it to her.
I didn't love her enough. I despised myself.

"You'd better leave."

"I don't want to leave you like this."

"Like what? How do you see me? A sick woman? A
wounded animal? A sad case?"

"I don't really understand you."

"That's called indifference, you know."

Her look shattered me. It was the look of someone who
wanted to die. It wasn't desperate. It wasn't hopeless. It was
just vacant. There was no memory behind it.

276

I went to the door. She didn't speak. I didn't look back. We had nothing more to say.

I went down the stairs. I looked at the remains of the fire in the big grate. I smelled the old scent of burned hickory.

I put my hand on the cold wood of the front door. I heard the shot.

# 45

# THE HOTEL ROOM

I climbed the stairs slowly, dreading what I was going to find. I wondered where she had shot herself, which part of her body would display the wound. I could see her sprawled back on the bed, a gaping orifice in her head, her brains splattered, gray offal in a pond of blood already soaking into the bed covers.

I went into the bedroom. She was sprawled on the bed, lying on her side facing the window, away from me. She held the gun in her hand. It was smoking, like a cigar.

A cracking noise drew my attention to the mirror. A piece of silvered glass fell to the floor. The mirror was shattered. From where I stood my reflection was splintered. The bullet hole was in line with my heart. I walked around the bed to look at her face. She lay like a model in an enigmatic Helman photograph. Her eyes were closed. She spoke.

"You can tell your wife I'm going to hunt her down and kill her."

"What! You're not going to do anything. And Barbara's not my wife."

"Just tell her what I said."

I bent over her. "You're not going to touch her. If you try—"

"What are you going to do? Kill me? Is that what you want?"

"I want to stop you."

"You can't, Mason."

"We'll see."

I left the room, left the house. I should have taken the gun from her hand and shot her. Later, they'd call it suicide. That fucking gun scared me. And her talk of freedom. Freedom to kill, what kind of freedom was that?

I was worried for Barbara. Kate's diagnosis was right. Ursula had transferred her love-loathing from me and from herself, to Barbara. Would she carry out her threat?

I went to the office. I had a hundred calls to return. I couldn't even begin. I called Barbara as I had promised. She sounded better. I could hear banging in the background. The shop front was being boarded up. I told her to come over to the office.

"Don't go home. Just come right over."

"No, I have to go home."

"Barbara, do as I say." I softened my tone. Don't alarm her. "I've got a surprise for you here."

"I don't need any more surprises."

"This is a nice one."

"Is it nicer than the one you gave two nights ago?"

She came by in the late afternoon. She had changed her clothes.

"Dammit. I told you not to go home."

"I had to change. Don't be silly. Now what's the surprise?"

I was terrified of Barbara spending the night alone in her house. And I didn't want to take her to the beach. I had made a reservation at L'Ermitage for the night. We had a great two-room suite with a Jacuzzi. Barbara had always wanted to install a Jacuzzi in her own house. I made out that this was my attempt to cheer her up after the disaster of the shop. And it did.

"This sure beats that awful place in New Mexico," she said.

While Barbara played in the foaming tub, I planned the

278

evening. All the time I thought of Ursula, what she was thinking, doing, planning. I wondered if Ursula had finally used that gun on herself.

She had been right about one thing. I did see her now as a wounded animal, getting worse every day. I wanted to help her but I was frightened to go near.

"Where shall we have dinner?" Barbara was drying her hair.

"Why don't we go down to the bar and have a few drinks? And you know what I'd like? Let's have dinner in the room. They'll bring us anything we want."

I didn't want to leave the hotel. After a couple of double martinis she was pleased to be back in our suite. We ordered lobster.

During dinner Barbara began to wilt. The shock of the day was finally taking effect. The wine increased her tiredness. She yawned. I spooned some orange-flavored chocolate mousse into her mouth.

"I meant to tell you before," she said. "Ursula came into the shop today."

"She what!" In my head I had just put her away in a drawer.

"You didn't tell me she's been in the hospital."

"Didn't I? She had an accident. She's been off for three weeks. What did she say?" I tried to sound casual.

"She told me she'd had a dream about the shop last night. She'd known what was going to happen. She'd seen it in her dream. She came over to check."

"Why didn't you tell me this before?" I could feel my heart beating in my ears.

"It's not important. Maybe if she'd called the minute she'd had the dream . . ."

"What else did she say?"

"Just how keen she was to get back to work. That she was so angry with herself about her accident. She felt she'd let you down. You don't seem to have much luck with secretaries, do you?"

What was she trying to do? Why did she go to the shop? Was she apologizing? Or was she just being sinister?

"Did you tell her you were seeing me tonight?"

"No. Why should I? Anyway, I didn't know then. Why are you so concerned?"

After dinner we watched TV for a while. Barbara dozed in her chair. I undressed her and helped her to bed. She was exhausted.

"I want to make love to you, but I feel so tired," she said.

We went to sleep early. I was as fatigued as Barbara. My wife. Why had Ursula said that? Was that how she saw Barbara?

There was a knock at the door. I groaned. Was it room service to take the dinner trolley? What time was it? The room was dark. But the drapes were drawn. It could be day. I didn't feel as if I'd been asleep for more than an hour. Barbara moved beside me. The knock came again. Barbara sighed and got out of bed. She stumbled drowsily toward the door.

"Don't open it!" I was suddenly scared.

"I'll see who it is."

"No!"

I sat up. But it was too late. Barbara left the bedroom. She opened the door to the living room. There was silence. Even in the darkness of the hotel room I could see who had come in as clearly as if it had been broad daylight. It was she.

The gun was in her hand. She pushed Barbara back toward the bed.

"Get into bed," Ursula said coldly, kicking the bedroom door closed.

"What's the matter?" Barbara was still trying to understand it.

"Take off your gown."

I started to get up. I was naked.

"Take off your gown and do as I say."

Barbara looked to me for help.

"Ursula, stop this."

"Do as I tell you." She aimed the gun at Barbara.

Barbara was frightened now. Ursula came toward us both.

"What do you want?" Barbara looked at me. "What's going on? You know, don't you?" She was accusing me.

"Get into bed together."

Barbara took off her gown, pulling it over her head. She was quivering. The two women looked at each other, Barbara with fear and incomprehension, Ursula with hatred and deadly resolve.

"Put your arms around each other."

We did as we were told. Barbara's flesh was cold to the touch. I held her tightly.

"Ursula, put the fucking gun away."

"Now make love to each other."

I looked at her. I knew what she wanted. For Barbara and me to make love before she killed us.

Barbara tried not to cry. She held me, started to kiss me. I kissed her back. I wanted to reassure her. She suddenly became passionate, as if she understood everything, knew everything that had happened. Did she want to die in my arms?

Ursula stood at the end of the bed, the gun steady in her hand. She watched me.

"Make him hard."

Barbara took me in her mouth. My left hand was stroking the back of her neck. My right hand went from one breast to the other, gripping them in turn. I became hard. There was no preventing it. Barbara was taking me to my death.

I was distantly aware of Ursula's perfume. The lemony scent began to fill the room. Barbara pulled me on top of her, kissing and nipping my skin with her teeth. I couldn't see Ursula anymore. Barbara drove on relentlessly. My body tingled. I began to give way under her attack.

I had a fantasy that Ursula was behind us, taking her clothes off, sliding out of her dress, kicking her shoes away, climbing onto the bed on all fours. She joined us. The gun was . . . I don't know, forgotten. She herself was the instrument of my death.

In my head the three of us were together, entwined, aggressive and submissive, a single animal mating with itself, its three mouths open and wet, damp haired, slippery to the touch, ambiguous, amphibious, androgynous, inside itself, on the edge of reproducing itself. A moment of exploding immortality.

Barbara cried out in anguish. I groaned and shouted, "No!" But it was unstoppable. In my imagination the gun went off. Liquid fire poured into me through a hole in my abdomen. A fiery storm blew through the widening, expanding opening. It was snowing flames. I choked with the acrid smoke as everything inside me burned, like dried leaves in gasoline, went up in a chain reaction. You could see the furnace glowing and flashing red through my skin. I was alight and dying . . .

Consciousness returned. Barbara was holding me. She was crying. I moved away from her and looked around the hotel room. Ursula was gone.

"We've got to call the police." Barbara was shaking with sensuality and fear.

"No."

"What do you mean, no?"

"Not the police. I'll take care of it."

"How? The woman's crazy. She's crazy!"

"Yes, she is."

I held Barbara in my arms. She was afraid and exhausted. I rocked her until she was overcome by sleep.

While Barbara slept I struggled to think what to do. There were moments in the next two hours when I saw Ursula. She was back in the room with us. She was making up in the bathroom. Then she was pulling on her red panties. She was cleaning the dressing table mirror. Then she was sitting naked in the armchair, her legs hanging over the arm, writing in her Pillow Book. Writing. Writing. What was she writing?

Ursula vanished as I began to think, think headache hard. I physically gritted my teeth with concentration. It became clearer. I would write to her. Not one of those anonymous notes that had plagued me from the start with their insinuations, but a letter of instruction. Let's have it out once and for all. End the threats. Usurp the nightmares.

Looking around this hotel room as the dawn light was

visible, I remembered the beginning, like this, lying with Barbara in the Sierra Hotel in Artesia. Go back there, to that hotel. That was what Ursula would want. Of course. Face the demons where they were born. Didn't she try to take me back there herself? I remembered the scene at the airport. That's what the fight had been about. That's what she wanted. Take her back to New Mexico and settle it. Today. Now.

I sat at the writing desk and switched on the lamp. Using hotel paper, I drafted a letter. "Meet me at the Albuquerque airport. 12:30 today." I'd have to check the carrier and flight number. The last time Barbara and I had arrived around twelve-thirty. I wrote, "Be there without fail or . . ." Or what? "Or I'll go to the police." It was dangerous to write that, I knew. But then Ursula had a gun. You can't get more dangerous than that.

I mustn't use L'Ermitage paper. I looked in my briefcase for a plain sheet. I didn't have one. Maybe Barbara had some. I looked through her bag. There were blank invoices and letterhead for Pandora's Box.

Wait a minute. Wait a fucking minute. I looked at Barbara. She was sound asleep. How would it be if Barbara signed the letter? Don't change a word, just sign it Barbara Kovak. Ursula was jealous of Barbara, she wanted to kill her. This would be irresistible. Barbara was my ace in the hole. Ursula would go to Albuquerque expecting Barbara. But I'd be there instead. That was it. Perfect.

I decided not to enclose a ticket with the letter. I would do that, but Barbara wouldn't. I checked the flight number right away. I made a reservation for myself on an earlier flight. It was six-thirty. I had the hotel send the letter by messenger.

I could picture Ursula reading the letter. I wondered if she'd call me at the office. Well, I'd go in for a half hour before leaving for the airport. I'd give Diana a cover story in case Ursula smelled a rat and checked on me. Not bad.

I told Barbara to go straight home and not answer the phone, just return calls. Don't go to the shop until I've sorted out the insurance. I told her I'd call her later in the day. That seemed to cover everything. If Ursula tried to take her gun, they wouldn't let her on the plane. I was pleased with my tactics.

I wasn't clear what I was going to do when I got her alone. Somewhere in the depths of my thumping heart was the idea that I might kill her. No, that would be crazy. But not as crazy as the idea that she might kill me. I was getting excited where I had been nervous.

Out of that chrysalis came not such a nice guy, came a murderer. Was that what she had wanted all along? Someone to finish her off?

# 46

# TO WHOM IT MAY CONCERN

She was standing in the crowded concourse of the Albuquerque airport. She was smoking, looking around for Barbara. She was dressed in her impeccable black silk suit. Beside her high-heeled feet was a scarlet overnight bag. Weaving through the crowd, I contrived to approach her from behind. I wanted to give her a shock.

I did. I put my hand on her shoulder. She jumped and spun around. Her balance was upset. Perhaps because of her limp and her stiletto heels, she was about to fall. I had to steady her. I gripped her tighter than necessary.

"Careful." A sadistic moment.

"Are you together?" She was expecting Barbara. Good. She was confused. Perfect.

"No. I wrote the letter."

I kept my grip on her arm. Now she was feeling what it was like to be set up, tricked.

"I don't know why I did those things. I didn't mean them."

"Oh, but you did."

"I was jealous. I wouldn't do anything to her. None of it's her fault." She lowered her head and pressed into my shoulder.

"Please forgive me. Please."

She had never pleaded with me before. So was it genuine or a ploy?

"Let's go," I said. I held to my resolve. I had to get rid of her. After this we wouldn't see each other again. It was that simple.

I walked with her to my rented car, crossing the parking lot. From the air-conditioned interior we felt the blast of dry heat outside. She was quivering. I let go of her arm. I could tell it wasn't a put-on. It wasn't for effect. Maybe she would just leave on her own accord. Maybe.

I drove south on the main highway. She didn't ask where we were going. She knew I was headed for Artesia. She stared straight ahead. We had both made this trip before, but not together. We were going back to the beginning. We both knew we were near the end.

"I am sorry. I just couldn't help myself." She looked at me. Her eyes were liquid and gray. The terrible darkness had gone. This was Ursula at her most vulnerable, most dangerous.

"I understand," I said. "But I can't let you go on doing this."

The fears and imaginings of the last two nightmare days faded somewhat as we hit the open desert road. Nonetheless this was going to be it. I couldn't trust her to stay in her apologetic mood.

"Can we stop for a moment?" She pointed to a gas station up ahead. "I need the bathroom."

I pulled over. Before she got out she put her hand on my knee and gripped it. I looked down and saw the scar from the scissors incident in the Casablanca. I watched her as she limped toward the women's toilet. I didn't need gas but I was tempted by the Coke machine. I got two cans. I didn't remember ever seeing her drink Coke.

I was leaning against the car when she came out. I handed her the Coke can.

"Just what I need." But she didn't open it.

"I don't want to go back to that hotel."

"Why not?"

"There's no point. I've decided to leave you. I know that's what you want."

She opened the car door and reached back to retrieve her red bag. She clutched the bag in one hand and the unopened can of Coke in the other. She smiled awkwardly. It was like the good-bye moment after a casual one-night stand. She started to walk away along the side of the highway toward the distant snow-capped sierras.

I went after her. In her high heels she wobbled on the rough, stony surface. She turned to face me.

"Don't touch me. If you touch me, I won't be able to leave. Just let me go. I'm fine."

"Where do you think you're going?"

"Mexico."

I laughed. "That's Texas down there."

"After Texas it's Mexico." She turned and walked on. I wasn't sure what I felt. Let her go. That's what you want, isn't it? She's making it easy for you.

She stopped after a few yards, bent down, and took off her shoes, kicking them away. Then she walked on barefoot.

Go after her. You can't let it end like this. I jumped back into the car in the gas station lot. Two local cowboys had watched the whole scene while they gassed up their pickup.

"You sure she's worth it?" I heard one of them say, not for my ears.

I drove after her. Yes, she's worth it. Twenty yards on I stopped, got out, and picked up her shoes. I threw them into the car. They bounced on the backseat. I drove on, not fast, following the limping figure of the woman in black, so inappropriately dressed for this desert and climate, this down-to-earth Land of Enchantment.

I passed her, stopped farther up the highway, got out, and waited. I was still thinking what to say when she reached me. She ignored me.

"Get in."

She walked on. I could imagine what the stony roadside must have felt like under her soft soles. I caught up with her quickly, took her arm. She dropped the Coke.

"Leave me alone."

She started to resist, pulling away. I didn't let go. She pushed at me. There was desperation in her eyes. I held her frail arms. She seemed to be in physical pain.

A frozen-food truck honked loudly as it hurtled past. We were enveloped in a cloud of dust. It was blinding. Ursula shielded her eyes. I choked. I pulled her to me. I kissed her. I couldn't help myself.

"I can't let you go like this."

Her eyes were closed. She moved her face to mine, rubbed her cheek against mine. We looked at each other. Our faces were powdery masks from the dust. She seemed to have aged, her black hair now yellow gray. We were victims of a sudden fallout not far from Los Alamos. We walked back to the car. I put my arm around her. Suddenly, we weren't young anymore.

"Let's go up into those mountains," she said. "We'll find a place."

As I drove I looked toward the snowy range-tops. This had to be the last time.

"When I look at the mountains I always think of avalanches," I said.

We left the main highway and drove for nearly an hour before reaching the foothills. As always the mountains were farther away than they seemed. I became impatient. I wanted to make love to her. I wanted to be inside her again. I knew she wanted that too. The damned sierras constantly receded before us. I drove faster now. The road became increasingly rough. We didn't speak. We were busy imagining things and just as busy not thinking of others.

As I drove, the weather began to change. It became colder as we climbed up the winding mountain road. I switched off the air-conditioning and put the heater on. She kept a lookout for a motel or a lodge where we could get a room. We saw nothing. I began to think that coming up to the mountains was a mistake, a romantic notion.

We were traveling in a different country now, cold, with forbidding rocks, bad roads, oppressive clouds and snow patches that persisted all year round, white wounds that wouldn't heal. Ursula spotted a cabin through the trees.

"Let's try there."

"That's someone's house," I said.

"Maybe they're not home."

I stopped twenty yards from the house in a clearing among the trees. I wasn't crazy about this idea. We got out of the car. It was very cold.

I saw that the log shed/garage was empty, the wide wooden door fixed open with a rock.

"Let's try the door."

"Knock first." I didn't want to break in. Why did everything in our relationship have a criminal aspect?

She knocked. There was no answer. I looked around. A black crow yelled from the bare branches of a tree. She knocked again. Still no answer.

She turned the brass door handle, not expecting it to open, but it did.

"There you are," she said triumphantly. "Don't you understand, I want you." She took my hand and led me into the small stone-and-wood cabin.

In the main room a German shepherd appeared. The animal leaped at Ursula. He had been waiting. He hadn't barked a warning because he had been trained simply to attack. Ursula screamed. The dog snarled. She backed away, terrified.

I got down on my knees.

"What's the matter, boy? Where is everybody? We're not going to hurt you. Come on, boy." I spoke firmly and reassuringly to the dog. The dog growled, but he liked me. For some reason I found I had a way with this dog. I was practicing for the Akita I had ordered. I patted the animal, and looked up at Ursula. She was less scared now and impressed.

"Pat him," I said.

She patted him. The dog then raised his paw.

"Take it."

Ursula took and shook the dog's paw like a hand. Now we were all friends. Ursula kissed me on the cheek.

There was no one in the cabin. The people who lived there or maybe were just staying there had gone out for the afternoon. The place was so remote, they probably weren't afraid of being robbed. The smell of burned logs reminded me of her house. The dog went with us as we checked each of the four rooms in turn, the bedroom last.

The bed was unmade. The crumpled sheets, the cover half-fallen on the floor, the dented pillows, and a pair of red cotton panties at the foot of the bed, all gave the impression of the aftermath of sex.

As we undressed I felt we were following two other lovers. I had never really called us lovers to myself. We were a man and a woman. Now we were lovers.

We knew each other's bodies so well, so intimately, that there were no discoveries. We didn't need them anymore. Making love now was reconciliation. For the first time in a long while we came together.

After I don't know how long, she opened her eyes. They were soft and wet and green.

"I want to tell you something," she said.

"Anything."

"I killed Felicity. I want you to know that now. You must know it."

Everything slowed down. I hoisted myself up as if I had a pack on my back weighing two hundred pounds. There was a pounding in my head, but slow, like an ocean of blood. When I blinked, my eyes seemed to close for several seconds at a time. I could feel myself forgetting what I was doing as I did it. The present became a languid, rippling flashback.

She may have handed me the pillow herself. I couldn't be sure. She was ready for it. And I, without knowing it, was prepared. She didn't struggle. There was no gasping or twitching. She just fell asleep.

When I took the pillow from her face I had no conscious idea whether she was dead or not. Her eyes were closed. There was no nightmare expression on her face. She was kind, not leaving me a hideous mask to haunt me to my own death.

I leaned across her. I arranged her body. I closed her legs together. I folded her left arm, so her hand was resting below her breast. I straightened her right arm by her side. She was unbelievably beautiful. I picked up her clothes. By mistake, I took the red panties belonging to the woman who lived in the house, whose smiling wedding-day photograph watched me from the dressing table. I discovered it later. It didn't matter. I wrapped her clothes and shoes with her purse into her black dress and rolled it all up. When I left I put everything in the red bag in the car.

I would never see her again, alive or dead, except perhaps when I was asleep. Then I wouldn't be able to keep her out.

I dressed quickly. I looked at my watch. I hadn't taken it off. We'd been lucky. I'd been lucky. The owners of the cabin still hadn't come back. Another couple of minutes and I'd be out of there. I took one last look around the bedroom. It was a strange place for it all to end. I looked at her. Just a naked woman, that's what she was, unknowable. I had to kiss her one last time, had to. I chose her left breast in preference to her lips. I was afraid she might kiss me back.

I came out of the cabin. The sky over the mountains was steely gray. It was snowing fast. I patted the dog as the forlorn-looking animal wandered up. Huge flakes of snow stuck to my clothes as I got into the rental car.

In a few minutes all my tracks would be covered. It would be as if I hadn't been there. I didn't speculate what the people who lived in the cabin would think when they found her. Forty minutes later I entered the sunlight. I could see the long highway in the distance. It wasn't murder. Maybe it was revenge. It was certainly a crime of passion. Ursula had killed Felicity. She had killed Larry Campbell. Now she herself was dead. I decided that if I was caught I wouldn't deny any of it. I'd tell everyone I had been in the grip of an uncontrollable passion for this woman. Everyone would understand. If I got fifteen years, I'd be out in five. But don't think about it.

On the flight back to L.A. I looked through her purse. I found the airline ticket. It was one way, Los Angeles to Albuquerque. The rest of it was void.

I picked up my car from the short-term lot and drove directly to her house. It wasn't locked. I went up the stairs to the bedroom for the last time, the theater for so much madness, so many scenes that contradicted each other. My memories were already scrambled. It would take an age to put them into any kind of order, chronological or emotional.

I stopped in the bedroom doorway. I switched on the lights. The room had completely changed. The chaos that had once reminded me of the inside of her purse was gone. Now the room was immaculately ordered. Her clothes, which were so often scattered, had been put away. Her books were

290

shelved. The candles were fresh and white and waiting to be lit. It was a picture of neatness. The mirror was covered in a white sheet, a shroud to hide its shattered glass and the memories of its reflections.

I put her things away, the dress in the clothes closet, the shoes at the foot of the armoire, the underwear in the drawer where I knew she kept them when she could be bothered. I took one last look around the bathroom that had been wiped to a shine and perfectly tidied. It was as if someone had cleaned the place up before going on a long vacation.

Then I saw the envelope. I'd missed it before. It was propped up on the mantel behind the black lacquered box. On the envelope was typed "To Whom It May Concern." It was in the same style as the mysterious notes. Even before I opened it I realized that she must have written the others, to herself, to me. Weird cryptic love letters that meant nothing to anyone but us in our crime. I read the letter. It was handwritten.

I have found it necessary to kill myself. You will find my body somewhere in New Mexico, perhaps in the Sierra Hotel, Artesia. I don't know where as yet.

During the course of a difficult time of love I have killed two people, Felicity Elliott and Larry Campbell, both residents of Los Angeles. I did not kill Annabel Hart in New Mexico. I don't regret these murders, although they didn't achieve everything I had hoped for myself.

But for you, my darling, it is perhaps another matter. These lines will explain it:

Him that I love
I wish to be free—
Even from me.

All my love, always,
Ursula

I put the letter back into its envelope and returned it to the mantel behind the black lacquered box. If it eventually incriminated me, I would deal with it. She'd expect me to. I refused to cry as I left the house and drove to the beach.

It was night. I looked at my own reflection in the wide window against the silver ocean beyond. I stared down at the beach. The phone rang. It was Barbara.

"What happened?" she asked. "Did you find her?"

"Yes."

"And?"

"It's over," I said. "Nothing like that will ever happen again."